VOLCANO ROADS

VOLCANO ROADS

Peter Tonkin

This first world edition published 2009
in Great Britain and 2010 in the USA by
SEVERN HOUSE PUBLISHERS LTD of
9–15 High Street, Sutton, Surrey, England, SM1 1DF.
Trade paperback edition published
in Great Britain and the USA 2010 by
SEVERN HOUSE PUBLISHERS LTD

British Library Cataloguing in Publication Data

Tonkin, Peter.
   Volcano Roads. – (Mariners series)
   1. Mariner, Richard (Fictitious character) – Fiction.
   2. Watercraft police – Crimes against – Indonesia –
   Fiction. 3. Detective and mystery stories.
   I. Title II. Series
   823.9'14-dc22

ISBN-13: 978-0-7278-6828-2   (cased)
ISBN-13: 978-1-84751-200-0   (trade paper)

All Severn House titles are printed on acid-free paper.

Severn House Publishers support The Forest Stewardship Council [FSC],
the leading international forest certification organisation. All our titles that
are printed on Greenpeace-approved FSC-certified paper carry the FSC logo.

Mixed Sources
Product group from well-managed
forests and other controlled sources
www.fsc.org Cert no. SA-COC-1565
© 1996 Forest Stewardship Council
FSC

Typeset by Palimpsest Book Production Ltd.,
Grangemouth, Stirlingshire, Scotland.
Printed and bound in Great Britain by
MPG Books Ltd., Bodmin, Cornwall.

For Cham, Guy and Mark as always.

And for students, colleagues and friends past and
present at The Wildernesse School, Sevenoaks 1950–2010.
Non Nobis Solum.

ONE
Motion

The woman hung in the upper waters of the Java Sea almost entirely motionless. Only the sea around her moved, long waves running southwards under a steady breeze, letting her rise and fall while a desultory current was balanced by a gently making tide. She was facing downwards, towards the reef below, and the only rapid motion near her came from the pearly strings of bubbles she was sending rushing towards the gently heaving surface several metres above.

Her pale pink legs were spread and slightly bent at the knees so that the upward-pointing soles of her fins passed lazily in and out of the column of shadow cast down through the water by the sturdy little dive boat bobbing above her. The motionless heels just touched together and the yellow blades of the big broad fins spread like a mermaid's tail. Her arms were thrown wide, but bent inwards at the elbows as though she was hugging the slow, warm current like an invisible lover. A lover who ran slow fingers across the redness of her cheeks, past the yellow frame of her face-mask, over the silver circle of the regulator between her carmine lips and up through the spread black cloud of her hair.

The intimate motion of the water made the extravagant sinuousness of her tresses extend the shadow of the boat above. And the shadow of the boatman floating face-down in the water just beside it.

The full, curved body between the spread legs and the embracing arms was clad in a black dive suit so snug as to seem like a skim of oil painted on her. The yellow straps of her scuba harness accentuated the trim waist, as though to emphasize the fact that she had not sent up her emergency line, which was coiled with its bright balloon still uninflated at her right hip. But there was something about her, beneath the dreamy motionlessness of her body, something about the frantic panting of those twisting ropes of bubbles, that might have suggested to an observer that she should have sent up the danger signal long ago.

The woman's body cast a shadow like the dive boat's. A sharp-edged blade of darkness that reached down among the searchlight beams of sunshine to the dappled glory of the jewel-box reef below. The precise pool of darkness that she shed spread over the only other dark thing below her: the black form of her dive-buddy hanging hunched immediately above the multicoloured coral, as though his yellow scuba tank was a balloon keeping him just aloft.

Immediately below his face, bright orange anemone fish darted in and out of amber anemone tendrils. Common lionfish cruised by, striped white and gold, like the beaches on the nearby shore. Batfish and angel fish glittered like shattered rainbows. Deeper, fusiliers, dartfish, purple queens and tiny barracuda exploded away from the outward jab of an attacking moray as though someone had spilled a huge bottle of indigo ink across the blue-black depths.

A hawksbill turtle cruised by, close enough to make the buddy's body move a little. A single bubble escaped from his regulator and wobbled up towards the still form of the floating woman.

Like the still boatman in the water just above her, the inert dive buddy had been dead for some time now and the motionless woman herself had little more than half an hour left to live.

The four-masted cruise liner *Tai Fun* came speeding round the northernmost tip of the reef that extended the island princedom of Pulau Baya out into the Java Sea at top speed and under full sail, like a white gull stooping to drink from the sapphire waves. She was leaning decidedly to port, all her state-of-the-art sails spread as wide as the computers that controlled them would allow. Her deck was at the maximum slope accepted by the same computers, whose programmes balanced the requirements of ship handling with those of passenger comfort. The composite of her computer-perfected hull vibrated almost ecstatically and everything within it or above it thrilled – as though she were a clipper ship running homewards a century since. Her knot-meter was clicking up near forty – and what little rigging her twenty-first-century design allowed was simply singing in the breeze.

In almost every regard, *Tai Fun* presented a perfection of maritime motion allied to high-concept carbon-negative design. The sails that powered her did so in more than one way. Even as they pushed her forward, they used the sun's heat to generate electricity stored in the batteries whose ballast weight obviated much in the way of a keel. Electricity powered everything else aboard – including the motors that drove her when the wind was not so willing. She did what she was designed to do: she fused the height of luxury with the pinnacle of eco-responsibility, and, almost by chance it seemed, breathtaking beauty as well.

Tai Fun's owner, Richard Mariner, was standing in the four-master's forecastle pulpit, where the bowsprit would have been footed in an older generation of sailing ships. His left hand was braced against the eager tremble of the foresail's woven steel hawser, his right hand shading his eyes as they gazed dead ahead. Even so, his sturdy legs were spread against the tilt of her deck, flexing automatically against the ecstatic tossing of her racing head.

Like his ship, Richard was in a hurry, but he could not rob himself of one of the most spectacular sights he had ever seen; a vista that seemed to gain in breathtaking impact every time he experienced it. And so he stood here now, oblivious to the spray that soaked his silk shirt like fine rain, careless of the damage the cool monsoon of brine might be doing to his linen trousers or his deck shoes, like a massive figurehead carved of white Carrara marble.

As *Tai Fun* swooped round the point of the submerged coral outcrop, so the whole eastern panorama of the island opened up. Richard was used to thinking of Pulau Baya as being shaped like a huge raindrop curling across the lapis blue of the Java Sea. But with the north-pointing spear of the reef extending its nose, perhaps the island paradise would look more like a leaping swordfish if he could image it on Google Earth.

The tip of the sword-slim reef, round which *Tai Fun* was speeding now, led back, broadening beneath increasing shallows to the wide green face of the curling fish. The illusion of a gigantic fish head was intensified by the gape of an estuary where the Baya River issued out through the blackened, half-buried ruins of Baya City and what was left of the old port beside it. On Google Earth that would look like a marlin's mouth with a black beard clinging closely to it. The reason for all that destruction stood like a bulbous black eye high above the river mouth and the calcified city – the still-smoking crater of the mountainous volcano Guanung Surat. Behind the crater, giving shape to the head like a series of gills, ran the curving outflows born of that great eruption nearly five years since.

But then the shoulders of the great leaping fish-shape were defined by increasing bands of greenery as the irrepressible life of the place took firm grasp of the warm, incredibly fertile volcanic soil.

The lesser peaks that defined the mid-line of the island were clothed on this side in half-wild banana groves that ran up into truly wild jungle. Their more accessible lower slopes were regimented into farms groaning with an abundance of fruit and vegetables made possible only by a perfect climate extended by the natural fertility of the warm volcanic soil into as many as three harvests a year.

Lower still, beyond the modern farmsteads, villages, townships and twentieth-century infrastructure, the silver belly of the leaping swordfish extended into the dazzling curve of Baya Bay, where gleamed the most luxurious white sand in all of Indonesia – for mile after mile down to the island's tail. A tail that had been formed, like the fantastic man-made islands in the Gulf, by engineers and architects seeking to create fabulously commercial real estate.

And here at last Richard focussed the wide gaze of his watering eyes – even though at this distance, he saw it more in his imagination than in fact. Their ultimate destination: the towering seven-star luxury of the Greenbaum International Volcano Roads Hotel. Could he just see the topmost floors of the tower peeping over the horizon? He glanced back and up at the lookout in his nest at the cross trees of the foremast. The man up there, armed with binoculars, would be able to see the whole hotel front, right down to the marina where their anchorage was waiting. But of course it was the lookout's job to look for hazards nearer at hand, like the uncharted coral heads that littered the waters here.

Still, with the root of the reef sword beginning to break the surface and the sheer heave of the island proper reaching vertiginously skywards to that smoking peak so close above his right shoulder, Richard felt the wild, impatient excitement threatening to overcome him. As ever, he burned to have his beloved wife, Robin, standing there beside him to share the moment, but her preoccupations were far more practical than his; her focus infinitely more social.

Robin was in their stateroom changing, with a good deal more alacrity than he could summon up. For they were due at a full, formal reception to celebrate two events crucial to the fabulous island and its economy that were being held more or less at once – an economy dictated, even here, by the belt-tightening of the global credit crunch. They were attending the formal opening of Nic Greenbaum's latest hotel – and Prince Sailendra's wedding in the massive state reception room there.

Richard had a wide variety of responsibilities at the former event, for he had sought to bulwark his company, Heritage Mariner, against the economic downturn of 2009 and 2010 by expanding the business in several directions – one of which was into property development with Nic. So the Volcano Roads Hotel was part financed – and part owned – by Heritage Mariner.

Robin, on the other hand, had responsibilities at the second celebration, for she was Matron of Honour to the bride. Or as close as one could come to being Matron of Honour at a fundamentally Muslim ceremony. That, and the fact that they had had no opportunity for rehearsals, planning meetings or even discussions except in video conferences, made Robin jumpy and short-tempered, even when everything seemed to be plain sailing.

But they were running behind schedule now.

Richard released his grip on the foresail's hawser and glanced at the face of his trusty old Rolex. Dangerously behind schedule, in fact. Especially as *Tai Fun* was bringing the bride.

Inga Nordberg and her father Nils had wanted to arrive in Pulau Baya aboard *Tai Fun* for sentimental reasons. Nils had once owned her and the sister ships which made up Richard's High Winds line. Inga had met Prince Sailendra aboard the beautiful vessel and fallen in love with him as they had fought a combination of pirates and volcanic eruptions together. And it had seemed sensible enough to use the breathtaking wedding cake of a ship as part of the bride's inevitable journey south and east from Sweden where she and her family lived. But their flight from Stockholm to Singapore had been delayed. And then they had been all but trapped by the security closedown ordered by the Singapore government in reaction to a terrorist incident at Changi International itself. The airport – and with it all the other international airports in Malaysia – was closed for the foreseeable future, in fact.

If *Tai Fun* had not been at Richard's beck and call as owner, and had he not made the decision to depart from her gazetted schedule to rescue the marooned Nordberg family, the bride and her parents would probably still have been trapped with all the rest of the tourists stuck on the tip of Malaysia.

Richard sighed a little wearily now and turned away from the beautiful view, his mind switching over to his much less welcome commercial and social duties. Angling his tall, strong body against the tilt of the juddering deck automatically, still deep in thought, he took his first, reluctant step towards his state room, his shower and his monkey suit. But no sooner was he in easy motion than he was stopped in his tracks as events, once more, overtook him.

'*Emergency! Emergency!*' yelled the lookout. 'There's a body in the water dead ahead!'

TWO
Over

R ichard was back in the pulpit in an instant, almost hanging over the leading edge of it. His focus was dead ahead once again. This time, however, he was quartering the water immediately below the forecastle, the far horizon, the hotel and the various responsibilities it represented all forgotten for the moment.

Tai Fun's wild rush was also, for the moment, over. The foresail hawser was spinning, winding the all-but-indestructible weave of the heat-exchanging solar panel cloth around itself. The other sails, Richard knew, would also be furling in at top speed. The eager list came off the long, sleek hull and bare masts swept upright through the rushing air. The deck beneath his shoes shuddered as the engines sprang to life, then the rolling under full sail became the pitching under screws on full reverse.

The change in motion was so sudden that even Richard staggered forward a little until the safety rail around the pulpit held him. There, immediately ahead, he saw a little dive boat bobbing strangely and lumpily on the water. As though the cockleshell of its hull were secured on a short line to something moving to a different rhythm altogether. The heat and the brightness twisted it. Made it look like a bubble of tar sitting on an undulating mirror. A dive boat – but no boatman that he could see. No divers. And, for that matter, no other boats anywhere nearby.

'Where's the body?' Richard called. He used his foredeck roar, and even in the restlessness of wind and water it carried to the lookout. From his elevated position he could see more detail on – and even below – the dazzling glitter of the surface.

'Immediately beyond the dive boat, Captain,' answered the lookout. 'I think there's another there too, underwater. But can't quite estimate how far down . . .'

'Not swimming?' demanded Richard. 'Not diving?' The urgency of their mission flashed briefly into his mind. And Robin's likely reaction to further delay now. Not to mention Inga's. Or her father's. Or, more distantly but no less powerfully, the frustration of a multi-millionaire oil-magnate and a Prince of the Blood whose plans were likely to be damaged here. Plans curtailed – perhaps even over. 'You're absolutely sure?'

'Just hanging in the water,' confirmed the lookout. He hesitated, clearly taking a second look. 'I'm certain. Dead certain.'

A carefully chosen phrase if ever there was one, thought Richard, as he span back. But it was more than enough to convince him. Then he was pounding down the length of the deck. Social and financial plans were one thing. Life and death were quite another.

Standard 'Man Overboard' routine aboard *Tai Fun* dictated that the First Officer and her emergency team should swing out the lifeboat nearest to the incident. That would be what Captain Olmeijer would call for, no doubt, thought Richard. But unless someone was thinking very quickly indeed, this was likely to be the slowest and least effective of the alternatives. Particularly if all aboard began to assemble at their Emergency Stations. And they would soon begin to do so, he realized grimly as the sudden shrilling of the Emergency Stations Alarm showed that the captain had made his decision. For emergency stations were, by and large, beside the lifeboats too.

Richard pounded on, his mind racing, weighing the lookout's words and balancing them against the likely reaction to the familiar emergency summons. One body in the water beside the boat. Another further down. But that in turn supposed another somewhere else – for even in these waters, simple safety procedures required scuba divers to go down in pairs. That would be the standard – boatman and two divers. And that in turn would mean—

'Richard! What on earth is going on?'

Richard's thoughts had brought him past the upper restaurant to the deck-top stateroom he was sharing with Robin. And she now stood in the door of their accommodation framed in shadow like something out of a young sailor's fantasy. Her slim, firm upper body was encased in a tight basque that emphasized the slenderness of her waist and gave her more matronly bosom a considerable cleavage, which was as ill-contained in a tiny gossamer bra as her hips were in a lacy wisp of thong. Much in the same way, after thirty centimetres or so of pale pink thigh, her legs were encased in self-supporting stockings. Her feet were squeezed into silk pumps with fashionably high stiletto heels. The effect was, to put it mildly, arresting.

'Bodies in the water dead ahead,' he answered, sliding to a halt.

'My God!' Her ready sympathy wiped away the frown that had been gathering on her broad brow. 'How many?'

'Two. Maybe three. Looks like a scuba party gone wrong. I'm going for a Zodiac. Quicker than a lifeboat. Don't go to your emergency station, it's just . . .'

'OK. But I can't help! I'd slow you down . . .' Her hand went to the golden ringlets of wedding-ready coiffeur. 'I'd need to change.'

'Slip on a robe and get the doctor up,' he ordered decisively.

Any thoughts of further argument she might have harboured were swept aside by the arrival of the First Officer and her team at the nearest lifeboat. Only under their distracted gaze did Robin suddenly realize what a picture she presented. 'Oh! Sweet Jesus!' she spat and slammed the stateroom door.

'The doctor,' shouted Richard through the slatted teak. 'And tell him he'll need oxygen. Or body bags. Or both . . .' Then he was off again, full-tilt.

The aft sections of *Tai Fun* were designed almost like a theatre, with levels of deck stepping out and down from balcony to balcony all curving over the central features of the pool and the water-sports area. This was where the ship's Zodiacs were secured. Here the lower poolside areas were walled with changing cubicles, cupboards of snorkel gear and lockers full of scuba equipment. Richard had a favourite locker where he kept the set he liked the best. And, even though he had been planning on wedding, not diving, he knew it would be pressured up and ready to go. It always was because that was the way he liked it. He tore the locker open and pulled the kit free as though it weighed nothing. He put the regulator in his mouth and tested it, even as he scanned the sloping stern for the nearest Zodiac. And more than that, he thought, as the rubber-foul oxygen-rich mixture he favoured hit his system like the alcohol he never touched. He needed a boatman and maybe a dive buddy of his own. But the sounding of Emergency Stations seemed to have cleared everyone away.

Swinging the scuba gear over his shoulder, therefore, Richard raced on sternwards, his gaze focussed fiercely on a little six-man Zodiac he thought he could just about handle alone. But then the need to take the risk receded. As Richard ran past a pair of reinforced glass double doors, he caught sight of a picture that stopped him in his tracks. The doors isolated the ship's main weights and training facility from the poolside area. Framed in the glass, a huge man was seated on a multigym using the pec deck. He was wearing headphones and his eyes were closed as he concentrated on his rhythmic exercise. Clearly he was as unaware of the Emergency Stations signal as he was of the alteration in the ship's motion – or of the worshipful gaze of the blonde in the red skin-tight leotard shorts and minuscule tube top, also wearing headphones as she lazily pedalled the exercise bike beside him. Richard had met the man, but not the woman, earlier in the voyage. He couldn't recall his name, but he had been struck by the power and physical competence he exuded. He had seen him since, confident around the Zodiacs and the scuba gear. Precise, decisive, almost like a Royal Marine Commando or an officer in the Special Boat Service.

Someone had called him 'Bugis', Richard remembered – but that was more likely to be his ethnic origin than his name, certainly judging by the colour of his hair and skin. Or it could just have been a comment on how shipshape he seemed to be. The Bugis were *Orang Laut*, men of the sea; sailors all, who rarely came to land. Pirates too, in the past, when they had put sufficient fear into the Victorian explorers to become the 'Boogey-man' of legend. Certainly he looked like a massive piratical Orang Laut with his tousled midnight hair, bare chest and his baggy black exercise trousers. All he needed was a gold earring and a fearsome snake-bladed Kriss.

Without further thought Richard slid the glass door open and strode into the exercise room. 'Hey,' he called. 'Excuse me.'

The man's eyes opened. They were still a little dreamy with effort and concentration, but they cleared quickly when they registered who it was that was calling. The massive arms let the weights ease back. He had been pulling the better part of 100 kilos on each, Richard registered automatically. No wonder his chest and arms would have flattered Mr Universe. One huge hand reached up to pull the earphones free.

'Yes?' rumbled the bodybuilder.

'We have an emergency,' explained Richard. 'There are bodies in the water. Dead and dying.'

The still brown eyes regarded him seemingly without comprehension. The face remained absolutely still. The only things moving were the beads of perspiration trickling over his bland brown face and the rounded teak-dark overhang of his sculpted pectorals.

'I'm taking a Zodiac and some scuba gear,' Richard persisted. 'In case there are others deeper down. Will you help?'

'Sure.' The big man heaved himself massively erect. 'No problem.' He glanced across at the blonde on the exercise bike, easing his shoulders and flexing his upper arms. 'I'll be back,' he promised.

Richard and the Bugis pirate carried the Zodiac down to the slipway at the stern, pausing only to allow Richard to scoop up the fins and weight-belt that completed his diving outfit. They slid it into the water, then Bugis held it while Richard jumped aboard with his gear. A moment later the massive bodybuilder too was hopping carefully aboard. Six-man vessel it might be – but not for six men such as these. Had there even been a third with them, the inflated rubberized gunwales would have been awash, thought Richard as he knelt on straddled knees in the scuppers. He slipped the scuba straps over the shoulders of his silk shirt as his companion gunned the motor. As the Zodiac swept out round *Tai Fun*'s starboard side, he tightened the belt over his linen slacks and added the preset weight belt, hoping the fact that he was going down in clothes would not upset calculations that had been made for a wetsuit. Then he rose carefully and sat on the midship bench. He kicked off the deck shoes and reached for the fins, getting ready to go overboard if the need should arise.

The massive Bugis took the wider tack – and just as well, for as they drew level with the mast immediately forward of Robin's stateroom, the lifeboat smacked down into the water on their inner side. It sat for an instant between them and *Tai Fun* herself as the falls came free and the motor started up. Then the vessels powered forward side by side towards the sinister black blob of the little dive boat.

As they drew alongside it, Richard glanced at his watch again. He was veteran of enough emergencies such as this one to be well aware of the importance of precise time-keeping – for the ship's log, the local authorities' incident report and the post-mortem witness statement at the inquest if need be. Even so, he was surprised by how few minutes had passed since he had looked last, just before the lookout saw the dive boat and the body floating beside it. Smart work, he thought.

There was almost nothing to the little boat. Basic emergency equipment, outboard with some spare fuel. Solid-sided cold bag, no doubt full of food and drink, strong enough to serve as a spare seat. Little box at the side with an open top and a glass bottom giving a clear view of the coral reef and the divers down below. It would hardly have warranted a second look, had it not been for the blood in the boat and the corpse floating face down, its right wrist tangled in a line.

One glance confirmed that the boatman was dead. Richard wasted no more time on him. Instead he crouched over the side of his own Zodiac, looking fixedly down through the glass-bottomed box trapped between the inflated rubber and the wooden gunwale beside it. The first thing he saw was the still form of a diver far below, hanging just above the reef, surrounded by inquisitive little fish. The lack of bubbles told Richard's wise eyes that the diver was no longer breathing. So he grasped the sides of the box with steady hands and began to search for the buddy who must also be somewhere close by – though he was beginning to suspect they were too late to be of any use to any of them.

He saw the bubbles first, and his heart gave a great wrenching leap within his straining chest. Under the water, bubbles meant life. Eagerly, he angled the box until he could see where the string of lively pearls was coming from. And so at last he saw the dying woman. She was hanging surprisingly close at hand a few scant metres down. So close to safety, but so unsettlingly still. Seemingly frozen in the water like a beautiful fly in amber. Her spread legs, reaching arms and weed-wide silky hair formed a picture that would stay in his memory for as long as he lived. But even as he froze the image instantaneously into his mind, another, wavering string of bubbles began to wander towards the surface.

Without further thought, Richard had his regulator in his mouth and his facemask firmly in place. He gave a thumbs-up to Bugis and got one in return – though his companion's still, dark face was harder to read than the signal. He rolled into the water and started kicking down to her, coming out of the cloud of bubbles and clearing his ears as he went. His focus was all on that mysteriously motionless form; his intellect all immersed in how he was going to get her safely up to the surface and back aboard his ship.

It was not until very much later that he began to speculate upon what had gone on here. Why both the boatman and the buddy were dead. And why the woman was still just hanging helplessly unmoving in the water – if she was still alive and breathing.

THREE
Murder

It was murder getting the bodies back. Had Richard and his team been able to use the little dive boat it would have been easy enough, but the blood-spattered cockleshell was all-too-obviously an important piece of evidence – if not an actual crime scene. So loading it with sopping wet bodies was clearly going to be the last resort. The lifeboat itself was pretty full, though there was just room for the boatman once they had disentangled him from the line.

As Richard had observed coming out, the Zodiac would hardly hold himself and his massive companion, so it was perhaps fortunate that he was the only one with scuba gear – to begin with at least. Because that meant that he was the one who waited, hanging from the dive boat's gunwale, and then went back down for the dead buddy as Bugis sped the dying woman back to the doctor Robin had called. And that, at the time, seemed an entirely fortuitous circumstance. But his main – no, entire – preoccupation at first, of course, was the woman.

Richard swam down towards the woman carefully, torn between the desire to get her up and back to safety and the need to take the utmost care with what he was doing and what was going on around him. He was first-aid trained to Accident and Emergency level and he never forgot the First Aider's first commandment: *You're no good to anyone if you get hurt yourself.* So as he finned down through the sensuous warmth of the limpid water, fighting to disregard the distractingly physical sensations of diving while fully clothed, he was forced to speculate at last on what had actually gone on here, if only as a way of trying to ensure that nothing similar happened to him too.

The blood in the boat was suggestive of murderous violence but not conclusive proof. Richard easily constructed a simple, non-violent sequence of events, like an anti-Sherlock Holmes. There were sea snakes here that carried the most dangerous venom on earth. The buddy could have disturbed a nest of the creatures and been bitten to death instantly. The woman could have been going to help him and been bitten too. Badly enough to send her into toxic shock but not quite badly enough to kill her. And the boatman, panicked, could well have slipped, bashed his head, sprayed blood everywhere and fallen overboard unconscious. Such eventualities were vanishingly rare. But, as Richard knew from an enormity of experience, extreme rarity was not the same as absolute impossibility. Incredible coincidences were all too commonplace. Things that are generally agreed to be improbable have a habit of happening all the time.

But as he neared the floating woman, he observed no snakes. Nor indeed anything threatening enough to have panicked her into her deadly state. And yet, the way in which she was panting seemed to suggest terror. Perhaps enough to induce catatonia. Certainly, gasping for air like that was the next most dangerous thing she could be doing other than hanging helplessly down here, making no effort to swim up. For the rapid breathing would be using up her air supply at a truly dangerous rate.

Richard thought back over the years to his first scuba-diving lesson. *Slow and even breathing*, he had been told. Shallow gasps like she was using were a near-criminal waste of life-giving air. On the other hand, if she was catatonic with terror, having a hulking stranger suddenly appear beside her might just be all it took to trigger some kind of a reaction. Panic. Perhaps even heart-attack. But even as he speculated, the pearly string began to thin. His wise eyes warned him that the woman's tank was almost empty. He was only just in time. He would need to work very fast indeed.

Without further thought, Richard was in action. As swiftly as he could, he finned down past her, keeping clear, so as to avoid startling her as much as possible. Then with a dexterous twist of his body he reversed his position so that he was beneath her, looking up from as close as he dared – fighting to maintain a non-threatening distance.

Behind the eyepieces of her face mask, her dark brown eyes were wide. Terrified. But Richard was sure that his arrival had not triggered the terror. He had a deeply unsettling flash of insight into a mind trapped screaming for help and dying in a body that refused to respond – like a patient coming out of anaesthetic part way through an operation. He reached up gently, rising beneath her into closeness, and then into a more disturbing intimacy. He found that he was fighting the disorientating desire to identify with her, as though sharing her terror might lessen it for her. But it would also incapacitate him. *And where there's fear there's life*, he thought, grimly practical.

He reached out gently to touch the frozen fingers of her right hand.

The icy-pink digits flexed in response to his pressure. They did not push back. He took her arm. Positioned it gently. It stayed just where he had placed it, seemingly incapable of independent motion. Her body behaved almost like a puppet. A helplessly choking puppet. He wondered if she could have suffered some kind of stroke. He had heard of seizures that struck that fast. Embolisms. Thromboses. But never of three people struck down the same way at the same time on the same dive. Not without some external cause.

Richard's mind was working at lightning speed, ranging in ways that his conscious thoughts simply could not keep up with. The touch of the fingers, the look in her eyes, the lack of resistance as he took her arms, told some deep part of his understanding that only her most basic functions were still working, no matter what the explanation. She could breathe – was breathing the last dregs of an empty tank. She could think – was feeling utter terror. She could blink and cry – was doing so now, in fact; though on reflection he was not certain that she was actually communicating with him after all.

Some kind of rictus or catatonia seemed more likely the more he thought about it. But what could cause such a thing? He glanced around for sea snakes once again. Then returned to her almost at once, reassessing her situation as he prepared to act. Her lungs could pump. Her brain could think – on some level at least. Her heart could beat. But that was all. If he tried to replace her regulator with his own and give her some of his oxygen-rich mixture, it was unlikely that she would have sufficient control to benefit. A gentle touch of the rigid pinkness of her jaw suggested that he would never prise her own mouthpiece free in any case.

He glanced down the length of her body and was shocked to find himself struck by the rosy curves of her modest cleavage. Between the teeth of the partly open zip front, the tops of her breasts were crushed together like the blushing cheeks of a baby's bottom. Covered with goose-bumps though they were, they reminded him all too forcefully of Robin in her enticingly revealing silk basque. *Grow up*, he thought fiercely; *get a grip, for goodness' sake!*

He lowered his gaze still further and reached down to her waist. Fumbled among the straps and buckles there. Her dive belt had a quick-release and he opened it, still holding her right arm with his left fist. As the belt fell free, releasing her natural buoyancy, Richard started finning up towards the surface, keeping pace with his own bubbles and holding her close. It was unlikely that either of them would get the bends rising too rapidly from this depth – but of course he had no way of knowing how deep she had been before he arrived – or how careful she had been in coming up. *Tai Fun* had all mod-cons and a ship's sickroom pretty well equipped to handle little diving accidents, but she did not stretch to decompression chambers. So, better safe than sorry – as long as she had a last few lungfuls of compressed air left.

As Richard eased the woman up through the last few metres below the surface, he found himself in a distractingly strange situation. Her long brown hair almost made a tent around his head and shoulders, flowing down like skeins of liquorice silk. He was hesitant to look too deeply into her eyes, for fear of empathizing too deeply with the naked terror there. So it was that he found himself looking at the ridged pipe that joined her regulator to her air tank. And he noticed something that he hadn't noticed before. As she breathed, so a tiny thread of bubbles escaped from the pipe as well. Incongruously, he was put in mind of childhood Saturdays. Of sitting in the garden with the wheel of his beloved Raleigh bicycle half disembowelled as he searched for punctures on the inner tube. Of the bowl of tepid water where the half-inflated tubes writhed like eels and the tell-tale skeins of bubbles that marked the otherwise invisible points where he would place his patch when the rubber was dry.

But even as Richard watched, the last few bubbles came and went. With gathering desperation he shook her hair out of the window of his face mask and looked up. The surface was perhaps a metre away. He finned for it with all his might and burst out of the water beside the Zodiac like a breaching whale. At once the silk of the woman's hair closed around him once more as though it was full of static – or he of magnetism. Her lifeless body attained weight in his arms and her tank added to it. The pair of them fell back and began to sink once more.

But Bugis was there. He reached his broad strong hands down and caught the woman under her armpits, lifting both her and Richard upwards effortlessly. Richard at last let go of her and slid back down the length of her, striking his forehead against the belt buckle of her scuba gear and against the solidity of her pubic bone, ridged as it was with the fastenings of her wetsuit's gusset. Her flushed thighs briefly straddled his cheeks and then the water closed over him again.

A moment later he pulled himself up by the line around the Zodiac's inflated side. He spat out his regulator. Even as he did so, he felt the Zodiac begin to move. 'CPR,' he bellowed. 'Can you do CPR while you steer?' He pulled himself up, twisting against the gathering drag of the water, straining to peer over the side of the vessel and make sure that Bugis had heard him. But one glance into the Zodiac told him all he needed to know. The woman lay in the crook of the huge man's right arm while his left fist gunned the outboard to full throttle. And, like Prince Charming come to rescue Snow White, he was pressing his lips to hers, giving her the kiss of life as he steered for safety.

As the Zodiac powered away towards *Tai Fun*, Richard swung round in the water, almost overcome by a sudden weariness. Weighed by his scuba gear, it was almost all that his suddenly exhausted body could do to splash across to the lifeboat. But no sooner had he reached the solid gunwale than he was almost brutally distracted from his physical, mental and emotional exhaustion. 'Look at this, Richard,' called the First Officer.

'I'll need a hand up,' Richard answered.

At once a pair of brawny fists took the shoulder straps of his scuba gear and lifted him up until he could look into the lifeboat itself. And there, laid out reverently in the scuppers, lay the boatman. His ankles were precisely together allowing his broad bare feet to point calloused toes at the sky. The knees were alike aligned and the turn-ups of his shorts were a matching eighteen inches above them. His brightly printed Hawaiian-patterned T-shirt clung to his skinny torso, tightly enough to show his ribs, even under the broad spread of his folded hands. The pattern's gaudy brightness was extended, brightened, by the great gouts of red that almost rivalled the plumage of the scarlet macaws and crimson birds of paradise that made up the bulk of the pattern.

His nose, like his toes, pointed religiously heavenwards. His eyes were closed and his jaw bound like Marley's in *A Christmas Carol* by a handkerchief to keep his mouth from lolling wide. Between the conservative white of the handkerchief and the flamboyant excess of the Hawaiian shirt, his throat lay like a pale ivory column. And exactly halfway down the column it had been cut. Cut so surely and severely that, in spite of the fact that there seemed to be only one knife-stroke, the windpipe and the blood vessels around it gaped in apparent wonder at what had been done to them. Gaped so wide that the tube of gristle lay open like the ruptured join of two hoses. Behind and around them, muscles gleamed like the carcass of a rabbit on a butcher's slab. And behind those, in turn, shone a pallid glitter of white where the vertebrae of the neck lay partially exposed.

'That's it,' said Richard. 'If there was ever any doubt, it's over now. This is murder.'

And one of the crewmen, a native islander from Seram, shivered, looked suspiciously around at the empty, apparently innocent face of the nearby sea, and said the one word which, under the circumstances, Richard probably least wanted to hear: '*Bugis!*'

FOUR
Bugis

Richard swam back down towards the dead man on the coral shelf. As he cleared his ears and went through the automatic diving routine, he found that his mind was distractingly preoccupied with wry thoughts about ethnic stereotyping. One sight of a cut throat had made the islander in the lifeboat think of Bugis pirates – had made Richard himself doubt for an instant the wisdom of giving the dying woman to a Bugis rescuer. And yet there were millions of Bugis living in the area. Many were seafarers. Indeed, some by tradition never came to land. They moved around in fleets of little craft that were effectively floating villages. And most of these were good honest fishermen, eking out an increasingly precarious living in the face of dwindling fish stocks like fishermen all over the world. Their traditional lifestyle sidelined – brought to the verge of ruin – by the greed of the big national and multinational fishing fleets.

But many more Bugis were coastal farmers, city dwellers, businessmen. To see them all as pirates was as thoughtlessly racist as supposing that all Scotsmen wore kilts, ate haggis while swilling whisky, and only took time off counting their money to dance the Highland Fling or to organize drunken brawls on Sauchiehall Street on a Saturday night.

And yet . . .

And yet . . .

As Richard neared the stationary, sinister body of the second diver, he dragged his mind back to the present. There was now no doubt that the boatman had been murdered. He could not yet begin to explain what had happened to the woman but foul play might well have been involved there too. So it was his duty as he saw it to observe everything near the dead diver as minutely as possible – for this might be a crime scene every bit as important as the blood-spattered boat. And it was all too probable that he was the only person who would ever get a chance to examine it in any detail. He slowed his descent therefore and moved to one side so that he could observe and mentally record.

From time to time in the past, Richard had relied on his strong visual memory, which was bordering on the photographic. It was not unusual for him to see more than he understood, only later coming to comprehend the relevance of some detail keenly observed, unconsciously recorded, then half forgotten until the vital moment.

So Richard narrowed his eyes and began to sweep his keenest and most focussed vision across the area at whose heart the dead man floated. He observed the way the coral formed a ledge that reached outwards like a crusted shelf, then plunged vertically, vertiginously, over a cliff that fell away into a blue-black abyss.

The dead man was perhaps fifteen metres down, the level coral shelf a metre more beneath him, stretching away in relative shallows as far as Richard could see to north and south. But three metres or so behind the lifeless flippers, the coral cliff plunged into the depths. On the ledge and the upper reaches of the cliff, the corals and the fish that swam among them were jewel bright and dazzlingly colourful. The clarity of the water compensated for the liquid's tendency to bleach out the yellows and reds in the spectrum and to favour the blues. Under a white flashlight, Richard calculated, the reef would be more lovely still, full of rubies and garnets where now there were a few emeralds but mostly sapphires, turquoise and aquamarine. Except for an area immediately below the diver himself.

Immediately below the diver, the corals were dull and brown, as though they had been washed with crude oil. And in this gash of lifelessness floated one or two fish, their bellies towards the distant surface, as dead as the diver watching them. Richard swam closer, his interest piqued. Almost without thought, he found himself reaching out to touch the diver's motionless shoulder. At once, on some deeply atavistic level, he was torn with indecision. His conscious mind continued to inspect the reef. His subconscious recoiled in terror in case the dead man should come back to ghastly life at the first touch. And unconsciously, perhaps, he was already bristling with tension and suspicion that there was something badly out of kilter here.

So that when a broad hand closed on Richard's own shoulder at the very moment he took hold of the dead man, he jumped with shock and let out such a yell that he nearly lost his regulator. He leaped back through the water, and his motion set the dead man dancing. But then Bugis thrust his head and torso into the whirling current between them. Richard took a moment to recognize the man for his face was distorted by the facemask and regulator. But there was no mistaking those massive teak shoulders. Nor the perfectly sculpted pectorals against which he pressed a message board.

Get back aboard as fast as you can, it said in Robin's distinctive copperplate. *This woman will die unless we get her to hospital at once.*

Richard nodded to show that he understood, then Bugis and he took one strap each and they hoisted the last corpse up to the surface by its scuba gear.

The lifeboat was gone, as was the diveboat – no doubt in tow. The twelve-man Zodiac bobbed in its place, and the blonde girl from the exercise bike was holding the outboard control – no mean feat as the thing was powered by a massive matched pair of Johnson outboard motors. Bugis went aboard first, as lithe as a seal landing on an ice floe. As he spat out his regulator, he turned and reached down, pausing as he waited for Richard to hand the dead man up.

In order to do this most effectively, Richard had to turn the corpse to face him and so, for the first time, he found himself face to face with the second murder victim. So close that their regulators almost touched. The man's eyes were wide and staring, bloodshot. Apparently filled with terror. The brows above them were raised in a permanent rictus that creased the skin trapped by the face mask. His nostrils were flared. His dripping hair was literally standing on end. Had his jaws not been locked around his useless regulator, he would have seemed to be screaming. But in Richard's experience, terror brings pallor to a frightened man's cheeks. This man's cheeks were bright red. And that made him think of the dying woman's cleavage. Which in turn made Richard begin to suspect that . . .

As Bugis's hand gained half purchase on a strap, Richard spat out his regulator, let go with his right hand and slid his face mask up to take a long, thoughtful breath of good fresh air, his mind for the moment distracted from its forensic train of thought.

Bugis grabbed the second strap of the scuba tank and slid the corpse up out of Richard's grasp. The sudden pressure on the tank made the straps strain around the corpse's torso. The dead man seemed to breathe out, pushing the pressure in his regulator up enough to release a disquieting hiss of air. Richard found his face

full of rubber-stinking dead breath. He hardly noticed the stale
rubber smell – his mouth and nose had been filled with it since he
put his scuba gear on – but there was something else that suddenly
made his head spin and his heart race. Something unexpected. He
looked up automatically, only to have his eyes filled by a thin stream
of water from a leak in the diver's air hose. Then the flippers flapped
into his face like the tail of an escaping dolphin and that pushed
all other thoughts away.

With his mind clearing and his suspicions shelved, if not forgotten,
Richard in turn pulled himself out of the water. No sooner had he
rolled into the Zodiac than the young woman gunned the motors and
the bow climbed on to a considerable wave as the inflatable powered
back towards *Tai Fun*. The full-throated roar of the big Johnson
outboards combined with the rumble of the headwind, the slapping
of the hull against the bow-wave and the tumbling hiss of the wake
to make conversation impossible. The body, still frozen in a half-
crouch, had rolled on to its side as though trying for a half-hearted
foetal position. This was neither the time nor the place for closer
examination, so Richard sat back, set about shrugging off his scuba
gear and started to assess the damage he had done to the clothes he
had worn through the adventure so far, but he was soon distracted.

Bugis and his companion had not chosen the larger Zodiac on a
whim. Clearly the big bodybuilder had seen as clearly as Richard
that the six-man would not be big enough to take them all. Indeed,
with the four aboard, even this one was sitting pretty low. But it
was the power that they clearly needed most of all. For *Tai Fun* was
by no means waiting for them. As Robin's message had stated, the
woman would be dead if they didn't get her some state-of-the-art
medical attention soon. And the nearest – best – hospital available
was in the basement of the Greenbaum International Volcano Roads
Hotel. Towards which the glorious white ship was already powering,
her sails at full-stretch and straining, her deck tilted and her sleek
hull racing forward.

The young woman brought the Zodiac round tight behind the
racing ship, thrashing the last knot out of the racing motors. And
she needed to do so, for the Zodiac was not designed for speed
– like Richard's beloved Cigarette Launch *Marilyn*. Forty knots
was her top whack, as it was *Tai Fun*'s, and for a moment it
looked as though Richard and his companions were going to be
left behind. But Bugis and the young woman were an excellent
team. As she squeezed the last drop of power from her motors,

so he gathered up the line in the Zodiac's bow and threw it forward to a team that were obviously awaiting them on the last lip of the dive deck. It was a good throw, expertly caught and whipped round a winch in one fluid motion. Then they were being dragged aboard, up the slipway that made up *Tai Fun*'s sternmost section. As they began to come aboard in a great wash of foam, Bugis pulled on the straining line. The woman throttled back on the motors and rocked their screws up out of the water. And Richard stooped to gather the dead man's body, ready to carry him aboard.

The Zodiac creamed up on to the slipway and settled. Willing hands cinched the bow-line tight and grasped the rope that ran around the gunwale, steadying the inflatable. Richard started to straighten with his unwieldy burden, but no sooner did he do so than another pair of strong brown arms joined his own to make a cradle for the corpse. And so he and Bugis carried the dead diver aboard together.

They didn't have to carry him far. There was a gurney waiting at the poolside, held by the doctor's assistants overseen by Eva Gruber, clearly doubling her First Officer duties as navigator with those of Medical Officer. 'The doctor's with the woman,' she explained brusquely, flipping a sheet over the body the instant they laid him down. 'He can't work out what's happened to her but he's in touch with the medical team at the hotel. There's a good deal he doesn't understand – not least what's the matter with her legs. Or her breathing come to that. But they'll be waiting to admit her the instant that we dock.'

'Her legs?' demanded Richard, following in her wake as she led the gurney team towards the ship's infirmary. 'Could it be the bends? That might explain the breathing problems too. I had no way of knowing how deep she'd been or for how long. But she was out of air when I got to her. I brought her up pretty quickly . . .'

'He thinks not the bends. Luckily. The nearest decompression chamber is in Surabaya.'

Robin was waiting by the mysterious patient's bedside. She had slipped on a simple sun dress and swapped her high heels for more practical deck shoes. But the outfit clung strangely and a little suggestively to her constricted shape and the feet thrust into the canvas footwear were still adorned by sheer silk stockings. 'I knew you'd come here first,' she said as he walked in. 'Pay your respects and move along, Buster. Look at the state of you! You'll have to shower again and get dressed in record time. We'll be there before you know it and I'm not about to have you coming ashore looking like a tramp and letting Heritage Mariner down.'

But her tone robed the acerbic words of any real sting. And as he looked down at the sleeping woman's pink-cheeked face – what he could see of it around the old-fashioned oxygen mask – she raised her hand and stroked the square line of his jaw. But the instant she did so, she started back as though she had been discovered doing something embarrassing. 'Oh. Hello, Captain,' she said. 'I didn't hear you come in. I don't think you've met my husband. Richard, have you met Captain Kalla?'

Richard looked up at her. She didn't usually gush this effusively. Then he looked across at the new arrival, a courteous negative rising to his lips. Where it froze.

For standing in the doorway was not the stranger Richard had been expecting. Instead, still dripping wet and wearing nothing but his swimming trunks, his hand politely extended at the introduction, was the man Richard had been thinking of as Bugis.

'Kalla,' said the muscular giant. 'Jahan Jussif Kalla.' His bland gaze switched from Richard to Robin, then settled on the sleeping beauty on the sickbed as he continued, 'Captain Mariner and I have worked well together, ma'am, but we haven't yet been formally introduced.'

'Captain Kalla,' continued Robin, as though unaware of the gently forceful interruption, 'is Nic Greenbaum's new head of security at the Volcano Roads Hotel.'

FIVE

Greenbaum

Within the hour, *Tai Fun* was riding easily at anchor in her allotted place under the shadow of the Greenbaum International Volcano Roads Hotel. It was a little after 4pm local time. The long, lean vessel was all a-bustle as excited passengers got themselves ready to go ashore. A wide companionway had been lowered, reaching in easy steps from the deck to a floating stage. This sat steady in the water, for the wind of the early afternoon had dropped and a calm had settled, bringing with it unruffled waters undisturbed by a gently falling tide. The sun was beginning to settle through the cerulean of the cloudless sky. It would be dark soon after six, when the fireworks were due to soar across a full and flawless moon.

Between the stage and the nearby Marina Reception steps, a flotilla of launches bustled busily, trying to make up for the time *Tai Fun* had lost already. The first of these had been waiting anxiously for the four-master's arrival, with the hotel's doctor and a medical team aboard. The mysterious woman was the first off and into their care, with Richard, in evening trousers and little else, keeping anxious watch from the rail outside his stateroom. He had been torn between a strange kind of jealousy and a poignant pang of relief to see Captain Jahan Jussif Kalla's massive form follow her stretcher solicitously aboard.

Next off were the woman's two dead companions. But by the time they were moved, Richard was wrestling with the fastenings of the incredibly chic little formal cocktail dress that Stella McCartney had made for Robin before the Mariners left London en route for Singapore, *Tai Fun* and Pulau Baya. Only when Robin was satisfied, and stood before the full-length mirror making tiny final adjustments like a blonde Audrey Hepburn on her way to *Breakfast At Tiffany's*, did he turn to the equally testing matters of wing collars, shirt-studs, cufflinks, cummerbunds and black bow ties.

By the time Robin was satisfied with her dress, accessories, jewellery and hair, Richard had finished tying his white bow, tightening his waistcoat, and was replacing his battered Rolex with the sleek gold Malvern chronograph by Christopher Ward of London that she had chosen for this occasion. Then he reached for the exquisite new handmade black lightweight Merino tails that replaced the familiar, favourite but slightly battered jacket that Gieves & Hawkes had made for him to celebrate the Millennium. He donned it with a slight nostalgic pang – as he had felt when the new watch replaced the Rolex. At least the black mirror-shiny patent leather party shoes by Lobb of London were snugly familiar, he thought.

But when Robin turned round, satisfied with her own appearance at last, she gave a satisfied little chuckle. 'Now you really do look the part, my love!' she purred, reaching up automatically to straighten his already perfect bow tie. Over her shoulder he glanced at his reflection in the mirror. He was not a vain man by any means but he did not disapprove of what he saw. The new jacket fitted perfectly, and was so light that it hardly seemed to be sitting on his broad, square shoulders at all. The wing collar stood clear of his broad, determined chin with the tie returned to the military perfection he always sought. When he touched the white bow thoughtlessly with his left forefinger, the sleeve of his jacket slid back to reveal the gleam of gold on the double cuff and the matching curve of his new watch. The whiteness of the starched cotton shirt emphasized the rich deep blackness of the jacket. He raised one eyebrow sardonically and met his own blue gaze with the slightly lopsided grin he now wore courtesy of an adventure in the China Sea. An adventure that also left him with a piratical scar along the line of one cheekbone, like the duelling scar of an old-fashioned Prussian Count. Robin patted his blue-black hair like a little schoolmarm with a huge but outstanding student.

And even as she did so, there was a rap on the door. 'The bridal party is ready to go ashore,' called the Chief Steward.

And Richard's grin spread. '*Showtime!*' he whispered.

The tall, slender, ash-blonde, apparently glacial, soon-to-be Princess Inga Nordberg had selected the design of her wedding dress with this precise moment in mind. Robin knowledgeably watched the young woman hesitate for an instant at the top of the companionway, her father aglow with pride at her elbow, as she glanced down towards the wedding-cake confection of the bridal boat waiting below. And at the slightly unstable flight of steps suspended between the two.

Most brides decided on their ensemble with the church in mind, thought Robin in ready sympathy. Or the reception. Or the wedding photographs. But when Inga had talked through the wedding plans with her matron of honour, Robin had said simply, 'If you and Sailendra insist on using *Tai Fun* as the wedding vehicle and you simply *must* arrive in your wedding gown, then it all turns round that companionway, Inga. Getting off *Tai Fun* in full matrimonial rig, down a companionway and into a launch without going ass over tit will be all but impossible. So if you don't want to change in the hotel itself, then that's the bit I'd focus on, my dear. And we'd better warn the bridesmaids too. High hems and low heels or there'll be twisted ankles, broken wrists – and a hell of a lot of underwear on display a good deal earlier than planned. Though of course you can all add little bits and pieces when you're safe ashore.'

Inga glanced back at Robin and flashed her a grateful smile.

Then, lifting the exquisitely embroidered hem of her white gown above the lace bows of her sensibly heeled white silk pumps, she stepped confidently down, hardly needing to lean on her father's steady arm at all. Richard and Robin followed immediately behind. Robin did need to lean on Richard for she had been less willing to take her own advice than the bride – or the bridesmaids who followed on behind – had been.

The reception party waiting to hand them up the marina steps was led by Nic Greenbaum himself. Dressed in an almost exact reflection of Richard's Savile Row magnificence, Nic still looked indefinably American, even before he opened his mouth to let loose that familiar Texan drawl. The Crash of 2008/09 seemed to have made him leaner – as it had burned the last fat away from his companies. A couple of billion dollars' worth of fat by all accounts, with plenty of lean meat left on the corporate bones. His face was angular, his badger-grey beard shorter and squarer cut. On their first meeting in the Long Bar of Singapore's Raffles Club, Nic had reminded Robin of a tough American Santa Claus. He didn't look much like Santa now, she thought. More like Abe Lincoln would have looked like if he had made it out of Ford's theatre, grown a moustache and lived to an active old age. But when he caught her eye and gave an ebullient wave, she grinned and waved back at him, as elated as a child approaching a Christmas grotto.

As they all stepped ashore, Nic gave the bride's cheek an avuncular peck and her father's hand a squeeze, but it was clear that he was really focussed on the Matron of Honour and her escort. 'Robin!' he boomed. 'You look fit to eat. Richard. My man!'

Robin took one look at the approaching bear-hug and yelled, 'Nic Greenbaum! If you mess up my—'

Nic smoothly segued the massive embrace into a swift hug and swung round to give Richard's hand a hearty shake. 'We have business to discuss. You, me and Sailendra.'

'In due course,' agreed Richard. 'But the bridegroom prince will have one or two more pressing priorities just at the moment, I suspect.'

'Do tell!' laughed Nic, easing his long, lean frame between the Mariners and taking each by the elbow. So the three of them followed the bride and her father up the steps and in through the Marina Entrance of the huge seven-star hotel – the most luxurious and magnificent outside what was left of the exclusive Saudi Riviera.

The huge white marble reception area was already thronging with the great and the good – their hangers-on and their acolytes.

TV crews and news reporters jostled with yet more TV crews and commentators – social, political and fashionable. Paparazzi swarmed, their invasive excesses courteously restrained by punctilious hotel security staff.

As the three of them entered the dazzling throng, however, Robin's mind suddenly took a darker turn. Her eye was not caught by the perfectly dressed men – wearing everything from royal robes to black tuxedoes. Nor by the bewildering variety of women – looking like a flock of Birds of Paradise flown down here from their protected virgin forests high on the volcano slopes. Her attention suddenly fixed on a plain white-uniformed nurse fighting to get through the careless throng. A nurse on a vital mission, clearly, thoughtlessly stymied by the uncaring bustle of the sybaritic guests and the ruthlessly rude photographers – until Captain Kalla appeared at her side and guided her safely through. His blue jeans and open-necked shirt made him stand out as clearly as her plain white uniform had done, independently of his massive size and irresistibly decisive movements. Making them both seem normal. Workaday. Real people doing real and important things amid this mindlessly self-indulgent bustle.

But when Robin looked across at Nic she saw her old friend's angular face darken in a fleeting frown to reflect her own dark thoughts. He raised his hand to his lips and she saw a flash of a microphone almost as discreet as Richard's gold cufflinks. 'Someone get to the chief of security and tell him I want him in a monkey suit by the time the ceremony starts,' the hotel owner ordered. 'I'm not about to let anything or anyone in this hotel look less than absolutely perfect, today of all days!'

It suddenly seemed to Robin that the eyes of the entire world must be on the island, the hotel and the dazzling ceremonies. And yet how tawdry they abruptly seemed to her under the current life-or-death circumstances. The only man who seemed to have his priorities right was the one too busy saving lives to get out of his jeans and into his penguin suit. She looked around, her eyes more jaundiced than ever. Social commentators thronged, agog at the range of celebrities attending. Financial correspondents stood counting the euros, pounds and dollars – roubles, yen and RBM – represented by the international money-moguls there. All of them as hungry as sharks at a feeding-frenzy for the promise of profits that would pull them out of the shadow of depression. Political pundits tapped their palm-held computers, calculating the power of the men and women called together from parliament and palace alike, every one equally thirsty for the life-giving political water of positive publicity and the illusion that they alone could bring hope like Moses in Egypt.

And none of them paid any attention to the little nurse or the tall man guiding her towards the Infirmary door – unless they were swinging round to face him with a curse or an insult in rude reaction to his courteous but insistent pressure to pass them by. Insults and curses, she noticed, that froze into cowardly silence when they saw just how big and powerful the casually dressed Captain was.

And yet, like it or not, Nic, Richard and she belonged here amid the vapid glitter as surely as Inga; as surely as Prince Sailendra himself. As the three of them moved forward towards the Grand Reception Room where Sailendra himself awaited them with his Council and the Island's leading Imam, every eye they met recognized them. Every face they saw smiled acknowledgement. Every head nodded familiar greeting. Every group and individual before them fell back out of their way – allowing them to breeze on past in exactly the opposite manner that Captain Kalla had been forced to proceed. Not only did they belong in places such as this, they were the natural leaders of circles such as these. Whether they liked it or not.

But even so, Robin felt increasingly trapped. She wanted more than anything to follow Captain Kalla and the nurse, to find out how the rescued woman was. But she had a duty as Matron of Honour that bound her as tightly as a straightjacket. 'I wonder how that poor woman is,' she murmured to Richard as they were ushered into the waiting room beside the Grand Reception Room.

Richard glanced at his gold watch then shot a calculating look into the Grand Reception Room itself. Their places were clearly marked and reserved near the seats occupied by Prince Sailendra's court. Sailendra himself was seated on his great gold-leaf throne, a vision in gold brocade and white silk trousers with curling-toed slippers and high, feathered turban straight out of the *Arabian Nights*. As Richard squinted through, the prince leaned sideways, apparently relaxed, talking to his chief councillor and the expectant Imam behind a hand encrusted with sufficient jewels to stock Asprey's in Bond Street or Tiffany's on Fifth Avenue.

'I'll see what I can find out before I go in and await events,' he promised as the waiting-room door was shut against him. And his promise lightened Robin's heart as she turned to oversee the final preparations for the swan-princess Inga Nordburg and her gaggle of over-excited bridesmaids.

SIX
Dr Dhakar

Richard explained to Nic what little he didn't already know about the adventure of the drowning woman while the pair of them were easing through the crowd towards the door marked 'Infirmary' that Captain Kalla and the nurse had entered earlier. But he did so only after a quick man-to-man – partner-to-partner – about how the late arrival of *Tai Fun* with the bridal party had reversed the proposed order of Grand Opening followed by Royal Wedding. 'That's life,' Nic concluded philosophically, relieving a waiter of a tray of gourmet nuts and offering them to Richard. 'We'll do the Grand Opening tomorrow and hope the guys and gals aren't too hungover to appreciate it. Now, bring me up to speed with what's going on in the real world of Life And Death.' Richard nodded, chewing on a mouthful of cashews and almonds, cleared his throat and began to speak.

The brief and focussed conversation that followed was more than mere indulgence – even the bits that were simply repeating what Nic already knew. It was Richard's first opportunity to work through his own memories. To begin to look for some kind of pattern. Some kind of clue.

'And she was just hanging there, five metres down . . .' Nic said, his voice full of wonder.

'Like one of those toy divers in a bell jar I had when I was a kid,' confirmed Richard, pulling the door wide.

As the door hissed shut behind them, they found themselves in a corridor that led inwards towards a stairwell and a lift shaft. After the brightness and buzzing bustle of the reception area it was almost unsettlingly quiet here. Richard repressed the desire to shiver – and not because it was cold. Quite the opposite, in fact.

'She couldn't move or anything,' said Nic round a mouthful of nuts.

'She could only just breathe as far as I could see. And she couldn't do that too well.' Richard looked round at the service areas under their flat white light. They were beautifully decorated and elegantly tiled, though he suspected that very few guests would be expected to come out here – except in an emergency.

'You'd have thought a shark or something would have taken her. Completely helpless like that. And there must have been blood in the water from the boatman at least.'

'There were no big fish anywhere nearby,' said Richard. 'There wasn't even anything big hunting along the reef itself.'

'Well it's a mystery that beats the hell outta me!' Nic pressed a button and the lift car hissed up towards them from the Infirmary level below. It took two seconds to rise two levels and when the door opened Richard was surprised to find how big the lift car was. Big enough to hold a couple of hospital trolleys, of course, he thought as he stepped in beside Nic. Still thinking about recent events but beginning to plan ahead a little too, he took the opportunity to check his reflection once again in the big mirrors that made up the inside walls of the lift. If the scrum in the reception area was anything to go by, they were all likely to be on TV before sunset. Independently of what was likely to happen when Pulau Baya's police authorities arrived to look into the two mysterious deaths.

'Let's hope Dr Dhakar can shed a little light,' continued the American and punched the button marked INFIRMARY in red. The minute the car began to sink, Nic lifted his right hand to his ear, touched something there, and said, apparently to his own frowning reflection, 'Captain Mariner and I are checking in the infirmary now. Keep me up to speed with the timetable for the Grand Reception Room. And I want a countdown before anything important happens. Captain Mariner and I need time to get back to our places. Now, security for the prince, count off on my mark and report your situations. Mark.'

Richard glanced across at his companion and for the first time noticed the tiny little Bluetooth earpiece he was wearing. 'Are you overseeing security yourself?' he asked, surprised. Nic was not a man to keep a dog and then go barking himself.

'Until Captain Kalla's kitted up and in full charge,' answered the hotel owner shortly after a tiny pause. 'Then I'll just be kept up to speed.'

The lift hissed to a stop. The doors opened and Richard stepped forward at Nic's side. And the illusion that they were in a top-flight hospital was complete. A short corridor led to two double doors, one on their right and the other almost straight ahead. On the left it led away into the bowels of the building. The two pairs of double doors were steel-panelled so that they could be opened by the impact

of a speeding trolley. Indeed, the faintest of marks on the pair opposite showed Richard that this had happened recently. As did a pair
of marks on the door and a series of rubber tracks on the padded
linoleum of the easy-clean floor. Though the doors were closed
now, a hum of conversation came from beyond them.

On the other hand, the other doors, the ones on their right at the
end of the corridor, were open. They revealed a room that was obviously a mortuary. Here the bodies of the boatman and the buddy
lay on a pair of stainless-steel autopsy tables. The buddy's gear was
piled on a third table. Beside this stood Captain Kalla clad in nothing
more than white cotton boxer shorts and black silk socks.

Nic gave an exclamation of surprise and irritation. He turned on
his heel and strode towards the mortuary, with Richard quizzically
at his shoulder. As they moved, however, a slim female arm appeared
out of the shadows handing over a pair of black evening trousers.
And by the time Richard and Nic made it to the door itself, Kalla
was stepping into them, moving steadily from one foot to the other,
with his broad back turned.

They arrived not only part way through his dressing, but part
way through a conversation as well. Their footsteps silenced by the
padded linoleum, their presence masked by the way the captain and
his assistant were concentrating on the job in hand, Richard and
Nic paused and eavesdropped for a moment.

'. . . I can't see any further security implications either for *Tai
Fun* or for the hotel,' he was saying to the blonde woman who
had controlled the Zodiac so adroitly. 'I guess we can leave this
to the local guys now and get on with our day job.' He fastened
his waistband and reached for a snowy cotton shirt.

'It's a bit of a coincidence, though. You were right to double-
check,' she said as he shook it out of its sharp starched creases,
pulled the crisp white material over his head and set about tucking
its tails in. 'I mean what are the odds? Today of all days? Here of
all places?'

'Well, Dr Dhakar will alert me if and when the woman wakes.
Or if she learns anything important from examining the corpses.
She won't be doing an autopsy – not until the investigators arrive
and decide on which pathologist they want for the post-mortem
work. But she might shed some light. In the meantime we'll still
stay on high alert.' He reached for a bow tie, looped it adroitly
round his neck and expertly began to tie it using a polished steel
surface as a mirror.

'You mean you're ditching the James Bond rule?' purred the woman, her voice coming mysteriously out of the shadows beside him. 'The one that says: *Once is happenstance, twice is coincidence, three times is enemy . . .*'

'Yeah,' he said. 'We go straight for *enemy action*. And stay on high alert until we know different.' He picked up a black leather shoulder holster and slid it on with the same practised ease he had used to tie the bow at his throat. He pulled a big boxy automatic that looked to Richard like the new Walther 9mm. He slid it in and out of the quick-release holster three times with dazzling speed. Then he reached for the black DJ that the blonde was holding for him. 'I think that's our best option,' he continued without turning. 'What do you think, Mr Greenbaum?'

'I agree,' said Nic, unfazed. 'Better safe than sorry. How long have you known we two were here?'

'Since you arrived, sir.' He straightened the black DJ and buttoned it. Then he turned, slipping an earpiece into his ear and settling the little curve of mic against his jaw where the minuscule transmitter could pick up any speech vibrations most effectively. He glanced across into the shadows and his blonde right hand stepped forward. She too was settling into place a tight-fitted, low-cut party frock, and Richard realized with a bad-boy frisson that she had been getting dressed behind the door as the captain had been getting dressed in front of it. Either way, in the tight black little couture number, she would have matched that of any of the guests and she, like her boss, could pass unremarked anywhere through the excited throng upstairs. If she was carrying a weapon of any size at all, Richard speculated, it must be strapped to her inner thigh, and very high up it indeed. For even her little clutch bag seemed too tiny to contain anything except a compact. But then he remembered a friend in China who had favoured a Rohrbaugh 9mm that was smaller than his palm . . .

'Now, is there anything else you want to discuss, sir, before the sergeant and I go to work?' rumbled Captain Kalla.

'No, Captain.'

'Thank you sir.' The captain's finger touched the tiny earpiece. 'Right people,' he said, apparently to the corpses lying either side of him. 'Now listen up . . .'

Nic and Richard stood back courteously as the massive security team leader and his sylph-like aide strode past with a whisper of cotton and slither of silk in a cloud of purposefulness and perfume.

Richard and Nic turned to follow them, but as they did so, the
second door opened and a tall woman bustled out. She wore a
white coat open to reveal black robes. A headscarf covered her
hair and was fastened beneath the determined jut of her chin.
Round, gold-rimmed glasses glinted fiercely, but failed to hide
the wide brown, frowning eyes. 'Who are you?' she snapped in
English. 'Why are you hanging around here? More security men
I suppose . . .'

Captain Kalla paused at the lift. 'No, Dr Dhakar,' he answered
easily as he punched the button to open the door. 'Mr Greenbaum
owns the hotel. Captain Mariner found your corpses and brought
your patient up.'

'Captain Mariner.' The doctor's rather fearsome gaze fastened
on Richard at once. 'I need to talk to you.' Her certainty over which
of them was which made Richard suspect at once that the formid-
able woman had recognized her employer straight away but chosen
not to acknowledge him.

'Perhaps later, Doctor,' Nic overrode Richard's answer. 'We have
important duties to perform.' As if to emphasize his words, the lift
door whispered open. The captain and the sergeant stepped in side
by side.

'As do I!' she snapped. 'Saving this poor girl's life! And if this
man can help me then that takes precedence over a social celebration, no matter how important.'

'The doctor's right,' said Richard. 'You go on, Nic.' He caught
Kalla's eye and a broad brown hand effortlessly held the lift door
wide. Nic hesitated. Then he reached up and took the Bluetooth
out of his ear. 'This'll keep you up to speed at least,' he said, dropping it into Richard's palm. Then he strode over to the lift and the
three of them were gone.

Richard turned to the doctor, sliding the warm moulding of the
earpiece home and dismissing at once the background hum of security babble over the open channel. 'Now, Doctor,' he said amenable.
'How can I be of service?'

The doctor turned on her heel. 'I have a problem,' she snapped,
as though the problem were all his fault – as indeed in a way it
was. 'I have a patient who is being very slow to respond to my
treatment. This means that the condition is worse than I had
suspected – or is different to what I diagnosed.'

Either alternative sounded from the doctor's tone to be equally
unthinkable, thought Richard, wryly amused. And it sounded as

though the patient was going to find herself in as much trouble as her rescuers, should she be unfortunate enough to wake up any time soon.

The diatribe was enough to get them through into the infirmary, however. Here the young woman lay apparently comatose under the watchful eye of the nurse Richard assumed was the one who had accompanied Captain Kalla down here earlier. Like the doctor, the nurse wore a white coat over traditional Muslim dress. Unlike the doctor, her round young face was folded into a look of sympathetic concern.

The unconscious woman's face was easier to see now, for the old-fashioned oxygen mask had been replaced by a more up-to-date nose tube. She was breathing more easily, it appeared to him, and did not seem to require any pressure to assist her. Her cheeks were paler now, too. The disturbing darkness had gone from her lips. The bare arms that lay outside the back-folded sheet were ivory now, not rose. She was connected to a heart monitor which registered her pulse rate as being elevated, but not dangerously so.

'May I . . .?' asked Richard without thinking, and he lifted the sheet to reveal a low-cut hospital gown, and the upper slopes of the breasts beneath.

'What are you doing? Cover the poor woman at once!' spat the doctor. And Richard obeyed instantly, stepping back apologetically as the nurse restored the pristine folds of the sheet. In his preoccupation he had utterly failed to take account of the sensibilities of the conservatively attired women. But he had seen what he wanted to see – in several regards.

'When I found her,' he said slowly, turning to face the outraged doctor, 'her skin was flushed pink. The colour was striking. Her breathing was extremely fast – as was her pulse. It seemed to me that she was only able to continue breathing because of the pressure in her air tanks and later in the pure oxygen the doctor aboard *Tai Fun* put her on. I have to say, Doctor, that despite what you said, your treatment is working well, whatever your initial diagnosis has been. It has certainly cured the most disturbing symptoms. Have you examined her dead companions yet?'

'Not yet,' answered the doctor more guardedly, perhaps a little mollified by the confidence of his tone and the relevance of his remarks.

'Then perhaps it's time we did so,' suggested Richard. And he turned on his heel, leading the doctor decisively out of the infirmary and into the mortuary. 'We can, perhaps, discuss my initial observations of her condition while we see whether his is any different.'

'But why should we do that, Doctor?' asked the nurse, no doubt surprised at her boss's willingness to follow the abrupt and discourteous Western man.

'Because,' said Dr Dhakar, 'our treatment has alleviated her symptoms, although I am by no means certain why, so making her condition more difficult to assess. While his death, and the consequent fact that we have tried no treatment at all, will have made his symptoms – probably much more serious – also much more permanent.'

'And therefore easier to diagnose,' said Richard grimly. 'Because I have a nasty feeling that the quicker we get to the bottom of what's going on here, the better it will be for all concerned.'

SEVEN
Professor Lok

D r Dhakar led Richard and the nurse through into the mortuary. Oddly, the first thing he noticed – probably because the doctor saw them too, and tutted in disapproval – was the tray of nuts Nic had taken from the waiter upstairs. Nic must have put them down on the table with the dead man's diving equipment while Richard was preoccupied with Captain Kalla and his willowy assistant. Richard had taken a mouthful or two on the way down – but not many, for he had been talking too much to risk either choking or spraying. The sight of them made his stomach grumble now, however, for he had missed lunch for one reason or another, and it was coming up to dinnertime with little prospect of food in the near future. He grabbed a liberal handful, therefore, and slipped them into his mouth all at once. Then, chewing contentedly, he followed the two women to the mortuary table.

It was the nurse who made the first step in their investigation, for the moment she got a clear view of the dead diver she gasped and began to speak in rapid Bahasa Indonesia, the language of the islands. Then, glancing at Richard's uncomprehending face, she switched into broken English. 'I know this man! He is famous! He is on television. What is his name? He is a . . .' She lapsed, her vocabulary overtaxed.

'A naturalist,' supplied Dr Dhakar. She too looked at Richard, frowning. He tried to conceal the fact that he was still chewing a mouthful of mixed nuts. 'Like your Sir David Attenborough.'

'Like Steve Irwin,' confirmed the nurse, nodding forcefully. 'His name is Professor Lok.'

Dr Dhakar looked down at him more closely. 'I have heard of Professor Lok,' she said more gently. 'Not just a naturalist. A famous conservationist. Tell me about how and where you found him, please.'

Richard swallowed. Swallowed again, to clear his throat of a particularly persistent salted almond. 'Well . . .' he began. And he took the doctor through the details he had stored in his capacious memory in expectation of just this question.

But as he talked, Richard's subconscious mind continued to distract him with increasing persistence. For it seemed that the atavistic section of his brain that solved problems for him while he was asleep, could work things out while he was awake as well. Especially when aided by such random sensory associations as a mouthful of persistent almonds. So, at the end of his description of the professor's discovery, the rescue of his sleeping buddy next door (whoever she is) and the recovery of his murdered boatman, Richard concluded, 'And I think I know how he died.'

'So do I,' snapped Dr Dhakar brusquely. 'Poison.'

'The girl next door must have peen poisoned too,' said Richard forcefully. 'Though what sort of poison could have done so much damage to two people so far apart in the water . . .'

'Nevertheless, it must have been poison,' nodded Dr Dhakar. 'But how was it administered? And why did it kill him but not her? We need to know that too before we can use the knowledge to help the woman most effectively.'

'I think I know that too,' said Richard, reining in his enthusiasm. 'Some part of it at least.'

'Well?' demanded the doctor.

'Have you studied their scuba gear?'

'Of course not! Why would I waste my time on anything so foolish? I have been looking for snake bites, poisonous stings from fish or jellyfish. Even for stingray strikes!'

To forestall the doctor's next objection Richard held up Professor Lok's air hose.

'I think there's something wrong with this. And, as I recall, there might have been something wrong with hers as well . . .'

But no sooner had Richard delivered himself of this forceful little speech than its subject appeared. The doctor and the nurse had turned back and were all half crouching over Professor Lok. Richard was standing at the third table still holding the air hose above the plate of nuts. They all had their backs to the door.

It was a guttural choking gasp that alerted them to the arrival of their patient. They turned. The doctor and the nurse closed ranks, hiding the dead professor with the combined breadth of their hips. Richard scattered the plate of nuts across the tile floor as he dropped the scuba gear and started forward.

The young woman stood crucified in the doorway, holding herself erect with the simple strength of her grasp on the uprights. The plain white hospital gown looked unsettlingly like a shroud – a grim concept given currency by the ghostly pallor of her face, the depth of her dark-ringed eyes, the sepulchral wildness of her hair.

'*Tengku*,' she whispered, heartbroken.

Her trembling grip failed; her quaking legs let her down. She sank to her knees. Her eyes rolled up. She pitched forward, her face slapping down with a report like a pistol-shot into the scattering of almonds on the floor.

Richard stepped forward once more only to be waved back by the doctor's peremptory hand. The doctor and the nurse were beside her in an instant, lifting her solicitously between them and carrying her out of the room, one arm over each pair of shoulders.

Richard watched them go, his face folded into a frown as he started to reassess matters in his agile mind.

The hospital gown was of a standard, universal type. It was one-piece, wrap-around, secured up the back by four ties. And the women's actions more than undid the work their protection of their patient's modesty had done in the face of Richard's thoughtlessness fifteen minutes earlier. They took the patient's arms over their shoulders, taking a wrist in the grip of their outer arms, and linked their inner arms around her trim waist. Above the linked arms, the gown gaped across wide, muscular shoulders that still bore the faint traces of the scuba harness. It gaped below them as well, allowing a glimpse of equally muscular, athletically defined buttocks to eyes more salacious than Richard's. But below the pale cleft moon of firm flesh, muscular thighs fell to strangely formed knees and surprisingly stick-like calves. Impelled by his brain rather than by any of his lower impulses, Richard found himself studying those legs carefully as they vanished all too rapidly out through the door, but lingered in his memory. With his mind still full of what he had seen, Richard stooped and gathered the scattered nuts together with his hands, piling them back on the plate – which miraculously had not shattered on the tile floor. Then he straightened, replaced the plate beside the scuba gear and turned.

After a moment more of thoughtful pause, Richard strode purposefully past Professor Lok. He stopped by the inner table, looking fixedly down. The boatman lay, his eyes and mouth reverently closed, his throat obscenely agape, even allowing for the fact that the back of his head was held by a simple metal support. A support whose forward thrust was augmented by the considerable knot at the back of the dead man's headdress. The headdress was a simple, traditional island thing. Woven of a traditional island design, it matched the simple loincloth that the boatman had been wearing. Only the bright Hawaiian-style shirt, all parrots, macaws and birds of paradise, struck a more modern, Western note. But even that was hardly strange. It was exactly the kind of shirt that would be found on stalls in any of the local markets – either in New Baya City or further afield in Surabaya or Jakarta. All in all, the boatman was thoroughly unremarkable.

Except that it was this man, Tengku, who the patient had been looking at when she fainted in the doorway. In the company of the late Professor Lok, the Indonesian equivalent of two of the most famous naturalists in the history of worldwide television, she had called out to the boatman.

Why?

Richard unfurled the dead Tengku's fist. He had expected to find this hard to do, but there was surprisingly little rigor mortis. The stiffness of death had either come and gone, or was yet to come. Delayed, perhaps, by the warmth of the water the man had floated in. Or by the almost total loss of his blood. Or by some other factor likely to affect a state that was much less inevitable or reliable than detective writers would have us believe.

The palm was disturbingly pale, made almost waxy by near-total blood loss compounded by immersion in the sea. It led down from a slim wrist to long, almost artistic fingers. The little spade of ivory flesh was relatively unlined. The boatman was, perhaps, even younger than he had looked. The pads at the roots of fingers and thumb were infinitesimally darker than the surrounding flesh.

Darker from one angle. Paler from another – there were blisters
there. Blisters rendered almost invisible by the lack of blood in the
flesh of the hands themselves.

Richard turned the hand over. The long fingers, darker on the back
than on the palm-side, reached past neat, almost delicate knuckles to
well-maintained, almost manicured fingernails. On one finger there
was a paleness where a ring had been, and the knuckle below it was
skinned and seemingly a little swollen.

Richard found himself tutting, sucking flakes of almond from
his teeth and frowning with concern. He had spent his life on and
around the sea. If there was one thing he knew all too well, it was
what boatmen's hands were like. Boatmen's hands were broad.
Delicate was among the last words one might apply to them. The
nails were usually broad and thick, salt-coarsened, split and splintered. Boatmen rarely in his experience wore rings – oars, poles,
the controls of outboard motors wore them through too fast. Sea-
salt ate at anything less than pure gold. Gold was hard to come by
for honest boatmen. Only pirates wore gold as a rule. The palms
of boatmen's hands were coarse and calloused. The horny-handed
matelot was by no means a fantastic figure. Even a youngster like
Tengku here would have had thick, lined, spatulate hands. With
wood-worn, rope-coarsened callouses, not dainty little blisters.

These were never the hands of a boatman. They were the hands
of a student. Or an office worker. Or, given the situation, even of—

'Ah,' said a quiet voice from the open doorway, a quiet tenor,
lingering on the aspirate. 'Captain Mariner. Mr Greenbaum said I
might find you here. I see you have already made the acquaintance
of poor Detective Sergeant Tengku Suleiman.'

EIGHT
Inspector Kei

Richard swung round during that first long, almost sibilant
sigh of 'Aaaaah . . .' Then he stood in courteous silence
during the rest of the little speech, studying the speaker
closely. The stranger was a short, plump man of early middle years.
His olive-skinned face was round but by no means soft. His eyes

were brown, apparently tearful and slightly bulbous but their gaze seemed sharp and keenly intelligent. The mouth was full, yet it was bound by tight lines. The chin was rounded but decisive. And in the midst of all this contradictory physiognomy stood the aquiline nose of some desert chieftain forbear. It looked as though somewhere back along the long line of the newcomer's ancestors, the Arabian mortal explorer Sinbad had found favour with the Indian goddess Parvati; Kali at her softest and most loving. And all of this interesting – aptly arresting – conflict was contained in the perfectly tailored, immaculately pressed uniform of an inspector of police.

The inspector strode forward, his peaked cap tucked under his left arm, extending his right hand as he came. His perfectly polished shoes crunched over an errant nut or two, and he raised his voice a little on the next few words. 'My name is Kei,' he introduced himself, pronouncing his name to Richard's unsubtle Western ears like 'Key'. 'Inspector Kei. I am here to look into the tragic death of Professor Lok, his assistant and the boatman who was one of my most trusted sergeants.'

Richard reached out and shook the inspector's hand courteously, his mind crazily seeking ways of avoiding references to the unsettling aptness of the fact that Inspector Kei should be looking into the death of Professor Lok. But the punctilious officer paid no attention to him. Like the patient from the room next-door, he seemed much more concerned with the late detective.

After a while, he looked up. His sad, spaniel eyes glanced keenly past the late professor, as though he could see through the wall into the adjacent room. 'And how is she? Still alive by some kind of miracle, I hear?' He talked as though Richard knew who *she* was.

'Yes,' answered Richard carefully. 'The doctor and I were just discussing how such a strange thing could happen to two people out diving. Both at once . . .'

'I think she was doing a great deal more than *diving* with Professor Lok,' said the inspector. He crossed at last to the second table and looked down at the dead conservationist. His gaze was not approving.

'But she was more worried about the detective sergeant, I believe,' probed Richard.

'Yes. They were close friends . . . Ah. I see. My observation has misled you, Captain Mariner. She and Professor Lok worked together. Nothing more than that. It would not be speaking ill of the dead to observe, I believe, that she did all the work while he earned all the plaudits, the publicity and popularity. She was the fierce and widely feared voice of conservation. He was a *television person-ality.*' The severe lips twisted fastidiously, as though the gently emphasized words had a bitter taste. 'A popular personality, but in many ways merely her mouthpiece. As I say, it is a miracle that whoever did this took such care to ensure *his* death and yet they seem to have left *her* still alive.'

Richard opened his mouth to observe that, unless the fainting fit and the blow to the head that followed it had done the patient next door a great deal of unexpected damage, Inspector Kei would be privy to at least some of the answers he sought in the not-too-distant future. For the woman was awake and could answer his questions for herself.

But all at once the murmuring in his ear that had been issuing distractingly from the Bluetooth suddenly claimed his full atten-tion. '*Captain Mariner. It is Kalla here. Can you come up to the Grand Reception area at once; your presence at the ceremony is required . . .*'

'On my way, Captain Kalla,' answered Richard at once, and then hesitated, courtesy demanding that he at least explain what was going on to Inspector Kei.

'Ah,' said the Inspector accommodatingly. 'I expect that was your summons aloft, Captain. I was supposed to warn you that it was imminent. I forgot. I have been derelict, I'm afraid . . .'

But as Richard crossed to the lift, he found himself oddly in the grip of the strongest suspicion that the Inspector had not, in fact, forgotten. That he was never derelict. Never negligent, care-less, remiss or lax. That he never did – or failed to do – anything neglectfully.

That Inspector Kei simply never did anything without good and sufficient reasons of his own.

The Grand Reception Rooms were thronged with silently expect-ant people. Hundreds of the richest, best-connected, most famous, powerful and influential people on earth stood, resplendent, in a hush of simple anticipation. Richard walked on tiptoe along the half familiar aisles and rows, brutally replacing his speculation about Inspector Kei with his clearest memory of the diagrams he and Robin had studied during their hours of preparation, listing the proposed placing of everyone standing here. And he needed that mental map to guide him swiftly and soundlessly to his place, like a priest arriving late to Easter Mass at the Vatican.

Apparently by coincidence, the ceremony got under way the instant he was in place. And as the formalities unfolded at a pompous velocity that reminded Richard of a supertanker under tow, he found that his grumbling stomach was grateful for those few sustaining handfuls of cashews, peanuts and almonds. But he would be more grateful still for a good, square meal. As a way of distracting himself, he began to look around. Robin was easy to spot, up there beside the fairytale figure of Inga. Inga stood all in white, seemingly plucked, dress and all, from the pages of Hans Christian Andersen. And she in turn stood beside Sailendra who looked even more like something from the Arabian Nights now that he had risen to his full height and revealed the true splendour of his wedding costume.

Next, the distracted Richard found the tall, silver-haired figure of Nic Greenbaum in his perfect New York tailored evening dress, his jacket square cut, unlike Richard's which swooped into tails that would have flattered Fred Astaire. Beside Nic was his long-term partner, the ravishing Gabriella Cappaldi, dressed in the kind of couture normally only glimpsed on the red carpet during Oscars night. Couture exquisitely judged to set off the Mediterranean glories of Gabriella without detracting in the slightest from the almost Arctic perfection of Inga.

Inga, who was by now in fact no longer Inga Nordberg at all, but Princess Inga of Pulau Baya. Much as, so many years earlier, Grace Kelly had suddenly ceased being a picture-perfect movie star and started being Princess Grace of Monaco.

A ripple went through the assembled throng at the decisive moment, a whisper as subtle yet as all-pervading as a breeze through a barley field. Richard was distantly relieved – Robin had been concerned that some of the guests might applaud and spoil the moment. But he was more consciously focussed on his search for the next guests on his mental list. Well, not guests, precisely . . .

And oddly, even as Richard brought Kalla and his cool blonde assistant to mind, the captain's voice crackled in his ear. 'Captain Mariner, this is Chief of Security Kalla. Can you possibly make your way to the main door, please? It's important, sir.'

Richard was in motion at once. Long before it began to occur to him that Robin would probably never forgive him for his embarrassingly late arrival and his shockingly early exit, he was picking his way back through that mental map like a bomb disposal expert through a minefield. But when he reached the doorway there was no sign of Captain Kalla. He paused, a little nonplussed, almost suspicious of a practical joke. As he turned on his heel, a frown gathering, however, Kalla's assistant appeared. 'Please come with me, Captain Mariner,' she said brusquely. 'Chief of Security Kalla has gone on up.'

'Up? Up where, Miss . . .' Richard asked, still more than a little confused.

'Up ahead,' she answered shortly, flinging the two words back over the lightly tanned square of her shoulder, above the black top of her incongruously strapless gown. 'And my name is Hilary Johnson. Hilly for short, or at social events. Assistant Chief of Security when things get formal.'

'And which is this?' Richard asked, as he followed the determined woman to the main bank of elevators. 'I mean we're leaving a party and heading into a security situation by the look of things. Which may or may not be arising because of a couple of murders, now I think of it.'

She flashed a surprisingly wide smile at him as she hit the lift buttons. 'I think you can call me Hilly, Captain,' she announced. 'No matter what we're headed into.'

'Then you had better call me Richard,' he answered as the lift doors whispered open and he stepped into the fragrant interior with her. 'Richard. Come what may.'

Part of the seven-star luxury offered by the Volcano Roads Hotel involved the kind of service fondly if fictitiously recalled from 1920s' America. There were bellboys in swanky uniforms in serried ranks at reception. Concierges and maitre d's at every desk and doorway. There were butlers and valets – gentlemen's gentlemen to rival Jeeves himself assigned to every suite. Chambermaids and housekeepers ready to assist the ladies in Jeeves' place. Chauffeurs ready to drive the guests wherever they wished in a fleet of white Rolls Royces. Skippers aboard a range of pleasure craft thronging the marina. Pilots waiting with helicopters beside the heliport on the roof. And lift-boys in the elevators ready to push the buttons for the guests.

'Twenty, please,' said Hilly as the pair of them stepped in. The doors slid shut a centimetre or two behind Richard's tails and they were off, powering up the heart of the building at rocket-speed. Richard had never ridden in NASA's space shuttle, but he suspected its lift-off could hardly have been any faster than this.

'Have you any idea what is going on now?' he asked.

Hilly shrugged. 'One of the new men noticed something odd

going on out in the harbour part way through his normal security check. The Chief will want to bring you up to speed himself, I guess,' she answered noncommittally.

But no sooner had she answered than the lift car was slowing and Richard hadn't even time to speculate before the doors were opening and Hilly was striding forward, every inch the Assistant Chief.

Richard followed the determined woman down the exquisitely fitted corridor, already suspecting their destination, though as yet clueless as to why they were headed there. He had had more than a hand in the design and construction of the place and he knew that this corridor would lead them to the series of suites along the hotel's frontage overlooking the marina.

On the twentieth floor, these suites were furnished with particularly wide balconies, designed to give especially spectacular views along the island's length towards the distant, smoking volcano. And, indeed, to serve as observation platforms where, in the absolute lightlessness of certain nights, the stars seemed close enough to touch. And to aid these observations they were all supplied with a top-of-the-range astral telescope, its lenses – by Zeiss or Bausch & Lomb – able to focus on the smaller craters of the Moon. So, as it happened, were the thirtieth, fortieth, fiftieth and sixtieth floors. But not the tenth, which was still full of leisure facilities, shops and restaurants – as indeed were the upper storeys below the heliport up on the roof.

It seemed likely to Richard, therefore, that they were heading across the twentieth floor towards the front of the hotel because Kalla wanted to show him something best seen from one of the balconies here, with or without the aid of telescopes. The ground had been still and the air undisturbed, so it seemed unlikely that Kalla would want to show him the volcano. It was rapidly approaching sunset, but nowhere near dark, so that they were unlikely to be stargazing. Richard knew before he followed Hilly into suite 2020, therefore, that there was something happening in the marina. And, if the day so far was anything to go by, he calculated grimly, it was likely to be something bad.

And he had come to this conclusion even before he reached the balcony itself and saw the worried frowns on the faces of Chief Kalla and Inspector Kei who were waiting for him there.

NINE
Pirates

Richard stepped out through the gap between the plate-glass sliding doors and on to the airy vastness of the balcony. Hilly slid out behind him, lithe as a cat. Inspector Kei stepped forward, his mouth opening, but it was Kalla, crouched over the telescope like a gorilla looking down a bamboo stick, who spoke. 'We got trouble, Captain Mariner.'

'Events are unfolding far too rapidly for my taste,' emphasized Kei. 'I have been called up here even before I got a chance to finish interviewing Dr Dhakar. Even before her patient began to wake up. I have a nasty suspicion that we are being manipulated . . .'

Richard's hurried footsteps rang urgently as he strode across the white marble towards the balcony's forward rail. 'Trouble in the marina or the anchorage beyond it,' he reasoned aloud as he moved. 'Boat trouble, and something outside either police or security experience, or you wouldn't be waiting for me before you did something about it. And I agree with the Inspector. Someone is pushing and pushing to keep us off-balance here. But who? And why?'

Kalla pulled himself erect and gestured. His broad hand invited Richard to replace him at the telescope. Richard glanced down towards where it was pointing, then stooped, hissing with concern. He guessed at once that Kalla had been observing *Tai Fun*. And the moment Richard looked through the eyepiece he could see *who*, if not yet *why*.

The beautiful four-master was surrounded by half a dozen traditional Bugis native *prahus*. At first glance it looked as though the natives had gathered to welcome the visitors into Pulau Baya's most exclusive anchorage – and no doubt as far as anyone observing things from the marina itself was concerned, that's just what seemed to be happening. But the telescopic lenses designed to plumb the deeper craters on the Moon and discriminate the rings of Saturn told a different story. Apparently almost close enough to touch, flashing in the last of the light, the unnerving range of knives and clubs the *prahus'* crewmen flourished as they swarmed silently aboard leaped into the clearest possible focus.

Richard straightened, took the two further steps needed to reach the end of the telescope, put his hand over the lens and turned the instrument carefully sideways. He did all this silently, his face folded into a thoughtful frown. He had a shrewd suspicion that he knew why they had waited for him, he thought grimly. To call himself an expert on piracy was going too far – but not much. He had attended United Nations briefings on the problem. He had even led discussions with the American Navy after the latest incident off Somalia.

Ironically, Somalia bordered one of the few sea areas east of Africa where Richard had *not* fought pirates in his time. But he had been aboard the blazing results of their desperate profession there. Robin and he had tackled piracy head-on in the Gulf, in the China Seas, and in Indonesian waters themselves. He had smuggled Special Forces troops aboard vessels in the hands of Terrorists racing west across the Atlantic. He had taken back control of SuperCats stolen by Russian Mafia people-smugglers on the Great Lakes of North America. He had fought his way through oil platforms in the hands of desperate Jihadists.

'There are only two choices,' he said quietly. '*Pay or play.*'

'I see that,' rumbled Kalla. 'But . . .'

'But,' said Richard, patting the carefully positioned telescope, 'this has given us the greatest advantage we could hope for. If no-one aboard the pirated vessel has seen the lens flashing and realized they are being watched, then we have the element of surprise. If we chose to *Play*, we must work fast and hit them hard – before they have any idea we even know what they are up to. Or we can wait for them to get organized, settle defences and strategies and let us know what their demands are. And get ready to *Pay.*'

'That could leave us with no other realistic options, I'm afraid,' said Inspector Kei. 'I remember an incident off Somalia where the whole might of the US Navy was held in check by four men in a lifeboat.'

'Four men with a hostage,' added Hilly, her voice a thoughtful contralto.

'The problem with striking back at pirates as I recall it,' continued Kalla, 'the problem beyond the hostage question, is that anyone trying to outsmart the pirates is usually going aboard a vessel they don't know. That, and the fact that it is difficult actually to board most vessels in the first place; certainly once they get under way. Then you find yourself going into a situation you aren't familiar with, and up against an enemy that knows you're coming.'

He let the observations hang in the air. Richard saw at once where this was going. None of the usual problems apparently applied to them at all. They had prior knowledge of what was going on and could act before the pirates knew what had hit them. Or they could if they acted now. *Tai Fun* was designed with a poop-deck area that was easily accessible even from small boats like the Zodiacs they had used to rescue the living and the dead in the medical facilities below. There were half a dozen people here who knew every inch, deck and passageway of *Tai Fun* as well as they knew their own back yards. And a number of them had fought pirates aboard this very vessel in these very waters not all that long ago.

'We don't have all that much time to think things out,' prompted Kalla, his voice rising infinitesimally with tension. Richard nodded. He too could see that *Tai Fun* was getting ready to sail. But if he knew Eva Gruber the Navigator, First Mate Larsen the Sailing Master and Tom Olmeijer the Captain, they would be going about their business as reluctantly as possible, hoping to slow the process, praying that someone would see what was happening. Would understand the implications. Would come to rescue them . . .

Abruptly, Richard was in motion. 'Right,' he snapped. 'Mr Kalla, how are things going down at the reception?'

'It's in full swing, sir.'

'Can we call half a dozen people out without causing undue concern?'

'Depends who they are, sir.'

'I'll need to talk to Nic Greenbaum, my wife, whoever's in charge of the marina – the harbourmaster if there is one for the anchorage. The leader of the Island Council, I assume and . . .' He turned at the opening of the great glass door. 'I'll need to talk to Prince Sailendra. He won't want us to do anything without at least consulting him.'

As Richard led the little group through the cavernous vacancy of the twentieth floor, they continued to discuss alternatives. The island princedom had no standing army, air force or navy. In these regards as in so many others it was part of the loose federation of states that made up Indonesia itself. The nearest professional soldiers were, like the nearest decompression chamber, in Surabaya. The nearest serious command centre was in Jakarta. The island really only had its local emergency services – fire and medical facilities – and its little almost token police force. Inspector Kei, for instance, would be based on Java. Which threw up another question now Richard thought of it. Precisely what was Kei's role and responsibility here? Was there a chain of command all waiting to follow him out to the beautiful island?

A question instantly dismissed before it became a distraction from the more urgent and immediate train of thought.

Pulau Baya's indigenous police force would likely be over-stretched keeping an eye on the important guests here alongside performing their normal duties, Richard thought as he returned his mind to the matter in hand. This would be especially the case if Kalla and Nic decided to commit many of the hotel's security staff to the enterprise they were about to undertake. And it seemed to Richard quite likely that Nic would want to do just that. As Richard had a stake in the Volcano Roads Hotel, so Nic had an interest in the High Winds fleet, and shared an almost parental affection for the beautiful *Tai Fun*. More than that, he would want this situation resolved swiftly and positively before any bad publicity damaged the order books for the fabulously expensive suites they were hurrying through even now.

But here at least the current situation seemed to be on their side. The hotel itself was not yet open. Floor above floor stood fully staffed but as yet empty of guests. After the formal opening ceremony there was due to be a quiet 'shakedown' period as the great and the good, currently at the reception below, were entertained, dazzled and sent happily on their way. But there were only a hundred or so of these – and fewer than that of vital importance. And, into the bargain, most of the heads of state and one or two of the corporate giants had brought their own security people with them. Nic Greenbaum was the only exception to that rough rule – except, of course, thought Richard wryly, that Kalla, Hilly and the hotel security were all his hand-picked team.

The lift opened cavernously in front of them. 'Lobby please,' said Richard to the lift-man. The others stepped in behind him.

'Where have these people come from?' asked Richard, turning as the doors hissed closed. 'Piracy is an economic crime. In Somalia the pirates became so troublesome because there was war, drought, starvation inland. Risking their lives on the sea seemed preferable to the men that went out in those little boats to raid the shipping lanes. Is there anywhere near here where things are getting that desperate?'

Kalla and Hilly shrugged. Clearly their security briefings had not been widened that far yet. Inspector Kei frowned and Richard had an instantaneous suspicion that the proper civil servant found himself momentarily trapped by his position. No member of the Indonesian elite was going to admit too much too soon to passing strangers – especially ones with the power and influence Richard could wield if he felt the urge.

So it was the lift-man, chosen for his post because he spoke good English but as yet untrained in the arts of servile deafness and social invisibility, who joined the conversation and answered the question. 'It is the great logging companies,' he said. 'They are to blame.'

'What do you mean?' asked Richard gently.

'All the islands north of here – everyone knows it – all the islands between Makassar and Martapura, almost as far as Singapore itself. The giants such as Luzon Logging have taken all the forest down. Have bought the land or bribed the landowners. They grow nothing but biofuel. There is work in the fields but little pay. And nothing to buy with the pay. And nothing to eat but the oil-seeds. The palms and the corns and the rape. Rape. That is what it is indeed. So what are the people to do? The Bugis turn to the old ways as *orang laut*, men of the sea. Even the Dyaks are no longer *orang utan*, men of the forests. Even the Dyak are *orang laut* these days!'

Richard turned to Kalla. 'I thought Nic had taken Luzon Logging down. The last time Robin and I were here, the Greenbaum Corporation had Luzon Logging in court with proof of racketeering, drug transportation, illegal logging, land-grabbing, wildcatting, smuggling of endangered species, corruption, God knows what else . . .'

Kalla shrugged. 'They must have got good lawyers.'

Richard swung round to face Inspector Kei. 'Do you remember anything of this? Luzon Logging must have come across your desk in one form or another!'

The punctilious policeman cleared his throat. 'Luzon Logging of Del Monte Avenue, Manila, is one of the largest and most influential companies in the east. I am aware of many accusations that have been made against them. I am not aware that any such accusations have managed to stand up in court.'

'Luzon Logging doesn't only deal in endangered species,' said the lift-man darkly, lent an utterly unexpected fluency by an almost awe-inspiring bitterness. 'It deals in justice too. It doesn't only rape the virgin forests, it despoils the law itself. It doesn't only bribe landowners. It bribes judges. And whatever it cannot control, it kills. That is why nothing ever stands up in court.'

TEN
Council

They met in an impromptu council chamber, and made their decisions there as swiftly as only a collection of truly powerful people can. The room itself was The Volcano Roads Hotel's version of an intimate dining room cum conference facility. Done out in a style that might have graced the more vivid pages of Joseph Conrad's, Rudyard Kipling's or Nicholas Monsarrat's Far Eastern novels.

Its walls were covered with patterned silk in place of wallpaper. Amongst the original prints and paintings of every noteworthy or breathtaking harbour from Ambon to Hong Kong, there were spiders, scorpions, centipedes, moths, butterflies and tiny birds, mounted in almost Victorian style. And in the middle of two facing walls, looking at first glance like huge TV screens, there were matching aquariums, filled with dazzling ranges of the most colourful fish to be found along the rivers and reefs of the island princedom.

For a moment after he entered, Richard found himself overwhelmed. Wondering whether the rare creatures in the tanks and on the walls, like the magnificent mahogany table in the centre of the overpowering room, had been ravaged by Luzon Logging out of some long-ruined virgin forest at vast, illegal profit. As if to reflect what he was thinking, the sun, framed in the tall window opposite the stately doors, sank away into a low grey miasma that seemed to have leaped from the sea on the distant, western horizon. And it was dusk.

Perhaps something of Richard's dark thoughts haunted the suddenly shadowy ether, for as Nic strode in he read his old friend's expression. 'All from carefully controlled and guaranteed renewable sources,' he said, stroking the magnificent table as though it had been a Kentucky Derby winner. 'Now, what's this all about?'

As Richard swiftly explained and Nic's own expression began to darken with simple outrage, Hilly came in with Robin close behind.

'Here you are!' said Robin, sounding unsettlingly like a mother discovering an errant child briefly lost in a shopping mall. Apparently torn between anger and relief. 'I know you don't like formal occasions much, but skipping out on a Royal Wedding really takes the cake.' Then the full effect of the room hit her and she fell unaccustomedly silent for an instant, gaping ever so slightly.

'Talking of things being taken,' Richard riposted grimly, slipping his words into the quiet like a salesman's shoe into a door, then he pulled her into the conversation as well.

Prince Sailendra himself arrived next. He had been able to escape with unexpected ease because this part of the celebration itinerary required that he retire from the more rigid formalities and change into a less formal outfit. And the princess was on her way to the prince's suite with this intention too.

The prince, still in his full regal magnificence, fitted right into the room; indeed he seemed to notice nothing excessive about the place as he strode purposefully through the doorway, looking keenly round. Kalla followed like a massive, fatherly shadow behind the royal shoulder, but Richard was struck by how much the island's ruler had matured since last they met. How little he needed either shadow or father now. And rightly so. The late king's last will and testament, a mirror of his own royal father's, and those of regal generations before that, dictated that this man would become King in turn within the year, on his thirty-fifth birthday. This new maturity was reflected in the respect with which Councillor Nona, Leader of the Council, treated him. And the quiet authority with which he dealt with Parang, his diffident private secretary.

As soon as Sailendra entered, with his little entourage, the meeting came to order and the prince took the chair as of right. 'Report, please,' he ordered, sweeping the skirts of his formal gold-embroidered red silk jacket to one side as he sat at the table's head. He gestured and the others also sat. Except for Kalla, his narrow eyes exactly level with the scarlet bird of paradise plume that topped the prince's turban, framed against the huge mahogany double doors that matched the table, hung within a darkly gleaming mahogany doorframe fit to flatter a palace. This room alone explained at once Luzon Logging's almost incalculable profit, power, greed and menace.

Richard took the lead, with Nic adding outraged monosyllables of support.

'And how long has elapsed since you observed the pirates board *Tai Fun*?' demanded Prince Sailendra as soon as the brief report was made.

Richard glanced at his formal gold timepiece. 'Ten minutes, your majesty.'

'You have acted fast. Well done, all of you. Ten minutes. Knowing you, Richard, that will have been more than long enough for you to have formed a plan . . .' He leaned forward.

But before Richard could speak, the door opened and Inspector Kei ushered in a man not unlike himself, in a quasi-naval whites. 'The harbourmaster, your majesty,' he said.

'The very man we need,' said Richard. 'Now, your majesty, what I had thought was this . . .'

'I guess there must be some pirate blood in those veins of yours after all, Richard,' said Nic ten minutes later still as they all went hurrying about their allotted tasks in Richard's simple but promising plan.

'Seafarers' at least. We're not called *Mariner* for nothing,' answered Richard.

'*Morgan* might be apter, though.'

'Very funny, Nic. But tell me, why isn't Luzon Logging dead and buried? When we last talked you and Gabriella were all set to tear them down, dirty deal by dirty deal.'

'Sorry to disappoint, old friend. I have guys from New York on the case that make John Grisham, *LA Law* and *Boston Legal* look like The Muppets and still they've all got bloody noses. These guys play hard ball. Why do you ask?'

'Something the lift man said.'

'The lift man? Do tell!'

But as it happened, the pair of them were heading for the lift anyway. It seemed petty – almost time-wasting – but if they were going to take on a ship-full of pirates, they would have to look less like leading men from a 30s' movie musical. Unless, of course, they were hoping to defeat the pirates by tap-dancing them to death. Or, more likely, by reducing them to helpless laughter. Either way, they were planning on a quick change out of white tie and tails. Nic, of course, was staying here and so his clothes were in his suite. Richard silently blessed the good luck which had dictated that Robin and he should have ordered overnight cases ashore soon after they had disembarked themselves.

Richard and Nic parted company outside the lift and Richard crossed to the suite that Robin and he had been due to share after the formal reception. He opened the door, already preoccupied with the contents of his case, trying to remember what post-party outfits he would find in there. Fit to go pirating in. And he stopped, as effectively wrong-footed here and now as he had been rushing to the Zodiacs in the hope of rescuing the bodies in the water in the first place. And by the same arresting sight. But this time Robin was wrestling her torso out of the frilly basque sublimely unconscious of what her contortions were doing to her thong. The self-supporting stockings lay like silken snake-skins across the back of a chair. A suspiciously practical array of dark blue clothing lay scattered across the bed.

'Robin! What . . .?'

'Don't be so dense, lover. I'm coming with you.'

At least he had the good sense to keep moving as he entered an argument he knew all too well he had little chance of winning. 'But why?' he demanded, shrugging off his tails and tossing them over her stockings on the chair-back. He removed his shoes by ruth-lessly treading on the heel of each with the toe of the other. He kicked them aside.

'Why not? And don't give me all that twentieth-century sexist guff. Gabriella's coming too. We can help. We both know *Tai Fun* every bit as well as you do. I'm First Aid trained and she is too – the equivalent at least. And she's championship standard with any pistol you give her. We can both handle ourselves and you know it.'

Richard shrugged off his braces to dangle at his hips and flung back the top of his ancient leather travelling case. He reached in for the all-but indestructible khaki suit that he had counted as his 'good luck' clothing ever since he had worn it safely into the dark heart of the western African jungles and – more importantly – safely out again. He had gone in after Robin, kidnapped by freedom fighters. And brought her out again. Then, grimly facing the fact that she had in fact got *herself* safely out of the jungle, he stepped out of one pair of trousers and into another.

'OK,' he said, looking down to button his trousers. 'You win.'

Robin glanced over at him as she reached for her trousers. Although he was still wearing his starched shirt and wing collar, for a moment or two as he straightened, fastening the khaki waistband across his slim waist, it seemed to her that he looked a good deal less like Fred Astaire and a little more like James Bond.

Which Robin found reassuring, for she was nowhere near as confident as she seemed, and would need a good deal of help and support if she was going to make the switch from Ginger Rogers to Lara Croft.

And Lara Croft was a name that occurred to Robin a little more than five minutes later when she and Richard met the determined Gabriella Cappaldi with the fuming Nic in tow. One glance at Richard showed that he too saw the resemblance. But he had little time to linger over it, for his attention was claimed at once by Nic. And as Robin approached her sister in crime, the two men fell in shoulder to shoulder and strode off towards the lift, their every lineament and gesture seeming to reflect their anger and outrage.

The overwhelming conference room was now the base of operations. Richard led the other three in through the huge mahogany door to be confronted with the sight of Kalla and Hilly kitting themselves up for action. Like Robin and Gabriella, Hilly had swapped couture for practicality and now wore jeans and T-shirt. Unlike Gabriella and Robin it seemed unlikely that anyone had questioned her right to do so. Kalla had simply slipped a black top over his white shirt. Satin tape still gleamed at the seams of his matt black evening trousers. Behind the pair of them, piled on the table under Inspector Kei's watchful eye, lay the hotel's armoury and most of its security equipment.

And, behind the table, standing tall, his face set every bit as determinedly as the women's – and for much the same reason – stood Sailendra. He had removed his turban and his silk jacket. His ceremonial trousers were tight and dark, as practical as Kalla's. He had been wearing shoes that in the interim had been exchanged for thick-soled black riding boots. And, most strikingly, over the white silk of his high-collared shirt he had strapped a police-issue black Kevlar stab-proof vest.

'Hurry,' he snapped as the others arrived. 'Parang informs me that the rest of the security team is waiting for us down at the marina and the harbourmaster has already selected the vessels best suited to your plan, Richard. We just need to get suited up and on our way.'

'Suited up and tooled up,' growled Kalla. He slid a sleek grey pistol into the fading light. It looked to Richard's knowledgeable eye like the Glock .45 GAP so popular with Special Forces. 'Your Highness and you other gentlemen may sort out your plans and your command structures between yourselves and lead us where you will. But I know my duties and my specialisms. And I know all about friendly fire. So I get to say who gets the guns. My big, broad back is too tempting a target to have anyone I haven't vetted carrying firearms behind me.'

ELEVEN
War

Although it was dark in the marina – and, indeed, across the eastern seas where they were bound – the top of the soaring hotel astern was still bathed in blood-red sunset light and the helicopter that lifted off it blazed like a golden dragonfly. Richard sat in the lead boat, content to be at Sailendra's shoulder with Robin in turn at his. If and when they got aboard *Tai Fun*, Nic would be at the prince's other shoulder and Gabriella at his. It was a classic little chevron shape, echoed by the one that Kalla, Hilly and a couple of trusted security guards would also make when they went into action. Echoed in turn by the surprisingly intrepid Inspector Kei and four local policemen, all armed to the teeth. Everyone in the three five-member strike teams was clad in stab-vests and helmets. Those destined for the outer wings also carried powerful torches strapped to their thighs. Everyone had some kind of a flash-light on them. And a police-issue nightstick. At least one team member had CS gas or pepper spray. Each team leader carried a Taser in case there was a non-fatal way of proceeding. But they planned to recover *Tai Fun* and her crew, no matter what it took.

Kalla had counted ten pirates climbing aboard, all armed with knives and clubs as he was watching through the telescope and waiting for Richard to arrive. Fifteen rescuers armed with Glocks, SIG-Sauers and Desert Eagles, most of them with red-dot sights, as well as all the less lethal equipment, seemed a sufficient counter-measure. But Richard at least remembered all too well how four determined Somali hostage takers in a lifeboat had kept the US Navy itself at bay.

The Bluetooth device in Richard's ear whispered. He had grown so used to it that he had almost forgotten it was there. 'Chopper pilot says he can see *Tai Fun*,' Kalla informed the warrior prince. The big man was laden with the central communications gear as well as everything else. And Sailendra's secretary Parang was with the harbourmaster and Kei's right-hand man in the marina office, which doubled as command centre for the moment.

'Tell the chopper to stay high and clear,' Sailendra warned. 'We don't want to alert them.' He gestured back at the harbourmaster's assistant who was in charge of power and demanding more speed as he spoke to the Chief of Security.

'Point taken, your majesty. But they're under full sail, running with no lights. Although the hull is white the sails are black. Can you see where they are?'

'No.' Sailendra waved for more speed and the other boats also accelerated across the shadowy water as the men and women aboard saw the added urgency in the lead vessel's velocity. The boat's hull started slapping more urgently through the water. The thick, dark shadows attained substance as they moved, becoming a humid head-wind. Even under full sail, *Tai Fun* would not be making much speed through the heavy evening calm.

'Then he'll have to stay around like Captain Mariner said he would, until we have some sort of visual at least,' Kalla answered.

'Then we need to make more use of him,' said Richard quietly, well aware that his voice would carry across the ether to the two other boats growling along in chevron behind this one, riding the V of her wake. 'Make him earn his keep. Can he see where they're heading?'

'No,' answered Kalla a moment later. 'It's too dark. And he doesn't have the kind of radar needed to pick things out at sea level.'

Neither did the three boats the harbourmaster had found for them. These had been selected because they were capable of running at speed in relative quiet. They were long, low-hulled fishing vessels – more like Richard's much loved Cigarette speed boat *Marilyn* than proper attack boats. None of them was large or well-equipped enough to run to long-range radar. Fish-finders and Kelvin-Hughes depth metres were about all they had to hand. But Richard's plan was to get them aboard and re-secure *Tai Fun* long before they got out into the deep and dangerous shipping lanes.

And thankfully the stillness of wind and water also came to their aid. For over the throbbing growl of the speed boat's motor came the coughing grumble of a much larger motor up ahead. A moment later Richard's nostrils twitched as the all-too-familiar smell of diesel fumes came through the oily calm. 'Bingo!' he whispered. 'The Chief has got them using the emergency diesel engines instead of the electric motors. Now we have noise and scent to follow. And, when we get closer, there'll be light from the exhausts even if they're running absolutely dark in all other respects.'

Robin, unaware of the fact that he was wearing the Bluetooth, assumed he was whispering to her. 'Yes,' she agreed. 'You're right, my love.' Then she added, 'And of course the sound of the big diesel engines will drown out the noise of our little motors as we come up behind her. Unless they're keeping a very careful watch indeed they won't even know that we've caught them until we're all safe and sound aboard.'

'Right!' said Richard, impressed by the simple logic of her reasoning. 'Thank God you're not chasing after me!' he added wryly.

'You should be so lucky, Buster!' she snapped.

Their friendship with Prince Sailendra was close enough and of sufficiently long standing for him to whisper, 'Stop flirting, you two. Everything you're saying is being broadcast on the open Bluetooth channel. And I think we're just about to go into action!'

Richard's simple idea was based on the assumption that the main objective was the recovery of *Tai Fun* with its crew safely aboard and the theory that rats are most dangerous when they're trapped. More experienced tacticians amongst them had honed it, but no-one had disagreed with it or sought to better it. The moment that the fleeing vessel's poop gathered into a pale cliff topped with two tiny red exhausts, therefore, the plan went into action. The three boats approached the landing area abreast. There was just room for all of them to sit with their bows snug against the water-level slipway that lay at *Tai Fun*'s stern. As she was running under diesel power through a near calm, there was no heel on the deck and so it was easy enough for the three teams to walk in single file up their respective boats and step silently aboard the larger vessel.

Immediately, Sailendra and Kalla led their teams to port and starboard around the outsides of the main accommodation while Kei's men secured the after area behind the ship's gym, positioning themselves carefully in the unfamiliar facilities by going exactly where Richard had suggested that they go. The fishing boats fell back into the shadows. By the time they had vanished into the darkness, so had the Inspector and his little team. Their function was to oversee the evacuation of the pirates – even at the cost of a couple of Zodiacs. They were supposed to get involved only if the natives tried to take hostages overboard with them. Or if they proved desperate enough to make a fight of it.

That was the plan, at any rate.

Richard tiptoed along the lower deck, just close enough to Sailendra to see his almost shapeless shadow in the darkness. He trusted that Robin was away on his own left shoulder, equally far out. If he looked right, he could just see Nic's lean shape outlined every now and then by a glimmer from the sea or sky. And he guessed Robin would be keeping tabs on Gabriella in more or less the same way. Robin and he would probably be invisible to their friends, however, for they were in the darkness nearer midships. And just as it was hard to see them, it was almost impossible to hear them, for the darkness seemed to have intensified the all-pervading grumble of the diesel engine. Although he was sorely tempted to relax a little by the near-perfect camouflage and the ease with which things had gone so far, he knew that it would be fatal to do so. He was the survivor of so many harebrained escapades – so many hair's-breadth escapes – precisely because he had learned never to drop his guard. Even though they were apparently a vastly superior force closing in on an ill-armed and ill-prepared enemy, he behaved as though he was point man for the Light Brigade going full-tilt for the Russian guns. It seemed to him to be an attitude of mind from which Colonel Custer, for instance, could have bene-fited at Little Big Horn. Though to be fair it hadn't done either the British or the US Cavalry much good on either occasion.

'There must be men on the bridge overseeing the ship handling,' he whispered almost soundlessly into the Bluetooth. 'And if the diesels are running there's probably someone with the Chief down in the engine room – they'll have to have some light down there at any rate.'

'But there's no light anywhere else,' returned Kalla, his voice intimately close and clear. 'I guess that means there's no-one in the main areas.'

'Unless they're setting traps,' whispered Sailendra.

'They'd only do that if they were expecting company . . .' Kalla's voice drifted off as he began to speculate on the implication of what the pirates were doing – and *not* doing.

But Richard was ahead of him. He had been in this situation
before on *Tai Fun* herself and had been struck at once by the difference in the pirates' behaviour now. In both cases *Tai Fun* had been
severely undermanned – with little more than a skeleton crew. But
in the first case, the pirates, having secured the bridge, began to
search for stuff worth stealing. They had ransacked the common
parts and carried their booty – and their captives – into their
prahus. They had only ceased – and begun to reverse – this process
when they had decided to take *Tai Fun* in her entirety. And they
had only done that because they had a friendly vessel nearby
willing to aid and abet them.

A vessel owned, as it happened, by the Luzon Logging Company
of Del Monte Avenue, Manila.

'Kalla! Is the chopper still there?' Richard asked suddenly.

'Yeah. As per your orders. He's our guardian angel until this is
all over.'

'Tell him to fly on ahead. I think there's a larger vessel up ahead.
Or it could even be a small island . . .'

'You mean these guys are going somewhere? Somewhere
specific?'

'Could be.'

'Then we'd better get a move on!' came Sailendra's distinctive
voice, its tone most regally peremptory. 'Richard, I'm as close to
the bow as I can get. Do I go up or down?'

'Up,' said Richard without a second thought. 'You too, Kalla.
We have to start at the bridge to stand any chance at all.' And it
was only as he said this that he snapped open the flap of his holster
and pulled out the Glock .45-calibre handgun he had been issued
with earlier. But he did not switch on the red-dot sight yet.

Each little arrowhead began to creep up the outer companionways, moving silently from boat-deck level to bridge-deck level.
The companionways were wide enough to allow both Richard and
Nic some room between their padded shoulders as they followed
Sailendra, a seemingly ceremonial four steps down. With the women
four steps back again, they made a procession as Victorian as the
conference room in the distant hotel – that glimmered still like a
pale candle on the horizon far astern. Richard used the proximity
to show Nic that he had his pistol out and the American silently
held his up as well.

Richard and Nic spread out a little as they stepped on to the
bridge deck four steps behind Sailendra. Richard held his gun at

arm's length, ready but pointing at the deck, safety off and one shell in the chamber, his thumb on the familiar switch ready to activate the red-dot sight. The deck was wide and seemingly empty, though there were pools of shadow deep enough to conceal a good number of people. A little way across stood the bridge itself, one mast soaring from the midst of it up to a flaccid black sail. Starlight gleamed fitfully on the bridge's clear-view windows. It was impossible to see who was in the bridge behind them. Who was looking out and keeping watch.

Suddenly the thought of ten pirates out there in the darkness was intensely unnerving to Richard, even if they were only armed with clubs and knives. Even if they had been aboard for little more than half an hour, scarcely time to do more than subdue the crew, deploy the sails, start the engine and get under way. Probably not sufficient time to break into the ship's tiny armoury. *Probably* not . . .

And as though picking up on Richard's restless thoughts, the evening breeze suddenly gusted in behind *Tai Fun*. The sails above Richard and his team thundered and filled, the masts and lines creaked like a forest in a storm. The deck beneath them tilted as the long hull came to life. A wall of diesel fumes swept up from the stern towards the bow, hitting both little teams at once with the unexpected potency of pepper spray.

The pirates appeared from nowhere.

The first Richard knew of them was the sight of an arm reared across the sky above his head, a lethal-looking panga glittering in starlight whose brightness was intensified by the tears in his streaming eyes. Shocked and disorientated, Richard pulled the Glock's trigger like the rawest untrained recruit. He was lucky not to shoot himself in the foot. The .45 round exploded into the teak deck between his toes and the pirate's. Splinters flew. Richard was wearing heavy boots – the pirate was not. The pain must have been like a hornet attack round his ankles. That and the deafening sound of the shot were enough to turn his blow. The panga's heavy sword blade whispered past Richard's helmet and glanced off his padded shoulder.

Robin's torch beam pierced the grey fumes of the exhaust like the blade of a Jedi sword. Now it was the pirate's turn to be blinded. He staggered back, shouting.

Richard began to bring his gun up. His thumb found the switch and the red-dot laser light leaped out. Only now did it occur to him to look for Sailendra. 'Your majesty?' he called. Silence and secrecy were now clearly redundant. 'Sailendra?'

'Here!' the answer came from the shadowed deck at the foot of the bridge-house wall. At once the torch beam found the dark shape of the crouching prince. No sooner did it do so than Kalla was crouching at the royal shoulder. 'Where are they?' he demanded hoarsely, his voice echoing strangely through the Bluetooth in Richard's ear.

And, with disorientating suddenness, Kalla's voice gathered in volume, though he was clearly no longer talking to Richard or Sailendra. 'What? Where? Dead ahead? Richard! We must turn *Tai Fun* at once. There is something massive dead ahead. The chopper pilot says . . .' But what the pilot said was lost in the rapidly accelerating swirl of events. A fusillade of shots echoed up from the after deck where Inspector Kei and his policemen were stationed. Followed by shouting and screaming. And another fusillade. It sounded as though there was a pitched battle going on up there.

Long before the second burst of gunfire, Richard was on the bridge. Robin arrived at his shoulder as his hands clasped the spokes of the big old Mississippi riverboat's helm. There was no time to discuss, or even to decide. His hands were in motion even as she arrived. The helm was hard over before Nic and Gabriella joined them. Some deep, unreasoning instinct had made him turn across the wind, so that the angle of the deck steepened. The sails bellowed and the rigging groaned, shouting as the full weight of the stirring night wind sought to push the sailing ship over – but only succeeded in swinging her more rapidly round.

Nic and Gabriella staggered across the bridge and started looking after the captain and his officers lying trussed on the deck. Richard stared wide-eyed ahead, watching in horror as the darkness began to resolve itself into the black steel wall of a huge container ship's hull.

But then, as the second burst of shooting rattled out, so the black steel began to slide sluggishly sideways, like an onrushing tidal wave turned by a submarine reef. Computers clicked and rattled, automatically adjusting the trim, keeping the hard-bellied sails full of air. Robin's wiry strength joined Richard's in pushing the big wheel hard over. He reached forward and pushed the engine controls to FULL AHEAD, and another automatic system answered, sending the engine monitors racing into the red as the screws thrashed the water to foam under the ship's low flat counter.

Containers gathered squarely above the onrushing steel wall. Cranes and stubby masts cut black outlines against the starry sky.

On the top of one of the containers, seemingly leaning against one of the cranes, the figure of a man looked down at them. As the sailing ship heeled harder and harder over, so another figure joined the first. Richard had the instantaneous, photographic impression that the men were dressed in native costume, as the pirates had been. Then the container-ship's forecastle gathered. The side flared out slightly as though the steel tsunami were breaking over them at last. Someone on *Tai Fun*'s foredeck – Kalla as likely as not – shone his torch beam upwards and the ship's name lit up, white on black: BOUNTY. Then it was gone as *Tai Fun* swept under the forecastle head and sailed clear.

TWELVE
Battle Zone

'They attacked us,' insisted Inspector Kei, apparently unruffled by Sailendra's questions. Now that the action was over, the inspector pulled the Bluetooth device from his ear and put it in his pocket. 'So we returned fire. It was self-defence.'

'But how?' demanded the prince. 'They were only armed with knives and clubs. How could they pose such a threat?'

The inspector's gaze fell, apparently coincidentally but pointedly, on Richard's shoulder. The pad of his body armour was gashed deeply where the pirate's panga had glanced off it.

And Sailendra himself had the grace to run his hand over the tender welt on his forehead where he too had been struck. With a surprised expression, he discovered that the goggles that he, like everyone else, wore on the helmet front, were hanging down, neatly severed across the nose piece by a sword blow that had nearly done more permanent damage. The lenses were both starred with cracks. He tugged the ruined eyewear free then he, too, pulled his redundant earpiece out. 'Even so . . .' He gestured. When he moved his hand the ruined goggles swung like little pendulums. The air around them seemed to stir, thickened with a stinking grey miasma of gun smoke that had yet to dissipate.

They were on *Tai Fun*'s after deck, at almost exactly the spot where they had come aboard a scant half-hour since. The watersports area was bathed in light now, for the ship was back under her captain's command and Tom Olmeijer had restored power to all areas, although it seemed that only moments had passed since the pirates had disappeared. In all probability, Richard thought, Sparks the radio operator was still talking to the harbourmaster, reporting the safe recovery of the vessel. And indeed, to Sailendra's secretary, Parang, reporting the survival of his prince.

The open-ended U shape, walled inboard with mounting tiers of balconied decks, seemed to give a new meaning to the term 'theatre of battle'. The deck itself was littered with brass shell cases and seemingly awash with blood. There were black pocks of bullet holes in the dive lockers and the glass doors into the ship's gym were lucky to have survived intact.

One of the Zodiacs lay on the lip of the slipway, its tether still secured. The rubberized sides were smeared with blood and spoke of a last panicked attempt by outgunned and desperate men to escape from the killing zone. Although the bloodstained Zodiac remained, there was no other sign of the vanished buccaneers who seemed to have been blown overboard by the withering fire unleashed by the policemen.

Except that the pool, its crystal surface heaving a little as *Tai Fun* turned on to the homeward tack, contained one last pirate, floating face down, spread-eagled in a sluggish cloud of blood.

Richard glanced up from his examination of the dead man. The instant he had crouched down a moment earlier, he had noticed with a strange pang of fellowship that the bare feet floating just beyond his reach were quilled with splinters. On the bottom of the illuminated pool immediately below the man lay the *panga* that had gashed his shoulder armour. In the brightness of the underwater lighting its blade was as badly marked as the dive-locker doors. The blade alone must have been hit by a dozen bullets. He didn't want to speculate how many had riddled the man holding it. But he was glad that his erstwhile enemy was floating face-down.

Especially when Robin arrived at his side and reached down gently to grasp his shoulder. He looked up at her and, apparently coincidentally, the back of her hand stoked the flat plane of his cheek. He straightened, still with her hand on his shoulder, suddenly aware that it was tender. Bruised. He shrugged gently, easing the muscles and bones. 'Well, it's done now,' he said decisively. 'This is a crime scene. It was even before the shooting started. The local authorities will want to look into the matter, I'm sure. Get an estimate from the inspector and his men of how many pirates were killed or wounded. Your Majesty may wish to institute an inquiry. Or the inspector's masters might. But our immediate objective must be to get *Tai Fun* safely at anchor and return you, sir, to your guests and, more importantly, to your beautiful bride. Then bring a proper investigating team aboard.'

But Richard had something else he wanted to do. Two things, in fact. Each of them equally immediate. As soon as he had said what needed saying, therefore, he was off. Striding purposefully along the route they had followed so hesitantly in the dark, he went to the foot of the companionway. Then, instead of climbing towards the command bridge, he went in and down. As he stepped in through the doorway, swinging it wide with his broad left hand, he almost unconsciously eased the Glock in its holster with his right. And that was how he found out Robin had followed him.

'What are you up to, Richard?' she demanded.

'Shhh!' he cautioned.

'What?' came Kalla's voice in his Bluetooth. He reached up to switch it off, then paused, remembering that Inspector Kei and Sailendra had already removed theirs. Speaking quietly to Robin, he communicated with the security chief as well. The security chief alone. And perhaps that was no bad thing, given what he suspected.

'The Chief,' Richard said to Robin, as if those two words must explain everything to both of the people who could hear them.

'What?' she demanded, but at least she had lowered her voice now.

'If the Chief started the diesel engine then he's in the engine room,' Richard explained to his two-part audience as he crept as swiftly as he dared and as silently as he could down through the accommodation areas towards the engineering section. 'And the pirates won't have let him go down there alone.'

'You think there's still a pirate down there with him?' whispered Robin.

'I'd lay fair odds on it,' he breathed. 'The engine's still running. He hasn't come aloft or rung through to the bridge as far as I'm aware . . .'

The engine room was at the end of a short corridor down in the bowels of the ship. Its door was very slightly ajar, but not far enough to allow the room's occupant much of a view out. Richard tiptoed forward, with Robin at his shoulder. He was by no means certain of what he would find, so he eased his Glock out and switched the red-dot sight on. Then, holding the weapon two-handed with straight arms, as he had done earlier, he followed the intense ruby speck along the deck until he reached the jamb of the door.

'Stay back,' he breathed to Robin. 'I'm going in.'

Richard hit the half-open door with his shoulder and whirled into the room, crouching as he brought his gun up. Going down on to one knee to ensure a steady firing platform. His wide eyes registered an instantaneous impression of two men standing together, one in front of the other. Details leaped into focus as he settled his right knee firmly on the deck and swung the red dot smoothly upwards.

The Chief, hands bound in front of his chest with silver duct tape and a square of silver tape over his mouth, sat very still – with the long serpentine blade of a Kriss knife at his throat like a steely silver snake. There was a wide-eyed face half hidden by the engineer's head, a slim body shielded except for the fist holding the knife. The fist trembled. The razor-sharp blade nicked the engineer's skin just above the throb of his jugular vein.

The red dot dominated Richard's vision, racing up the Chief's white overalls, leaping over his shoulder to dazzle the pirate's wide eye. The brown face flinched. The red dot stopped, zeroed in on the pirate's skull between the outer orbit of his right eye and the thrust of his ear, just under the garish red of a piratical Bugis headdress. Range maybe two metres. Six feet max. *An easy shot*, some cold and deadly corner of his mind was calculating. Even past the Chief's right ear.

The Chief's eyes clamped tight shut. His whole face screwed up.

The pirate's eye widened in shock and surprise.

Richard squeezed the trigger.

And a stream of spray hissed above his shoulder, seeming to follow the beam of the red dot, giving it substance, like mist defining a torch-beam. The spray hit the pirate in his wide-eyed face, just where the bullet would have gone a second later.

Richard registered what it was an instant before the backwash hit him. So he took avoiding action without further thought. As the Chief went to his knees, still holding his breath, Richard rolled backwards, also holding his breath, allowing the red blade of light to cut through the misty atmosphere, the red dot speeding across the deckhead above the choking pirate. He brushed past Robin's legs as he moved and kept on rolling. Robin stepped forward, her eyes shielded by goggles, and grabbed the engineer by the shoulders. The Kriss rattled on to the deck as the pirate clutched his eyes. His screams were falsetto, almost girlish. Richard rolled right out of the engine room as Robin dragged the Chief bodily over him into the corridor, then slammed the door.

'Are you OK?' she asked. 'Richard! Are you OK?'

Richard guessed it was safe to try and breathe then. 'OK,' he answered. 'OK, Chief?'

'*Merde*,' swore the wiry Frenchman. 'I got a face full of that fornicating pepper spray. I'll need to wash it off before I dare open my eyes. Breathing is difficult enough! And my skin is on fire! God's death, Robin! You are a bad woman to piss off!'

Kalla arrived then, with Hilly and their team in tow. Richard pulled down his goggles, held his breath once more and went into the engine room with them. The atmosphere was as thick as the smoke-filled field of fire beside the pool. But it was marginally less lethal. The pirate was puking helplessly on the deck, his face swollen and his eyes streaming. He held his headdress in his hand and had clearly been trying to wipe his face with it. Richard retrieved the Kriss as Kalla and one of his men pulled the choking boy to his feet. And it was only then that Richard realized how young the pirate in fact was.

As the security team dragged the slight brown body out, Richard used up the last of his carefully held breath in shutting down the engine, resetting the bridge telegraph to ALL STOP and switching on the air filters. The filters were designed to clear the room of smoke or fumes in case of fire. Pepper spray would be no problem, he thought. Then he switched off the lights, closed the door behind him and took a deep breath of the relatively clean air out here.

Kalla and his men had taken their captive down to the end of the corridor, then paused as though wondering what to do next. There was no sign of Robin and Richard guessed she must have led the chief off to wash his face as requested. 'Kalla,' Richard called.

The big security chief turned. 'Yes?'

'You need to check the ship. There may be more of them left aboard.'

'Yeah,' said Kalla wryly. 'I guess I'd better get to them before Mrs Mariner does.'

Richard gave a grunt of laughter. 'And before Inspector Kei does,' he added pointedly.

Kalla looked at Richard calculatingly for a moment longer. Then he glanced at the choking boy and nodded once. 'Yeah,' he said again. But this time his tone was grim.

Richard's next urgent port of call was the bridge. With Kalla and his men securing their prisoner and sweeping the ship in search of others, he could turn his attention to the next unresolved mystery of the night. 'I really would like to know,' he said conversationally to Captain Tom Olmeijer, Sailing Master Larsen and Navigator Gruber, five minutes later, 'just what in hell's name a bloody great container ship is doing sitting in the middle of the Java Sea with no running or riding lights, no radio and no kind of warning to any other vessels nearby.'

Tai Fun was running easily across the night wind, heading back towards the tall white blaze of the Volcano Roads Hotel that stood like a beacon on the horizon dead ahead. Eva Gruber was standing over the Collision Alarm radar, keeping an eye out for pleasure craft as they approached the outer reaches of the harbourmaster's jurisdiction. Larsen was keeping an eye on the depth-metres measuring the distance between the keel and the coral heads beneath. Sparks was indeed still in communication with both Parang and the harbourmaster in the office overlooking the marina. Richard had not chosen the most convenient moment to make his demand – reasonable though it was.

Tom shrugged accommodatingly. 'Sparks,' he called. 'Were you able to make contact with any vessels nearby?'

'No, Captain,' called the radio operator from his little shack behind the bridge. 'Only the harbourmaster and the general traffic and shipping information channels.'

'Does the vessel register on your radar, Navigator?' Tom asked, turning to matters nearer at hand.

'Not at this setting, Captain,' answered Eva Gruber. 'If I widen the calibration then I'll set off the collision alarm.'

'Richard?'

'I think it would be worth it, Tom.'

'Very well. Widen to twenty miles please, Navigator.'

'Resetting Collision Alarm, Captain. Twenty—' Eva's words were lost beneath the alarm, which warned them that the marina was much less than twenty miles distant and on a dangerously convergent course.

But Richard paid no attention to the alarm. Instead he crossed to Eva's shoulder and focussed all of his considerable attention on the green bowl of the radar itself. The contact line swept round, showing the bright wall of the marina ahead, then it reached out and back as the radar dish on the masthead above them sent its signal out across the Java Sea.

'There she is!' breathed Richard.

The contact was more than ten miles distant, on their port after quarter, receding at the same speed as they were moving forward. It was a surprisingly big contact – shockingly so even to Richard, who had so nearly run into it. It sat squarely on the screen like a raindrop on a watch-face as the hand of the contact line swept on past it. But there was something about the fading signal that brought a frown to Richard's broad forehead. A modest rash of smaller contacts lay clustered brightly around it. 'I don't know,' he said. 'Something just doesn't look right . . .' He looked down for a moment more in silence, narrow-eyed as the alarm continued to sound, though Eva Gruber set the volume to its lowest setting. 'What was her name?' he mused, trying to make some kind of sense out of his observations and suspicions. '*Bounty*?'

And even as he said this, so the radio operator came through on to the bridge. His slight frame was puffed up with unaccustomed importance. He was almost literally big with news. 'I've just received a general alarm,' he said. 'The container vessel *Ocean's Bounty*, five days out of Manila bound for Surabaya, has apparently just been taken by pirates somewhere in the Java Sea!'

THIRTEEN
Somalia

'But this is ridiculous,' raged Sailendra. 'We are not in Somalia here! This is Indonesia. Piracy is a thing of the past. A legend from history.' He had shed his stab vest and scarred helmet to reassume his ceremonial jacket and turban.

The rescue party had returned. The wedding reception was over, except for the lingering music of the dance bands still keeping the youngsters and the diehards dancing. The prince had fulfilled his social and ceremonial duties. And, before he retired to fulfil his equally important matrimonial duties, he and a select group of his most powerful and influential guests were gathered in the conference room discussing what was going on in the seas around his island. The huge mahogany table was laden with cordials, tea and coffee. And, for those who indulged in it, alcohol. Most were dressed in the costumes of their countries or in evening wear of a more Western type. Only Richard and Nic were out of place, still in their workman-like pirate-hunting clothes. Though they too had left their body armour aboard *Tai Fun* under the watchful eye of Inspector Kei, guardian of the crime-scene. Kalla, too, was absent. He had gone off with Hilly to see to their one captive. The pirate was little more than a boy but they were treating him as though he were a dangerous man. Or seeming to, at least. Both Kalla and Richard were concerned that he should not meet the same fate as his confederates – so they were keeping him clear of Inspector Kei for the time being. Also, Robin's application of the pepper spray had been too liberal and had resulted in an allergic reaction. The boy was helplessly blind, his face swollen to gargoyle proportions.

The room was Victorian in more than one respect. No women were allowed to overhear the men's deliberations. Or to breathe the cigar-smoke-filled atmosphere redolent of some old gentlemen's club in London. Though what was true for women was true of secretaries also – or perhaps of lower-class smoking materials. Parang was exiled to the hotel's lesser smoking areas to indulge his passion for American cigarettes.

Richard looked up at the Victorian walls, thinking that Sailendra's version of the 'distant' past was hardly historically accurate. He sipped a fragrant cup of Java coffee. A brew so famous that at one time or another it had just been known as *Java*. Hadn't there even been a song and a dance called 'The Java Jive'? Dreamily, in the grip of post-action euphoria, he tried to pull his mind back to the matter in hand. Pirates.

In the days when this room had represented the pinnacle of modern fashion, Joseph Conrad and Rudyard Kipling had written with horror of the Bugis pirates who had haunted these waters. When Victoria was still Queen Empress, they had sailed stealthily out of their secret villages, slitting throats and stealing women and spiriting away the children of the Raj. And both of the writers had been out East and *knew*. Knew what frightened their Western friends and readers, at least.

And the fiendish Sanda Khan – the Bugis leader who faced Rajah Brooke of Sarawak in Nicholas Monsarrat's historical novel *The White Rajah*, long before their roles were reversed in the animated series once beloved of his children – was an island pirate *par excellence*. Or he was in the eyes of the British and the Dutch in the 17, 18 and early 1900s.

But then again, thought Richard wryly, sipping more of the scented coffee, history was only useful if people could apply its lessons to the present – and learn from them. 'Your Majesty,' he said, putting down his coffee cup and speaking even before his thoughts were fully formed. 'Gentlemen. Piracy is no longer a tribal leaning. A tradition passed from father to son almost in the genes. No longer a way of life to be followed by one generation because an earlier generation lived like that before them. Like so many others, modern piracy is an *economic* crime. And a desperate one at that, because as far as I can see it is one of the riskiest and most dangerous enterprises a man can undertake.

'The Somali pirates who have proved such a nuisance off the horn of Africa in the not-too-distant past were driven by a combination of factors. Their country was in turmoil. In the grip of both anarchy and starvation. There was neither a living to be had nor a legal system to be relied upon ashore. Their lives were so desperate that it seemed to make sense to them to get aboard their little boats and attack big ships in the shipping lanes, no matter what the risks. It was agreed by the United Nations, I believe, that the best way to stop them was to give them a better life at home rather than to make things more difficult for them at sea.

'It is a lesson, I have to say, that goes back to Roman times. So we can literally learn from history. When Pompey the Great cleared the Mediterranean of pirates fifty years before the birth of Christ he not only took away their ships, he gave them farms far inland so that they would not be tempted back to sea again.'

'But how is this relevant?' demanded the chairman of the Singapore and Seram Shipping Company almost pettishly, wiping his bald bullet head with a huge silk bandana. He was perspiring with outrage rather than with heat in the carefully air-conditioned room. Especially as he had a frosted bucket full of ice at his elbow and a cooling glass of chilled champagne well within reach. He found it too difficult to fit his portly person into his famous collection of sports cars. He collected Bentleys now. A stir of agreement went round the table as the better part of twenty tuxedoed and silk-robed business moguls, sultans, kings and princes nodded their heads in agreement at his words.

'I believe it is relevant, Dr Jurong,' soothed Richard, focussing all his attention on the businessman's frowning, sweat-slick face. 'Consider, sir, what has been happening in Indonesia during the last few years. Since the death of President Suharto, the firm grip of the centre has weakened. You cannot deny it. The state of Indonesia has begun to dissolve into its constituent parts, like the old Soviet Union did both after Stalin's death and more especially after the collapse of Communism. Combined with that, there is the increasingly uncontrolled rapaciousness of companies such as Luzon Logging . . .'

Richard hesitated infinitesimally as a whisper of shock ran round the table, as though he had called on the Devil himself at Mass.

'These companies do not of course bring anarchy in the same way as war has done to Somalia. But their activities destroy natural lifestyles – or they can do so if they are not controlled. They can drive people off the land, and leave them little alternative but to follow the Somali model after all.

'It is a matter of record,' he persisted, raising his voice slightly against the continued rustle of disbelief, 'that vast areas of virgin forest have been simply ripped apart for their ancient timber. Areas have been cleared on a scale almost comparable with the decimation of the Amazon rainforests. Often by the same companies – or their more anonymous offshoots. And we all know that the cleared areas are not farmed so as to protect the indigenous communities whose original lifestyles have disappeared with the priceless hardwood trees. With the ruthless and relentless slash and burn. Instead, the naked hill slopes are squeezed for quick-buck profits. They are put down to fuel crops, not food crops. Or to plantations of bamboo and rattan destined for Chinese furniture factories. Or ramin groves that will one day become pool cues. Or they're given over to the production of consumables for export that no local can dream of affording. Like the farms in Africa where they grow salad crops, fruit and vegetables destined to be packed in aeroplanes and flown to European markets while the local people starve. Under a combination of circumstances like this, with central government and law enforcement failing while traditional ways of life are being destroyed in search of short-term profits for vast, powerful and faceless conglomerates, it is little wonder that the islanders dabble in piracy.'

'But this is fantasy,' said the Sultan of Sabah, his cut-glass tones reminiscent of Eton College and Kings Cambridge, where he received a First in Classics and captained the polo team. His stable of polo ponies remained the most successful east of India. And the most fabulously expensive.

'I hesitate to disagree, sir, but I'm afraid I must do so. Prince Sailendra, could you tell His Majesty which company was involved in stealing vast tracts of virgin forest from the slopes of Guanung Surat before the volcanic eruptions?'

'Luzon Logging,' answered Sailendra, frowning.

'And at least partially as a result of this, what did the island fishermen turn to?'

'Piracy,' allowed the prince reluctantly. 'But . . .'

'I am sorry to interrupt, Your Majesty, but may I ask which company has been most active in pressuring you into planting biofuels on those same mountain slopes – in preference to your own preferred crops of rice, bananas and ground nuts for local consumption as well as export?'

'Bogor Biofuels,' answered Sailendra.

'May I ask, Your Majesty, what form this pressure has taken?'

'It has been both legitimate and less legitimate. Court cases undertaken on behalf of farmers – real and fictitious, with any kind of claim to the land. You may remember the late Councillor Kerian.' The prince's long, mobile face twisted at the name. It had been Councillor Kerian who had led the rush back to the old Bugis pirate ways. A decision supported by his contacts in Luzon Logging. A decision that had cost him his life in the end. 'A writ was issued in Councillor Kerian's name giving rights to vast acreages of the most fertile mountain slopes. It took a great deal of time and money to prove that it was entirely spurious. My people have been bribed and threatened. I myself . . .' The prince fell silent, frowning thunderously.

Richard eased himself courteously into the silence. 'And is there any particular company, sir, which has been especially interested in taking advantage of the local oil deposits just off the northern coast of Pulau Baya, even though drilling for oil is likely to infringe the UN ruling on areas of outstanding natural beauty and might jeopardize the fish and shrimp farms you are planning to set up there?'

'Pontianac Oil Enterprises. And I see at once where this is leading. They used the same tactics. The same threats and promises. Now I think of it, I believe they even used the same lawyers to dispute my sovereign right as Pulau Baya's crown prince to influence what was done in my island's territorial waters . . .'

Richard swung round further, his icy gaze raking over the faces round the table until it rested on Nic Greenbaum.

'Nic?' he said crisply. 'Have you ever heard of Bogor Biofuels?'

'Yes,' came the equally crisp reply. 'Bogor Biofuels are a subsection of Luzon Logging . . .'

'Pontianac Oil Enterprises?'

'The same.' Nic's gaze raked round the table, every bit as icily as Richard's. One by one the other gazes met his then fell away. 'Pontianac Oil Enterprises is a subsection of Luzon Logging, Del Monte Avenue, Quezon City, Manila.'

Richard leaned forward, his face set and his expression at its most intense. 'You see what I mean, gentlemen?' None of them would meet his eyes. 'Even here. *Even here.* If someone of the stature and reputation of Prince Sailendra is the subject of this kind of thing, what chance is there for desperate villagers whose lands and livings are in ruins, whose families are starving, who have nothing to their names except their knives and their *prahus*?'

The impromptu meeting broke up then, but Richard, Nic and Sailendra lingered over their coffee as the hotel servants moved silently around them, clearing away. 'I don't think I convinced them,' observed Richard a little grimly.

Nic gave a cynical bark of laughter.

But it was Sailendra who said, 'They have too many vested interests. Overlapping concerns. Wheels within wheels. Companies such as Luzon Logging do not just fade into smaller concerns with different names; they cast nets of influence and power. No matter how rich and powerful a man might become, there is always something else he wants. And there are always people offering to supply these wants. At a price. And all of these men work for someone.'

'And all too many of them work for Luzon Logging or their subsidiaries,' supplied Nic.

'We're surrounded by Faustus after Faustus,' concluded Richard. 'All just begging to sell their souls to the devil.'

'And it seems that Mephistopheles has moved his headquarters up from Hell and into Del Monte Avenue, Quezon City, Manila.'

FOURTEEN
Cut Throats

Richard and Robin were complementary opposites. This was one reason that their marriage worked so well. The euphoria that came from surviving danger and defying death filled him with physical relaxation and mental stimulation. It filled her lithe body with restless energy. It made him want to talk into the wee small hours then go to bed to sleep. It made her want to go to bed as soon as possible – with sleep the very last thing on her adrenaline-jumping mind.

The fact that Robin had not been called to the men-only conference added to her restlessness, a mental frustration compounding the physical fizz. She became a creature of burning, impatient motion. She went up to her suite and showered off the stench of gun smoke. She changed out of her pirate-fighting gear back into her party outfit, basque, thong and all. And she went down to join the diehards whose mission was to party all night – in one way or another.

With Richard still nowhere to be found and the door of the conference room still courteously closed to her, Robin next went in search of the bride. She found Inga, less than happy but quiescent – as befitted a trainee princess – seated, talking to a range of passing female guests, and then Robin was off again, hunting excitement. And, in her present mood, excitement came in trousers.

Robin found Parang first. She found him deep in conversation with a square, powerful-looking Japanese man whose round-bellied body would have been far better suited to Samurai armour than to the dinner jacket he was currently wearing. They were discussing something in a slim black-leather briefcase, which Parang was holding on his lap as he sat on a spindle-legged chair. But as soon as it became obvious to the two men that Robin was not going to leave them alone, the Japanese man gave a slight but formal bow, and vanished. Parang put the briefcase behind a chair against the wall, stood up and turned towards her.

Prince Sailendra's private secretary was a courteous but slightly diffident young man. He was happy to talk to her – especially about

the prince, who he worshipped. Or about the prince's wide circle
of famous friends, to whom he was happy to introduce her, if she
would allow him to search them out. These were luminaries of
stage and screen whose credits stretched from the West End to
Hollywood via Broadway. He would even call the Japanese man
back, for he had been nominated for the Nobel prize . . . But she
wanted no social, intellectual or artistic stimulation.

Robin wanted to dance.

Parang was a disappointment on the dance floor. He was well
tutored in a range of Western Terpsichore, indeed his slight figure
and impeccable tailoring, sterling-silver cigarette case and the black
lacquered cigarette holder he occasionally affected seemed to have
plucked him bodily from *Top Hat* or *Shall We Dance?* Nevertheless
he moved with formal frigidity, keeping his sensuous partner at
arms' length, as though he was dancing with an extremely ancient
Grand Duchess whose dignity, temper, corsage and bone structure
might all be equally fragile.

'Antonio Banderas isn't here, I suppose?' she demanded at last,
as he tried to achieve a tango – and managed it with absolutely
none of the dash, style and fire Antonio achieved opposite Catherine
Zeta Jones in *Zorro*. He thought she was serious and actually began
to look around, wreaking final destruction on his footwork – and
on her dancing shoes. Not to mention the tingling toes within them.

If Messrs Banderas, Depp, Clooney or Pitt had been there earlier,
they were long gone now, however. Or they were locked in that
bloody conference room with her equally bloody man, Robin
thought, ruthlessly dumping poor Parang as she went in search of
tighter trousers and looser hips.

She lingered in the wide doorway of the ballroom, her restless
gaze sweeping easily over the reception areas, unconsciously struck
by the way the ballroom doorway commanded an almost perfect vista
of the comings and goings right across the front of the hotel itself.

And, to be fair, the restlessness was not all confined to Robin and
her trim, burning body. For there was in fact a fair bit of coming
and going still, despite the late hour and the length of the celebrations so far. As she followed a deeper, darker, pounding beat out
of the more formal atmosphere of the ballroom, so she found that
there were people of all ages in all imaginable costumes, coming
and going, singly, in couples, pairs and groups. There suddenly
seemed to be a strangely wild undertone to the evening. But then
she looked around at the beautiful but conservative public areas and

gave herself a mental slap. *Get a grip, girl*, she thought. *This is just a hangover from your pirating adventures.*

'Why are pirate jokes funny?' she asked herself quietly. 'Because they Arrrr . . . Aharrrr . . .'

Then, under the cool professional gaze of the hotel security team, who were no doubt assessing her mental state even as they watched her, she crossed the main reception and followed the throbbing down to the hotel's massive night club. Here, a cavernous seating area surrounded by bars and fast-food grills led through into a hazy vastness filled above by the wheeling beams of disco lights and below by whirling, gyrating bodies.

Robin took a flute of champagne from one of the open bars and sipped it speculatively, feeling the bubbles rising to her head while the chill of the alcohol went dangerously deeper. She realized that on top of everything else, she was drinking on an empty stomach. But somehow the tempting-looking chicken kebabs and prawn satays were not quite tempting enough. Unlike that timeless jungle beat of the disco. She discovered with surprise that her champagne flute was empty. She took another. With a third in her hand a moment later, she stood hesitating like Eurydice at the gates of the Underworld. But only for a moment more. Then she drained the glass and turned away. The temptations of that dark and sweaty dance-heaven were aimed at her children, not at herself.

And there behind her stood Chief of Security Kalla. He looked more like a star from an action movie than a leading man from a musical, even though he had changed back into his perfectly fitted evening wear. Even so, she was desperate, and no longer entirely sober. 'Captain Kalla,' she demanded. 'Can you dance?'

'Call me Jahan Jussif, Captain Mariner,' he invited.

'Only if you call me Robin, Jahan,' she answered.

They fell in side by side and walked away from the disco.

'I thought you and Ms Johnson were an item,' she said a little later, as the pair of them sailed sensuously around the perfectly polished, exquisitely sprung grave of poor Parang's dancing career.

'We have a professional relationship,' he answered lightly.

'What does that mean?' she probed a little recklessly.

'We maintain a proper distance,' he answered, with just the trace of a disapproving teacher in his tone.

She raised a disbelieving eyebrow, but said nothing more on the subject of their relationship. Though the lady herself continued to occupy her thoughts for a moment more. 'Where is she, by the way?'

'Babysitting.' The one was unexpectedly – unaccountably – more serious suddenly.

'You have babies?' she asked, amused at the thought, not quite picking up on his tone.

'We have a hurt and frightened pirate who is hardly out of his nappies,' he explained.

'Ah. And Hilly's babysitting him like a good little *professional* – while you play the field?'

'Perhaps.' Kalla's tone lightened again, betraying little more than companionable amusement. She glanced up at him. His expression was courteous but somehow removed. His sculpted mouth curled in a tiny, almost self-satisfied smile. His hooded hawk's eyes were distant. He manipulated her easily across the dance floor once again, dictating her movement – and his own position – with the firm pressure of his hand on the small of her back. Just where the basque met the thong beneath the tissue-thin silk of her dress.

'Except that you're not, are you?' she demanded suddenly, almost childishly.

'Not what?' The dark eyes glanced down at her, then up again.

'You're not playing the field. You're up to some kind of James Bond trickery.'

'What do you mean, Robin?' Again with that teacherly tone.

'I mean I'm not a dance partner. I'm some kind of cover that allows you to keep watch through the ballroom doors while you play at dancing with me.'

'Do you mind?' he admitted cheerfully. 'I rather thought you would enjoy being in a James Bond situation.'

'Listen, Jahan Jussif, there are days when my whole bloody life seems to be part of a James Bond situation. I just wish Mr Connery would be where I want him to be – when I want him to be there – just a little bit more often!'

'Mr Connery?'

'Or Mr Brosnan. Or Mr Craig . . .'

'Your taste in men is wide,' he teased.

'My taste in men is singular. In all the senses of the word,' she said, a little dangerously.

'And yet here you are, dancing with me,' he flirted.

'Only because my personal Bond is still stuck in with Prince Sailendra,' she countered. Then, characteristically, she changed tack. 'Who are you keeping watch for?'

He glanced down again, still wearing that irritatingly self-satisfied little smirk. But at least he paid her the courtesy of answering without prevarication or excuse. 'The pirate says his captain will come to get him. Probably tonight. Says he will chop his way through the guests to get him if need be.'

'You believe him?' This was a change of subject with a vengeance, Robin thought.

'He's young and frightened. But he could be telling the truth,' said Kalla, his voice a little husky.

'You think a pirate captain will come after some kid?' Her tone was sceptical.

'I think the pirate captain would if he is actually his daddy,' countered Kalla carefully.

'OK.' Robin suddenly found his hands were tighter on her and the hard wall of his body more insistent against her. He almost crushed the breath out of her. Something in the basque creaked dangerously. She realized that she had been fighting him to get a better view out through the doors. Fighting hard enough to make him fight back now. Somewhere deep inside she clearly gave the pirate boy's story as much credit as Captain Kalla did. She looked up, frowning, and he was watching her. The little smile was gone. 'There's more?' she demanded.

He nodded once. 'I told the kid what happened to his friends to loosen him up a bit. He saw the one floating in *Tai Fun*'s pool in any case.'

'And?'

'The kid says his daddy'll cut his way through to him. Then cut the throats of everyone who came aboard *Tai Fun* tonight out of revenge for his murdered crew.'

'Cut-throats to a man,' she said, slightly less lightly than she meant. 'So now I know what it's like to get given the black spot. And you don't look much like Blind Pew. You certainly don't dance like Long John Silver, I'm glad to say.'

Robin allowed her tense body to relax a little and he whirled her around again. And she suddenly realized that he had come after her on purpose. The pirate had told him about his father's likely revenge and Kalla had made sure Hilly was safe and then had come out looking for Robin. Just in case. He was dancing with her now so he could keep her safe while he watched Hilly's back. Suddenly almost achingly grateful, she tightened her grip on him, taking some comfort from the hardness under his perfectly tailored jacket. 'Is that a Glock .45 you have there, young man,' she continued, still fighting to lighten her tone. 'Or are you just really pleased to see me?'

He glanced back down with a grin and managed a fair Humphrey Bogart. 'I always have time for a wise-cracking dame.'

'Is that a quote?' she asked, sidetracked.

'Made it up on the spot,' he answered. And swung her round again, his eyes raking the main reception area outside. 'It seemed apt. But I can do you a quote about girls who want to sit in my lap. While I'm standing up at the time . . .'

'I know that one,' she countered. 'And the one about playing it again. Have you warned Richard, Nic and Sailendra?'

'Not yet. I will if the going gets tough.'

'Let's not wait till then,' she suggested, slowing her movements as the dance music stopped. Stepping back, as he was doing, and applauding with formal courtesy, she said most forcefully, 'Let's warn them now, Jahan Jussif.'

Kalla looked down at her. He read the expression on her face. He nodded. 'You go,' he decided. 'You stand as much chance of getting past the bodyguards on the door as I do. I'll stay here for the moment and keep a weather eye out.'

'*For a one-legged seafaring man*,' she half whispered.

'Another quotation?' he asked gently.

'As if you didn't know,' she answered, turning away from him at last and beginning to hurry across the dance floor.

Robin had only just reached the doorway when Parang appeared again. The prince's secretary seemed to materialize out of the shadow by the stairwell over beside the lifts and come staggering forward horribly into the light.

But even at that distance he claimed the whole of Robin's attention. He would have done so because everyone nearest to him stepped back, shocked, and one or two started to scream. He would have done so, even had he not been clutching at his throat, and opening and closing his mouth in silent screams above his white-bunched knuckles. He would have done so because of the fact that his starched white shirt-front and waistcoat were running red with blood.

'Kalla!' shouted Robin and was in motion at once.

While everyone near the secretary was hurrying away from the stricken man, Robin was running towards him. She shouldered her way through the crowd, her wide eyes fixed on the choking face. Her first-aider's mind was occupied already with trying to work out how best to treat a wound like this one. Because she had no doubt over what had been done to Parang. And that meant that, in spite of her *Treasure Island* quips about Black Spots, Blind Pew and Long John Silver, there were in fact pirates somewhere close by.

And they really were cutting people's throats.

FIFTEEN
Maze

B y fortunate coincidence, the two men standing closest to Parang were wearing white silk evening scarves. Both were frozen with horror at the secretary's terrible situation and neither even registered the fact that Robin stole their finery, let alone chose to object.

As Robin ran across the reception area, her mind had been a whirl of speculation, all of it focussed on how best to treat wounds such as these. Had she not seen the scarves, then she would probably have stripped off her self-supporting stockings – for something long and thin was obviously required, something which would do as a makeshift tourniquet. Something that could be tightened enough to put pressure on the wound itself and stanch the flow of blood without actually strangling the patient.

But evening scarves were bound to be better than stockings. More accessible and much easier to acquire. Less likely to raise eyebrows than rummaging around at the tops of her thighs, come to that. Though for once in her life she could probably have stripped off almost unnoticed.

'Handkerchiefs,' she shouted as she pulled the white silk affectations free from the shoulders of the nearest gentlemen guests in a double flick of silk and tassel. 'I need something to make pads with!' One man instantly reached into his pocket and brought out a neatly folded and clearly unsullied linen square. Though under the circumstances, thought Robin grimly as she added it to the bundle in her hands, cleanliness was next to irrelevant. Then it occurred to her that her helper was showing suspiciously quick thinking for just another casual witness.

But all irrelevant thoughts were swept aside at once. Robin was standing face to face with the choking man. It took all of her strength of will not to be sucked into the helpless depths of his stricken gaze. It was like rubbing noses with a drowning puppy. 'You must take your hands out of the way so I can help you,' she said gently. As she spoke, she steeled herself. Heaven alone knew what she should expect. A hot pulsing shower of blood in all probability. Was it horses or people who could pump blood thirty-two feet straight into the air, she wondered, some half remembered titbit from school science lessons surfacing dangerously. It was shock, she knew. Still with the bundle of silk and linen in her fists she took his shaking hands and pulled them down.

She looked down as she did so, peering past the blood-crusted, palsied tremble of the fingers into the gaping pit of the throat. Skin sagged flaccidly, like the neck of a turkey waiting for stuffing. Incongruously supported by the precise knot of a bright red bow tie. The blood-thick tubes within also reminded her confusingly of preparing the Sunday roast.

But then her reeling mind began to take a firmer grip. There was no pulsing spray of scalding blood after all. Therefore no major artery had been severed. The red gristly tube of white-ridged wind-pipe seemed intact; certainly there was no foam of escaping air. No slit lip in the ridged tube flaring out and sucking in below the almost architectural structure of the Adam's apple. The blood, which seemed to have gone everywhere and then settled and begun to set like stage gore, seemed to have come from the smaller veins beneath the skin rather than the major vessels deeper within the structure of the gaping neck itself.

Robin saw and understood all this in an instant. Then she was pressing the folded hankie to the most dangerous-looking bloody area, and wrapping the scarf around it with careful fingers, praying that she would get the delicate operation completed before she went into shock and her hands began to tremble helplessly. But even as she did so, the staring eyes in the dead white face rolled up and the knees began to sag. 'Shit!' she screamed, her language height-ened by shock and desperation. 'Will somebody *please* hold this poor man up while I see to him?'

Once again, it was the man with the hankie who was quickest-thinking. He grabbed the fainting Parang by the shoulder. 'Tom!' he shouted to his scarfless companion. 'Get this poor guy's other arm!'

'And for God's sake hold his head!' she snapped. An obedient fist came in and grabbed a handful of Parang's hair. Robin leaned forward, suddenly crushed between three close-pressed male bodies. She fed the scarf round Parang's neck and pulled it tight. 'Pressure,' she said, unaware that she was speaking aloud. 'Pressure not strangulation.'

'Good thinking, lady,' said the young man who was not called Tom.

Robin glanced at him and was shocked by how close his face was. He had a square jaw, bright blue eyes and a shock of dark blond hair. He looked like Brad Pitt. Disturbingly so, given that she had been thinking about him and George Clooney just a little while earlier. She glanced back at once, tying the first scarf off neatly and swinging the second round on top of it, even as the blood began to soak through the fine white silk.

'Brad,' she said without thinking as she tied off the second scarf. 'You and Tom have got to help me get this man down to the Infirmary. Can you do that?'

'I guess so. Though I have to tell you the name is not Brad,' said the quick-thinking stranger. 'It's Scott. Come on, Tom.'

'OK, Scott,' said Tom. 'You lead. I'll follow. Keep firm hold of his hair though. I can see a lot of this lady's good work coming adrift if his head starts rolling around any.'

So Robin, Scott and Tom carried Parang to the lift. Robin pushed the button and then stood transfixed by the amount of blood her hand seemed to have smeared across it. Her stomach rebelled then, and the steely smell of the stainless steel doors compounded with the smell of blood to make her feel faint in turn. She regretted at once the champagne she had taken and the good solid chicken she had left.

When the lift doors sighed open she staggered in. Tom's spare hand grabbed her upper arm and held her steady. She looked at him gratefully and found him to be a dark-haired, brown-eyed boy with a virile moustache. Like Scott he had deep laugh-lines round his eyes emphasized by his tan. Though neither of them was smiling now.

The lift dropped with a speed that made her feel even dizzier. But she sobered up surprisingly swiftly when the doors whispered open. The infirmary area was eerily still and silent after the terrified bustle upstairs. Robin stepped forward into the passageway and looked to her right. The door into the mortuary stood very slightly ajar. It was dark in there, thought Robin, as she staggered out of the lift with Tom and Scott carrying Parang behind her.

The whole of the area seemed to be dark. Silent. Seemingly empty – though she knew well enough that there were at least two corpses lying in the mortuary, staring at the ceiling. And the girl, the doctor and the nurse were still somewhere in the Infirmary.

'Hello!' called Robin, taking another step forward as Scott and Tom carried Parang out. 'Is there anybody there?'

Her voice seemed to echo strangely and for some reason her hair stirred uneasily. 'Doctor?' she called. Then, lowering her voice, she continued, 'I don't suppose either of you two is armed?'

'What?' said Scott. 'Why would we be armed?'

'Well you look like a couple of Captain Kalla's security men to me,' she answered. 'I mean, look at you. If you're a pair of hair-dressers you're sure as hell in the wrong job . . . Help here! Is there a doctor or a nurse down here?'

And the Infirmary door swung open just wide enough to let the doctor come out. Apparently unaware of Robin and her burden for an instant longer, the doctor turned, holding the door as the nurse pushed a wheeled gurney out into the corridor. 'Doctor!' called Robin.

And at last the doctor turned, seeming to register the horror of what was going on. 'Quick!' she ordered. 'Lie the poor man on here.'

Robin, Scott and Tom were quick – and happy to obey. At once the doctor was bending over Parang. 'Nurse!' she ordered. 'Bandages, now! And bring my mobile phone. I must get an ambulance here from New Baya City at once!'

She looked up at Robin and the two men. 'Thank you,' she said icily. 'He is in good hands now. You may go.'

'Now just wait a minute,' said Robin, her breath simply taken by the abruptness of her dismissal. The rudeness of it. After all she had done.

She hesitated, with Scott and Tom at her shoulder, suddenly – almost insanely – ready to make a fight of it.

'There is nothing more you can do except get in the way and undo the good you have done so far!' snapped the doctor. 'Now go!'

Captain Kalla entered the conference room dragging a pair of disgruntled bodyguards in his wake. 'We got trouble, Your Highness,' he said. 'Your secretary's been attacked. The princess is safe but she needs you with her, sir. I have to get you two and Mr Greenbaum to safety now.'

'Right!' Sailendra was on his feet at once. 'You can fill in the details as we go. Nic? Richard?'

'Where's Ms Cappaldi?' demanded Nic, coming to his feet as swiftly as the prince.

'She's with Princess Inga, sir.'

'And my wife?' asked Richard.

'She's with Secretary Parang, Captain. She's taking him down to the Infirmary. Two of my best men are with her. As soon as he is safely under the doctor's care they will bring her up to the safe rooms.'

'I'll go down to her, just to be sure,' decided Richard.

'Your decision, Captain. Can't say as I blame you. Got your Bluetooth? Good; we can stay in touch then. Your Majesty? Gentlemen?'

Richard ran across the reception area, his eyes everywhere. There were fewer guests in evidence now but more staff and security people. He skidded to a stop by the lifts. It was not until he looked down that he understood just why the floor was so slippery. And then when he reached for the lift button he saw the great smear of blood on the brushed steel.

'Kalla?' he said as he stepped into the lift car, his eyes focussed on the trail of blood across the floor. 'Just what has happened to Secretary Parang?'

'You'll see,' came the terse answer.

But Richard saw precious little a moment or two later when he arrived in the corridor. Here he discovered Robin hesitating in the face of the doctor's icy dismissal. The doctor herself was crouching over a gurney in the corridor, trying to replace a couple of blood-soaked silk scarves with some proper bandaging round Parang's throat.

'Are you alright, darling?' he asked at once.

'I'm fine,' answered Robin. Though she looked pale and shaken. Her face and hands were brightly smeared and several thousand pounds' worth of couture had apparently been reduced to bloody rags.

'She is in shock,' said the doctor. 'I have told her. She would be better to have a hot shower and a warm drink then go to bed. You and these gentlemen would be much better searching for whoever has done this. I can take care of things now. You are only in the way.'

Richard looked at the Infirmary door, frowning. 'Isn't there anything you can give her? After all . . .'

'Sir!' The doctor straightened. 'I have more than enough to deal with, trying to keep this man alive until an ambulance arrives. I do not have the time or the inclination to leave him bleeding to death while I find some pills that would do a job equally well done by a hot shower and a cup of tea. Take your wife away and leave this to the experts, please!'

That was more than enough for Robin. 'Please, Richard,' she said. 'Please!'

Richard put his arm round Robin then. With the two young security men in tow, they crossed to the lift car and stepped in. He pressed the button for his floor. As the lift car hurtled upwards, he looked down, frowning with thought, wanting to discuss the night's events with Robin but hesitant to do so in front of two more strangers.

There was something going on here that he couldn't quite fathom. Something more than piracy, bad though that was. Something deeper, darker. It seemed that there was a pattern forming here – but he couldn't quite work it out yet. No matter how he racked his brains and tried to re-examine the evidence – such as it was – he simply couldn't get a grip on things. It was incredibly frustrating. He felt utterly trapped and at the same time uncharacteristically helpless.

He felt like a blind man in a maze.

The lift stopped at the main reception. Kalla was there. He put his hand on the door and held it wide. 'Mrs Mariner! How are you?' he asked, shocked. As he spoke, he jerked his head and the two security men stepped out.

'I'll live,' she said. 'But the doc says I need a shower and a nice cup of tea.'

'Then that's what you must have. I'll get one sent up. Richard, we're going over this place with a fine-toothed comb. Then the inspector's going over it again as likely as not. He's moving *Tai Fun* to somewhere more secure at the moment but then he'll be double checking my work here. Do me a favour, would you?'

'If I can. What?'

'Stand back for a while. Look after Mrs Mariner. Get some sleep. If there's anything I think you need to know, I'll bring you up to speed in the morning. Deal?'

Richard felt Robin's arm tighten round him and in spite of the nagging worry at the back of his mind, he said, 'OK. Deal.'

SIXTEEN
After

Five minutes later Richard was undoing Robin's blood-soaked basque. The dress lay crumpled on the bathroom floor and the bloody ruination of Robin's poshest ever frock was complete. The shower was full on, and belching steam. He undid the last hook and dropped the basque on to the dress as she wriggled out of the thong, stepping forward into the cloud of steam.

'You know you've even got blood on your bottom?' he said helpfully.

'Then why don't you get yourself in here and help me get it off?' she demanded.

He had an instantaneous vision of himself like Cary Grant in some old half-remembered movie stepping fully clothed into the shower. And he might almost have been tempted to do so, but a discreet tap on the suite's main door stopped him. He closed the shower door. He closed the bathroom door. He crossed the main area and opened the main door. A tall waiter stood there bearing a tray piled high with food and drink. There were sandwiches, cold meats, bowls of fruit, nuts, olives and dates. There was Perrier, cordial, coffee, tea, milk. All in Thermos flasks. 'You,' he said to the waiter, 'are a life-saver. Thank you very much.'

He put the tray down on the bedside table after he had closed the door. 'Food's here,' he called through.

'Later,' she said.

And in his wide and pleasurable experience, that could only mean one thing. He began to pull off his clothes at once, feeling a sudden surge of energy. And mercifully, just before he went through to join her in the shower, he remembered to take the Bluetooth out of his ear.

Not for the first time in their active and exploratory love life, Richard found he had good reason to be glad of non-slip shower mats. Then, after they had towelled each other languorously dry, they made love again a little less adventurously and athletically. But a great deal more satisfyingly.

Afterwards, like kids on a camping adventure, they picnicked in the middle of the huge bed, taking extra care only to keep spills and crumbs to an absolute minimum.

Then, as they had been directed by almost everyone they had talked to recently, they tucked down to get some well-earned rest.

But Richard could not sleep. His mind was a whirl of worry and speculation. And he hated being in situations where he could not help out – or at least stay up to speed with whatever was going on. At last, with Robin snoring gently on his left shoulder, lulled as always by the steady pounding of his heart in her ear, he reached across with his broad right hand and picked up the Bluetooth device. He slipped it into his ear, adjusted the volume, and brought himself up to speed.

So Richard did not remain out of the loop although he was isolated in his suite. The Bluetooth in his right ear communicated on its open channel with Kalla who was leading a top-to-bottom search of the hotel. Not so much a search, it soon transpired, as full Code Red security sweep.

Every now and then he would swap a quip with Hilly on the open channel until she too pleaded exhaustion and closed her channel with an assurance that her charge was sleeping soundly – and that she proposed to do the same. And anyone who even dreamed of tapping on Suite 2020's door before morning would get a short sharp answer. From the Glock .45 as likely as not.

At the same time, Nic had put a Bluetooth in his own ear – standard issue in the secure area – and he all but held a conference while he discussed plans with Sailendra and the other relevant guests who were staying up with him into the wee small hours. While Richard listened to the distant overlapping conversations he filled his time by increasingly sleepily visualizing the faces of the speakers and trying to work out what they were doing – and precisely where – by the sounds in the background of their broadcasts. Hilly's for instance had been pretty echoey. She must have been sitting by the big double doors looking out over the balcony towards the harbour, he calculated.

'We'll postpone the formal opening ceremony,' Nic grated. Distracted from thoughts of Hilly at once, Richard could almost see the frown on that lean, white-chinned face as the billionaire made his decisive calculations. 'What's the point of a ceremony in any case?' Nic continued distantly in Richard's head. 'To raise the hotel's profile. Get some publicity going. Well, for the moment we've got all the publicity we can use. We'll have to wait and see whether the publicity is good or bad.'

'This incident will bring publicity for the whole of my country, not merely for the hotel,' observed Sailendra regretfully.

'Don't worry, Your Highness,' Kalla interjected – from the lift by the sound of things. 'We'll get this all sorted out. It will do Pulau Baya more good than harm in the long run. Wasn't it Oscar Wilde who said "There's no such thing as bad publicity?"'

'Perhaps,' answered Sailendra, 'But if so, he probably said it from a cell in Reading Gaol.'

'No,' said Kalla bracingly as the doors hissed open somewhere near him. 'He probably said it in the Ritz Hotel in Paris. That's where he ended up, isn't it?'

The Bluetooth conversation returned to Nic then as the businessman discussed plans to scale back the opening ceremony and worked through the implications of getting the guests and the celebrity performers back home safely and securely. The long-serving legendary rock band re-formed for the occasion would be shipped on to their next gig in Australia. The young gun rivals to their iconic status would be wafted back to their recording studios in LA. The London Symphony Orchestra would return home without having unpacked so much as a triangle or cymbal, but they were due in a recording studio too – to add the soundtrack to the latest summer blockbuster, half of whose A-list cast were also in the suites upstairs. Or so it seemed.

At last Nic observed, almost cynically, that managing the publicity wouldn't be too much of a problem. Most of the reporters here worked for Greenbaum International Broadcasting's radio and TV networks. All of the columnists worked for Greenbaum International Publishing's magazines and newspapers.

Richard's attention drifted further and further away from Nic's deliberations, though they were likely to impact on his own life and business for some time to come. The soft buzzing of Robin's snores and the reaction to the excitement and action – not to mention the soporific effect of a full stomach – were beginning to overcome even his seemingly limitless reserves of strength and energy.

Increasingly distantly, Richard could hear in Kalla's voice every time the security chief reported another floor checked and clear the growing frustration and anger of a man feeling personally responsible for a situation that was by no means of his own making.

And then, with startling suddenness, it was morning. Richard awoke to the feeling that Robin was no longer snuggled warmly at his side. And that someone somewhere had just closed a door. And that the air in the suite was filled with the delicious odours of bacon, eggs, toast, tea and coffee.

The Bluetooth hissed in his ear, the static suggesting that everyone else had switched off and/or fallen asleep at last. The sleep had rearranged Richard's own priorities a little too.

Robin was out on the balcony enjoying a typically hearty breakfast in the seemingly eternal sunshine. Richard rolled out of bed, slipped on a robe and strolled over to look down at the pile of crisp bacon piled beside her fried eggs and wholewheat toast. It seemed like ages since he had eaten anything hot. He tried a rasher. The flavour was pleasant but unexpected, somehow.

He looked down at her, still chewing, eyebrows raised. 'It's beef bacon,' she said. 'Indonesia's mostly Moslem, remember. And those sausages are beef too. And chicken.'

In the end Richard took a cup of coffee and some toast into the common area and flipped up the screen of the laptop on the desk there. When the familiar Google logo came up, he typed *Professor Lok* into the search box.

There was a range of entries, the most recent of which referred to the breaking story of the professor's death. Richard found one with a video feed and was rewarded with a recent TV interview. It was a local broadcast but it had been syndicated now that the professor's death was international news and there was an English translation. The professor was explaining how smugglers were decimating the wildlife of the islands, and of the seas around them. With all the sparkle and charisma for which he had apparently been famous, Lok was giving an exhaustive list of the endangered species – apes, insects, arachnids, birds, crustaceans, corals, fish . . .

The video had been shot in the professor's lab at the university, and although the cameraman had clearly been briefed to keep his lens squarely on the pretty interviewer and her charismatic interviewee, nevertheless it was possible to see that there were other people at work there. And after a couple of goes, Richard managed to freeze the video picture on the head and shoulders of a woman in a white coat busy at a bench behind the professor's shoulder.

On the right breast of the white lab coat beneath the familiar face, not quite concealed by the familiar tumble of black silk hair, there was a white square of security ID covered with print. The words on it were in the written form of Bahasa Indonesia and meant nothing to him at all. But Richard knew a name-tag when he saw one.

Richard had a near photographic memory. So that when he typed the unfamiliar characters into the Google search box, up she came – in a choice of text or image – with the impenetrable script helpfully translated. A moment or two later, he had a full-length picture of Ms Sheherezade Aru, BSc (Hons), MSc, doctoral student, University of Jakarta Marine Section. The picture showed her standing tall in her white lab coat half turned towards the camera as she lingered at the top of the steps up into Professor Lok's lab.

In each hand, holding her body elegantly upright, there was a crutch. And the angle of the shot – clearly a candid shot snapped from the bottom of the steps – emphasized the thinness of her calves.

Richard didn't really need to see the potted biography listed under the University's Marine Department website to know that Sheri Aru had suffered from infantile paralysis – or Poliomyelitis, as Google helpfully explained – commonly known as Polio. She had, it seemed, contracted the disease in childhood and been lucky to survive. There had been no need for an iron lung. And the calipers she wore at primary school had been removed in her teenage years. She would need the crutches for life, however. Or she would do so whenever she walked on land.

But a little further research was needed for Richard to discover that Sheri was currently undergoing treatment under the Kenny regime and was taking bromocriptine to control the tiredness and pain that her busy academic lifestyle and rigorous diving schedule brought to her weakened lower limbs.

SEVENTEEN
Sheri

*ON THE CONSERVATION OF CORAL COLONIES IN THE
JAVA, BALI AND FLORES SEAS*

*From a proposed Doctoral thesis by Sheherezade Aru,
BSc(Hons), MSc. University of Jakarta, Department
of Marine Biology*

Richard scrolled down the document that Google had discovered for him and then translated for him, smiling with almost paternal pride as he waded through the meticulous maths of the basic research and then read the smoothly translated, increasingly outraged words of Sheri Aru's inescapable conclusion.

'The decimation of all the major coral colonies in the Java, Bali and Flores seas therefore has several origins,' Richard read, his interest caught at once.

'The variations in salinity arising from global warming plays its part, though we must admit that the melting of glaciers and polar icecaps could seemingly hardly be more distant as causes go.' Richard found himself nodding, though his eyebrows were raised. *Melting icecaps, indeed*, he thought.

'The increase in population densities on the land-masses around these waters does contribute more immediately and massively, however. It is a well-known fact that the pollution from the coastal cities in China and Japan have infested our seas. Indeed, cities further inland such as Nanjing pour their effluent into rivers such as the Yangtse and it still ends up in the waters we are discussing here. As well as those cities, huge urban conglomerations in Vietnam, Cambodia, Laos, Thailand and especially in Malaysia all generate almost immeasurable amounts of rubbish and waste, most of which washes down into the waters of the East Pacific and the China Seas. And thence, again, into the waters under consideration here.

'Such is the expanse of detritus caught up in the centre of the Pacific gyre that, like the seaweed of the Atlantic's more natural

Sargasso Sea, it is visible from space. And I don't mean from the low-orbiting satellites that generate the detailed pictures for Google Earth.'

'That's my girl,' whispered Richard as he read the polemic. 'You get good and angry!'

And so she did:

'Even more immediate, however, is the increase in pollution from the exponential expansion of shipping passing through these areas into and out of the Banda Sea, the Celebes and Sulu Seas and, most of all, the South China Sea. The expansion in trade has kept increasing, even through the spikes in oil price and the economic downturns of the early twenty-first century.

'It is hard to over-estimate the damage done by these ship movements in terms of water disturbance, compounding the variations in salinity. In terms of what we might call human pollution – everything from the impact of excrement (and the chemicals used to control it shipboard before it is dumped over the side) to the damage done by plastics, cleaning chemicals, paints and thinners, down to the ubiquitous drinks bottles and aluminium cans. And in terms of industrial pollution – by which I mean mostly oil. Bunkerage, tank-cleaning, illegal cargo-dumping. The percentage of oil per hundred litres of water in the Java Sea has risen by seventy-five points over the last ten years alone.

'Oil is doing damage in more innocent pursuits as well. Even the exponential expansion of the tourist industry plays its part in adding to the danger and the damage. For we have recently proved that scuba divers and snorkelers who have come to view the reefs with no intention of damaging them at all have in fact deposited globules of their suntan lotions that the fish and reef life-forms find poisonous.

'But all of these pale into insignificance beside the damage done by species smuggling. Like elephants decimated for their ivory or tigers hunted to near extinction for their so-called magical properties; like whales chased relentlessly for their oil, their blubber and their meat, the great fish of the reefs are being wiped out for profit. Appendices One through Forty list the decline in numbers of specific reef-dwelling fish such as Crocodile Needlefish, Cornetfish, Saddleback Groupers, Giant Trevally, Greater Amberjack, several species of Sweetlips, all the larger Emperor Fish, Damsel Fish and Parrot Fish, Scribbled Filefish, Lion Fish of all sorts. As well as these, reef visitors like all species of turtle, dugong and more sensitive whale species are vanishing, from the Pygmy Killer to the giant Sperm. And the reefs are dying with them.

'Like the jungles that were once their homes, these reefs belong to the islanders. And so do the rare breeds of fish that swim in them. It is perfectly legitimate for fishermen to trap and sell rare and valuable fish in the old traditional ways. These ways do not harm the environment and they give the sea-faring peoples a legitimate and traditional income.

'But the demand for rare breeds of coral-dwelling fish far outstrips the supply that can be produced in the old ways. It is compounded not only by the massive growth of markets in India, China and Japan but by the infiltration of even the remotest communities by less and less legitimated "dealers". And by the ease with which such contraband species can be transported in the hugely expanded transport networks we have already described. And this offers the chance of inflated profits to organizations who are as happy to decimate the reef walls in the same way as they have raped the mountain slopes above them.

'In place of lines and fish traps, these men come with scuba sets and gas guns. They train the innocent – starving and desperate – villagers in simple diving techniques and give them quotas to fulfil. The process is simple. A diver dons a snorkel set. He places a cartridge of poison gas in his gun – the gas is usually cyanide. A pull of the trigger will release a stream of cyanide bubbles through a needle-thin barrel of the gun. The diver goes down to search the reef. If he finds a fish, he pushes the gun into its face and pulls the trigger. The cyanide bubbles infest the gills and stun the fish. The bubbles are directed almost literally with pin-point accuracy because the point of the gun barrel is so fine. The stunned fish floats helplessly and is easily scooped into a keep net.

'But this is by no means the end of the matter. The cyanide gas dissolves in the water and a solution of cyanic poison rains on to the reef below, killing everything that it touches. Smaller fish and crustaceans die at once. Corals, together with the plant and animal life-forms living on and around them die more slowly. But they do die. A gang of half a dozen snorkelers with their gas guns can strip a square mile of reef of all its marketable fish in half a day. And in the week after the area had been cleared, all the other life forms will also die.'

Richard sat back suddenly, eyes wide, as the penny dropped.

'As will any divers who come across the smugglers while they're working on the reef,' he said aloud. 'Especially if the needle-sharp barrels of those cyanide guns are shoved into their air hoses and a couple of squirts of cyanide gas get fired into their regulators!'

He sat back, staring at the screen, trying to control his horrified imagination as it delivered a nightmare vision of Sheri Aru wrestling her more powerful opponent while the ruthless poacher pierced her air pipe with the point of his gun. And she froze there, knowing that a moment later she would be breathing pure cyanide. Knowing that her only hope of help had already choked to death away down on the reef they had come here to protect.

He pulled himself to his feet, sending the chair skittering noisily back across the floor.

'What is it?' called Robin from the balcony.

'I know how Professor Lok was murdered,' he answered grimly. 'I'd better go and tell Inspector Kei.'

'What?' she called. Her knife rattled down on to her breakfast plate and her own chair scraped as she rose. 'What brought on this revelation?' she demanded, sweeping through into the suite.

'She told me,' said Richard simply. 'Sheri did.'

'And who on earth is Sheri?' demanded Robin as she crossed the room to stand behind him, looking down.

Richard clicked up the picture and Robin stood with one hand on his shoulder staring at the computer screen. 'A very striking woman,' she allowed. 'Show me where she explains to you about Lok's murder and the attempt to murder her,' she said after a moment of thoughtful silence. And he clicked up the relevant page of the thesis.

'She won't get her doctorate writing like that,' observed Robin thoughtfully. 'But I see what you mean. I think we'd better print this off and take it down to Inspector Kei.'

'Good thinking,' said Richard, who hadn't thought of printing the relevant pages off at all.

Richard met the inspector in the lobby. Kei had been forced to surrender the more important crime scene aboard *Tai Fun* to a superior from Jakarta and he clearly didn't like it. Especially as his command seemed to have been reduced to one silent constable. But he was willing to talk to Richard and Robin as soon as he saw the possible importance of their discovery.

'Gas guns, pushed into divers' airlines. How terrible,' he said, apparently shocked. But he glanced back down at the papers, seemingly needing more proof to convince him of Richard's theory.

'We should be able to prove it,' Richard insisted forcefully as the inspector tugged sceptically at the tip of his nose while he glanced down the final page of Sheherezade Aru's doctoral polemic. 'The scuba gear is all piled in the mortuary beside the bodies of Professor Lok and your sergeant from the boat.'

'Sergeant Suleiman,' said Kei, his dull tone impossible to read. 'Tengku Suleiman.'

'Just so,' said Richard after an infinitesimal pause. Then he continued, 'I'm certain I could find the little hole where the gas gun pierced the air pipe. There may even be residue in the regulator. And, of course, the professor's body is showing the classic signs of cyanide poisoning. I even smelled the odour of bitter almonds on his breath . . .'

'We all smelled almonds,' said Kei thoughtfully, capitulating and leading the way to the lift. 'Someone had scattered peanuts, cashews and almonds all over the floor. But as to scuba gear . . .' He shrugged. The lift arrived and the three of them stepped out. As yet aware of nothing at all being out of kilter, they walked swiftly to the infirmary.

Kei swung the door wide. The little room certainly did smell of nuts, Richard thought guiltily. And the distinctive almond smell was there all right. But he saw at once that something else was not where he expected it to be at all.

The two bodies lay precisely as he had left them, awaiting a more thorough post-mortem examination no doubt. But the third table was empty. All the scuba gear was gone. 'What's happened to all that gear?' he demanded.

Richard crossed to the table. There were water drops on the stainless steel of the surface, but they were hardly conclusive. His mind raced. On the one hand the scuba gear was vital evidence. Anyone wanting to make it harder to find out what was going on here might well take it for that reason. On the other hand, the scuba gear was state of the art. Worth a great deal of money to anyone daring – desperate – enough to risk taking it. If they had any way of transporting it unobserved, of course. He had better ask Kalla for a look at the footage from the security cameras, he decided. In the meantime, protestations and arguments were probably redundant. And would almost certainly do more harm than good.

He found himself wondering how much policemen got paid and whether flogging off a couple of scuba sets would do much to add to that income.

'Do you have a list of everything that your men found in here when they searched the place last night?' he asked, flashing a warning glance at the frowning Robin in case she too was wondering about policemen's pay, and keeping his voice easy.

'I have schedules of every room in the hotel,' said Kei accommodatingly. 'Lists of everything they should contain – and of what my men actually found in them. It is standard procedure.'

'May I see them for this room?'

'I don't see why not.' Kei took them to the infirmary, punctiliously closing the door of the mortuary after him and turning the key in the lock. His every careful movement seemed to say: *We are careful and reliable. You can trust us.*

Richard looked around the neat, tidy little infirmary, frowning with the first stirring of suspicion and concern. It was completely empty. Both beds neatly made with sheets but no blankets. Presumably everyone he had seen here earlier was on their way to hospital now. The thought was there and gone in an instant. Because, in amongst all the neatness and the tidiness, there were one or two things that made him frown. Doors not quite perfectly shut; a medicine cabinet fractionally ajar despite the label that said in several languages KEEP LOCKED AT ALL TIMES. When the nurse came back on duty he must check. But in the meantime, his main focus remained on the missing scuba gear.

Kei took a little briefcase off the floor, placed it on one of the beds in a manner that would have brought the wrath of the doctor down on his head – especially as it went straight on to a clean white sheet – opened it and produced a pile of papers. One glance was enough to show Richard that they were simply printed lists of contents – such as he was used to seeing in each section aboard his ships. They had no doubt been supplied by the manager – or whichever member of the hotel staff was responsible for the rooms. Thankfully, but not surprisingly given the provenance of the Volcano Roads Hotel, they were in English.

With the practised ease of a captain completing a ship's inspection, Richard scanned down the sheets of paper, noting the items that had been ticked as being present and crossed as being absent. He frowned over the much less legible lists at the foot of each flimsy describing things discovered in the rooms that were not on the lists. *One male corpse, cause of death unknown,* for instance. *One male corpse, cause of death cut throat.* But no mention of a set of scuba diving gear complete with fins and dive belt.

He glanced up at Kei, who was clearly waiting for the return of his paperwork. He glanced down again, however, thinking that he might not get such an easy chance again to check out those nagging little inconsistencies that had been bothering him since he came into the room.

'And when did your men complete the search of this room, Inspector?'

The punctilious policeman checked his watch. 'Only an hour or so ago. We moved *Tai Fun* to a secure location. I reported to my superior officer who arrived from Jakarta in the small hours. Then we completed the search. We used the lists supplied by the management because there was no sign of the doctor or the nurse at that time, of course. There was no sign of anyone who could not be accounted for. It is not obvious who attacked Prince Sailendra's secretary or why. But the matter is out of my hands now that my superiors have taken over . . .'

Richard nodded absently. 'And you checked with the hospital that everyone arrived safely?'

Kei shrugged. 'We were very busy, Captain . . .'

Richard nodded again, his mind moving from being absent to being positively distracted. He put the mortuary's list at the bottom of the little pile and swiftly scanned down the infirmary list, to where it said:

'Secure box I 27 Contents: restricted drugs – opiates, painkillers, antispasmodics. Parlodel (bromocriptine).' The square beside it was crossed. The medicines from the open SECURE cupboard were missing, along with the doctor and the nurse. And Sheri.

'One box bandages various.' With a cross to show that it was gone.

'One bottle oxygen.' With a cross to show that it was gone.

'Cupboard I 3 – six white doctors' coats.' With a cross showing that they were gone.

'Cupboard I 4 – two sets of crutches, standard design. Adjustable aluminium tubing with rubber ferrule, moulded handles, sprung forearm clips.' With a cross denoting that they were gone.

And, more tellingly still: 'Alcove I 4A – two collapsible wheelchairs.'

With a cross denoting that they were gone.

It was at that moment that Richard's Bluetooth came alive. And at a volume that very nearly deafened him, Kalla bellowed in his ear, 'Alert! Alert! Suite 2020 is open and empty. Ms Johnson and her prisoner have disappeared. I say again, they've disappeared!'

EIGHTEEN
Sherlock

The security tapes were frankly a disappointment. Richard wasn't sure at first what he had been hoping to see, but there was nothing in the colourful comings and goings that raised his suspicions at all. Certainly there was no sign of Hilly and the pirate boy coming or going anywhere through the night, either alone or accompanied by mysterious strangers.

Kalla allowed them to join the search without question. 'Fresh eyes are always welcome, I guess,' he said, sounding suspiciously desperate as he put them in a corner of the security centre.

He had reason to sound frustrated at the least, thought Richard grimly. The moment it had been established that Hilly was not where she should be and that no-one had any idea where she or her prisoner were, Inspector Kei and his superiors had taken over. Richard could see their point – and so could Nic and Sailendra who were both consulted. These were the local men. Law and order was their responsibility. Kalla, Tom, Scott and their teams might be well trained; might be friends and colleagues of the missing woman. But they were security consultants in a situation requiring proper policemen. So they were dismissed to their security area while police work was carried out elsewhere.

But at least they had access to their tapes. Though of course there were no 'tapes' as such, thought Richard as he settled down to go over them. Everything observed by the hotel's security cameras was stored digitally on the central computer's hard drive. One computer in the corner could access everything. No doubt Kei had a computer somewhere in the more official areas, looking at exactly the same footage as Richard and Robin were watching. All they had to do was log in time and location, then up it came. Often with a choice of camera angles. A diversity of sound systems. An almost infinite variety of zooms.

'What were you expecting?' Robin asked after the first half-hour. 'A bunch of colourful guys with a couple of parrots, too many cutlasses and too few legs?'

A stir of half-suppressed laughter showed that Kalla and his security team appreciated Robin's humour, weak though it was. Almost anything would be welcome if it relieved the tension and frustration they were all feeling, she thought. Hilly was never far from their minds – nor was the fact that they had been forced to relinquish responsibility for finding her to Inspector Kei and his bosses.

'I wasn't expecting pirates at all,' Richard answered slowly. 'Not obvious ones at any rate. And certainly not Long John Silver. Or even Sanda Khan.'

'Then what?' Robin asked. She could almost feel Scott and Tom raising their eyebrows, wondering the same thing.

Richard thought back to the rooms. To what should have been there but, along with the women, was missing. 'Putting it all together,' he said slowly, 'what I think I'd be looking for is a tight group of half a dozen or so people in white coats. All walking close together. Bunched around two wheelchairs. Close enough together so you couldn't see exactly what or who was in the chairs – in any case the occupants bundled up in blankets. You noticed that the blankets were gone from the beds in the infirmary? Though they weren't mentioned on Inspector Kei's list. There was bandaging missing too. Enough to tie someone's legs together, I would think. They'd be walking close enough together to conceal the number of knives ensuring quiet and obedience. And at least one gun. A Glock .45 calibre . . .'

'Now wait a minute,' said Robin. 'You're going too fast for me here. Take me through this step by step, would you?'

Richard glanced up at her. In the gloom of the security room he could see the pale ovals of three other faces looking over towards him. 'Two wheelchairs,' he said. 'One for Sheri Aru. One for the scuba gear. Blankets bundling them both up well enough to hide exactly what – or who – was there. From the casual observer at least. Maybe even from security cameras. Because I think we're looking for more than one woman and an escaped prisoner. I think whoever came into the hotel last night took Sheri and maybe the doctor and the nurse as well.'

'But why – when?'

'I'm not sure why. Let's just push the logic on that – what there is of it – and see how far we get. When? If I'm right they acted just after Parang was attacked. They used the confusion as cover. It's the one really random thing that happened. It's the logical place to start. They may even have been in the infirmary or the mortuary while you were talking to the doctor, Robin. And she wouldn't have dared give anything away because they had Sheri Aru as a hostage. Captain Kalla, I know you talked to Hilly well after the Parang incident – but there was something about that conversation that struck me as odd . . .'

'Yeah. Me too,' said Kalla. 'So push on. See where your logic takes you. What have we got to lose?'

'OK. So what was it? Five people in white coats and two wheelchairs? Well, I can see them using a wheelchair for the scuba gear,' allowed Robin grudgingly. 'But why Sheri Aru? She's likely to be pretty nifty on crutches, all things considered.'

Richard was silent for a moment as though her observation had triggered a new series of thoughts. But then he answered, speaking slowly to begin with, but then with gathering speed and certainty. 'That's what I thought at first. But she's still pretty unwell. Lucky to be alive. I'd say there was something about whatever medication she was on that lessened the effect of the cyanide. Or maybe the cyanide gun she describes in that thesis wasn't loaded properly. Whatever. I'm almost certain she was still too unwell to walk.

'But if they took her then they took her for a reason. That makes it likely they know who she is. So they've taken some crutches for her when she gets better. And some of her medication in the missing medicine chest. Which makes it look like they plan to keep her alive – or to have that option at least. And the doctor and the nurse to look after her in the meantime. And what was she on in the infirmary?'

'Oxygen,' said Robin, the penny beginning to drop.

The first penny of several, as things turned out.

'Oxygen. Which is missing. Along with the scuba gear – also filled with oxygen. You see where I'm going with this?'

'I'm not sure,' persisted Robin. 'Next step, please, Mr Holmes.'

'The doctor and the nurse were in white coats anyway. They put Sheri in another one. And that left five more.'

'At least two men to break in to the infirmary, especially if they were threatening enough to scare the doctor and the nurse. I can't see one man alone pulling that off!'

'Good point. So, two men in the infirmary – maybe three. Three coats down and two to go.'

'And one set of crutches.'

'And the bandaging, of course. Yes. So the way I read it is that they – whoever *they* are, but pirates seem most likely at this stage – broke into the infirmary and did what we have discussed. But that was only part one of their mission. In their white coats and whatever a couple went on up to Suite 2020. They probably took the doctor up there with them. I can't think of anyone else outside the team that Hilly would have let in. Especially as the young pirate was still pretty badly affected by the pepper spray.'

'Yeah, I get that,' said Kalla grudgingly. 'Hilly would have opened up for the doctor . . .'

'The moment that she did they overpowered her. Slung one of the spare white coats on her and the other on the kid. Had them back out in an instant and down to the infirmary before you could say *knife*. Which of course they didn't need to say any longer, did they? Because Hilly had taken their armaments to a whole new level. She had a Glock, didn't she? A .45 the same as yours, Kalla?'

'Yeah. I got that the instant that you mentioned it.'

'But she wouldn't have been a happy lady. And I guess that an unhappy Hilly is a considerable handicap in all sorts of ways. So. What to do with her? Knock her out? No, they needed a fast getaway, which was why they had loaded the wheelchairs. Knock her out and put her in the second chair? No, because it was full of oxygen canisters and scuba gear. Kill her? No, they want hostages at this stage because whatever they're up to is starting to look a little complicated. And there are suddenly a hell of a lot of people on their case – from a range of agencies. And more in prospect, too. I mean, look at those Somali pirates who kidnapped the American captain. Suddenly they were up to their necks in FBI and Special Forces . . .'

'Point taken,' said Kalla. 'And these guys have got us on their sorry tails into the bargain . . .'

'So what *did* they do?' demanded Robin.

'Well, I guessed at it when I was thinking of Sheri and the crutches. You said she was pretty nifty with them. And I'm sure she was – and that would be another reason *not* to put her on them. Understand? And yet for someone who's pretty nifty *without* crutches, someone who's likely to be trying all sorts of tricks – but someone who they need to get moving pretty swiftly . . .'

'Hilly. Yes,' said Robin, seeing where his logic was leading.

'They used the bandages to tie her legs together and gave her the second set of crutches,' he explained. 'I reckon the second set in case Sheri needed hers for any reason. Or in case they needed Sheri's wheelchair. Whatever. There was no way Hilly was going to get up to any tricks under those circumstances.'

They all sat around for a moment, gaping at the apparently unassailable logic he had exercised.

Then he rather undermined his status in their eyes by saying in his most modestly English fashion, 'Of course it's all guesswork really. But it seems to fit with things as I observed them.'

'So,' summed up Kalla slowly, 'if we assume your guesswork's good, Captain Mariner, then we're looking for four pirates dressed in white coats wheeling two wheelchairs. One full of assorted equipment and the other with Ms Aru. They have a doctor and a nurse in white coats with them and of course Hilly in the last white coat – who's on crutches into the bargain!'

'That's about the size of it,' said Richard.

'Then why in hell's name can we not see them?' demanded Kalla, gesturing at all the bustling security screens with a frustrated sweep of his hand. 'And why was I able to talk to Hilly later on?'

'Well, it was on open channel and it sounded echoey to me so it may have been coming from any distance,' said Richard. 'We can be pretty sure that there's no reason to believe she was still in Suite 2020 other than that she said she was.'

'Even allowing that,' said Kalla, swinging back towards the security footage, 'why can we not *see* them?'

'Because they found a way of moving outside of camera range,' said Richard simply.

'But how?' asked Kalla.

'It would have been quite a feat to pull off, certainly,' continued Richard. 'In fact, I'd guess that it would be *so* hard to do that if we worked out how they pulled it off, we'd also have worked out where they went. And maybe even where they are right now. Look. Why don't you all wait here and continue going through the tapes. I'd look particularly hard for any sign of the doctor and a couple of guys in white going anywhere near Suite 2020. In the meantime, let me walk the ground. See what I can come up with. You'll be able to watch me if I'm wrong.' He gestured at the live feed from the security cameras. 'But if I'm right, then you'll hardly see a thing.'

Five minutes later, Richard stood outside the locked and police-taped doors into the infirmary and mortuary, looking thoughtfully around. He was imagining the white coats, wheelchairs, crutches. Five desperate men and three women. He saw at once that he had miscalculated slightly. For there must have been a gurney too. With Parang on it. And, now he thought of Parang, he began to wonder . . .

He looked up at the ceiling. 'No cameras here,' he said to himself. 'That's a good start.'

'But there's only one way to go,' said Kalla in his ear, listening, obviously, even if he was unable to look. 'Stairs or elevator.'

'There's no camera in this lift either, is there?' said Richard. 'I mean it's basically a service lift. Completely different to the big lifts on the other side of the reception area. No lift men. No internal security cameras.'

'No,' answered Kalla. 'No cameras in the service elevators. But there's one that covers the doors as soon as they open up at ground level.'

'Not quite, I think,' said Richard gently. 'I noticed a little blind spot just at the left side. Where the stairwell opens just beside the door.'

'But I thought we agreed they couldn't have used the stairs,' said Kalla. 'And that camera covers most of the doorway. There's no way they could have got five people and two wheelchairs past it.'

'And a gurney,' added Richard thoughtfully. 'I forgot poor old Parang. Still,' he added as he pushed the button to call the lift car, 'if they didn't go up then I'd guess they must have gone down.'

As Richard stepped into the lift car, Kalla suddenly added, 'Still and all, I find it incredible that they could have moved without anyone even seeing them!'

Richard pushed the button. 'I agree,' he said. 'And I think someone did see them when they first moved. Someone who became part of the final plan.'

'Who saw them?' demanded Kalla.

The doors hissed open. Richard had pushed the UP button. With one eye on the lobby camera, Richard moved sideways. Immediately beside the steel jamb to the lift door was a vertical curve of wall opening immediately into the stairwell. Here, on the top step, there was a great gout of congealed blood. And at one side of it just the outline of a naked footprint.

'Parang saw them.'

NINETEEN
Out

Richard reached into the lift and pushed the button, then he stepped back. He stood and watched the doors begin to close. Then he walked swiftly but thoughtfully down the stairs, talking quietly into the Bluetooth headset, able to explain his thinking much more easily on the hoof as he hurried down.

'They couldn't have smuggled all those people and the wheelchairs up in the lift, I agree,' he said. 'And they certainly couldn't have got them all back down the stairway. But one man holding someone at knife-point is another matter. Two men up in the lift and out of the corner, avoiding the security cameras. One man who ran back down the stairs after he pushed his victim, cut throat and all, out into the main reception where he very swiftly and naturally became the centre of attention. Distracting everyone from what might be happening down below. Or out back.'

As Richard spoke, he glanced at the stair carpet. On every second step there was a thick smear of red where the man with Parang's blood on his foot had leaped silently and swiftly downwards. 'Did your men see the blood on the stairs when they swept the hotel?' he asked Kalla.

'Nope.' Kalla's voiced dripped with chagrin. 'I don't think the police saw it either,' he added defensively. 'The carpet is very dark.'

Richard arrived at the infirmary level soon after the lift. It stood waiting with its doors open and Richard pushed his hand in to keep them wide as he thought. 'But why Parang?' asked Kalla distantly.

'I'm afraid he was almost certainly caught out by his little vice,' said Richard. He hit the button and the lift whispered almost silently down once more. 'But there may be more to it than that. We'll get a better idea when I get down to the next level.'

The lift doors opened once more. But this time they revealed a huge, shadowy space, its simple vastness emphasized by the low roof and dim lighting. The rough concrete of the floor was marked with parking bays, most of which stood empty. Beyond these, the better part of sixty metres distant, a secure cage which looked large enough to hold a modest herd of elephants contained the hotel's fleet of white Rolls Royces. Beyond it leaned a kind of shanty hut, empty and dark at the moment, where the chauffeurs could relax. Beyond that again, rack after rack of maintenance equipment. Also securely under lock and key.

On this side of the cage, the concrete was banded with white road-markings and hatched delivery areas and drop-off zones where, it was clear, the bulk of the hotel's supplies would be delivered. At the distant outer doorway of the huge underground car park, a massive barred security gate was closed across a roadway half as wide as a motorway. This led away in turn into the morning dazzle of the gardens behind the hotel and further away into the eye-watering distance. The figure of a security guard stood against it, black against the distant daylight, like a statue carved in anthracite, casting a huge shadow inwards across the floor.

But in here it was still only dimly lit. The lift doors hissed closed behind Richard as he stood taking in the strange vista, and the whisper seemed to fill the place as though the nearest shadows were full of snakes. When Richard spoke, his voice echoed eerily. 'I'm in the underground garage,' he said. 'Did your men go through here?'

'They went down for a look-see,' said Kalla, his voice distracted suddenly. 'What can you see?'

'Wheel marks.' Richard crouched, his eyes narrow. There was a range of wheel marks and tyre tracks to choose from, most of them from a variety of treads that told of cars, vans, and lorries of various sizes coming and going here. And the diesel stench of the still, sultry air attested to their presence almost chokingly. Thinner marks told of trolleys, laden and less so, that had blackened the rough concrete with their slick black wheels, or had disturbed the gritty dust that still bled from the new-laid concrete floor.

But Richard was not paying much attention to these. He was focussed on two sets of narrow wheel marks that ran side by side in parallel through the grit, but seemed to come and go like the dashes and dots of Morse code across the floor, obliterated here and there by the marks of shuffling feet. And a third, slightly thicker set beside them.

Two wheelchairs and a gurney.

But here, closest of all to the lift door, lay a cigarette butt. It had not been smoked to the stub. Instead, the whole cigarette had been dropped after just a puff or two then lain on the floor there, untouched and undisturbed, slowly burning down. A long grey scimitar of ash curled unbroken to the brown cork tip. 'Now this is a case where smoking really and truly could kill,' said Richard grimly to himself. 'As poor old Parang found out the hard way.'

He had the ability to distance himself from the natural outrage – while he was in this particular mood at least. In crises, he always thought first, acted next, felt last, and usually saved his most intense feelings until well after the action and reaction were safely past. 'They needed a diversion,' he decided, still speaking to himself – but aware that Kalla was probably still listening in to his thoughts. 'Certainly poor Parang proved to be an exceedingly effective one. And perhaps he knew too much. Recognized some person or saw some detail that might put their plans at risk.

'Whatever,' Richard continued thoughtfully. 'They had a plan, even if they were willing to wing it a little if an unexpected opportunity presented itself.'

He focussed on the tyre tracks again. 'Now these tracks don't deviate,' he explained to Kalla quietly. 'They go in a straight line. These guys knew exactly where they were headed. And, of course, as we're in cynical mood,' he mused, 'they could have had someone calling to them and guiding them to the best way out. And perhaps *that* was the person Parang saw.'

'But then it would only make sense to cut Parang's throat,' said Kalla suddenly, making Richard jump – even though he knew with the certainty of a true believer that his thoughts were being monitored from on high. 'If whoever was guiding the pirates out was someone who needed to stay here unsuspected. Someone who appeared to be working for us but was really working for them. A spy . . .'

'*Now* you're getting there, old chap,' said Richard, with a grim sort of gallows cheeriness. 'That's the kind of thinking we need. Was there anyone at all thinking like this last night, do you suppose?'

'I guess not,' admitted Kalla.

Slowly and carefully, like a bloodhound following a scent through water, Richard followed the intermittent wheel tracks straight across the underground car park to the inside of a wide door. He tested the handle. 'I'm at the inside of a big pair of double doors,' he said. 'They're locked.' He laughed. 'One up for security.'

'Stable doors and bolted horses spring to mind though,' observed Kalla. 'They should be secured at all times, though. They're the main door out on to the loading dock.'

'I know,' said Richard. 'And that fact makes me wonder again about whether there was someone holding it open last night that Parang was unlucky enough to recognize.'

'But they went out on to the dock,' said Kalla.

'A natural thing for them to do, what with them being pirates and all,' said Richard, thoughtfully. 'The harbourmaster's office is on the other side. And he's got a key . . .'

Kalla needed no further prompting. He started barking orders into his Bluetooth. A moment later the key grated in the lock and the left side of the big double door swung wide.

Richard hesitated, dazzled by the brightness. But as his eyes began to clear so they saw *Tai Fun*. Her tall side seemed to be a few scant metres distant. Her masts towered away up out of their view, sails furled tight. The elegant sailing ship had been tethered in the secure area of the working dock, as out of place as a model from *Vogue* on the cover of *Shipfitters Monthly*. Standing on her weather deck, beside a short, fat man in a baggy suit, was Inspector Kei. If he saw Richard looming in the dark gape of the doorway, he gave no sign.

Richard stepped out into the airy, ozone-smelling brightness then, with a murmur of thanks to the harbourmaster's assistant who stood there with the keys. His eyes were still busy on the ground. But the concrete out here was more regularly used and recently cleaned into the bargain. There were no more easy clues to find for the moment.

Richard looked away left and right, therefore, narrowing his eyes against the glare. The left-hand vista showed a loading dock curving away towards the more exclusive marina area beneath the shadow of the soaring hotel. To the right, the dock passed in front of the harbourmaster's office before it ceased to be a dock at all and became a metalled spur of the wide road that ran away through the grounds and up towards New Baya City.

'This is about as far as we can get just using our eyes,' he said. 'We have to use our tongues for a while.'

The harbourmaster and his assistant looked like father and son. He was a big, burly, lightly bearded, white-haired ex-boatman. He had the experience and ready intelligence of an ex-pilot. Both of which he was. He spoke several languages, one of which was English – as suited his position and responsibility. His fingers, forever spoon-shaped from years of handling ropes and oars, were calloused and salt-cracked. Entirely unsuited to the computer keyboard with which he monitored – dictated – the comings and goings of ships in his harbour. And, indeed, on occasion, the comings and goings of helicopters high above. His son had his father's eyes, his father's virile curls – though in ebony still, not ivory – and would soon have his father's hands. Richard took to them at once, seafaring men all together.

'Last night?' said the harbourmaster, echoing the last words of Richard's first question. 'Last night was madness. I take only limited responsibility for anything that occurred last night!'

Impressed by the man's ready willingness to take any responsibility at all, under the circumstances, Richard began to probe gently. 'I am most interested at this stage by any comings and goings on the dock out there. Is there any kind of log?'

'There were more than I could begin to remember, let alone record! I have all the ships' movements, of course, though Inspector Kei relieved me of much responsibility by insisting what should go where. Especially with regard to *Tai Fun* – which I would never have placed in the working dock. But he insists that she is a crime scene now and she must be held securely under guard – and close by. And in any case, I should not complain, for my time was more than a little taken up once the helicopters started to come and go in such numbers. My training as an air-traffic controller is extremely basic – emergency work only, really. And the equipment, excellent though it is, was not really designed for such intense work.'

'I see,' said Richard sympathetically. 'So you were pretty busy here. But you would have logged all ship movements?'

'Certainly. I or my son would have done so.'

'The system is manual?'

'It is when the automatic computer record is switched over to monitor sky movements instead of sea movements.'

'Of course. So for some sections of last night I would have a detailed computer record of every helicopter movement . . .'

'As I have said . . .'

'But the record of ship movements would be in the written log.'

The harbourmaster's eyes grew narrow. 'You do not strike me as being slow of understanding, sir. What is the point you are making?'

'I am trying to establish whether it might or might not be possible for a small boat, hardly bigger than a *prahu*, to creep in and out unnoticed when the air traffic was at its most intense.'

'It is conceivable, sir. But it is unlikely. Not without the boy having seen it.'

'And did he see any *prahus*? Picking up several people at this dock. With at least two wheel chairs, perhaps? And a trolley?'

'No. And remember, even if he missed it – which, as I say, is highly unlikely – the police guard on *Tai Fun* must have seen it.'

'Ah yes. The police guard. But before I disturb Inspector Kei and his men, I just want to check one more thing. Road traffic.'

'Road traffic?' The harbourmaster's face went blank.

'Yes. The inland end of the dock here becomes a spur of the main road up to New Baya City. Is there any record of what traffic went up and down there at all last night?'

'No, sir! Of course not! The pair of us are responsible for water traffic and air traffic. No-one will have kept a record of road traffic except for the security guards on the main gate to the hotel grounds. And I have to tell you, sir, that last night, what with one thing and another, the gates were effectively unmanned. But as for road-traffic – it was hardly like rush hour in New Baya City. Nothing came and nothing went.'

TWENTY
Vanishing

Kei met Richard at the head of the gang plank as though the inspector were actually *Tai Fun*'s captain. He was to a certain extent the commanding officer, Richard thought as he shook hands formally with the punctilious man. For Captain Tom Olmeijer, his officers and crew had all been sent ashore long since. But Kei was the only senior officer aboard, Richard thought shrewdly. Or he was if the plump man in the neat suit had disembarked while they were talking to the harbourmaster. For he must have been Kei's superior – the one who arrived from Jakarta in the wee small hours.

Kei continued to shake Richard's hand with lengthy formality. Sufficient in fact to make Richard more than a little suspicious that the policeman was up to something. 'To what do I owe the honour of this visitation?' asked the inspector courteously with only the faintest hint of irony in his voice.

'I don't actually want to call you away from more important matters,' answered Richard, his tone also carefully calculated.

'But I was wondering whether it would be possible to talk to whoever was keeping watch aboard last night.'

'We are policemen, not sailors,' Kei observed. 'There was a man on watch – various men at various times, in fact – but they were policemen, not a watch-keeper as you might mean the term. They wrote no logs. They reported to me anything they thought sufficiently important . . .'

'Then perhaps, if you have time,' said Richard blandly, 'you wouldn't mind helping yourself. I was wondering whether your watchman noticed several people in white coats and one on crutches, pushing two wheelchairs and a gurney out on to the dock down there. And if he did notice them, whether he saw where they went.'

'Well,' answered Kei guardedly, 'you would need to be specific as to time. We spent much of the night moving *Tai Fun* around the outer and inner harbours. However, I would be happy to take you through our comings and goings . . .'

Richard seemed to stand outside himself, listening to this verbal fencing with gathering frustration. He had not come down here to practise his arts of Eastern courtesy or to listen to lengthy guarded diplomacy and he really could not understand why Kei was being this coy and precious. He glanced away from Kei and looked around the deck. Abruptly he thought he caught a furtive movement out of the corner of his eye. And in a moment of revelation he realized that they were being spied upon. By whom and for what reason he had no idea. But his natural instinct was to do something about it. He looked back at Kei, frowning with his new understanding. Kei refused to meet his gaze, seemingly focussed on their verbal fencing.

'Can we perhaps go below?' asked Richard abruptly. 'I for one could do with a drink.'

Inspector Kei stopped mid-sentence and turned towards him, his expression unreadable. Then he gave a bland smile. 'Of course,' he said equably. 'The servants all went ashore with the crew last night. I am effectively alone on board. But I know where everything is kept. I believe we can manage a cup of coffee. Or tea.'

Over coffee in *Tai Fun*'s main passenger lounge, with acres of open space all around them and no chance for anyone to overhear them – unless Kei was carrying some kind of bug himself – the inspector was much more businesslike and precise. Almost forthcoming, in fact. Before they had emptied their first cup of coffee, they managed to establish a simple sequence of events both ashore and at sea.

At the time Parang and Robin were dancing, and while Richard was in the Victorian reception room, *Tai Fun* had still been in the outer harbour. Tom Olmeijer, his crew and all the ancillary workers such as cooks and cabin staff were ashore – in the hotel with everyone else in fact. Kei and his small command had been on board alone, their initial sweep of the ship complete, their statements about the deaths of the pirates written up, guarding the crime scene against the arrival of his superiors and a forensics team from head office.

Then, out of the blue, Kei had received a radio message. On the orders of Kei's approaching superior, who radioed down from his inbound helicopter, *Tai Fun* was to be moved into the inner dock. The senior policeman had begun to feel airsick; he had no intention of compounding this with seasickness. *Tai Fun* should move at once, the message emphasized. He refused to come aboard her until she was safely secured and as still as possible.

Because Captain Olmeijer and his crew had been sent ashore, a skeleton crew had had to be summoned back out to move *Tai Fun*. A good deal of time had been wasted in the enterprise – but it had in the end delivered *Tai Fun* to her present secure and convenient location.

At the moment Parang's throat had been cut – established to the nearest hundredth of a second by the clock on the security video – the beautiful vessel was only just beginning to enter the inner dock. It was then that Kei had come ashore to oversee the police search of the hotel and greet his recently arrived commanding officer. And remain ashore with him – because *Tai Fun* was still not safely secured and at rest.

The ship had continued to be moved towards her present location in Kei's absence. He had returned aboard only after the whole hotel had been searched from top to bottom – with no clear or satisfactory result – and after his superior officer was satisfied that the vessel was absolutely still. By which time *Tai Fun* was in fact safely in the anchorage where she was sitting now.

'So the long and short of the matter,' summed up Richard, 'is that during the crucial half-hour or so, *Tai Fun* was still moving in from the outer harbour. She had a skeleton crew aboard but no formal watch-keeper. The ship handlers would have been glued to their instruments or maybe keeping an eye out for smaller vessels going in and out of the marina. You yourself were ashore, but a few of your men were still aboard overseeing security in your absence. If your men were on deck in any case, it is unlikely they would have been keeping any kind of lookout.

'Meanwhile, ashore, the hotel was in furore as we know. In the dock area here, the harbourmaster was focussed on his helicopters and his son was guiding *Tai Fun* to this anchorage – both using instruments.

'And somewhere during all of this, several people came invisibly out of the hotel and simply vanished. It's like one of those Victorian detective stories. Locked room mysteries. We need Sherlock Holmes, or Dr Thorndyke; Hercule Poirot or Father Brown . . .'

As Richard was completing this grim little summing up, Robin arrived. She was clearly full of news and bursting to tell it. Over her right shoulder she carried a slim black plastic case that was the perfect size to contain a laptop. As she crossed the empty room towards the men she overheard Richard's last few words.

'Whether or not any of your detectives was involved, it looks like some of them managed to vanish a couple of times earlier in the evening as well,' she said by way of announcing her arrival. 'Kalla sent me,' she explained as the men looked up. 'He thinks he's solved part of the puzzle. Is that coffee? I'd love some.'

Kei rose courteously to pour her a cup and, as he did so, she slid a laptop computer out of the black carry case she had slung over her shoulder.

'Has he indeed?' asked Richard. 'What and how?'

'I'll show you,' said Robin, opening the computer and switching it on. 'We have remote access here, don't we?'

Kei took the opportunity to freshen all their coffees, then the men stood behind the vital, vibrant woman as she accessed the hotel's network and typed in the security codes needed to enter the security system. 'Kalla says he may have to kill me later,' she joked. 'These codes are as precious as the access codes for the CIA mainframe at Langley, the NSA's and the White House's all put together.'

As soon as she had finished speaking, Robin brought up the familiar security camera footage they had been studying all morning. 'Look,' she said, switching dexterously from one camera to the next. 'You have to pay pretty close attention, but it'll be easier if I run a couple in parallel. Split screen rules. This is the footage from lift cameras one and two going up and down from the main lobby. Pay particular attention to lift two.'

The pictures ran in parallel. Lift men sat, stood, sat. People got in and out, apparently having gone nowhere. The time clocks ran. The clock on lift two jumped – went out of sequence with lift one for exactly a second. Then it went back in sequence. 'That's clever,' said Richard. 'Run that by me again, would you, darling?'

The sequence was repeated. That single second of time in lift two vanished once more – like a test of Einstein's laws of time and motion. 'So nothing we see on lift two's camera can be relied on,' said Richard thoughtfully. 'Someone's fiddled with it. There may be only a second missing on the clock but there could be hours of missing footage. I recognize the lift man. He's the one I had that extremely illuminating chat with. Looks like we'll need to have another chat with him now. Any idea where he is?'

'Yes,' said Robin. 'And no. I know where he's *not*. He's not where he should be. He's gone. Vanished. Neither hide nor hair of him anywhere in the hotel.'

'Hmm,' said Richard quietly. 'Suspicious. But I think we'll find there's more. Freeze lift two's camera on the missing second, would you, darling?'

Robin obliged. The time clock sat, its nine-figure read-out showing hour, minute, second, hundredth, at the foot of a still picture of an empty lift. 'He's vanished there, too, hasn't he?' said Richard. 'Darling, can you scroll through the footage from the camera outside Suite 2020 until you get that same time, please? Put it where you have the footage from lift one. I want to see them side by side.'

Robin obliged. The hundredth of a second counter whirled. The second ticked up. The numbers matched. The footage from Suite 2020 flickered.

'Take it back,' ordered Richard. 'Roll it one frame at a time.'

And there was the proof. There and gone so vanishingly fast that only someone certain it existed would ever have seen it. During the one-hundredth of a second when the figures matched exactly, the lift man was outside the lift, in the corridor, looking up at the camera. One-hundredth of a second earlier he was not there. One-hundredth of a second later he was gone. 'Now that,' said Richard, with simple awe in his voice, 'is what I call a vanishing act!'

'That's not detection,' said Robin. 'That's science fiction. How in hell's name did he do that – and how did you work it out?'

'I have no idea how he did it – and by lucky guess,' answered Richard. 'But I'd say we now know how our suspects were able to move around the hotel during the vital missing minutes without the security cameras picking them up.'

'But we still need to work out exactly how they vanished all together,' said Robin.

'I think we're getting there,' said Richard. 'I just need one or two last pieces of the puzzle and I'll know.'

It was Inspector Kei's superior, Superintendent Hatta, who inadvertently gave Richard the next – last – piece of the puzzle. And this was apt enough, for he was in many regards the Javanese equivalent of Richard's inspiration Hercule Poirot. He was rotund and balding. He gloried in an oiled moustache. He was as precise in his dress as a Flemish milliner. And, under normal circumstances, he had a mind capable of amazingly acute insight. But these were not normal circumstances.

Superintendent Hatta was a man who disliked moving very far from his desk, unless to his favourite eating place or to his home. Or, very occasionally and under carefully controlled conditions, to the scene of a crime. In spite of his elevated rank, he was a man of uncommonly conservative habits. He had to be particularly careful what he ate or drank, and was normally fastidious to the nth degree about how he travelled. The journey here had undermined what little intestinal fortitude he normally enjoyed. The helicopter ride had come very close to undermining his personal dignity by requiring him to empty the contents of his considerable stomach into a brown paper bag, and only the fact that he had taken a large number of motion-sickness pills saved him in the end.

The mere thought of going aboard *Tai Fun* threatened to undo the good these numerous and potent tablets had done – and so Hatta had ordered her into the inner harbour and into the securest dock available. He had, however, fortified himself with a further ingestion of seasick pills before venturing up the gangplank.

Superintendent Hatta had been trying to make sense of Kei's report through the haze of a considerable overdose, therefore, when Richard had first caught sight of his neatly suited figure out of the corner of his eye. And even though the vessel was absolutely steady, he had been overcome with *mal de mer* in the moment before Richard came aboard.

Kei of course had suggested the superintendent should go ashore, but Hatta had decided to remain aboard with almost drunken insistence. Kei had no idea where best to put a superior who was behaving in such a strange manner. But he held Hatta in a great deal of personal regard, and was simply too fond of the man to consider showing him up in his present condition. And he was all too well aware that the reputation of his commander – of himself and indeed of his own force – could well be at risk here.

Richard's arrival could hardly have come at a worse moment. He welcomed the inquisitive Englishman aboard in his most distractedly guarded manner, all too well aware that his mysteriously intoxicated chief was wandering somewhere nearby. At least the blessed inspiration of going below seemed to offer Hatta the chance of getting ashore unobserved. A particularly wise move in Kei's estimation, as the smell of good strong Java coffee was likely to have an almost emetic effect on the superintendent.

But as it turned out, Robin's arrival had forced Hatta to retreat once more and it was only the combination of her rapid disappearance below and the extra-strong whiff of coffee that came immediately after that made the semi-conscious superintendent move. He staggered out on to *Tai Fun*'s deck, therefore, and made a break for the gangplank. But *Tai Fun* was a boat not a building. Even secured as she was, nevertheless she sat in the water. Her side was pressed against the solidity of the concrete walled dockside, but separated by rubber fenders which sat, like the gull-white hull, in the tidal swell of the harbour.

Just as Hatta reached the top of the gangplank, *Tai Fun* gave a little dip. Her side slid down the grumbling fenders as the water beneath her heaved. And the water was not all that heaved. That one tiny movement undid everything the superintendent's fortitude and considerable overdose had done. He rushed to the rail and hung helplessly over the side. His whole world shrunk to a burning point of acute, almost volcanic discomfort.

But, as is often the case, that first eruption, considerable though it was, brought almost instant relief and clarity. So that Superintendent Hatta, even as he reached for the huge scented Thai silk handkerchief he always carried with him, and began to wipe his unfortunately bedraggled moustache with it, found himself looking down into the face of a man floating almost upright in the water, the shoulders of his black tuxedo wedged between two fenders, his eyes, his mouth and his throat all gaping wide.

TWENTY-ONE
Invisible

As the chopper whirled in above the gleaming towers of New Baya City's burgeoning financial district, racing in towards the King Jayavar Clinic, Richard guided the lively conversation to its conclusion.

'Of course it had to be the ambulance,' he insisted – though no-one had actually disagreed with his conclusion. 'What else could have come and gone almost unnoticed through the confusion last night?'

'What else could have picked up a doctor, a nurse, a couple of patients and several people in white coats without arousing undue suspicion?' added Robin, leaning forward earnestly. 'Like that story Richard kept on about. Where no-one noticed the murderer coming or going because he was disguised as a postman.'

'G.K. Chesterton,' explained Richard, irredeemably literary. 'One of the *Father Brown* stories. The case of *The Invisible Man*.'

Kalla nodded, willing to be persuaded by the ambulance theory, but sublimely unmoved by Father Brown. Already half convinced by the confirmation offered by the gate-security team, in fact. Because they had confirmed that an ambulance came and went past them last night as soon as he thought to double-check. They hadn't thought twice about it. The doctor had warned them to expect an ambulance. An ambulance had come and gone. The doctor had said it was an emergency so they'd simply waved it through. No, they hadn't looked inside . . .

'But why dump the prince's secretary in the harbour like that?' demanded Inspector Kei.

'Basically, I'd say it was simple logistics,' said Richard. 'They had Ms Aru in one wheelchair and the oxygen in another – though we might well find that stuff at the bottom of the harbour into the bargain if there was oxygen in the ambulance itself . . .'

'They had the young pirate blinded with pepper spray,' interrupted Robin. 'They obviously wanted him out of our clutches before he got taken to the United States or wherever and charged, like that other young pirate from Somalia . . .'

'And of course they had Hilly,' added Richard. 'That echoey garage was where she answered the last call from. With a gun at her forehead or a Kriss at her throat, as likely as not . . .'

'So. Two invalids. And, what, five other people?' concluded Kalla, grimly. 'The doctor, the nurse, the pirate who cut Parang's throat, the lift man, and Hilly.'

'A bit of a squeeze,' allowed Kei, 'even allowing that it was a big vehicle.' He looked down at the screen on Kalla's iPhone, which was displaying the frozen image from the gate's security camera that showed the ambulance pulling out. It was a big, boxy, strangely old-fashioned looking vehicle. Its high, square rear-section was painted white and marked with a red cross, a red crescent and more local medical signs. And the logo of the King Jayavar Clinic, Sailendra Square, New Baya City. He looked up again, a little queasily, thought Richard. Certainly, the whirling leap of the heli-flight explained why they still had the inspector with them instead of his seasick boss. 'And poor Parang was probably dead by then in any case,' he added grimly. 'Only Robin's phenomenally quick thinking had kept him alive up to that point. But I dare say the man who cut his throat in the first place would have been less careful of his welfare.'

'He must have been hiding in the infirmary while your men and I delivered Parang to the doctor,' said Robin with a shiver. 'Keeping Sheri Aru as a hostage to ensure everyone's co-operation. That explains why they brought the gurney out . . .'

'Then, soon after you left,' concluded Richard, 'they wheeled everyone out, took them down in the lift and through the underground garage. I'd guess the lift man met them there – it was probably he who got the key and let them out on to the dockside as the ambulance arrived. They'd have been safe enough in the garage because everyone was still upstairs looking for the pirates who had attacked Parang.

'Then they cleared the decks of their dead wood, so to speak, and slipped everyone else aboard. They'll have done that carefully and subtly. No-one on the dockside seems to have noticed anything going into the water – though *Tai Fun* was still coming in from the outer harbour, according to the inspector here, so her berth would have been clear. And there's no reason I can see to suppose the ambulance men had any suspicions. They probably just saw a medical emergency under control, with the doctor clearly in charge. So they loaded up and off they went.'

Kalla's iPhone sounded. He put it to his ear. He held a brief and cryptic conversation and then nodded.

'That's the King Jayavar Clinic,' he said after a while. 'Just confirming that they dispatched an ambulance as requested but no doctor because they were told a doctor was already on the scene. And they're expecting us in fifteen minutes. The director himself is going to meet us, I understand.'

Director Aquina could have been Superintendent Hatta's elder brother, thought Richard as they shook hands. Except that he was, if anything, neater, more precise – and a great deal less seasick. His suspiciously perfect hair shone like black varnish on either side of his perfect rule-straight parting. His equally black and shiny moustache turned up through precisely ninety degrees beneath his fastidiously chiselled nostrils. When he smiled, as he did often, a little gold gleamed modestly amongst the Hollywood-white perfection of his dental work.

'This is a terrible business,' the director announced, waving them to a range of chairs as he enthroned himself behind a massive mahogany desk, sliding his hands down his hips and buttocks as he did so, to prevent the tails of his ivory silk suit jacket from becoming untidily creased.

Behind the director stretched a panoramic window so wide and bright as to effectively mask his urbane face with shadow. The view was of such breathtaking beauty and bustling industry as to be positively distracting. In the blaze of morning light, the rooftops of the city gleamed like scattered jewels as they mounted the iridescent emerald slopes of the central mountains. Mountains whose sheer, stark watersheds seemed to saw at the sapphire sky like sharks' teeth. Away beyond the director's beautifully tailored left shoulder, high above even those jade-green fangs, the plume of smoke that Guanung Seurat volcano belched unceasingly upwards was carried away from the island by the steady pressure of the monsoon.

In January the monsoon blew from west to east, Richard thought inconsequentially. In June it blew from east to west. And as the island lay perfectly north/south, the monsoon always carried the smoke away. His eyes wandered to the right, beyond the volcanic plume, beyond the end of the window itself. And there, high on the wall, just beneath the director's doctoral certificate, in pride of place above a dresser full of Indonesian artefacts reminiscent of the Victorian room in the Volcano Roads hotel, a polished brass plaque was screwed to the wall.

King Jayavar Clinic. Sponsored by DelMonte Medical Facilities Limited. One of the DelMonte Medical family of clinics.

'. . . a full internal enquiry,' the director was saying. 'That one of our vehicles should have become embroiled in such a dreadful incident. Piracy! Kidnapping! The murder of His Majesty's private secretary!'

'But, Director Aquina,' interrupted Kei, 'where is the vehicle now? Do you have it secure? Where are the people who were aboard it?'

Director Aquina stopped mid-flow. Even with the full tropical light behind him, it was possible to see that his mouth was hanging open. 'But I thought you realized. I believed you had been informed . . .'

'What?' asked Richard, glancing back from the polished perfection of the brass plaque, his senses stirring, understanding at once that there was a vital oversight here. Adrenaline was already beginning to flood his system, quickening his heart-rate and sharpening his perceptions.

'The ambulance! It has not returned to us at all! I supposed you knew. It is not based here. We do not use such old-fashioned vehicles in our premier facilities, you understand. It was out on the road and available so we sent it at once. But it has not come back here. It is from our little polio clinic at Bandar Seri township over on the west coast and it seems to be returning there.'

To emphasize his point, the director rose and hurried across the office to a map on the wall. Richard was up at once, striding over to join him, eyes narrow.

The map showed the island looking indeed like a leaping fish – a swordfish truncated, for it did not show the slim blade of the north-pointing reef. The round black eye of the volcano stared out of the headland at the north. The river-mouth gaped as though it was chewing on a steel hook. The old city was marked brightly along it as though the buildings were not half-buried now by metre upon metre of pumice, ash and mud. The in-curving belly of Bandar Laut Bay reached down from the ruins of the old, lava-covered city to the almost geometric perfection of New Baya City itself.

Then in the far west, beyond the curved lateral line of the central watershed peaks reaching south from the volcano to the tail where the Volcano Roads Hotel stood, there was the back of the long green body. Here the land heaved westward in solid, almost muscular swathes until it reached the outward curve of the western shore.

Here too a fishy feature was concealed by the fact that this was a map and not a chart, Richard thought. Stretching away under the plain blue water like the sail-fin of a marlin was the area of outstanding natural beauty that the UN was trying to protect – with the vociferous support of the late TV star and naturalist Professor Lok.

And there, right at the lower end of that invisible fin, stood the port and township of Bandar Seri. The director was gesturing and talking in apologetically explanatory tones but Richard was paying little attention. He was looking at the red line denoting the road. It wound almost drunkenly through the steep mountains, its way dictated by the folding of the rocks and the meanderings of the torrents that chopped their way relentlessly through them, powered by the deluges brought by the monsoon winds that kept the volcanic smoke and ash at bay. Director Aquina was pointing to the red line winding into the eastern foothills with a pencil. That was where the ambulance was at the moment.

'And you are certain they are returning to Bandar Seri?' Richard demanded, interrupting the emollient flow rather rudely.

'Certainly. All of our vehicles have a simple identification and tracking device aboard. It is often vital that we know which one is where.'

'But you can't just contact it and tell the driver to stop – or even to return?'

'Unfortunately not. The two-way seems to be out of order. Like the vehicle itself, it is not in the first flush of youth . . .'

'And in any case,' emphasized Kei with surprising forcefulness, 'it seems certain to me that if they tried any such thing it would simply result in two more cut throats.'

'There is that,' allowed Richard. 'On the other hand, as far as I can see there isn't anywhere obvious for them to stop off – or turn aside, come to that. Until they get to Bandar Seri itself. They're bound in by the mountains until they're almost in the outskirts.' He looked at his watch as he asked, 'And just how far is that?'

Robin realized what he was thinking first. 'You think you can catch them up, don't you?'

'Well, I know where they're going and I know they can't get off the road that will take them there – not easily at any rate. So, if we can get the chopper fuelled up for that length of flight and up in the air in time – and of course if Inspector Kei will agree to get us flight clearance in time – then yes. Yes I do.'

Kinabal Surat, the island's second-highest peak, fell away below them less than an hour later. If Richard had looked back – something he very rarely did – he might have seen the reflection of Director Aquina's panoramic window lost in the dazzle of the city far below. Certainly, if the director sitting invisibly behind it had the leisure to swing round in his leather-bound, gimballed and castored throne to look out, he would have seen the chopper just beginning to settle out of the hard blue midday sky behind the solid green saw-teeth of the mountain range.

But the director was otherwise occupied and Richard as ever was looking fiercely forward. He had never been to this side of the island but he had talked at length to Sailendra about the prince's adventures here during the hours before the volcanic eruption that had led to their first meeting and their friendship. The details had been so vivid that he felt he knew the place quite well. It came as no surprise, therefore, to find the upper slopes, still thickly forested with virgin jungle, falling swiftly into semi-cultivated areas where the red banana and mango plantations surrendered unwillingly to the required regimentation of modern farming techniques.

And below them, he saw as though for the hundredth time the shining scimitar blades of the stepped paddy fields that led down the lower mountain slopes towards the urban sprawl of Bandar Seri's more elevated suburbs. The township itself came as something of a surprise, for Sailendra's stories of this place had been set further north, and some years since. The town had grown almost as fast as New Baya City back behind them. It was a considerable manufacturing centre now, a busy port and, if various plans went well, a potential oil-terminal.

The bustle of shipping was a surprise too, though Richard's wise eyes soon saw how the big ocean-going vessels were all following a strictly controlled deep-water sea-lane towards the south of the busy port. To the north stretched the tell-tale shallows of the great reef that was the UN's current conservation target for the area. Here the paler blue of the shallow water was dotted with little fishing smacks and dive boats like the one that had started this whole adventure.

The only feature that threatened the tranquillity of the scene was the oil-drilling platform standing at the north-west corner of the shallow reef, footed in the deep water and, Richard knew, waiting for final permission from the conservationists before it sank its first exploratory well. He would have been much happier to see it there had it been owned by BP or Shell. But it was the property of Pontianac Oil Enterprises, he thought grimly. And, through them, of the ever-present, secretive and all but invisible Luzon Logging Company, of Del Monte Avenue, Manila.

TWENTY-TWO
Rescue

'You know,' said Robin, 'there's no guarantee that they'll still be aboard if and when we catch up with this ambulance.'

Richard dragged his gaze in from the far horizon and met her steady grey eyes. 'Maybe there's more of a chance than you think,' he countered. 'If they're serious about holding Sheri Aru then they aren't going anywhere far – with her either in a wheelchair or on crutches. I can't see them dashing through the virgin rainforest with her lying on a gurney either. No. If they want to keep her close then they'll stick to the road. And then it'd be logical to stay with the ambulance as long as possible.'

'OK. I see that. But maybe she's just an incidental. You know, expendable.'

'I don't think so. They've gone to a lot of trouble to hang on to her. And if she was expendable then she'd have been floating in the harbour with Parang.'

'Maybe she is.'

'No she's not,' called Inspector Kei, who had been in contact with headquarters and various outlying police stations right throughout the flight. 'My divers have just finished checking beneath *Tai Fun*. One corpse and one gurney. That's all.'

'OK,' allowed Robin after a short silence. 'So they don't want to kill her – or Hilly by the look of things.' She switched her steady gaze across to Kalla's worried frown. 'But what's to stop the men we're after just leaving the women where they are and simply dropping out of the back of the ambulance? Then, I don't know . . . Getting aboard another vehicle. Maybe even hitching a lift. Disappearing into the hills?'

'Well, the kid's still likely to be pretty blind,' observed Kalla. 'That was one hell of a dose of pepper spray that went into his eyes. I'd say he'd need to be sedated and treated by a competent medico for a while yet. Hitching would certainly be out of the question. No, he'd need the ambulance as much as Ms Aru would.'

'And whatever else they are – why ever else they're there – the kidnappers seem to be pirates,' added Richard.

'So?' Robin drew out the monosyllable, quavering slightly, her voice uncertain as she strove to approve his logic. It would be much safer for everyone concerned, she felt, if Richard was right. Or right enough to have some kind of a handle on this.

'So I'd guess they're heading for water.' Richard gestured ahead at the boats bobbing just beyond the rising heave of the town. 'It's what pirates do.'

Robin was on the verge of pointing out that they had just come *away* from pirate waters, when the outskirts of Bandar Seri swept under their landing gear and suddenly everyone was craning to look down. Except for Kei, who was talking quietly to someone at Bandar Seri's main police station.

Bandar Seri was now the oldest occupied settlement on the island – except perhaps for one or two Dyak villages up in the hills. It was the opposite of New Baya City in almost every way. Even from up here, thirty metres above the tiled and palm-thatched rooftops, it was clear that this was a city of ceiling fans, not air-conditioning. Of slatted shutters, not double glazing. Of low verandas, not high rises. It was a place where the Volcano Roads Hotel would have stood out like a sore thumb – but its Victorian room would be right at home.

The town's low, colonial-style buildings sprawled in organic outgrowths rather than regimented suburb blocks. Streets wandered haphazardly between them, their way dictated by something much more natural than the urban planner's ruler. They wound lazily, in almost serpentine patterns, down towards the main heart of the town, a heart apparently broken by the slow swell of the Sangsang River. It was the Sangsang whose broad, tidal mouth opened into the docks. Whose relentless flow had deepened the shipping lanes far out to the south of the great square reef. Wandering like tributaries towards it, the lazy boulevards stopped in a timeless, almost convivial way to open into squares, four wide thoroughfares coming together like old friends for a chat. Clustering round brightly coloured gardens or neatly trimmed little coppices like ancient roués flirting with pretty young girls. Then they wandered off again, to lose themselves beneath broad-branched trees, which seemed to have moved down here from the jungle like Dyaks or Orang Utans, slightly out of place, and still half wild.

And there, suddenly looking very modern indeed by contrast, was the ambulance.

Even as Richard's eager eyes fastened on it, it vanished under the green of a massive half-wild tree that looked for all the world like a cedar. 'Got it!' Richard called exultantly. 'Now where's it going?'

Inspector Kei stopped talking into his radio and leaned forward. 'That road leads down to the river,' he said. 'And to the clinic. The clinic actually backs on to the river,' he added, with characteristic precision. 'It is housed in what used to be the old River Pilot building.'

'Perhaps they're really going home,' said Kalla.

'Then perhaps we can get there ahead of them,' said Richard grimly. 'Inspector, is there anywhere we can put this thing down close by the clinic? Somewhere with more space and fewer trees maybe?'

'There is King Jayavar Square. And that is where the main police station is located too. I will radio ahead and warn them of our plan . . .'

No sooner had Inspector Kei contacted the station once more than the ambulance was in the open again. It was easing forward at the heart of a gently swirling stream that seemed to be made up of brightly coloured but old-fashioned vehicles. Volkswagen Beetles, miraculously preserved. Subarus, Kias, Toyotas and Hondas in models, styles and colours that hadn't been fashionable for a decade or so.

There was now no doubt in Richard's mind: the boxy vehicle was headed straight for the clinic. A glance forward showed a fairly simple layout. The roadway that the ambulance was following would open in a kilometre or so into a big square not unlike Parliament Square in London, except that there were shrubs instead of statues. The river side of the square was closed off by a long, white-painted two-storey building with an official-looking frontage. And, the chopper's elevation revealed, a covered section overlooking the river that seemed half-veranda and half-jetty. It could only be the old River Pilot's headquarters. The clinic.

Roadways ran to one side and the other off the square, following the river, well in from the shore so that other important-looking buildings could stand along the riverside itself, most of them, by the look of things, converted out of warehouses. Between them there were open spaces that had once been docks and landing points but which were now obviously car parks. The two largest straddled the clinic and they were both already partly occupied with ambulances and motorcars.

Across the river road, at right angles to the clinic, stood another languidly official-looking building with a car park at its rear. This car park was full of garishly painted DayGlo cars that could only be police patrol vehicles.

Blessedly – and unusually as far as Richard could see – the square itself was not full of trees. Inspector Kei was right: they could land here. As the ambulance came down out of the slow swirl of traffic, therefore, and entered the brightly coloured, fume-belching whirlpool of the square itself, Richard glanced back at Kei to confirm that they were going to land as soon as possible. The iron taste of tension suddenly filled the back of his throat. Or perhaps it was the first stench of diesel coming in through the chopper's window. He looked over at Robin but she too was looking steadfastly downwards.

And then, as it sometimes did for Richard, the world seemed to go into slow motion. The ambulance swung into the square and slowed, signalling that it was going to cross the traffic towards the clinic. As it did so, two long black limousines joined the colourful swirl of old-fashioned vehicles, like sleek sharks swimming with multicoloured turtles. They stayed behind the ambulance as it crossed the traffic lanes, apparently unaware of their presence. But as it eased across the river road towards the clinic's car park, they closed in with all the relentless focus of new arrivals at a feeding frenzy.

'We need to go down as fast as possible, I think,' rasped Richard. 'Inspector, are those black limos yours?'

'No,' answered Kei, his voice suddenly tense. Then he was barking orders into his radio again.

The ambulance turned across the traffic into the car park beside the clinic. On the square side there were gates but they were hardly security gates. On the river side there was a walkway down on to the old jetty.

'They yours, Kalla?'

'How could they be?' answered the big security man. 'I don't have any security people down here!'

'Then just what the hell is this?' demanded Richard. 'Inspector, I would most strongly suggest that we need to get this helicopter on the ground right now!'

As soon as the ambulance entered the car park, it accelerated towards the river. The two limousines followed it in and did the same; speeding up, spreading apart and slewing sideways as their doors began to open and men in suits began to tumble out. All of them wore dark glasses. Each of them was reaching for his left armpit.

That was the last thing Richard saw with any clarity for several minutes. The chopper began to settle into the centre of the square and even though it was well-grassed, a good deal of dust was kicked up by the down-draught. The change of perspective also blinded him. From three storeys up in the air, he came down to street level all too swiftly. The wall of traffic and the cloud of choking fumes above them made an all-too-effective barrier. And that was before the whirling chopper blades tore a tornado of red dust from the ground.

The car park remained clear in Richard's mind's eye, however, with the ambulance heading for the river's edge and the limousines spewing black suits at an alarming rate. But his real eyes were confronted with the sides of cars, vans and lorries as soon as they cleared of dust. Stooping under the slowing whirl of the idling chopper blades, he pounded forward, still deep within the grip of his primal hunting instinct, seeming to move with the slow grace of a swimmer pushing against the current, reaching unconsciously into the gaping vacancy below his own left arm. He had a vague sense that Robin was behind him and that Kalla was massively with her. And that Inspector Kei, probably much more sensibly, was lagging a little behind, still trying to raise back-up from the police barracks.

It seemed ridiculous to Richard that he should wait for the crossing lights. He had seen so many films where the hero simply hurled himself into a rushing river of traffic and danced like a bull-fighter from fender to fender unscathed. But this was real life. Even Volkswagen Beetles could be lethal, given the correct velocity. But the lights were quick to change and the green man appeared before his more suicidal James Bond instincts got the better of him.

Richard's slight hesitation at the crossing gave the others a chance to catch up and so the four of them erupted into the clinic's car park side by side. Kei had his service revolver out of its gleaming holster and Kalla had his big Glock at the ready. But no-one was running wildly forward. There was a wall of men in suits closing off the rear of the car park. In the centre of the line was a tall man whose grey hair gave the lie to his lean but unlined teak brown face.

'Van Leir! What are you doing here?' called Kalla, giving the Dutch name a strange intonation halfway between 'Leer' and 'Liar'. As the big security man slowed, so the others slowed with him. Kalla's gun hand went up and he made a dumb show of re-holstering the Glock.

The man called Van Leir looked at them dispassionately. His eyes were so blue as to appear almost white in the dark face. Unlike Kalla, Van Leir was obviously of mixed race. Somewhere in the distant past, perhaps when this town had still been in the planning stage, a Dutch freebooter had loved a Dyak girl. And here, generations later, was the unsettling result. The brown skin might make Richard think of jungle hardwoods, but the blue and white eyes made him think of ice. And that strange combination of wildness and coldness seemed to characterize the man. That coldness and an almost tangible air of threat. When he raised his right hand, even the intrepid Robin flinched. But the hand was empty. Extended in a cool handshake. One professional recognizing another.

'Kalla,' said Van Leir, his voice light and dry, the voice of a dusty academic. 'I thought I recognized the description. And this will be Inspector Kei. There is no need for your weapon, Inspector. Nor for your officers, now that I see them arriving. We have everything well under control.'

Richard stepped forward, surveying the scene over Van Leir's shoulder. The ambulance stood with its doors open. There were the black pocks of bullet holes high in its white-painted side. The stench of gun smoke hung on the still, thick air. The driver and his mate lay face-down on the ground by the gaping driver's door with their hands behind their heads, fingers laced across their necks. The doctor stood in the dark mouth of the cavernous rear. Her hands were raised in the universal sign of surrender but her body protected her patients. There were signs of pale movement behind her.

But there, beyond the strange frozen picture, there was much more active movement. Richard stepped forward until his shoulder collided thoughtlessly with that of the unyielding Van Leir. Five figures – two in white coats, the rest in jeans and T-shirts – were scrambling aboard a motorboat at the end of the little jetty which extended the narrow path down from the car park and out into the river. Even as Richard stopped, his focus absolute and the beginning of a frustrated outrage building in his chest, the motorboat turned out into the current. The motor caught. The little vessel powered away.

And a tall man stood in the stern of the escaping craft, looking back, seemingly straight into Richard's eyes. Seemingly into Richard's eyes alone.

And, but for the lines of a generation in age, it was the face of

the pirate he had fought with aboard *Tai Fun*. The pirate whose face
had hardly been out of his thoughts since. The pirate whose feet
he had filled with splinters and slowed at some vital moment of the
fatal escape attempt. The pirate whose body he had last seen floating
dead in the tall ship's swimming pool, riddled with bullets from the
guns of Kei's murderous command.

TWENTY-THREE
Confined

In spite of the old colonial appearance of its exterior, the interior
of Bandar Seri's King Jayavar Clinic was as modern as any hospital
Richard and Robin had ever been in. The private suite at the rear
of the building might boast a teak-floored balcony that stood above
a series of jetties reaching out into the lazy brown swirl of the Sangsang
River. But instead of French windows stepping out from the ward
on to the veranda, a solid wall of double glazing confined the patients
and their atmosphere as effectively as a wall of prison bars.

The view it commanded overlooked the broad reach of the estuary
and the lightly forested downtown area opposite, where the malarial
swamps had been reclaimed centuries since. And the hill slopes
above them were peopled a little more recently by elegant residences
that might have been at home in old New Orleans. But the view
was kept at a carefully clinical distance. And the miasmas that arose,
laden with a range of flying pests and timeless infections, from the
inward and outward wash of the tides, were scrubbed and sanitized
by the air-conditioning before they were allowed entry, like a dirty
urchin permitted to visit an enchanted princess in a fairy tale.

It was here that Richard first met the young woman whose life
he had saved at the beginning of this adventure.

But Sheri Aru was by no means at her best. She was lying propped
up in a hospital bed she would have given almost anything to get
out of. She might have been still in clinical shock from her near-
death experience. She was certainly still shocked on quite another
level by the murder of two good friends, an affront brought agonizingly closer by the fact that she had spent most of the interim asleep.
She was still further outraged by what she had awoken to in the

back of the speeding ambulance. And she was frustrated by her experiences since, right up to the present. But she did not feel ill, or weak, or in need of hospital treatment.

She found herself now caged like a mountain tigress not only by deceptively soft pillows in cool starched pillowcases, but also by rigidly tucked sheets with creases sharp enough to cut and blankets in hospital corners. She was also trapped by barrier after barrier of medical, legal and security procedure.

The room in which Sheri was lying seemed to symbolize the whole almost cripplingly restrictive situation. From where she lay cribbed, she could see the river down which her kidnappers had escaped. She knew the vanished pirates to be the men responsible for the murder of her friends. Or at least she was certain that they knew who the murderers were. She felt strong, fully recovered, full of a burning desire to pursue them and bring them to justice. But the doctors wouldn't even allow her feet to touch the floor, let alone bring her crutches. Instead, they were insisting on test after test after test.

And when she was finished with the doctors, she knew, there would be the police, occupied now with their debriefing of Dr Dhakar and her nurse. And beyond the police, there stood the mysterious Van Leir and his sharply suited cohorts. And beyond them, all too wearying experience warned her, there would be the local and international press, hungry for the story of Professor Lok's demise. All of them ranged between her and what she was almost literally burning to do.

But the only people on whom she could take out her whirlwind of frustration were the tall, tanned, faintly familiar Englishman with sky-blue eyes and a white scar on his cheekbone like the duelling trophy of an Austrian count, and the willowy, grey-eyed blonde at his side.

'This is ridiculous!' she raged with bitter frustration, beating the bed covers that bound her thighs like a strait jacket. 'We should be chasing those murderous pigs down the river and out on to their ships. There should be patrol boats, helicopters. The inspector should be locking the lot of them up for what they and their friends have done!'

'*We* should,' agreed Richard equably. 'I'm not so sure about you, though.' He paused, trying to work out the best way of fishing for information without angering and alienating the frustrated young woman further.

'And is anyone chasing them?' she demanded, pouncing on his silence like a leopard on a lamb, her voice quivering with outrage. 'Anyone at all?'

'Apparently not,' said Richard curtly.

'Though we can't be certain,' soothed Robin. 'I'm afraid we're as far out of the loop as you are at the moment. Meinheer Van Leir has introduced a sudden but impenetrable wall of silence around us. I think they only allowed us to come in here and visit because they wanted us safely out of the way while they got on with things.'

'*They?*' snarled Sheri. 'Who are *they?*'

'Don't you know?' asked Richard gently.

'Well, Inspector Kei seems to be in charge still,' Robin explained patiently, shooting her inquisitive husband the shadow of a frown. 'He's questioning the doctor and the nurse.'

'Though he's been on the phone to Superintendent Hatta almost non-stop since we got here,' temporized Richard, eyes narrow, hoping that the names and ranks would mean something to her. Which apparently they did. She seemed as familiar with Kei and Hatta as she seemed to be with this place.

'And that Van Leir. As I say he's certainly in the thick of it,' Robin continued bitterly, unconsciously aiding Richard's subtle interrogation.

'Whatever *it* is,' snarled Sheri.

'Well, at least Kalla seems to have gone off to debrief Hilly,' said Richard bracingly. 'He'll feed back what he knows, I expect.'

'If and when he learns it,' sulked Sheri, her tone changing suddenly. 'Hilly won't be wanting to spend too much time with him until she's checked up on her brother.'

'Her brother? What's her brother got to do with anything?' asked Robin as Richard's hand tightened on her shoulder.

'Hilly's brother's here,' said Sheri as though even an ignoramus should know what she was speaking about. 'He's part of the reason she came to work in this place.' Faced with the utter incomprehension in the expressions of her visitors, she grudgingly explained, 'Hilly's younger brother Steve. He came east backpacking a year or so ago. Caught viral polio somewhere up in the hills. Family's Christian Scientist or some such and didn't believe in vaccination. No-one realized what was wrong with him until far too late. He's in an iron lung next door.'

Richard eased the door open. The instant he did so he heard the rhythmic wheeze of the machine. Heard it even before he registered the murmur of conversation, though the words were a good deal louder. Heard it because he had been listening for it, of course.

He opened the door wider. 'May I come in?' he called, moving forward confidently as he did so.

Hilly was sitting at the bedside of a pale-faced young man who was all too obviously her brother. Richard would have known it even without the persistent wheeze of the machine that was doing his breathing for him. A function it was apparently able to perform even though he was sitting up, his head on a level with his sister's. Kalla was standing massively behind her and the three of them had obviously been locked in a pretty intense conversation. Richard's inquisitive antennae twitched, as they always did when he thought he had come across something he didn't quite understand. Something that made him suspicious.

Richard took another step forward, his eyes fixed on the iron lung, surprised that it was so neat and unobtrusive. It was almost lost beneath the razor-sharp creases of the sheets, only partly on view because the stiff cotton had slid down off it. It was white and clinically moulded, reminding him irresistibly of the armoured breastplates worn by Darth Vader's Imperial Stormtroopers in the old *Star Wars* films. The young man's arms lay above the sheets, apparently fully functional. A range of amusement and communication equipment lay on the bedside cupboards around him. Laptop, iPod, iPhone. Something that looked like a games console. There was a 48-inch flat-screen TV hung on the wall at the bed-foot and if the young man looked to his right, there was a panoramic window with a view across the river to match Sheri's.

'Hi Hilly,' said Richard as he took all this in and immediately started to calculate its implications. 'I'm glad to see you looking so well. That was a nasty experience. No ill-effects?'

'Hi Richard. Nice of you to be concerned. No. I guess I was lucky.' Hilly looked up at Kalla, clearly ill at ease, almost embarrassed. 'Thanks for coming after us.'

'No trouble. As Jahan Jussif here must have told you. He's an excellent boss. He wasn't going to stop until he had you back again, all safe and sound.'

'Yeah,' she said. 'I know. Richard, this is my brother Steve. He's had—'

'Polio,' said Steve. 'I guess he knew, Hilly; it's a polio clinic after all.'

'How do you do?' said Richard, crossing to Steve's bedside and offering his hand. 'Richard Mariner. I'm sorry to meet you under these circumstances.'

'Ah. A plain-speaking man. More honest than most. And it's good to meet someone that looks me straight in the eye instead of straight in the lung.' Steve seemed to run out of breath then. He waited until the lung wheezed some oxygen into his chest. 'So. You're a friend of Hilly's?'

'An associate of Hilly's and Jahan Jussif's here.'

Steve grunted. 'Right. So what do you make of this mess then?'

'I'm still weighing things up, I'm afraid. Lots of new information keeps coming in. But at the same time there are things I haven't managed to find out yet – like what Dr Dhakar's told Inspector Kei. And exactly who were the men who spirited the young pirate away. Let alone how they managed to do it so easily . . . And I haven't really had the chance to think it all through yet.'

'Do tell. And what's the latest bit of information that you have got your hands on?'

'You are.'

Steve gave a wheeze of wry amusement, as though his iron lung was laughing. 'And where do I fit in, then?'

'You certainly brought home to me exactly what this place is.'

'The polio clinic? You reckon that's important, do you?'

'It's certainly coincidental, given Sheri Aru's condition . . .'

'Not so, you see. Or maybe less so than it appears. This is the best polio clinic on this side of the world. Maybe the best *in* the world. Certainly since the disease was wiped out in the western hemisphere in 1994 there aren't too many clinics like this back home. The last case in the States was, what, 1979? And in any case, the old medical insurance and blue cross wouldn't run to much in the States. At least the dollar's still pretty strong out here. Which explains why I'm here.

'And Sheri's local. So this is her hospital in any case. Though I have to say, that girl is my inspiration. When Hilly here called to tell me you'd pulled her aboard *Tai Fun* in that state I nearly took up my bed and walked, as the Good Book has it. Didn't do me any good, though, to be brutally honest. The stress of it all but knocked me flat – I was out of it for a good few hours afterwards.'

'Well,' said Richard. 'Sheri seems well recovered now. And I'm glad to see you are too. She's absolutely bursting to get out of here, I think.'

'Well, I should guess she would be,' said Steve. 'Tomorrow was going to be the Big Day after all. For both Professor Lok and Sheri.'

'Why?' asked Richard, thinking for a moment that the TV star professor and his lovely researcher must have been about to get married. Like Sailendra and the lovely Inga. God! Had that wedding only been yesterday?

'Because,' said Steve, in much the same tone as Sheri had used, as though he were addressing a moron who didn't really speak his language properly, 'tomorrow is when the Marine Conservation Area on the reef out there and the underwater lab that oversees it is due to be opened. I guess that's why this guy Van Leir and his ace security team are here.' He squirmed round to pull Hilly and Kalla into the conversation once more, clearly picking up from the point they had reached before Richard opened the door and interrupted them.

'It's a huge project, designed by Sheri, so she says, though Lok was taking all the credit as usual. It's been all over our local papers for weeks, though I guess the celebrations on the far side of the island have hit the news services in a bigger way. But the plan is for the whole reef to be a closed conservation area. And the underwater lab will oversee it, catalogue it, do experiments, whatever . . . And it's all been sponsored by the oil-rig guys. Van Leir's guys. Pontianac Oil. Same outfit that are working so hard on the conservation of the virgin forests that I went to visit before I got infected. What are they? Bogor Biofuels. The big boss honcho is on his way out from Manila for the opening ceremony, so I'm told. And he'll be paying us a visit into the bargain, which is why Van Leir's men have been all over the old clinic like bears at a barbecue.'

'Of course,' said Richard. 'Of course I see it now. The name should have warned me, but . . .'

'What?' asked Hilly, frowning. 'What name should have warned you about what?'

'DelMonte Medical. It's another associate. They all go together. DelMonte Medical, Bogor Biofuels and Pontianac Oil. They're all parts of Luzon Logging! Now just what in hell's name is Luzon Logging up to here?'

'Well, I guess you'll find that out tomorrow,' said Steve. ''Cause like I say, that's when the head man himself is coming out here to open up the Conservation Area. You could stroll right up and ask him, I suppose. If you can get past Van Leir, of course.'

'The head man's coming, you say? Then he must think this is really important. And I don't suppose a little thing like a dead professor will stop him either,' said Richard, his cold gaze sweeping over Steve, Hilly and Kalla as he spoke. 'Not if he's still got the almost as famous, much more photogenic, famously crippled researcher to share his photoshoot with.'

Kalla nodded thoughtfully, frowning as though he too was beginning to see a distant light in the dangerous darkness. 'Now that's what I'd call positive publicity,' he said.

'Publicity like that,' emphasized Richard, equally thoughtful, 'could turn a company's reputation round in a moment. From zero to hero. And then some.'

In his mind he was already ticking off the ways in which this one masterstroke could wrong-foot Nic Greenbaum and his lawyers all at once. Make everyone forget the illegal logging, the slaughter of endangered species, the blackmail, bribery, piracy and murder. Publicity like that could turn even Sailendra's head. Put Bogor Biofuels back on the map with Monsanto and the rest. Get Pontianac Oil permission to start their rig offshore drilling into the vast field they believed was there. A field that might bring them up with Texas Oil. Even this close to the reef that they were apparently helping to protect. The area of outstanding natural beauty they were seemingly committed to preserving.

A company like Luzon Logging would do *anything* to get a chance like that, he thought.

Anything in the world.

And perhaps they already had.

'Or perhaps,' he said, voicing his darkest thoughts aloud in spite of the confusion on the three faces in front of him. 'Perhaps there's even worse still to come.'

TWENTY-FOUR
Mephistopheles

'**G**ood afternoon, all of you, and welcome to this momentous ceremony. As many of you know, I am Professor Satang Suang Sittart, Chief Executive Officer of the Luzon Logging Corporation.' The speaker's face twitched as though experiencing an electric shock.

Richard eased himself forward in his chair, his gaze fixed, his eyes narrow and his pulses racing. He realized that the pained twitch was meant to be a welcoming smile. Ridiculously – but powerfully – he felt like James Bond confronted by Mr Big. Dr No. Ernst Stavro Blofeld.

It was early the next afternoon. Richard and Robin had spent the interim busily engaged in a range of activities that had, frustratingly, seemed to move them forward hardly at all. They would probably have been back in the Volcano Roads Hotel – or, conceivably aboard *Tai Fun* – by now, but for Richard's insistence that he must be here for this. Simply getting tickets for the exclusive little gathering had taken most of the morning – and all of the influence that Heritage Mariner, and then Greenbaum International, could bring to bear. And hardly surprisingly, Richard thought now, glancing around. There were enough dignitaries to make the security boys – and girls – edgy. Enough television and recording equipment to make the insurers go pale. But it had been a morning well spent after a well-spent, languorous night. They had spent the night in the Irian Garden Hotel's bridal suite. The hotel was the soul of Bandar Seri, a long, low, colonial-style building surrounded by carefully tamed jungle on the lower slopes opposite the polio clinic, high enough above the river to be mosquito-free. Their dinner, taken almost *al fresco* on the grand veranda, had been soporifically satisfying, a fine balance to the invigorating beauty of the view across the estuary. And so they had passed the night in the bridal suite much as any honeymooners might have done.

Like the entry to the CEO of Luzon Logging's carefully staged presentation, it had taken a certain amount of influence to get rooms in the Irian Garden, but Richard had put matters in hand the moment he and Robin left Steve Johnson's room at the polio clinic. Then the afternoon had passed in a whirl of activity. They had talked to Inspector Kei, who laid open little about what Dr Dhakar or her nurse had exposed in their interviews about their adventures in the ambulance and the events that had led up to it. What little they did manage to glean from the tight-lipped policeman simply seemed to confirm Richard's version of events. Especially his suspicions about the tall old pirate who had looked so fixedly at him out of the back of the escaping boat. The blinded boy's wild threats of rescue by his father had been inaccurate – or inaccurately translated. The boy's father had been lying face-down in the pool, his feet full of splinters and his torso riddled with bullets. The pirate captain who had come to rescue him – and had slit Parang's throat in the process – was his grandfather.

And that was important, it seemed, because while the dead father had been the captain of one sizeable but single pirate vessel, the grandfather was the headman of the pirates' floating township. The admiral of the pirate fleet.

Richard had passed this information down the line to Nic Greenbaum with a warning to tighten up security at the Volcano Roads still further – something the laconic Texan had been able to do without lifting a finger, for Superintendent Hatta's extra men had arrived. And, in spite of the fact that the superintendent seemed to have found his sea legs and insisted on using *Tai Fun* as his HQ, everywhere in the hotel and the marina beside it was seemingly awash with policemen. Under the circumstances, Nic had suggested, he would keep Kalla's deputies Tom and Brad together with the rest of their solid security team with him. Richard should keep Kalla and Hilly until things in Bandar Seri were more settled. On the one hand, Nic had calculated, Parang's death had led Prince Sailendra and his new wife to postpone their honeymoon and remain in the Volcano Roads for the immediate future, adding to the security requirements there. On the other hand, if the devil in charge of Luzon Logging was about to appear – with or without a puff of green smoke – Richard himself might well need solid back-up.

As Luzon Logging's CEO courteously repeated his opening welcome in Bahasa Indonesia and then again in Japanese and Cantonese, a very civil devil paying careful attention to his guests, Richard had the opportunity to take his initial measure of the man. And something made him wish he had brought a longer spoon. No matter what language he spoke in, the voice was sonorous, slightly nasal. A carrying light baritone that hardly needed the enhancement of the speaker system. The English phrases were spoken in an accent that Richard couldn't quite define. Perhaps an American twang? American at one remove – spoken English lessons given by someone who had learned their additional language in the States. In one of the Dutch states of New England, somewhere north of New York – New Amsterdam as was, when the Stuyvesants were top-dog – and somewhere south of Boston. The strangely melded accent that this had left him with was one of Dutch cadences, balanced with eastern gutturals and – worsened by the way his teeth were set – long, lingering and gently sinister sibilants. The hissing sibilants were particularly striking because of the professor's love of oratorical devices such as the relentless alliteration which he seemed to employ in the naming of his subsidiary companies. Just as it echoed the sibilant alliteration of his own given name.

Like his accent and his security chief Van Leir, Sittart was of mixed race. His mouthful of a name and the way he pronounced it were proof enough of that. But, physically, he seemed as pure-blood Bugis as Kalla. He was a man of early middle years who stood a little above medium height. His slight stature was flattered by a combination of exquisite tailoring and elevator shoes. His apparent youthfulness enhanced, oddly, by the fact that he was shaven-headed. In the humid blaze of the afternoon sunshine, augmented both in heat and brightness by the television lights and outside broadcast cameras, his cranium gleamed like a bronze cannon ball.

But it was by no means spherically formless. Hard-edged shadows revealed the vertical ridges of his temples as they ran up above his wide, square forehead almost like horns curling under the glistening skin of his scalp. There was a decided ridge rising in the centre of the skull, like some kind of helmet crest. It ran back from the very top of his head towards the neck and, when he leaned forward to look down or to read from his notes, Richard could almost trace it running away beneath the edge of his starched white collar.

But the top and back of Satang Sittart's head were nothing compared to the front of it. Beneath the square forehead with its pronounced temple-ridges sat two long, almost Japanese eyes, the black-brown irises all but lost between heavy upward-sloping lids emphasized by an extravagance of long, curling black eyelashes that would have flattered Cleopatra. Above the hypnotic intensity of these, startlingly black eyebrows swept up to pronounced points then plunged down again, their shape emphasizing the temples too. Beneath the eyes, Sittart's cheekbones were as sharp as the temple ridges and as sloping as the eyes. They came together in the centre of his face exactly on the bridge of a long, thin nose with fine, pinched nostrils and an almost geometrically square tip. Their outer ends reached round to the centres of neat, tight, perfectly balanced ears.

Beneath the nostrils, Sittart's upper lip was long, deeply divided by a central valley so strong as to make one expect a sensuously full mouth below it. Certainly, the valley in the peanut-butter skin beneath the nose was echoed by a cleft in the square chin that would have demanded a sensuous masculine Venus-bow from any self-respecting portrait artist.

But nature had not been so kind. The mouth was thin – not quite a lipless gash, but almost so. The mouth of a moray eel, perhaps, rather than that of a tiger shark. And the teeth that gleamed secretively – even when he gave that shallow grimace of a smile – were as separated, fine and sharp as those of any ancient Dyak cannibal.

Perhaps in honour of the occasion, Sittart had decided against the fashion of wearing formal suits with open-necked, untucked shirts. At his throat, beneath a defined Adam's apple, sat the elegantly massive knot of a wide tie woven of expensively coarse gold silk. The simple richness of it reached down across the immaculate white of an old-fashioned cotton shirt with starched collar and double cuffs secured by heavy gold links. It vanished between the lapels of a single-breasted suit jacket exactly the colour of the sand on the tropical beach that formed the background to the speech. The perfect creases of the trouser-fronts fell from the jacket skirts to the dark tan of the parade-ground polished shoes, their tops sitting astride a square gold belt-buckle as perfectly as the ridges of his temples sat astride his forehead.

Richard leaned over to Robin, who was surveying the scene as intently as he was himself. 'What do you think?' he asked.

'That's not a man *I'd* want to get on the wrong side of,' she answered. 'I wish you all the luck in the world – and then some – if *you* have any intention of pissing him off.'

'Oh how well you know me, my love,' he began.

But she only answered, 'Shhhhh! He's back into English again.'

Satang Sittart straightened to his full five-foot-eight, almost sparking with restless energy. He raised his right hand and extended his arm in a wide gesture. 'My friends,' he hissed. 'What you see behind me is the future. The future!' He paused. 'The future in more ways than one.'

What his audience in the makeshift seaside arena could see behind him was a wide expanse of pale golden sand, artistically framed with palm trees, some clearly imported for the occasion. The palms were designed to enhance the vista of the sand, the sea beyond it and the reef lying shallowly beneath the waves rolling lazily in from the horizon to whisper rhythmically up the shore. The imported trees on his right hid Bandar Seri's nearby suburbs and the commercial docks at the outreach of the Sangsang River's mouth. Those, natural and thinner, groves at his left shoulder did not quite conceal the solid grey of the oil platform just beyond the boundary of the reef itself.

The wide-swept arm reached wider still, however, seeming to ask the hand-picked audience to look away to their right, north along the forested slopes of the island to the tall peaks of the

watershed, thick with priceless virgin jungle, and the smoking
caldera of the great volcano beyond.

'And what is this future of which I speak?' Sittart dropped his
arm dramatically. Took hold of the edges of the simple lectern, which
was all that stood on the open stage with him. All except Van Leir
and his security cohorts, who were guarding the stage itself much
in the same way as the local constabulary, augmented by Kei, were
guarding the perimeter – or three sides of it at least – on the lookout
for vengeful pirates. Though if the blood-spattered, bullet-riddled
after deck of *Tai Fun* was anything to go by, thought Richard
inconsequentially, the thicket of palm trees behind the speaker's
right shoulder were probably full of police sharpshooters with semi-
automatics covering the apparently unguarded beach.

Apart from Sittart and his lectern, Van Leir and his men, the
stage contained an empty chair with Professor Lok's photo, A2 size,
in an ornate gilt frame resting on the seat and propped up against
the back. And another chair bearing the slight, tense form of Doctoral
Student Sheherezade Aru, newly released from DelMonte Medical
Facilities Limited's Bandar Seri King Jayavar polio clinic to be the
guest of honour in the dead man's place. Clearly, in Sittart's view
at least, she was the inheritor of the dead man's mantle.

As Sittart clutched the lectern and seemingly sought to meet the
gaze of each person there, in preparation for revealing the nature
of the future he had in mind, Richard also looked around the rest of
the audience. Director Aquina of DelMonte Medical's main King
Jayavar Clinic in New Baya City was there. As were representa-
tives he recognized from pictures Nic Greenbaum had shown him
when they were discussing Bogor Biofuels and Pontianac Oil
Enterprises. Also, more surprisingly, perhaps, there were Dr Jurong,
the chairman of the Singapore and Seram Shipping Company,
together with the English-educated, polo-loving Sultan of Sabah,
both last seen in the overpowering Victorian room at the Volcano
Roads Hotel just before Parang got his throat cut.

'*We* are the future,' announced Sittart, dramatically if a little anti-
climactically. 'Princes and Sultans fighting to guard the priceless
heritage of their lands. Their lands and the equally priceless seas around
them. Shipping magnates seeking to transport their wares across those
same seas in the most economical and environmentally friendly manner.
Even in the face of lawlessness and downright piracy, as my good
friend Dr Jurong of the Singapore and Seram Shipping Company finds
himself at the moment. Rest assured, sir, that now the pirates holding

Ocean's Bounty have shown their hand you may count on Luzon Logging's full support!'

Richard swung round, frowning. So, as he suspected, the ship with which *Tai Fun* had nearly collided had been in pirate hands. And it was owned by Dr Jurong's company into the bargain. 'Curiouser and curiouser,' he whispered to Robin.

But she just said, 'Shhh! He's still talking!'

'And the future is with the logging companies such as Luzon Logging themselves, who fight to take as little as they can from the precious treasures of the rainforests. Who cut their trees not just for market but for the immediate benefit of the landholders and forest guardians as well as of the farmers who will make such good use of the land they clear. And who, even then, seek to protect the species that inhabit the forests, as well as the species that inhabit environments such as the reef behind me. The future lies with oil companies whose platforms are designed to protect the environments in which they work, on land or at sea, from the frozen Arctic to the sweltering gulfs nearer at hand.

'Companies which seek oil and pass it to their scientific departments so that they may balance the environmental damage it threatens with biofuels that will prolong the life of the oilfields as well as of the precarious planet that we all hold so dear. Biofuels that in the past have been based on extracts of plant-life and animal-life, the production of which have, in many instances done more harm in their production than they have done good in their employment!' He shook his head sadly at the bitter irony of the Catch-22 that Nature seemed to have thrown at himself and his good-hearted conservationist colleagues at Pontianac Oil and Bogor Biofuels.

'But Luzon Logging, Bogor Biofuels, Pontianac Oil Enterprises, using the kind of cutting-edge scientific expertise that has made our DelMonte Medical facilities world leaders in their fields, have gone a significant step further still. What you see behind you, Your Highnesses, ladies and gentlemen, is the Professor Ninoy Lok Memorial Conservation Area. A pristine reef environment sponsored and guaranteed by Luzon Logging, now and in perpetuity . . .'

He raised one hand, riding and quelling the sporadic applause, not yet finished with his announcement.

'Beyond it, between its outer edge and the oil platform you see on the horizon, is a stretch of water co-owned by Pontianac Oil, Bogor Biofuels and Luzon Logging, where Indonesia's first

Algae Production Facility is already under development. Algae does not damage rainforests. Algae does not pump out methane, or carbon dioxide or carbon monoxide. Algae, like virgin rainforests, can add to the health of the world. But when we harvest it, algae becomes an infinitely renewable fuel source that adds to the power of oil, cuts down the emissions of fuel and lengthens the lives of the oil fields. And, incidentally, what will the tiny creatures at the bottom of the food chain in our protected environment next door on the reef feed upon as they increase and multiply? Multiply and diversify, bringing back all the wonders of underwater Indonesia that teeter on the brink of extinction, from the tiniest angel fish to the greatest whale? Algae, my friends. Algae!'

And it was on this unexpected note, just as Sittart swung round, his arm raised once more, gesturing across the algae-filled waters towards the grey shape of the oil rig, that the container ship *Ocean's Bounty* arrived.

She came into the frame from the north, past the thinner grove of palms, thrusting herself relentlessly in front of the oil-rig but close enough to the shore to make it apparent that there was no danger of collision.

And that in turn seemed doubly fortunate because she was clearly in trouble and seemingly out of control. Her decks were swarming with the half-naked figures that Richard remembered from the near-collision with *Tai Fun*, figures that seemed to him to be pirates to a man. And, either from her foredeck or from the holds immediately beneath it, she was belching a column of thick black smoke that would have flattered an erupting volcano.

But worse was to come, for, even as the audience rose in horror, as though awarding the CEO of Luzon Logging a silent standing ovation, so the racing vessel's bows reared up on to the reef that Sittart had promised to protect. The men on the deck went down like skittles. The massive containers tore lose and broke apart, throwing the foremost into the foaming maelstrom of the water. And cascading goods and bodies, seemingly screaming with the voices of agonized flesh and steel alike, with a sound like half-drowned thunder, the vessel ran hard aground.

TWENTY-FIVE
Help

'This is a truly terrible situation!' said Professor Satang Suang Sittart. 'What can we at Luzon Logging do to help?'

Richard looked across and down at the frowning CEO, then up at his tall, icy security chief. Van Leir met his gaze with a cold, blank stare. An infinitesimal shrug settled the perfectly cut jacket over the bulge of the gun at his armpit, making it almost disappear.

They were all standing on the inland edge of the beach, looking out at the wreck of the *Ocean's Bounty* as she settled on to the jagged shoulder of the reef. Robin stood at Richard's shoulder and Sheri Aru stood at hers, her stance made slightly uneasy by the way her crutches were settling unevenly into the sand.

Sheri was unaware of her apparently shaky position. Her slim, powerful body adjusted to the shifting sand beneath her automatically. Her arms and shoulders flexed without direction – as her heart beat, her pulses throbbed and her ribs rose and fell. The crutches had been part of her life since before she could remember. Her gaze fixed with unsettling intensity on the still-screaming ship as her mind tried to calculate the overwhelming scale of the potentially disastrous wreck on the protected environment of her reef. The hull was no doubt doing untold damage to the delicate fabric of the corals. The impact of the containers that spilled over the bow would have compounded the ruin terribly. The contents of the shattered containers on the deck and in the water were probably spreading the damage further as the last of them cascaded into the shallow sea. Then, all too soon, there would be bilge water leaking if the hull was breached – heavy with waste matter from crew and engines alike. There would be oil leaking too, soon enough – bunkerage if nothing else. And that was all independent of what might happen if the fire got worse or – Allah forfend – caused the whole thing to explode. With a feeling of desperation growing within her, she looked across at the picture of her dead mentor and then around at the strangers by whom she was surrounded, wondering who there was left that she could trust.

On Richard's left stood Kalla and Hilly; beside them Inspector Kei who was in turn surrounded by a squad of heavily armed officers who had, in fact, materialized from the man-made thicket nearest to the town. Beside Kei stood Dr Jurong, chairman of the Singapore and Seram Shipping Company and, beside him, the Sultan of Sabah. One, it seemed, owned a good deal of the cargo and the other, as Sittart had just said, owned the ship herself.

No-one seemed ready to answer Sittart, for the man to whom the question was most obviously addressed – Inspector Kei – was on his mobile to his superintendent, seeking advice and, perhaps, orders.

'That's very kind,' Richard therefore said. 'What had you got in mind, Professor?'

'Retake the ship and tug her clear,' answered Sittart at once, glancing at Richard with a kind of electric energy in his eyes. Then he looked across at Robin and Sheri.

'That may be easier said than done,' suggested Richard equably, all too well aware of Sittart's glance – and where it was directed now.

'Oh, I don't know,' Van Leir answered on his CEO's behalf. 'If those are pirates aboard then they'll be pretty shaken up. I could take a team on a chopper out there and sort them out before they knew what hit them.'

The cold eyes flicked across to the semi-automatic weapons Inspector Kei's men were holding.

Richard nodded. It was, after all, more or less what he had done in his attempt to recover *Tai Fun*. But there was one vital difference. 'They'll see you coming,' he said. 'There'll be no surprise element.'

Van Leir shrugged. 'My guys can handle themselves,' he said, 'if it comes to a fire fight.'

Richard paused for a moment, looking blandly at the two men. Then he turned to Dr Jurong. 'Excuse me, Doctor,' he said quietly. 'But could you tell me how many officers and crew you have aboard *Ocean's Bounty*?'

The shipping man looked at Richard, frowning slightly. 'Twenty-five,' he answered shortly. 'Thirteen crew, six officers and two cadets. But the captain has his family aboard. Wife and three daughters.'

'Ah,' said Sittart as even Richard gaped a little at the unlooked-for details. 'I see where Captain Mariner is going with this, Mr Van Leir. Hostages. Publicity. Good publicity if we arrange a positive outcome for all the hostages aboard and especially the children. Bad publicity if they die. And we are here, after all, with a good news story that we do not wish to harm.' He glanced across at the doctor and the sultan with that strange electric twitch of a smile. 'Perhaps we had better prepare a ransom payment rather than an armed assault!'

'But surely the authorities will have something to say about that!' said Robin without thinking.

Sittart's long dark eyes snapped back towards her. The gaze, that she had already found unsettlingly direct, seemed to intensify. It was as though Sittart could see through her clothing all too easily – he had already, she felt, observed both herself and the restless Sheri as though they were naked. Robin had met men whose eyes seemed to do that to a woman automatically. But she had never experienced such intensity as she felt now. Nor had she ever experienced a physical reaction quite like the one she felt as soon as those black eyes burned past her modest clothing. Her skin rose in gooseflesh. Her breath shortened as her heart pounded. And her nipples clenched to flinty peaks. It was unsettlingly impossible to tell with any certainty whether this was lust. Or fear. Or something in between.

Now he seemed to be stripping away her flesh and bone, peering relentlessly into her mind. 'Ah yes,' he said quietly. 'The authorities.' He swung round to look at Kei. Robin almost staggered. Brushed against Richard's solid shoulder. Steadied herself.

And just at the moment Sittart looked at Kei, as though this was all part of some carefully staged act, the inspector broke off his connection with Superintendent Hatta. Seemingly unaware of the professor or of the tacit question lying unspoken between them, he said, with not a little wonder in his voice, 'The superintendent is coming at once. He will be here before dark and will assume on-the-spot control.' He glanced tellingly across at the TV cameras and the reporters swarming round them, held in check only by a line of Van Leir's courteously impenetrable men.

'Risking another chopper flight is he?' asked Richard, following Kei's revealing gaze.

'No,' answered Kei simply. 'He has commandeered your vessel, Captain Mariner, as it is still a crime scene and the subject of current investigation, though the centre of the case seemed to him to have moved here with the escape of Parang's murder into the Sangsang River. He is coming aboard *Tai Fun*.'

No sooner had he finished speaking than Richard's cellphone started to ring.

Richard would have had no real objections to Superintendent Hatta commandeering *Tai Fun* if the alternative was for her to be tied up at the Volcano Roads marina while the investigation was completed. Those guests and crew aboard who were not content to extend their vacation at the hotel had been spirited away with the symphony orchestra, the rock bands and the rest.

Typically, however, Nic Greenbaum had parlayed the superintendent's action into a situation that benefited him. The call on Richard's cell was the ebullient Texan announcing that he and Sailendra would be aboard as well, their places grudgingly allowed by the superintendent in return for their acquiescence in his scheme.

'Though I guess he wouldn't have stood up to a prince of the blood for very long anyways,' the Texan drawled. 'He's leaving Inga and I'm leaving Gabriella—'

'I'm not sure that would be the best option,' Richard interrupted. 'Gabriella's pretty expert on your business matters in the east, isn't she?' Richard glanced around uneasily, wondering who might overhear him if he spoke too plainly now. All too well aware that the time it had taken him to get tickets to this event had also given Sittart time to check up on him as well.

'She is that,' answered Nic easily. 'Especially on Luzon Logging and all their works. Why?'

'Well . . .' Richard, wondering vaguely if even the contact with Nic's phone was still secure, standing there on the foreshore, surrounded by Kei, Kalla, Van Leir, Robin, Sheri, Sittart and the rest, gave a carefully coded explanation of what exactly had been going on up until the *Ocean's Bounty* ran on to the reef.

The inclusion of *Tai Fun* in the investigation seemed to give her owners some kind of quasi-official status. And whatever Hatta had agreed with Nic seemingly put Kalla and Hilly into the frame as well. Certainly, when Inspector Kei moved the centre of his operations to the New Harbourmaster's building, he raised no serious objections when Richard and Robin tagged along with the security experts beside them.

Robin at least felt a little guilty about going with Richard. The look that Sheri shot her as Sittart closed in on her was little less than pleading. But the Sultan, and, oddly, Dr Jurong followed the CEO of Luzon Logging as he swept the marine biologist up towards the cameras. Any attempt to rescue her would have been too lengthy and far too public, she calculated. For Sittart obviously thought that there was another photo opportunity here. Another chance to drive his good-news story home. And the press seemed keen to let him try – to put it mildly! And to settle matters finally, Van Leir and his men swung in behind them, making something between a Berlin Wall and an Iron Curtain of black-suited shoulders and discreetly bulging arm-pits. So she reluctantly turned away and followed Richard and the others to Kei's police transport and the Harbourmaster's Office.

As soon as they arrived, Richard could see the wisdom of the policeman's decision. The office that Kei had chosen as his temporary headquarters gave a panoramic view not only of the harbour but also of the reef and the waters beyond it. Not only that, but the harbourmaster himself was more than willing to offer every assistance he could – supplying equipment from the simplest binoculars right the way up to the state-of-the-art communications and ship-management equipment he used to control his busy port.

And a quick-thinking, decisive – not to say ruthless – side of the inspector was revealed at once. Within ten minutes of arriving in the bright and spacious office with its spectacular windows, Richard was introduced to the man who might well have ordered the slaughter of the retreating pirates on the after deck of *Tai Fun*.

'Whether or not we decide to take the ship back by force or by negotiation,' he began, talking to the distant Hatta on his Bluetooth as he surveyed the grounded vessel with the most powerful binoculars to hand. 'I would assess that we have to contain the problem as swiftly as possible. We need some well-armed vessels here at once, as I'm sure the prince will agree. Do you wish to contact the Navy's Eastern Command in Surabaya or do you want me to do that, sir?'

In the silence that contained Hatta's reply, Richard crossed to the window and picked up a pair of binoculars himself. No sooner had he started focussing them on *Ocean's Bounty* than he sensed Robin at his side apparently doing the same.

Richard saw two things at once. The confusion on the deck was rapidly becoming reduced to order by an ant's nest of busy bronzed figures. And the smoke billowing up from mid-ships was thinning. Whoever was currently master of the vessel was rapidly gaining – or regaining – control. And, oddly, he found that fact worrying.

The only reason he could see for the ship being run up on the reef in the way she had been, was that the captain on the bridge had done it. Either as a desperate signal for help, or because his battle with the pirates had undermined his seamanship at a vital moment. Richard could see no ready reason for the pirates to do it – for the grounding simply robbed them of options and the possibility of profit should they want to sell the hull. No, he decided.

Unless someone was playing a deeper game than even he could see here, there was no other explanation.

There was no doubt that the pirates were in control of the deck now, he thought, adjusting the focus and sweeping his enhanced vision over the sloping deck. And the engineering areas too, he decided – where they were either fighting the fire themselves or presumably directing the engineers and GP seamen to do so.

'Think they've got control of the bridge?' asked Robin, who had obviously been thinking along the same lines.

Her question and his own suspicions made Richard focus on the broad dark line of the command bridge's angled clear-view windows. And even as he did so, the distant door from the bridge out on to the bridge wing opened and a tiny figure in a captain's whites stepped out, with a tall, lean figure half-concealed behind him.

Richard hissed and readjusted the binoculars to maximum magnification. But he knew deep in his bones who the second figure was long before his vision cleared.

The figure behind the captain was the tall man from the back of the boat that had escaped down the Sangsang River yesterday. And in his hand, pressed against the captain's Adam's apple, was the snake-bladed Kriss which, Richard would have sworn on oath, was the knife that had cut poor Parang's throat.

TWENTY-SIX
Gunships

*T*ai Fun came over the horizon at six, just as the sun was westering into the sea somewhere south of Sumatra. She made a breathtaking sight, for she came out of the golden sunset like a comet, her full sails seemingly aflame, heading unerringly into the wide mouth of the River Sangsang on the crest of the flooding tide.

But *Tai Fun* was by no means the first vessel to come racing to the aid of *Ocean's Bounty*, her captain, his family, her officers and crew. Two hours earlier, Richard had been standing at the window with the binoculars pressed to his eyes again – though *Ocean's Bounty* was apparently deserted now for all the activity he could see aboard. He knew the pirates and their captives still had to be aboard, however.

The sea between the harbour and the stricken vessel had been alive with little boats all afternoon, but none of them had sailed close enough to the container ship to take anyone off her – or get anyone aboard, for that matter. The only coming and going between the water and the deck had been the recovery of the men thrown overboard when the vessel struck. And that had been done swiftly and efficiently by means of ropes and lifebelts. Richard himself had watched the speed and efficiency of the operation, grudgingly impressed, then he had kept sporadic watch, in between the meetings and the communications sessions he had been a part of.

But there had been men with eyes on her at all times, under Kalla's orders. He wanted to know the instant that anyone got closer than hailing distance. But not even the journalists, who rushed down to the harbour when Sittart was finished with them, got any real joy. The flat-screen television on the harbourmaster's office wall had been tuned to the local news channels all afternoon, its pictures telling their own story so clearly that it didn't matter that Richard did not speak the local language.

Although he had kept his watch out of the window, he had also seen the press conference that Sittart and Dr Jurong had given. How they had pushed the nervous-looking Sheri forward to say something passionate about the ravaged reef. How the men had taken over again, driving home a series of serious points about the ship, the men aboard her and the danger it all presented to the environment they were fighting to protect – not to mention the captive men, woman and children they were fighting to save. Then the pictures had moved from the staged conference to the bustling docks and out, unsteadily but graphically, on to the restless water. But the reporters clearly got no real joy.

The only people likely to get anything positive from the afternoon, in fact, thought Richard, were the local fishermen's children. For the container that burst open and showered the waves with its contents had been full of old-fashioned wooden and plastic toys. As the reporters, in the absence of any hard news, were all too willing to show.

So it was that in the late afternoon, when the latest meeting had broken up for tea – or rather, given the location and colonial history of the place, for coffee and hot chocolate – Richard was staring out of the window once again when he gave an exclamation of surprise. 'Good God! That looks like an old Tribal Class frigate! I'll be damned if it isn't the old *Tartar*! I thought she'd been scrapped long ago!'

The frigate, now the KRI *Hasanudin*, was followed in from the west by two Andan class patrol boats, *Ajak* and *Singa*. The disorganized flotilla of little boats around the wreck seemed to split apart and draw back as the warships swept majestically in, like scum on the surface of a washing-up bowl retreating from a squirt of liquid soap. The three ships positioned themselves in the suddenly empty waters around *Ocean's Bounty* and remained on watch with the stricken vessel all too obviously under the wide range of guns they carried. And, as an afternoon soap-opera rolled its final credits, suddenly the ships were there on the TV screen as well, bristling with Bofors guns and Vickers guns, not to mention Oerlikon 20mm cannons.

When darkness fell soon after *Tai Fun*'s arrival, a fourth ship slid out of the eastern shadows. This was a Sigma class corvette and her armament made the old frigate's look almost antique. She had an unnerving range of anti-air missiles, Exocets, 76mm and 20mm guns and more torpedoes than you could shake a stick at. As soon as she arrived, the four warships switched on massive searchlights and pinned *Ocean's Bounty* against the night like a moth on black velvet. And the picture of them doing so on the news channel of the wall-mounted TV reminded Richard irresistibly of one of the framed exhibits in the Victorian room at Volcano Roads.

'Who is in contact with these people?' demanded Superintendent Hatta, who arrived at that moment, with Nic, Gabriella and Prince Sailendra in tow.

'No-one, sir,' answered Kei. 'We have been trying to raise them all afternoon but they will not answer the radio. That is,' he corrected himself punctiliously, 'the leaders will not answer the radio. I have had regular contact with the ship's radio officer, but he says the pirates will not talk to us.'

'Ah,' said Hatta. 'They are playing a waiting game.' He seemed to inflate slightly. 'They may well be waiting for someone who is in a position to hold serious negotiations.'

'Or waiting for orders themselves, perhaps,' said Robin, who had already discussed this idea with both Richard and Kei during their meetings. 'The pirates in Somalia might have started out as largely self-employed, but they soon found a range of sponsors. Maybe these guys are the same. Or maybe they want to be the same.'

'Or,' added Richard, sliding his thought in, for what it was worth, 'they are already in contact and negotiating. Just not over the ship's radio. And not with us.'

'If not with us,' snapped Hatta angrily, 'then I'd like to know with whom?'

By way of answer, Richard's gaze reached lazily over to the TV on the wall. Where Dr Jurong, the Sultan of Sabah and Professor Sittart were being interviewed yet again while Sheri Aru sat silently beside them, pale and hunted-looking, apparently overwhelmed.

Hatta's mouth opened. His moustache seemed to bristle a little. Then a look of thoughtful calculation suddenly filled his face. 'Why them?' he asked. 'Why them rather than us?'

'Because they own the hull and the cargo. Because they are the ones so desperate to protect the reef,' Richard explained.

'Because they have the money. And the smarts. And the choppers. And the tugs if they want – they're a shipping company after all. And they don't have one single inch of red tape tying their hands,' Nic expanded thoughtfully.

'Even so. They can only act legitimately through us . . .' Hatta was not so sure of himself now.

'If they want to act through us, then why are they not here?' demanded Kei, for whom their absence had been an increasingly serious source of irritation all afternoon. After a moment he grudgingly added, 'Sir?'

There was a moment of silence. Then Richard took the plunge and gave voice to a thought that had been occupying his mind with increasing force of late. 'Perhaps because they know that the last time the pirates dealt with you, Inspector, so few of them survived.'

'So!' exploded Kei. 'That's what you think, is it?' He swung round. Hatta looked down, refusing to meet his gaze. Nic looked away. No-one except Richard would look him squarely in the eye. At last the furious policeman came face to face with Sailendra himself, his countenance working, his tone beginning to shake with mounting anger. 'Your Majesty! You must understand at least. Your secretary! Parang!'

Sailendra took a step back in the face of the outraged policeman's passion; his lean aristocratic face folded in an uncomprehending frown. 'Parang?' he demanded. 'What about Parang?'

'Parang,' explained Inspector Kei, his voice trembling with outrage as he tore the words out of himself, 'was not the first to get his throat cut, was he? No! Tengku Suleiman was. My sergeant, disguised as a boatman to keep watch over Professor Lok and his doctoral student Aru as they looked into the smuggling of rare species. Tengku Suleiman. Slaughtered like a goat by these criminal barbarians. I tell you, I would kill them all without a second thought if I had them under my guns again!'

'So much of it seems to turn on those three murders,' mused Richard later that evening. 'But there's a heck of a lot more going on. I just can't quite get my head round it all. Not yet at least.'

They were on the veranda of the Irian Garden Hotel, seated at a table laden with the remains of dinner – and only still laden because Sailendra had waved away the solicitous waiters as they talked over coffee. Sailendra, Nic and Gabriella were staying aboard *Tai Fun* for the moment, for she was quite palatial enough to suit them. Robin, particularly, was keen to remain in the hotel's honeymoon suite, and Richard, knowing very well why, was happy to indulge her. As long as he had the strength.

On the way here, however, he had stopped off at the dockside ships' chandlery and bought himself the most powerful binoculars Zeiss produced, and had carried them across the river ferry and up in the taxi with him to the hotel. Robin had wondered why – until she had seen once again the view from the restaurant's veranda.

With the naked eye, Richard could scan a view almost identical to that from the harbourmaster's office. But the panorama was wider, and the most interesting parts of it, of course, much further away. Still, had Richard been of a mind to stand up and put the binoculars to his eyes he could have scanned the river-mouth and the docks, the downtown areas opposite from the harbourmaster's office to the police station and the polio clinic. He could see *Tai Fun* at her moorings and the ships in the harbour as well as those further out in the roadsteads.

He could see the beach where today's exclusive presentation had been made, and the reef that it so artfully overlooked. He could see *Ocean's Bounty* still wedged on the shoulder of the reef and the four warships keeping her so brightly under their guns. He could see – in the oddly reflected beams of their searchlights if nothing else – the oily heave of the algae farm. And further beyond it, right on the far edge of the horizon, lost in the shadows except for its constellation of warning lights, the oil-platform.

'What do you mean?' asked Nic, leaning forward.

Richard hesitated uncharacteristically, mouth a little open and eyes narrow as his mind raced.

'Talk it through,' suggested Gabriella. 'See where the logic takes you.' She too leaned forward, sweeping back over her shoulder a great fall of hair exactly the same colour as the black coffee in the cup she raised to her lips.

'Yes,' insisted Sailendra. 'We need to get the events clear – to help Miss Aru remember more clearly if for no other reason. I talked to Superintendent Hatta just before we sat down and the poor young woman can remember almost nothing of the first incident. And even her memories of the kidnapping and ambulance ride are both hazy and sketchy.'

'OK. We'll have to go over some old ground, laying foundations so to speak. But then we should be able to move forward more confidently. Stop me if there's anything that seems off track or out of the question. And remember, this is speculation.'

They all nodded.

'OK.' Richard drew breath slowly. Then he relaxed, leaned back and began. 'Professor Lok was getting all geared up for the announcement we heard today. Sheri was helping. The reef off Bandar Seri was just about to become their most famous endeavour. International business sponsorship. Ground-breaking biofuel technology helping to set up the perfect environment for the greatest underwater zoo ever. Worldwide publicity with any luck. So-on; so-forth. Then they get warning of fish smugglers. People like the ones Sheri had mentioned in her doctoral thesis. On another reef, granted, on the far side of the island up beyond Old Baya City. But it was a potentially disastrous danger to the project. It must have seemed well worth investigating.'

'Fish smugglers?' asked Nic incredulously. '*Fish* smugglers?'

'Endangered species; medical myths; illegal collectors – it isn't just Orangutans and tigers here. Or elephants and mountain gorillas in Africa. You know that.'

'OK. Fish smugglers probably exist,' allowed Nic. 'But how do you know it was them?'

'Sheri told me. Or her thesis and her near-death experience did. Stay with me for the moment.'

'OK.' Nic shrugged. He glanced across at Gabriella, who nodded, silently supporting Richard's contention.

'They alerted Sergeant Tengku Suleiman, who doubled as their boatman, and off they went,' continued Richard. 'Sure enough, something was going on at the reef. Two, maybe three people down there, up to something.' He held up his hand to forestall the questions. 'More than three and they wouldn't have risked going down. Fewer than three and the smugglers would never have got the drop on them. So. They went down to investigate . . .' He leaned forward, suddenly burning with intensity. 'Now, according to Sheri's thesis, the way fish smugglers work is with gas guns. Gas guns that have needle-sharp points and canisters of cyanide gas. The guns are designed to spray bubbles into the faces of fish and stun them. But the points are more than sharp enough to inject the gas into the air pipe of a scuba set. And there you have it – instant cyanide poisoning. They killed Lok. They nearly killed Sheri but failed – maybe the gun wasn't properly loaded. Maybe it's something else. I favour her polio medicine giving her some limited immunity, myself. And someone popped up out of the water behind the sergeant and cut his throat.'

'OK,' said Nic. 'That seems to hold together. But who are "they"?'

'On other Indonesian islands it's usually men from the coastal villages, but there's no village close by there. And Sailendra can tell us whether there are any likely contenders close enough to be in the frame.'

'No!' said the prince decidedly, at once, as loyal to his people as they were to him.

'Pirates, then,' said Robin. 'Pirates cut throats.'

'That's certainly what Inspector Kei seems to think. And we know there were pirates near at hand. They may have boarded *Ocean's Bounty* by then. They certainly took *Tai Fun*. And it was on the assumption that the pirates killed his sergeant that Kei slaughtered them when he got the chance. All except the boy that you took care of, Robin.'

Robin nodded.

'And the boy seems to have kicked off what came next. It seems most likely that Kei's men didn't kill all the pirates on *Tai Fun*'s after deck. At least one got away. Alerted the Pirate Chief – I'm sorry but I can't think of anything less melodramatic to call him – that his son was dead. And there was no news of his grandson. So he followed *Tai Fun* back to Volcano Roads and came looking.'

'Cut poor Parang's throat,' grated Sailendra.

'Quite so, Your Majesty. Cut Parang's throat and put into action a pretty elaborate plan. I've explained what happened already, but it still seems strange that a couple of pirates, apparently improvising as they went along, should have been able to come up with something so elaborate . . .'

Richard rose and began to pace the veranda, wrapped in thought. He was one of those men who reason best when in motion – if not in action. But no sooner had he taken a turn around the airy space than his cellphone started ringing.

'Excuse me,' he said, taking it out, glancing at the incoming call number and frowning deeply enough to tell Robin at least that he didn't recognize it. He put it to his ear. 'Hello?'

A babble of conversation ensued.

Instead of answering, Richard strolled across to the veranda rail, picked up the binoculars and pressed them to his eyes.

'Right,' he said after a moment more. 'Count on us. We'll be there.'

He closed the phone and slid it into his pocket, still staring fixedly through the binoculars. Then, almost unconsciously he raised his phone-hand and waved as though in reply to a signal.

'What was that all about? And what *are* you doing?' asked Robin.

'I'm waving to Sheri Aru,' he answered. 'She's at her window in the polio clinic. And she just called. For help, I think.' He lowered the binoculars and turned round.

'Part two of the photo-opportunity takes place first thing tomorrow. She's supposed to take an underwater camera team and some divers from Luzon Logging out on to the reef to show them the endangered species they have promised to protect.'

'So?' asked Robin, quietly.

'So she wants us to go down with her,' he answered thoughtfully. 'Sittart has it all set up and won't take no for an answer. She still can't remember exactly what happened to her the last time she went diving, but the thought of going down again has simply terrified the life out of her.'

TWENTY-SEVEN
Caligula

S atang Suang Sittart BA(Hons) MEcon, PhD, sometime visiting professor of economics at the University of the Philippines, Manila; Chief Executive Officer of Luzon Logging and senior board member of every one of its associate companies, sat at an ornate desk beside a broad window with a panoramic view almost as wide as Richard's.

He was in the main guest suite of Dr Jurong's exclusive, almost palatial island hideaway. The beautiful old building was situated a mile or so from Bandar Seri's northern suburbs on the lower slopes of the hills that overlooked the northernmost edge of the reef. The guest suite commanded a westward-facing view bettered only by the view from the master suite immediately above. The bedroom was furnished much in the same way as the Victorian room in the Volcano Roads Hotel. Its polished wood floor was strewn with price-less carpets. Its walls were hung with prints and pictures, pressed flowers and pinned insects, birds, arachnids. In one wall, also framed like a picture and larger than the biggest TV screen, there was an aquarium filled with exotic fish in all sorts, shapes and colours. But it was of no more interest to Sittart than the foot-long scorpion secured beside the bird-eating spider the size of a dinner plate.

Behind him towered a four-poster bed hung with gossamer curtains, light enough to be stirred by the ceiling fan which beat round lazily in spite of the fact that the air-conditioning was on. Away beyond the double-glazed French windows, across the balcony they opened on to, and above the tops of the manicured trees on the lower slopes, Sittart could see the container ship aground on the reef. He could see the naval vessels surrounding it and keeping everyone trapped aboard with that dazzling blaze of warlike bright-ness. The heavy heave of the algae-rich water like a sea of green oil. The angular constellation of lights that defined the oil platform. The genuine galaxies beyond, hanging in clusters, as though the sky was garlanded with vines laden with pearls instead of grapes. The promise of moonrise silvering the still, somnolent horizon.

Or rather, Sittart could have seen all this if he had troubled to look at the breathtaking view any more than he bothered to look at the old pictures, the dead creatures or the restless kaleidoscope of priceless fish.

But none of it held any fascination for Sittart. He was an austere man, little given to sensuous delight. He might have been a Buddhist priest. A Moslem Mullah. He certainly lived like a monk. He had no wife but Luzon Logging. No family but Bogor Biofuels, Pontianac Oil Enterprises, DelMonte Medical and the rest. He breathed shal-lowly. Ate sparingly. Drank nothing except water. He walked softly. Spoke quietly. Slept frugally – in three twenty-minute power-naps during the day and never more than four more hours in the middle of the night. He wore silk and tailored linen only on special occa-sions. He travelled rarely and only when the most important business called him out of the office where he lived alone on top of the Luzon Logging tower that dominated Del Monte Avenue, Quezon City, Manila. And where he wielded power almost equal to the power of the great Roman emperors Tiberius, Nero or Caligula.

It was the power that drove him. The certainty that he could dictate the lives of millions of other creatures, from the merest algae to the Sultan of Sabah. And he loved doing so every once in a while. Loved feeling that he could reach his hand out in secrecy and silence in the dead still of the night – and this one would be ruined or that one made for life.

In many ways, he recognized, he was as drily avaricious as a miser, living in rags, freezing and starving rather than employing the glittering riches he would rather hoard than spend. For what was the purpose of power if it was not wielded to give the powerful man a little personal pleasure and fulfilment? And, one might suppose, the greater the power, the greater the pleasure – bound only by limits of inclination and imagination.

But Sittart knew his western history as well as he knew his global economics – and himself. He knew that with power such as he could command came the threat of insanity like the madness of the Caesars. He had read his Suetonius and his Procopius as well as his Gibbon; his Friedman and his De Soto as well as his Keynes. The Historians as well as the Economists.

He knew all about the archaeological speculation that it was the lead pipes in their palaces that led Tiberius to turn the whole island of Capri into a perverted pleasure dome which would have shamed Coleridge's Kublai Khan. That led Nero to burn Rome, slaughter Christians, murder his mother and declare himself a god. That led Caligula to sleep with his sister, prostitute the wives and daughters of the greatest politicians and make his horse into a Senator. Caligula, who once whispered, 'Remember: I can do *anything* to *anybody*.'

But Professor Satang Suang Sittart also knew the truth of the matter. It was not the lead poisoning that drove the Caesars mad. It was the power. It was the fact that Caligula was right and there was nothing that they could not do. That there was no-one that they could not do it to. The realization that there was no limit on earth and no punishment from the other gods in their heaven to forbid them anything. And so the things they did, testing the outermost edges of power and possibility, became, step by step, more and more brutally insane.

And every now and then, secretly for the most part, Sittart also had begun to test himself. To experiment with Caligula's theory. To test his control over those only a little less powerful than he was himself – some who knew him and some who did not – by seeing how much they would overlook, excuse, forgive. To demand acts of subservience from those around him. Or from their wives. Or their daughters. To spirit away unfortunates who took his fancy and who were never seen again.

And sometimes in that strange dark void between the spiriting away and the final disappearance, to see how much of his power he could make them bear. It was not psychopathic sadism – it was not so much the sexual suffering as the utter helplessness that excited him. He had the power and he knew it; he did not need to reassure himself of the fact. But every now and then he needed to test it on some hapless, helpless creature. Like Tiberius did. Or Nero. Or Caligula.

And at the moment, the thoughtful Sittart was utterly unconscious of the Victorian opulence by which he was surrounded, or the beauty of the tropic night outside his window. This was because he was watching the wide screen of his personal laptop sitting on the polished mahogany top of the ornate, antique desk. Mesmerized by the screen, which was filled with pictures from the hidden cameras in the polio clinic.

Earlier, Sittart had observed Hilly Johnson talking to her brother in his iron lung while the massive Kalla paced the room like a caged tiger. Now he was watching Sheherezade Aru, utterly naked and completely unaware, bending forward and steadying herself on her left-hand crutch as she reached with her right hand for the nightdress that lay on her bed like the silken skin of some legendary creature.

Sittart felt a strange sensation on his chin as though a fly was crawling there. He wiped it thoughtlessly with his hand. His fingers came away slick with spittle. His mouth was literally watering at the sight of the naked girl. How absolutely helpless she seemed to him. How completely desirable.

The last ferry across the mouth of the Sangsang left at midnight and Richard's guests were on it – power, wealth and aristocracy mixing with commoners like Antony and Cleopatra disguised amongst their subjects in Alexandria, as he wryly observed to the apparently drowsy Robin. The first of the next day left at six a.m., and the Mariners were on it, bright-eyed and invigorated by a short sleep after a bout of passion, a rush of adrenaline at the promise of adventure and the strongest cup of Java coffee they could bear. They were heading, via the ferry-port and the docks, for *Tai Fun* and their scuba gear. Then, with Kalla and Hilly in a local taxi, for the beach above the reef where Sheri Aru and the dive team would be ready to go at eight.

The ferry was a tidy, modern little craft, big enough to carry two-dozen cars as well as a number of foot passengers. But the timelessness of the river's tidal reach swept over the vessel's workaday modernity as easily as the fog swept in with the spring and out with the ebb. It was sweeping in now as the morning arrived with the miraculous swiftness of the tropics. It was a strange kind of battle between light and darkness, for the Sansang's mouth opened westward and there were the mountains to the east. As the sun soared up the eastern sky, and the tide swept into the river bringing the fog with it, so the burgeoning brightness seemed to thicken, to hesitate. It was as if the sun itself flickered. But then, riding over the back of the fog to stir the night-still air, came the first breath of the dawn wind. And the day exploded into place.

Richard, in the ferry's forepeak, found himself looking down on his left along the docks, past the upper works of the smaller vessels moored there to the white box that was the new harbourmaster's building. He strained to see past the featureless, functional building to where *Tai Fun*'s four tall masts stood above her larger, outer berth. Even as his eyes fastened on the lovely vessel beyond the ugly building, the first of the sun caught the panoramic windows with the blinding dazzle of molten gold. He was forced to blink his tears away. When his vision cleared, he found himself looking up at the floor of the balcony outside Sheri's room – though he saw it as the roof of the veranda that swept along the river-front of the clinic. Beyond the double-glazing, the place was bustling with activity already, for here on the ground floor were the common areas, the kitchens and the dining rooms for those who could be up and about. Then the ferry swung away starboard and began its approach to the northern dock.

They had come down from the hotel in a taxi and the driver had brought it across. As docking was completed, therefore, they climbed back aboard and settled back for the short ride to *Tai Fun*. As the taxi rolled along the dockside, under the long shadow of the tall ship, Kalla and Hilly loomed in chiaroscuro, flat black against the gold blaze, misshapen by the fact that they were carrying four sets of scuba gear.

'You want a hand with that?' called Richard as the two of them walked across to the gangplank.

'We got it,' called down Kalla. And, when he arrived on the dockside itself he continued, 'I checked it all. But you'll want to double-check your own rigs, I guess.'

A few moments later the scuba gear was in the taxi's boot and the four of them sat facing each other in the back.

Richard noticed nothing beyond the fact that the newcomers, like the Mariners themselves, had dressed with swimming gear replacing underwear, but Robin was more sensitive to atmosphere and she sensed at once that something was not quite right between Kalla and his right-hand woman. She leaned back in her seat, as deceptively somnolent as she had seemed to Richard at midnight last night, and she tried to work out what had stirred her suspicions.

It might be nothing at all, of course, thought Robin. An incorrect assumption when she had first met them that they were a couple, being readjusted now by the truth of a more coldly professional relationship. Or maybe Hilly's experiences at the hands of the pirates and in the back of the ambulance had deepened some natural reserve. Or maybe Kalla thought there was something about that adventure that she hadn't told him yet. And, given their profession and situation, secrets and suspicions could be very damaging indeed. The only thing more damaging at the moment, she decided as the taxi slid to a halt in the car park beside the beach, was to have someone thoughtlessly poking their nose in at the worst possible moment. She would see what Richard thought, she decided. Then maybe she would probe a little, later.

Immediately across the sand from the car-park gate there was a ramshackle dive hut, some clapboard changing rooms and open-sided public showers; a kiosk with a sign saying BAYA DIVE – GET DOWN WITH US! And there was a pier. At the pier's inland end, beside the kiosk, a raised platform the size of a modest room stood high enough above the sand to require four steps up. The wooden flooring was worn and smooth, its edges rounded, by the countless scuba divers who had sat here over the years. As indeed, a good number were sitting there now.

Richard and Kalla shouldered the scuba gear and led the little group across the still-cool sand. The women followed silently with the beach bags. The air was cool as well but it held the promise of fierce heat just around the corner. Calling greetings, they unloaded the gear on to the platform and started unbuttoning shirts and trousers. Outer clothing and beach bags went to the cheery young man with blond hair, a mahogany tan and an Australian accent in the kiosk who oversaw – among other things – a bank of lockers.

Richard and Robin both declined his offer of wetsuits and shrugged their scuba gear on with practised and economical movements.

Richard had just settled his weights belt round his trim waist and turned to check Robin's harness when he saw Sheri coming across the sand with the same focused and economical movements that Richard and Robin were using. Her progress was much steadier than it had been yesterday and Richard was struck most forcibly as he looked at her that it was not just in the water that she could be completely in control. She was wearing a gauzy multicoloured wrap substantial enough to protect her modesty – even in this Moslem society – but practical enough to be easily and swiftly discarded when she came to the water's edge. Over her shoulder was a beach-bag that rested across the small of her back and was clearly positioned so that it would not interfere with her powerfully purposeful movements. All in all, thought Richard, she made quite an arresting picture. Then he suddenly became aware that his was by no means the only head that had turned.

'Hey Sheri,' called the young man in the kiosk. 'G'day!'

'Hi Cobb,' she answered. 'My gear ready?'

'Yup. Locked and loaded.'

'Well, ladies and gentlemen,' she said as she swung round to the front of the kiosk and let Cobb pull her bag and robe free then lift her scuba set on to the bar so she could slip it on more easily. His movements revealed the fact that she was already wearing the high-cut, skin-tight wetsuit Richard had first found her in. 'Let's get this show on the road, shall we?'

She paused for a moment longer, looking at the faces of the film crew and the rest. Cobb slipped a net bag containing weight-belt, flippers and facemask over her shoulder. And she swung into motion once again, leading them up on to the platform then out along the walkway that stood above the sea's surface and the top of the coral shelf a couple of metres below it.

Back in the guest suite of Dr Jurong's residence half hidden in the jungle slopes above and inland, Satang Suang Sittart leaned forward once again. His long black eyes focussed on the laptop screen, which showed in intimate close-up the pictures from the camera immediately behind the determined marine biologist. As he watched, controlling his breathing carefully and swallowing almost convulsively, Sittart considered the backs of Sheri Aru's wasted calves, the sudden statuesque strength of her thighs, the muscular, almost angular, fullness of the deeply cleft, rubber-clad buttocks . . .

And the thought came to him out of nowhere that when Nero first tried to murder his mother Agrippina, he ordered that she should be drowned in a bay a lot like this one.

TWENTY-EIGHT
Reef

As the water closed over Sheri's head, she was filled with the familiar sense of freedom and power that went a long way towards keeping her sane. But at the same time, her fear-damaged memory stirred, making her heart pound with something more powerful and disturbing than the familiar rush of ecstasy. Without thinking, she curled into a ball, reaching down with her right hand to feel the reassuring handle of the big diver's knife that Cobb had slipped into the net bag with her weight belt, fins and facemask. It was strapped to the thin calf of her right leg in a specially adapted sheath. Its foot-long razor-sharp carbon-steel blade would see off everything, man and fish, up to the size of a tiger, a bull or a hammerhead.

What a pity she hadn't been wearing it when . . .

What a tragedy that *he had* been wearing one . . .

Her memory spasmed shut like a damaged muscle freezing into a cramp. Her heart pounded even more painfully and she fought to control her breathing, all too well aware how fast she was using up her air, panting with terror like this.

She angled her body and worked her flippers so that she could look up at the outer end of the pier where a smaller wooden platform stood on four tall legs founded on the coral nearly ten metres below. Through the restless half-mirror of the surface, her first buddy, Richard, plunged in. The big Englishman's reassuring bulk simply seemed to throw the water aside. His finely scarred face broke into a grin as he finned towards her. The grin was apparent almost entirely in the creasing of the skin around his excited blue eyes. His lips were stretched wide in any case – over the mouthpiece of his regulator.

His slim wife Robin followed, their refusal to be separated necessitating the unusual double-buddy system they were running.

But to be fair, Sheri felt she needed all the reassurance she could get. The steady grey eyes below the golden riot of the woman's hair crinkled at the edges and Robin gave the OK sign to Richard and to Sheri. Then they paused side by side and cleared their ears.

As they did so, the others plunged into the still water beside them. Kalla and Hilly first, then the TV crew. Sheri had considered wearing a mic and trying for some live commentary – but all things considered, she decided to do a voice-over later, after she saw what footage they managed to shoot. At least, now that they were underwater, she thought wryly, the second camera was keeping his distance. She had not liked the way he kept invading her space on land.

Hadn't liked it even though she had been blissfully ignorant that he had been secretly filming her and transmitting what his camera saw to Sittart's computer.

The nine of them fell in almost shoulder to shoulder as Sheri gestured towards the shallower water further out, where the reef gathered into an up-thrusting ridge before it formed a square-cut cliff edge and fell sheer for hundreds of metres. The most interesting section of the underwater environment was close to where the *Ocean's Bounty* was aground in a clear, brightly lit shallow area between the long dark hulls of the four warships still sitting in the deep water around the grounded container ship.

Sheri turned and started finning powerfully across the reef, heading unswervingly towards the wreck. The water all around them was clear and the colours breathtaking. The light was powerful, beams and blades striking down as the sun came over the top of the mountains, their effect magnified by the clarity of the water and the gentle up-slope of the reef. The tide was rising gently, as it had been since dead water at five, and there was no current to speak of.

The reef that was sloping up towards them was a dazzling vista worthy of any Impressionist painter, thought Richard; beyond the imagination of all but the greatest. If there was a base colour, he decided, it was the pale ochre of sandy coral heads. But these convoluted outcrops, effectively the dead rock on which everything else lived, were overlain with a breathtaking variety of living corals, seaweeds, anemones and other plant and aquatic animal life-forms that he could not begin to name. They formed little meadows of intense green, long streamers of sage and russet, gem-bright explosions of red and blue, all waving, pulsing, opening, closing to their own strange dictates under the overwhelming impulse of the incoming tide.

And in and out of the coral outcrops, over the iridescent meadows, flirting with the vivid dangers of the anemones, there were seeming millions of tiny fish in yellows, reds, turquoises, aquas and blues – depending on their nearness either to the surface or to the reef. Over the seaweeds, aquatic mosses and lichens that clothed the coral, beneath and among the constant darting of the swarms of tiny fishes, there crawled a living treasure chest. There were glittering starfish, octopi, hermits, gleaming long-spined urchins, the rich and velvety sea-cucumbers, the bright seahorses, the crabs, the darting shrimp, the DayGlo lobster and all the teeming, rainbow-coloured rest of them.

And over all of these there cruised the mid-sized reef fish. Schools of needlefishes, halfbeaks, soldiers and squirrels, trumpets, comets, ghosts and angels. Colours beyond the widest palate; numbers beyond calculation. And then, as the up-swell of the coral gathered before the final abyssal plunge, the big fish from the deep water that had come cruising in more speculatively, the grotesque groupers, the lean snappers, the dangerous silver-sided barracuda.

The cameramen and their buddies peeled away like fighter planes at a dogfight. Kalla and Holly drifted downwards, side by side, seemingly entranced. Richard, falling behind the rest as the rapture of the reef swept over him, was forced to shake himself free of the dangerous magic and power forward more forcefully until he was close to Robin and Sheri. Unlike the others, who seemed to have little purpose beyond watching or filming the fish, Sheri was clearly on a mission and Robin, good buddy that she was, stayed at her shoulder as she went to fulfil it.

After a very few moments indeed, Richard had worked out what Sheri's mission was. And it was the logical one, had he stopped to consider things from the marine biologist's point of view. She was going to assess the damage that *Ocean's Bounty*'s grounding had done to the priceless environment she was fighting to protect.

The first sign of the damage was the cloud of grit that hung in the water, suddenly. Invisible from any distance – for it simply faded into the blue-grey of the distance – it was suddenly all around them. The reef beneath them seemed a shade or two less dazzling, some of it dusted with the coarse silt, all of it toned down by the finer clouds still suspended in the water. Richard stopped as Sheri and Robin did, bringing himself vertical in the water, seemingly seated on the heave of the tide beneath them. From this position he, like they, could see the way the container ship's forecastle was jammed into the shoulder of the reef surprisingly close at hand. Although clearly hard aground, the long hull was nevertheless in constant motion, worked by the forces of current, tide and waves. And as it moved, so it ground at the living coral, generating more and more clouds of debris. It was clear to Richard at once that by no means *all* the local life forms found the disturbance of their environment a bad thing. Myriad little reef fish darted here, feeding on the tiny particles of plant and animal that *Ocean's Bounty* was stirring up. And where the little fish gathered in such numbers, there the larger predators also came. And the deep-water fish that preyed upon them. And so on up the food-chain. A barracuda drifted apparently aimlessly out from behind the captive hull, its two-metre length gleaming like the flank of a silver tiger. Away in the vertical column of shadow cast down into the depths by the old frigate's hull, a hammerhead lingered speculatively. The shark's precise dimensions were disguised by distance but it looked the better part of three times longer than the barracuda.

But to be fair the hull of *Ocean's Bounty* was not the only thing doing damage here. Its cargo was also grinding down the coral. There were four containers between the three divers hanging in the water and the hull that they were looking at. None of them sat squarely on the seabed. None of them sat still. Like the ship from whose deck they had tumbled at the moment of collision, they were being moved by the waters around them just enough to be working at the delicate half-formed peaks of coral that looked to Richard like white brains. Like heads of broccoli carved in ivory. Like naked cauliflowers.

The nearest of the containers gaped half open, its side clearly split by the impact of falling into the sea. Bizarrely, in and out of the dark mouth of the wound in its side, a crowd of plastic figures came and went, like swimmers not quite certain that they wanted to risk the water. They were a shockingly pink school made up not of fish but of Barbie dolls, some in their wrapping, some escaped. Their long yellow hair flowed like molten gold, showing how the currents beneath the rolling waves were working on them as they were sucked rhythmically in and out of their sanctuary.

The next container lay smashed wide and seemingly empty. Richard swam over towards it, his interest piqued by the strange sight of the Barbies, and suddenly wanting to know what else had been carried aboard the pirated ship. He glanced across at Sheri and Robin, carefully signalling to them where he was going. As soon as he closed with the container, he saw that he had been

mistaken. The sea bed all around the gaping wound in its side lay
under a sparkling carpet of shattered glass. Whatever had been in
here had been in containers of some kind. Not bottles – there were
no corks, caps, lids or labels. And the glass was white. Angular. As
he drew nearer still, close enough to peer into the shadowy interior, he saw a bird's nest of angular structures scattered all across
the floor of the thing, held inside by a lip of metal container-
side that had remained intact. The metal edges lay like roughly
sketched boxes, like mathematical nets. The biggest of them
almost coffin-sized, the smallest hardly bigger than a biscuit tin.
Richard actually put his head into the vacant space and looked
around. He reached back on to his dive belt and unclipped his
waterproof torch, shining its broad, bright beam into the eerie
dimness of the place. But there was nothing else to see. He clipped
the torch back into place, then lingered for a moment more, until
a particularly large wave swept by overhead and the whole thing
stirred. The skeletal shapes shifted. Glass cascaded elegantly, with
the grace of snowflakes. A strange tinkling filled his head.

Richard pulled himself out of the second container and looked
around. The cameramen had found the Barbies and were assiduously
filming them. Sheri and Robin were exploring the third container. As
he swam past them, Robin pulled out a red plastic fire truck big
enough for a child to ride upon. Sheri pulled out a model of a WWII
British Lancaster bomber. Richard recognized it at a glance. It was
what Guy Gibson's 617 Squadron had flown, laden with Barnes
Wallace's bouncing bombs on the famous 'Dambuster' raid against
the Nazis' industrial heartlands near the Rhine and Ruhr. It was almost
as big as the fire engine, its wing-span the better part of two metres
wide. There was obviously still air trapped within the solid fuselage.
Not much, but just enough to make it buoyant. For when Sheri let
it go, the plane simply soared through the water, heading inward with
the waves, as though seeking dams to bust.

The second film crew deserted the Barbies and followed the
bomber's elegant flight path towards the surface and the shore. And
they were fortunate in their choice. The Lancaster had reached the
upper levels, and was just beginning to lose its fragile stability when
the barracuda hit it like a squadron of Me 109s and in a moment
of spectacularly brutal savagery tore the model into pieces.

Richard looked away, with a scarce-believing shake of his head,
and went for the final container. This one lay nearest to both the
container ship's trapped bow and to the cliff-edge where the reef

fell away into the abyss. The inner sides of the metal box seemed to be solid and secure. But when Richard swam round the end, he saw that there was a narrow gap in the corner closest to the cliff. In and out through this, a multitude of little reef fish were swimming industriously in and out, like the Barbie dolls coyly appearing and disappearing, but in numbers and colours that made him think of bees swarming round a hive. Fascinated, Richard swam closer. The fish paid no attention to him except as an object to be circumnavigated. As he neared the narrow gap, the incoming and outgoing fish simply split into streams and bustled past him. But as they did so, they vanished into – or emerged out of – absolute blackness. Whatever it was that had them coming and going so remarkably, Richard would need to find some way of casting a little light on the situation if he was going to learn much more.

And the strange behaviour of the fish suddenly made Richard very keen to learn more. Even when he took hold of the edges of the split and fought to see into the container as he strained to pull the edges a little wider, still they bustled all around him in numbers he could not begin to estimate. Immediately that strange tinkling filled his head but he was concentrating so hard on what he was doing that it was some moments before he associated the sound with yet more broken glass.

And there was something else. Like the model of the Lancaster bomber, this container seemed to have enough air trapped within it to give it some buoyancy. As he laboured to pull the black-throated gap wider, Richard suddenly became aware that the whole container was slipping and sliding across the surface of the reef.

But Richard's attention was abruptly claimed by the success of his attempt to pull the gap wider. The sides yielded. An opening scarcely wider than his head was suddenly half as wide as his shoulders. But there it stopped. And even though the gap was wider, the inside of the container was still filled with absolute, impenetrable darkness. Keeping one hand in place, Richard reached down with the other and unclipped his torch again. Then, holding himself as steady as he could against the restless stirring of the whole big box, he shone the torch beam through the gap.

At first, all he could see was that swarm of fish, but it didn't take him long to realize that they were feeding. And once he worked that out, he was able to focus on what they found so tasty. The inside of the container was the size of a modest room and it seemed to be full of dead fish – seemingly almost as many dead ones as there were living ones. The dead ones were easy enough to spot because they were for the most part floating belly-up against the strange mirrored surface created by a great bubble of trapped air that seemed big enough to have filled about a quarter of the space. Most of the dead fish were in tatters, but it was still possible to recognize coherent shapes, especially those of fish that had been bigger in life. Or which had died and joined the food chain more recently.

Entranced, Richard strove to follow his torch-beam in through the gap, but his scuba gear caught at once, forcing him to fall back. And as he did so, he bumped into Sheri Aru. The unexpected contact made him jump so powerfully that he dropped his torch, but Sheri caught it and shone it back into the bustling interior.

Richard saw that there was something badly wrong at once. Sheri looked in at the strange frenzy, then looked across at him, her face stricken with absolute horror. The marine biologist began to gesture and frown, but Richard simply could not work out what she was trying to communicate. Then Robin arrived and Sheri swung round to her. A moment later the two women turned back to Richard, both of them gesturing that he should pull the gap wider. And he realized with a strange, sinking sensation in the pit of his stomach that Sheri was desperate to go in there.

He checked his watch. They had been out for a while but they should all have plenty of air left. And to be fair, the marine biologist was in her element. If anyone nearby knew precisely what they were doing it should be Sheri. But he could not rid himself of the certainty that this was a very bad idea. Still, in the face of the silent requests, he shrugged, took hold of the edges of the opening and pulled with all his strength.

Nothing happened, except that the sharp edge he was clutching cut his palm. He transferred both hands to one side, coiled his long body like a spring and put his flippered feet against the far side. Using all the strength of his massive frame he strained. Again, nothing – except that both hands were bleeding a little now. At last he let his feet fall and he hung in the water, shrugging apologetically.

Sheri handed Robin the torch. With brusque, efficient movements, she unbuckled her scuba gear and shrugged it off. With another long, lingering, meaningful look, she handed Robin the tank and retrieved the torch. Robin started sinking at once, for the tank was not buoyant. Richard grabbed first her shoulder and then the tank's shoulder strap. And when he looked up, Sheri was gone. Lithe as a moray, though dark as a conger in her black rubber wetsuit, she had eased her slim body through the gap and had vanished into the container.

Richard pulled Robin back to the unyielding gap. Inside the half floating metal box they could see the blade of brightness that was the beam of his torch. Sheri hung, surrounded by the feeding fish, pulling parts of their feast into the net bag she had carried out here with her. Working as fast as he could, Richard calculated. He glanced at the scuba gear Robin and he were holding then looked at his watch. *She's been in there more than a minute already.* She finished filling the net bag and turned, clearly preparing to swim back out to them. As she angled her body downwards, so the beam of the torch swept across the floor of the container. And there, among the broken glass and the strange skeletal boxes, she saw something else that caught her attention. Abruptly, she was in motion, swimming determinedly down towards it, following the steady beam of the torch. Richard looked at his watch again, frowning. *Two minutes and counting . . .*

The hammerhead came round the side of the container then. Had the extra weight of Sheri's scuba tank not pulled them down, the shark would have swum right into them. As it was, the sinuous length of it swept majestically just above their faces. From the alien stalks of its eyes past the slits of its gills and the brutal curve of its half-open mouth, past the underside of its widespread fins, along the speckled length of its belly with the claspers that proclaimed it a male, to the vertical scythe of its tail, the whole thing must have measured the better part of six metres – nearly eighteen feet. It wasn't hunting. It was merely exploring. Probably following the scent of Richard's blood. The little golden fish seemed to know that and they paid it little more attention than they had paid to Richard, moving out of its way but by no means scattering in panic.

But the shark's arrival had several unlooked-for consequences, each one potentially more dangerous than the last. Richard and Robin started back and cowered down, moving away from the opening in the container's side and taking the scuba set with them. The camera crews – like Kalla and Hilly – also swam clear, watching the lazy motion of the massive predator from a safe distance. Only the second cameraman, perhaps more foolhardy than his companions, pushed forward a little, lights on and camera recording.

And the current set-up by the great predator's apparently easy motion broke the delicate balance that had held the buoyant container in place. Even as Richard realized that the shark was coming round to circle the container once again, so he realized into the bargain that the big steel box was beginning to drift towards the edge of the cliff, bumping gently across the coral, and taking the trapped biologist along with it.

TWENTY-NINE
Container

S heri reached up for the Rajah Laut, then for the humphead wrasse behind it. Both of the fish were half-eaten but still clearly recognizable for what they were. And what they were was damn-near extinct. Holding herself just below the false surface of the air-bubble trapped in the container, she looked around at the half-consumed banquet of rare and endangered species. There were creatures here that were quite literally irreplaceable. Life forms whose worth was almost beyond price.

Unfortunately, they were priceless not only to environmentalists such as Sheri and biologists such as poor Professor Lok, but also to ruthless collectors, zoos and aquariums. So there were always men who were desperate enough or greedy enough to steal them out of the wild and sell them to the highest bidder, no matter what damage that did to genetic lines, species, habitats – or the world in general. The ecological destruction held in this one container was nearly incalculable. And the fact that there were so many unique and uniquely imperilled life forms all in one place would have told its own grim story – even had they not all been dead into the bargain. This was a kind of genocide, she thought, that Ninoy Lok would have equated with the Nazis' Final Solution, had he found this and lived to broadcast his findings.

Sheri's chest hurt so badly that her eyes filled with tears. And her horrified mind was so far removed from her actual situation that it did not at first occur to her that the pain had anything to do with the fact that she had been holding her breath for nearly three minutes now. She actually thought her heart was breaking.

The container shifted. Sheri's head filled with unearthly tinkling as shards of shattered glass lying scattered across its floor all shifted in sympathy. Still without thinking, she shone the torch beam down towards the source of the unearthly sound. And there, among the angular skeletons of the boxes whose sides had once been the aquarium glass that was tinkling all around her, she saw the one thing she had not expected to see here. The sight of it was so unexpected and so horrific to her that she screamed. And it was only when her chest was empty that she realized where she was and remembered what was going on.

It was as the shark came round the second time that Richard heard the scream. Even though it was deadened and distorted by the water, even though it was dulled by the sound of his own breathing, the hissing of the regulator and the rumble of releasing bubbles, he heard it clearly. Knew exactly what it was. Knew precisely where it had come from. Without further thought, he simply snatched the scuba set from Robin's grasp and drove it up into the shark's face like a Roman legionary with his shield. He did not hit the big fish hard. The shock to his arms of the solid yellow plastic carapace bashing the half-open jaw was no greater than that of falling forward to do push-ups. But the unexpected attack was enough to disturb the shark. With an outraged twist of its head and an arrogant flick of its tail, it was gone. And not a moment too soon, thought Richard. The container bounced up on to the final up-slope. The edge of the abyss was no more than five metres distant – a good deal less than the length of the departing predator.

Richard grabbed at the side of the gap at once and thrust himself into it. Sheri was back up at the inner surface, her head and shoulders pushed up into the bubble of trapped air as she all too clearly went about replacing the breath lost in that one terrible scream.

Richard slid the tank in through the gap, wishing he had thought to do this earlier. Then he pulled his own mouthpiece out and shouted her name as loudly as he could. Either the noise he made or the bubbles of breath he released alerted Sheri and she sank back into the water above him, gesturing as best she could. She seemed to be laden with all sorts of paraphernalia, not to mention a net bag full of dead fish. He held the scuba tank up towards her, but she shook her head and gestured again – she was coming out. *Good job too*, he thought, feeling the container slide another metre or more towards the cliff edge.

And then everything went mad at once.

Robin grabbed his shoulder and swung him bodily round to face the returning hammerhead. As she did so, his shoulder twisted agonizingly – the scuba set was still inside the container and it wedged there, its straps caught on something. Robin's arm went round him, doubling the size of the creature they presented to the incoming shark. Her other arm waved fiercely. The gesture was little enough, but it sufficed to do two things both at once. First, it jerked Richard's hand into a bird's nest of scuba straps and secured it there for the moment. Secondly, it turned the fish's charge. Angling itself almost arrogantly, the shark whipped past the corner of the container, seeming to brush the metal side with its tail. The current of its passage pulled the box forward once again.

Richard looked down and found he was actually hanging over the edge of the precipice. The coral cliff below him plunged down into blue-shadowed depths far beyond the reach of his eyesight or the sunlight on which it depended. He swung back, almost feverish with haste. The depths below held very little danger for Robin. But if the container went over and sank with Sheri still trapped inside it and Richard still tangled in the wedged scuba straps, then he and she would die. A short but intensely horrible death.

Sheri was immediately behind Richard, and even as he turned, fighting to disentangle his hand from the all but unbreakable webbing of the scuba straps, so she pulled a huge diver's knife out of her leg sheath. One swift movement of the razor-bladed carbon steel was enough to cut the strap that was caught on the box itself. But then, with a delicate precision and a care for Richard's skin which, under the circumstances he thought to be a little excessive, she started sawing at the bright yellow bindings that held his hand so helplessly.

However, Richard only had a moment to watch what she was doing with the almost surgically sharp blade, for Robin grabbed his shoulder once again and swung him bodily back.

The hammerhead made its second attacking run from out in the deep water under the shadow of the old Tribal Class frigate Richard had recognized as *HMS Tartar*. It came head-on towards them like a charging bull, its every lethally fluid movement speaking deadly determination. Still trapped by the tangle of straps and wedged helplessly against the corner of the restless container, Richard could only watch it come. He wished most poignantly that Robin would make a run for safety – but he knew she simply wouldn't. She had neither the time – nor the inclination – even to join Sheri in the relative safety of the metal-walled container. But, given where that was likely bound for, that was probably just as well. Once again he felt her arm tighten around his waist. He tightened his arm around hers in reply.

So that when Sheri, in a position now to appreciate the danger they were in, shoved the big diver's knife through the gap, it was Robin who grabbed it. As the shark closed with them, she began to wave the long steel blade threateningly, almost pulling herself out of Richard's grip as she sought to frighten the fish away. But Richard wouldn't let her go. So she pulled him forward as she lunged – and he felt the whole container slipping forward with him. He worked his hand and wrist among the tight tangle of strapping and felt it beginning to give.

But the balance was desperately fine now. The shark was coming onwards. Robin was slashing, stabbing and lunging out towards it. Every time Richard felt his wrist coming free another lunge would jerk it tight again. Another lunge that wrenched him and the container forward, inch by inch by inch. The container was teetering on the cliff edge. And Sheri, who would have been well employed in untangling the straps for him, for some reason seemed to have stopped helping altogether.

Then, as the shark closed in for the kill, its mouth gaping, gills wide, eyes rolled up ecstatically – as though already savouring the unaccustomed heat of its unusually warm-blooded meal – a long black tube thrust out of the container. Sliding across Richard's shoulder like a rifle barrel on a marksman's rest, it came, more than a metre of it, until he could feel the trigger guard against the sensitive flesh of his back. A tube that ended in a needle-sharp point that was already spitting a surprisingly accurate stream of bubbles straight into the oncoming shark's wide mouth.

And, big as it was, powerful though it might have been, the shark simply froze. All six metres of it went rigid. It came on, still impelled by the power of its charge. But it came like a log. It slowed, too, as the impetus went out of it, and by the time it had crossed the last couple of metres it had already begun to fall away. It struck the corner of the container where it was projecting over the cliff edge, a good few metres beneath their flippers. And, having struck the metal point, it seemed to bounce back a little, before it started to fall away, belly-up, the undersides of its eye-stalks and fins making it look to Richard like a strange kind of Cross of Lorraine.

The whole container heaved. Richard's hand came free at last and he pulled his arm out, turning to receive Sheri's scuba rig. Then Sheri herself slid out, reaching for the regulator with one hand and jamming it back between her lips. As soon as she released it, she gestured UP! with that same hand. The other hand kept tight hold of the underwater rifle that Richard recognized all too clearly as the cyanide gun

Sheri had described in her doctoral thesis. No wonder she had
screamed, he thought. It had been a gun exactly like this one that
had murdered Professor Ninoy Lok and so nearly killed her too.

When Robin grabbed him yet again he whirled back, almost dropping Sheri's air tank, half-expecting yet another shark attack. But
no. It was very nearly worse. As the three of them finned desperately for safety, the container finally gave up its unequal battle with
both tides and gravity. In the same elegant slow-motion that the
shark was using, it toppled over the edge of the cliff. Immediately,
the air trapped within it started to leak out. Skeins of silver bubbles
joined the swarms of golden fish all streaming out of the falling box
which gathered pace as it tumbled into the abyss. Soon it overtook
the shark, and the last thing the three of them saw before they started
for the surface once again was the hammerhead shuddering back to
life as the dead weight of airless metal hurtled by.

Two minutes later the three heads broke the surface, and the first
thing Sheri said to Richard was, 'Get me to the police station. I
have to talk to Superintendent Hatta!'

They towelled dry and dressed over damp suits without pausing to
shower or change. Cobb called for a cab as soon as they could call
instructions to him and by the time they were dressed a battered
Mazda was sitting in the car park behind the beach. As they rode
into Bandar Seri and began to ease through the downtown traffic
towards the police headquarters, Sheri told her story to Richard and
Robin, answered their questions and prepared to explain to Hatta
the details of what had happened to Ninoy Lok and herself – while
Richard confirmed in his own mind what had almost certainly
happened to their boatman Tengku Suleiman.

After calling for the cab, Cobb had also called headquarters and
warned the police to expect Sheri, Richard and Robin, so Inspector
Kei greeted them in the security area, saw them through reception
and took them up to the office he and Hatta were sharing while
they were here.

Sheri was quiet in Kei's presence, and Richard could all too
clearly see why. The long ride in the ambulance had left the marine
biologist in no doubt how outraged and grief stricken the pirate
chief had been about the slaughter of his people and the death of
his son aboard *Tai Fun*. Nor was there any doubt in any of their
minds that Kei had ordered that slaughter in revenge for the murder
of Tengku Suleiman.

'But it wasn't pirates at all,' Sheri explained to Hatta ten minutes later. 'I've talked it through with Captain Mariner and his wife. I have it all clear in my mind now.'

'Very well,' said Hatta. 'Tell me what you remember now. You have no objection if I record the conversation? You do not feel you need a lawyer present?' He moved several ornaments and bits of bric-a-brac on the table to make room for a recorder. Among these, Richard noted with wry amusement, was a coconut still in its green husk. A hole had been drilled in the top and a straw protruded. Fresh coconut milk was as much of a local delicacy as the red bananas, mangoes and fragrant Java coffee. The almost childlike simplicity of coconut milk in his lunch box seemed to open a new side to the fastidious Hatta.

'She has two witnesses,' pointed out Richard. 'And this is evidence freely given. It's not a confession.'

Hatta shrugged and nodded. Pressed a button on a CD recorder and gave the standard briefing. Time, Date, Location. Case title and number. Names of all those present. Who was giving the evidence. Then he sat back.

'Professor Lok got word that something was going on,' Sheri began. 'We were wrapped up in preparations for the opening of the reef, but even so he was worried about people stealing and smuggling endangered species from the far side of the island. He and Sergeant Suleiman had a meeting and decided the most likely situation was that villagers were being trained by illegal traders to take a few fish for profit. They thought we should check it out. The professor invited me because smuggling of this sort was an important section of my thesis. And I went along because they weren't expecting any real trouble – just a couple of villagers up to mischief out of their depth, easy to frighten. Sergeant Suleiman was hopeful that he would get the names of the men who were organizing the trade and smuggling the fish.'

'And the disguise?' asked Hatta. 'Why did he not go in uniform?'

'He didn't want to frighten them off.' Sheri shrugged helplessly in the face of the enormity of the miscalculation.

'But it wasn't villagers,' prompted Kei, his voice strained.

'No. I suppose we should have realized sooner. There was no village close by. The villages on that coast north of Baya City were destroyed when Guanung Surat erupted. There was nowhere nearer than half a day's boat-ride away, except for the old police dock in Baya City harbour that we used. Nowhere on Pulau Baya, at any rate. But when we got to the reef, there they were. Two men in wetsuits. We could see what they were doing at once. Professor Lok went over immediately to try and stop them and I paused only to take some of my medication before following him.'

Sheri paused. She looked around the room white-faced and sliding into shock as the vividness of her dreadful memory swept over her. 'But there were more than we realized. Half a dozen or so. They appeared from deeper down the reef cliff where we couldn't see them at first. We had been expecting villagers, remember. But these men were different. Deadly. They surrounded the professor. It took only an instant. I couldn't see exactly what they were doing but I started for the surface. But they caught me. Three of them surrounded me. The rest went up to the dive-boat. Two held my arms and a third one pierced the hose of my regulator with the point of his gun. I heard the hiss of the cyanide gas going into my breathing system. I held my breath of course. I tried to spit my regulator out but they held it in place and waited. The more I struggled against them, the more I needed to breathe. I had no choice. In the end I had to breathe. I cannot begin to describe . . . I cannot . . .'

'And who were these men?' demanded Hatta.

'Pirates,' spat Kei.

'No!' choked Sheri. 'That's just it! They weren't pirates at all! There was only one vessel nearby and it wasn't a pirate ship. It was *Ocean's Bounty*.'

'Precisely!' snapped Kei, a little desperately it sounded to Richard's ear. '*Ocean's Bounty*!' The Inspector gestured through the end wall of the office. In the harbourmaster's office next door there was a window that overlooked the container vessel and the warships still surrounding it. Here there was only a blank wall with a ceremonial Kriss hanging framed upon it. 'Full of cut-throat pirates!'

'I don't think so,' Richard said quietly. 'If you consider a couple of things I think you'll see quite clearly that it was the original crew, not the pirates at all.' He held up one long, steady finger. 'First, the fish we found had been put in glass aquariums and stored in containers. From the looks of things they would have been safe and sound until they reached their destination – except that the containers went over when she ran aground. Pirates wouldn't do that. Only a ship's crew with time and expertise could do that.' A second finger went up. 'And secondly, talking of cut throats, do you have a Kriss to hand? Ah, I see you do.' Richard rose, crossed the room and carefully unclipped the ceremonial dagger from its frame on the wall.

'In spite of its fearsome reputation,' he explained to the stunned policemen, at his most pompous and professorial, 'the Kriss is not a very efficient throat-cutter. As we found out with Parang. If pressed, I believe Robin will agree that although there was a lot of damage to the main veins and arteries in the neck, the rigid cartilage of Parang's epiglottis – part of the voice box – had not been badly damaged.'

Abruptly, he caught up the superintendent's lunchtime drink. 'Look.' He held the coconut against his chest and used the Kriss to slice through its lower section. Both women looked away, for the green nut did in fact look disturbingly like a head. And Richard's re-enactment was hardly the most sensitive way of proving his point.

But it was certainly the most effective. The green outer husk sagged graphically, causing Robin to go almost as pale as Sheri when she all too unwisely glanced back. But the dark hairy solidity of the milk-filled kernel inside the husk remained unscathed. 'It gets through the fibrous outer coating,' said Richard. 'But it doesn't cut the nut itself. Like it got through the soft tissue on Parang's neck but not the windpipe itself. Now, your sergeant's neck was very different, wasn't it, Inspector Kei? The blade that cut poor Suleiman's throat had all but chopped his head off. Through skin, muscles, veins and arteries, windpipe and damn near everything else. Sheri, would you oblige? Your knife?'

He took the diver's knife with its foot-long carbon-steel blade from Sheri's shaking hand and repeated the experiment on the coconut. He was lucky not to cut himself. After one swift lateral stroke, the whole lower section fell open. Husk, nut, everything gaped dramatically wide. And half a pint of thin white milk cascaded all over his shoes.

But his point was made. He placed Hatta's lunchtime drink back on the desk and returned the knife to Sheri. Then he turned back, frowning. 'Well?' he demanded.

'We have to get aboard that ship,' grated Kei. 'As soon as we can and no matter what it costs.'

And Hatta nodded. 'Would you recognize the men who attacked you if you saw them again?' he asked Sheri. 'If we got you on board the *Ocean's Bounty*, and let you look at the crewmen aboard? The masks and regulators wouldn't have disguised them too effectively?'

'I'll know them,' Sheri asserted, her voice a disturbing echo of the vengeful Inspector Kei's. 'Every time I close *my* eyes, all I can see is *their* eyes. Their eyes as the three of them watched me – and waited for me to die.'

THIRTY
Seppuku

Richard and Robin left Sheri going through her evidence once again, confident that the biologist and the policemen were now on the same page, the same team and the same mission. Richard's next mission, prompted by the less-than-happy Robin, was to get the coconut milk off his shoes and trousers before it went rancid and ruined some very expensive clothing.

The Mariners might be sleeping at the Irian Garden Hotel, but they still had their suite aboard *Tai Fun* and the beautiful vessel was moored a ten-minute walk from the police station, down the riverside promenade past the new harbourmaster's building. 'At least they seem to be singing from the same hymn sheet now,' observed Robin as they hurried towards the quayside.

'Yes,' agreed Richard. 'We seem to have a clear view of that whole episode. But it leaves the involvement of the pirates very much more questionable. And as far as I can see makes what happened in the Volcano Roads even harder to understand.'

'Well,' Robin allowed. 'Now that you only have that aspect to focus on, I dare say you'll have it worked out in no time.'

'Famous last words!' he teased.

But as things turned out, she was right.

They arrived aboard *Tai Fun* to find Nic, Gabriella and Sailendra partaking of a light luncheon. As the vessel was safely tied up in dock, the senior officers were available to fill out an unusually lively captain's table. Tom Olmeijer took the head as was his right, with Sailendra on his right and Nic on his left. Then Gabriella sat beside Sailing Master Larsen; Richard beside navigator Eva Gruber and Robin beside Nic to finish the circle.

In the midst of the lively conversation, and in spite of the fact that much of it centred around his exploits of this morning, Richard soon found himself overcome with fatigue. Born, he suspected, of two very active nights whether in the honeymoon suite or not, two early starts and two exhausting days. 'Look,' he said to Robin. 'Why don't we just finish up our meal, then I'll catch forty winks while the stewards sort out this coconut milk, and I'll be ready to go an hour or so from now.'

Robin had spotted several interesting little boutiques on the commercialized riverside promenade, and she knew that Gabriella and Eva, both intrepid shopaholics, would know of several more. So she agreed without a second thought.

Lunch was a light but fiery satay of chicken and prawn served on a light salad of noodles, pea- and peanut shoots. There was a salad of local fruits, and then coffee. Richard, skilled in the art of power-napping as he was in most other things, finished with a fearsome cup of thick black Java tossed back like a measure of tequila. 'Right, I'm off,' he announced to all and sundry. 'I have half an hour before the coffee hits. Get my head down for twenty minutes and I'll be a new man!'

'Oh! That's just what I need,' teased Robin. 'A new man! Can I choose?' But her words fell on deaf ears. Richard was halfway to the door.

The suite was perfectly prepared – cool and dark. Without even bothering to turn on the lights, Richard slipped off his jacket and tie. Kicked off his shoes, unzipped his trousers and put them in the double-door so that the cabin steward could take them and work his magic. Then his shirt went on a bedside chair, followed by socks and underwear, and he climbed into bed. He was asleep the moment his head hit the pillow.

The full effect of the coffee hit Richard's system right on queue twenty minutes later and he sat up, wide-eyed and fizzing with energy. He threw back the bedclothes and climbed out, going automatically into his morning routine. The flat-screen TV on the wall at the foot of his bunk went on, tuned to CNN, and it remained a brightly shifting background, whispering a constant news update as he padded through and stepped into the shower. Five minutes later he returned, towelling himself dry, and stopped dead in his tracks, frowning.

The face on the flat screen was familiar. He reached for the handset and turned up the volume.

'. . . *treating his death as suspicious. But police say they are not looking for anyone else at this stage. Dr Yoshimoto made his reputation*

*working in the field of biological fuel supplements and most recently
he led a study into the most efficient methods of extracting biofuel
from algae. It was for this work that he was nominated for last year's
Nobel Prize, though the eventual winners were the Cambridge Genetics
team led by Professor Blake. A spokesperson for Dr Yoshimoto's
employer, the Greenbaum Corporation, has expressed their shock and
sadness at the news, but it has not yet been possible to reach Nic
Greenbaum himself . . .'*

Richard closed his eyes. He was blessed with a very nearly photographic memory and he knew he had seen that face. But the name
was not familiar and he could not quite identify the occasion . . .

Robin opened the door then, full of shopping plans. She stopped,
surprised to find him still naked, standing staring at the screen.

'What?' she asked.

'This man, Dr Yoshimoto,' demanded Richard. 'Do you know
him?'

'Yes, of course. Well, I never met him, but he was there at
Sailendra's reception. He and Parang were thick as thieves. I
remember I had to drag Parang away from him to get a dance.
Which I have to say was a waste of time in any case. I guess Nic
sent him off home with all the rest. Why?'

'He's just died suddenly. Looks as though there might be something suspicious about the circumstances.'

'Oh! That's terrible! Does Nic know?'

'Apparently not.'

But Nic did know. By the time they found him still at the lunch
table ten minutes later, he was on his cellphone frowning. 'Gabriella,'
he whispered, briefly depressing the SECURE button so he could
talk without his contact overhearing. 'Get my laptop would you?
We seem to have something between an emergency and a crisis
looming.'

The ship's officers withdrew – out of courtesy if nothing else.
But Richard and Robin both had close contacts with the Greenbaum
Corporation. Sailendra had joined in on the finances of the Volcano
Roads project. Nic asked them all to stay, therefore, as he and
Gabriella started to assess what had happened and what implica-
tions it would have for their companies. Nic went on to the internet
first. Gabriella had brought her own laptop and went through a
series of security walls into the corporation's personnel files.

'There seems no doubt poor old Yoshimoto killed himself,' grated

Nic after a while, as he followed up the CNN news cast with Fox and the BBC online news services. 'Seems to have gone home, done the rituals at once and committed *seppuku* right there in his living room.'

'But why?' demanded Gabriella. 'He seemed fine at the reception. What could have happened? Something on the flight back to Tokyo? Something when he got back home to Kagoshima?'

'Did he leave a note?' asked the ever-practical Robin. 'If it was a formal ritual, he must have considered things pretty carefully . . .'

'No details yet,' said Nic. 'Maybe I'd better get over there. Gabriella, first flight out?'

'If he committed *seppuku* in the full ritual, then he must have left a death poem at least,' said Richard suddenly. 'But it can't have been *seppuku*. The police said they aren't looking for anyone else and you need a friend in *seppuku*. To cut your head off after you cut your stomach open. Well, not *off*, precisely . . .'

'God!' said Robin, faintly disgusted. 'It's like being married to the Encyclopaedia Britannica! There are some things, beloved, that we don't want to know – and which I personally don't want *you* to know either.'

'What's *jumonji giri*?' Nic interrupted.

'The explanation,' answered Richard grimly. 'That's the kind of *seppuku* where you *do* do things alone. If anything at all goes wrong then you just sit there in agony waiting to die. He must have felt there was a deep shame involved to have done that.'

'Either that or he had no friends,' observed Robin.

'He was a lonely man. Married to his work,' said Gabriella. 'Parents dead. Only child. No wife or kids. No family at all. No nothing. Unusual for a Japanese man.'

'A secret life?' asked Richard. 'Blackmail?'

'Must have been something pretty terrible,' said Gabriella. 'And there's not a whisper of suspicion on his file.'

'Even so, it's the most likely explanation. Statistically,' said Richard thoughtfully. 'He did something terrible – or thought he had. Just what the secret was – or what he did when the blackmail took hold—'

'But he had nothing worth being blackmailed over!' said Gabriella. 'We paid him well, of course – he was a world-leader in his field. But he lived modestly. His work was all he had that was worth anything as far as I can see.'

'So that's where we would need to look,' said Richard. 'Nic, did he say anything to you about his work when you saw him at the reception?'

'Nothing,' said Nic ruefully. 'But I was preoccupied. We all were.'

'Sailendra?'

'I never spoke to the man.'

'I know. But Parang and he were apparently friendly. Did Parang say anything . . .?'

'Parang?' demanded Sailendra, sounding shocked. He leaned back in his seat, frowning.

'What was his work?' asked Robin.

'Bio energy,' answered Nic and Richard at the same time.

Then Richard sat back like Sailendra, frowning, and let Nic finish. 'Turning algae into fuel. He was working on a formula . . .'

'Oh now, that's almost *incestuous*!' said Robin. 'I mean . . .'

'What?' demanded Nic, surprised by the intensity of her reaction.

'That the world expert on getting biofuel from algae was at a reception only a couple of hundred miles away from a place where Luzon Logging have this amazing new facility that no-one knew anything about, which *just happens* to be turning algae into biofuel. *And* only a couple of days before Sittart makes the big announcement! I mean, *Luzon Logging*! Excuse me, as my darling daughter is so fond of saying. Luzon Logging: Nobel laureates in the fine old art of blackmailing!'

'Parang!' said Richard, leaning forward to look at Sailendra, his gaze at its most piercingly intense. 'Could Luzon Logging have got their claws into Parang?'

'Yes,' answered Sailendra shortly. 'Yes, I'm afraid they could.'

'Enough to make him a conduit at any rate,' said Richard. 'We know he was talking to Yoshimoto. Then he was dancing with Robin. Then he was waiting around down in the garage. Got taken by the pirates, and so forth. But the question, surely, is who was he waiting for?'

'Well? Who?'

'Just before I take a guess at that, I need to just emphasize . . . Look. The pirates were seemingly able to move around the hotel invisibly. The security system had been tampered with. In both the lift and the corridor outside Suite 2020. Who could do that? Why? *Not* a bunch of pirates come ashore with no real plan other than to rescue a boy. They lucked into something else that had been much more carefully prepared for. Something involving Yoshimoto, Parang, the lift man, someone else, and the ambulance – which probably means the doctor or the nurse into the bargain. That ambulance – too much of a coincidence. Linking the one other critical person there with Luzon Logging. Don't you see? It had to be Hilly. Hilly was always going in the ambulance. Always coming here to the clinic – where her brother's life depends on DelMonte Medical. Yoshimoto gave Parang the research Luzon Logging needs to get into the biofuel business. Parang was waiting down in the garage for Hilly to arrive. After the cameras had been "fixed" and the lift man alerted. The doctor, as planned, had called for the ambulance. Hilly was due to take it to the clinic and they were going to pass it all to Sittart. But the pirates muscled in at the crucial moment. The whole thing went to hell in a handcart. Van Leir let them go because he didn't know what else to do. They took anything that looked promising with them and hey presto! Total cock-up!

'I'd lay pretty good odds that poor old Yoshimoto got home yesterday to find a message from Luzon Logging threatening some terrible reprisals because the stuff he was supposed to give them had gone astray. Parang would have been in line for a nasty shock as well, I dare say. But he at least is beyond their reach. And so is Yoshimoto, now. The enormity of his situation must have really hit him then. And out came the *sanbo* table, the *sake* for those four last sips, the *washi* paper for his death poem and the *kozuka* disembowelling blade or whatever. Or a *wakizashi* sword. He has a Samurai name, after all. A pretty famous one at that. And Samurai Bushido pride to go with it. Or he *had* . . .'

'So, oh Oracle,' interrupted Robin. 'Who has whatever Yoshimoto passed to Parang if Hilly hasn't and Sittart hasn't?'

The Sikorsky S 76 luxury helicopter swooped low over *Ocean's Bounty* and Sittart looked down, narrow-eyed, then up at the two men sitting opposite. 'Is the ransom money organized?' he demanded icily, his voice only just audible above the whirring rotors.

'Yes,' answered Dr Jurong. 'It is a fortune of breathtaking magnitude – so many millions of dollars! But it is in place.' He swung round in the deep-padded seat so reminiscent of top-flight first-class airline travel. His shoes squeaked quietly on the deep-pile carpeting. A pair of slim, tight-uniformed attendants stirred at the sound. They were twins and almost identical, a young man and a young woman. They had taken a lot of finding and had cost almost as much as the chopper in the end, if the Sultan was to be believed. But worth it in all sorts of ways. The Sultan's tastes in collections, pastimes and perversions ran far wider than polo ponies and spectacularly endangered fish. 'The Sultan has been particularly helpful. And not just because he has allowed us full use of his helicopter.'

'Thank you, Your Highness,' said Sittart.

The Sultan of Sabah bowed his head regally. 'We have mutual concerns here, old chap,' he said. 'There are items aboard that are of untold value to all of us.'

Sittart nodded coldly. 'I will make sure our people and our . . . ah . . . *associates* in Jakarta continue to expedite matters.' He glanced down at the long, sleek shape of the Sigma Class corvette whose captain had taken command of the situation as soon as he arrived. Whose orders came – intricately but ultimately – from that tower on Del Monte Avenue, even though Sittart himself was here instead of there.

'And the puppets nearer at hand whose strings we pull?' asked Dr Jurong.

'Them too,' answered Sittart gently but chillingly. 'This situation is one I wish to have resolved swiftly and advantageously, no matter what the price.'

'Or who pays it?' suggested the Sultan roguishly.

The flat-screen TV on the bulkhead showed a picture of Yoshimoto. The sound was turned down. They all knew a lot more about what had happened to the scientist than the news services did. And the reasons for his final actions.

Ocean's Bounty and the warships surrounding her fell away beneath them as the helicopter bustled on above the slow green viscosity of the algae-thick water. Twenty minutes later it settled on to the circular helipad that sat on top of the platform co-owned by Bogor Biofuels and Pontianac Oil Enterprises.

Twenty minutes later still, Sittart was alone with the rig manager, his drilling superintendent and the chief geologist. 'I am fed up with all this pussyfooting around,' Sittart was saying – or as near as he could get to the sentiment in his grating Bahasa Indonesia. 'We need to start bringing in some serious oil.'

'But sir,' interrupted the manager, who had been alerted – to put it mildly – by the way the chief bio-engineer had been simply frozen out of the conference. 'We are so close. The drilling we have been doing since we arrived on site has gone about as deep as we dare. If we hit a gusher, there is no telling what damage we might do!

As soon as we get our hands on Yoshimoto's work and perfect our algae treatment plant, then we will be able to—'

'Too much has gone wrong already,' snapped Sittart. 'This foolishness of Yoshimoto's will only complicate matters. Slow everything down, if we aren't very careful. And there are other things in hand that will complicate matters still further but still must be done. A power cut at the polio clinic at the very least. How could that stupid American woman have allowed the pirates to take the one thing she was to protect at all costs? Well, her worst nightmares are about to come true. For her brother and for herself. *Pour encourager les autres*, as the French have it – if for no other reason. I wonder if it is common for women to commit *seppuku* in the United States?' He lingered on the thought and the picture it brought unbidden to his mind. 'Well, she may well wish to end her life before I am through with her,' he snarled at last.

And, he thought, *there will be time for the other woman too. The biologist.*

'What are you all staring at?' he spat – literally, for he had started to drool at the thought of Sheri Aru. 'You will start the drill and proceed at full pace day and night until I bring Yoshimoto's missing files aboard or until you strike oil. And be damned to the United Nations and their Areas of Special Scientific Interest!'

THIRTY-ONE
Ransomed

Sheri's first interview with Superintendent Hatta had not been in the nature of a confession. Hillary Johnson's certainly was. The atmosphere was completely different. Although the damp stain on the floor remained and the Kriss had been returned to its frame on the wall, the coconut was gone. There would be no shenanigans with knives here. Under the law of Pulau Baya, Hilly was allowed up to three friendly witnesses if there could be no lawyer present. She opted for Kalla, Robin and Richard, though none of them felt particularly friendly towards her at the moment.

Hatta recited the litany of time, date, case name and number, and then listed all present. 'So,' he continued. 'Miss Johnson. You wish to explain things to us.'

'Yes,' said Hilly forthrightly. She was looking at Hatta with Inspector Kei standing at his shoulder, but Richard had the distinct impression she was really talking to Kalla, and hoping for some forgiveness there. How did the old hymn go? Richard wondered irrelevantly. *'Ransomed, healed, restored, forgiven: who like thee His praise should sing?'* Yes; that sounded about right.

'It was for Steve,' Hilly began. 'Though Steve knows nothing about it. They said if I didn't help them they would hurt Steve.'

'Who?' asked Hatta quietly. 'Who said this?'

'They never gave their names. They sent pictures of him in the clinic. Photographs in the mail sometimes or clips to my email account. With messages. Which were never signed.'

'I see,' said Hatta. 'Well, we will interrogate your hard drive when we have finished here. Proceed.'

'As far as I can see it was a really simple plan. Mr Greenbaum was bound to invite a range of his top employees to the reception and as the prince's secretary, that list would go to Parang. They were targeting Yoshimoto. I guess if Mr Greenbaum hadn't invited him then Parang would have done so and put him on the prince's guest list. But Parang was the key.'

'And do you know what sort of hold they had on Parang?'

'No more than I know what sort of hold they had over Yoshimoto.'

'The prince and Mr Greenbaum are looking into those questions now,' said Richard.

'As are we,' nodded Kei. 'It is only a matter of time.'

'But the answers are of limited relevance here and now,' said Kalla gruffly. 'We just need to know what Miss Johnson did and why she did it.'

'Indeed,' nodded Hatta. He turned his slightly bulging eyes on Hilly.

'Yoshimoto was to pass something to Parang. Parang was to alert me. I was to take whatever it was . . .'

'A briefcase,' prompted Robin. 'A black leather briefcase. I saw them exchanging it at the reception.'

'And I was to take it down to Doctor Dhakar and wait with her until an ambulance came. Then I would go aboard the ambulance, come here to the clinic and hand it over. It was vital I did that in person. That I went armed. That I guaranteed delivery. Then I would be smuggled back, no-one any the wiser . . . Oh, did I say that they were going to disable the security system so I could come and go undetected? They had placed the lift man as well as the doctor . . .'

'But it all went wrong,' Inspector Kei prompted grimly.

'And then some!' said Hilly. 'To begin with the medical facility was full of bodies, dying or dead. That made the doctor very nervous. Next, Mr Kalla put me in charge of the pirate boy. So he became a part of the whole thing. Then his grandfather showed up and cut Parang's throat. The first I knew about the mess it all turned into was when the doctor turned up at my door herself, with the lift man and a couple of pirates in tow. We all went down to the surgery and got everyone together. Moved everyone through to the garage and waited for the ambulance. Parang didn't last long so they shoved him in the harbour just as the ambulance arrived. I guess it would have been easier to kill off Sheri then too, because she was coming in and out of consciousness and getting to be a bit of a handful. But the doctor wasn't up for any more bloodletting and the old pirate seemed to calm down now he felt he had avenged his son and rescued his grandson. And he kept saying he wouldn't make war on sick women. Though that didn't stop him and his men feeling me up and taking anything they liked the look of – starting with Yoshimoto's briefcase. They had me trussed up like a Thanksgiving turkey and of course they had my gun so I wasn't in any position to stop them. And off we all went.'

'And what happened on the journey?'

'Nothing more. Conversation. They established that the kid was OK. The grandfather talked about getting some kind of financial revenge. Ransom of some kind. They might have mentioned *Ocean's Bounty*. They left us alone. Even the lift guy, who'd come along with us – he was useful as a beast of burden if nothing else. Sheri Aru needed looking after. And we three women couldn't do all the hefting and humping.'

'Very well. We will need to go over that in more detail, when we have finished talking to the doctor and the nurse. But let's move on. What happened when you arrived?'

'I can't really help you there either. I really had no idea what to expect. Anything from a welcome with open arms to a shootout. But these security guys just took over and everything seemed to move really slickly.'

'Mr Van Leir,' prompted Richard. 'We arrived just in time to see the pirates get away.'

'With the briefcase,' observed Kalla. 'I wonder why Van Leir let that slip through his fingers?'

'Didn't realize what it was? Wasn't expecting an ambulance full of pirates, women and witnesses? And we turned up just at the vital moment.'

'Don't ask me,' said Hilly. 'All I knew was that we stopped, the doors opened, everyone who could walk piled out except the doctor and the nurse and the next thing I knew we were surrounded by strangers. Then you guys showed up and that was that.'

'This is most unsatisfactory in any case,' decided Hatta. 'As I say, I will interview the doctor and the nurse. And the ambulance men. And I shall want a detailed description of this elevator operative who seemed to come and go so mysteriously. But much of that will have to wait. There are more urgent matters closer at hand. Not the least of which is a boat full of pirates surrounded by naval vessels sitting in what you Americans call my own back yard.'

'I don't know,' said Richard. 'But I've got an uneasy feeling that things are starting to move pretty rapidly. It's like being in the middle of a storm, you know? In the eye. We've a moment or two of relative calm before things really start going mad.'

'Yes,' said Robin. 'I feel that too. But it's frustrating. I've got this gut feeling that we need to get ready. But I'm just not certain what we need to get ready *for*.'

Richard and Robin were sitting with Nic, Gabriella and Sailendra in *Tai Fun*'s main entertainment area. The accommodation was spacious and, apart from the four of them, empty. Richard had already sent to the Irian Garden for everything that he and Robin had left in the honeymoon suite.

Sailendra leaned forward. 'Yes,' he said. 'I feel it too. It's like the feeling I remember from the hours before Guanung Surat erupted.'

'Yes,' agreed Richard. 'And do you remember, Robin, up the Yangtze a couple of years ago? Just before the earthquake started? Like that.'

Robin looked out across the wide mouth of the Sangsang. 'Except that the birds aren't all going mad,' she said. 'In fact everything out there looks pretty damn peaceful to me.'

And she was right. The sun was just beginning to settle into the lower sky, sending its late-afternoon brightness directly up the Sangsang River itself on top of a gently making tide. A gentle sea

breeze was following the surge of water as it pushed into the wide
arrowhead of the estuary. The windows of the houses, hotels, offices,
hospitals, clinics, all set in the bright green forests on the up-slopes
above the river banks, were shining as though newly gilded. Birds
were winging back from their afternoon forays into the forests
upriver or out into the waters beyond the tide. The ferry left the
southern shore and began to chug across the slick brown surface
of the river.

Robin's cellphone buzzed and she excused herself to answer it.
'Captain Mariner?' The voice was only just recognizable as Sheri
Aru's. The line was truly awful.

'Yes?' answered Robin automatically. It didn't really occur to
her that Sheri had got the wrong Captain Mariner.

'Can you come to the clinic? There's something I want to discuss
with you. Can you come alone?'

Robin looked across at the others clustered around the table,
locked in some critical discussion. 'On my way,' she said.

Sittart brought Van Leir and a local lawyer with him to arrange
Hilly's bail. There was no real difficulty because Superintendent
Hatta had no charges against her major enough to hold her in the
face of legal representation. And in any case, he was a Luzon
Logging man, body and soul.

Hilly was at first relieved when Inspector Kei came down to the
cell to which Hatta had sent her after the unsatisfactory conclusion
to their interview and told her shortly that bail had been posted.
She followed the policeman up the stairs to the main reception area.
In her imagination she saw Kalla waiting for her, grudgingly
forgiving, but ready to welcome her back into his affection and his
organization. So the truth of the matter came as an added shock.
She knew Van Leir slightly – well enough to have some grudging
trust for him. She recognized Sittart from the briefing he had given,
though she knew him from Kalla's files. However, if Van Leir had
not been with him she would have hesitated before accepting either
his assurance that posting bail was no trouble at all or his offer of
a lift over to see Steve in the polio clinic.

'Mr Van Leir assures me that you are a leading member of Mr
Kalla's security team,' Sittart said in his accustomed low tones as
he handed her into the back of the air-conditioned limousine, then
climbed in to sit beside her as Van Leir joined the driver up front.
He spoke English with a strange American twang that made her

think of the Amish farmers and Pennsylvania Dutch. He smelled of sandalwood. 'I am surprised he has not bailed you out himself, though I was surprised to learn Superintendent Hatta was holding you at all. It seems to me that your involvement in this situation was as the victim of a kidnapping and little more.'

'Well,' she temporized, easing away from the earnest man, trying to be subtle about it. She was more than a little repulsed by the way he sprayed her with spittle every time he used the letter 's'. She tried not to think of Gollum, escaped from *The Lord of the Rings* into real life.

'Still, anyone worthy of Mr Van Leir's interest is worthy of Luzon Logging's. After you have talked to your brother, you must contact my head of security. We are always on the lookout. Ah. Here is the clinic now. Did you know that DelMonte Medical is a subsection of Luzon Logging in fact? Oh yes. I shall come in with you if I may, and make the acquaintance of your brother. Stephen, is it?'

'Steve,' she said as she climbed out of the limo, closely followed by Sittart, with the most ridiculous feeling of some dreadful but formless danger sweeping over her.

Robin entered the clinic from the riverside walkway and ran up the stairs to Sheri's room, her mind filled with nothing more than a lively speculation as to why the biologist had called her. Certainly, unlike almost everyone else around her, she had no real sense of danger at all. It seemed likely to her that Sheri had called because she had remembered something important. But why on earth she should want to tell Robin rather than Richard – or even the police – she could not begin to guess. Or rather, she could not begin to guess until she entered Sheri's room.

Sheri was lying face-down on her bed. She was dressed in a light nightgown that was currently bunched up to her waist. A towel was draped decorously over her rear end but it only just covered the slopes of her strong-muscled buttocks. Like the shortest of miniskirts, too minuscule even to pass as the most brazen ballerina's tutu, the towel fell to the creases that crossed the very tops of her thighs. A muscular blonde nurse was working on the right thigh and calf as Robin entered. She looked up, using the back of her right hand to sweep a cow's lick of heavy hair out of her eyes. She nodded at Robin to come on in and then she proceeded, lifting the ankle vertically to massage the calf, inner knee and lower thigh. The sight revealed by the medical procedure explained to Robin at once why there were no men invited to this particular meeting.

'Hello, Sheri,' she said, crossing to the bedhead. 'It's Robin Mariner. What did you want to tell me?'

Sheri's face was white and drawn with pain. Her closed eyes seemed almost sunken and the skin immediately beneath them was dark. Robin suddenly got an all-too poignant view of what it actually cost the intrepid woman to behave in public as she did. She sat down, leaned forward as though the stricken biologist was her daughter lying in the hospital bed, took the left forearm that was crooked beneath Sheri's pillow, and spoke again. 'What did you want to tell me, dear?'

The dark-ringed eyes opened wide. They seemed huge. Dark and fathomless. With nightmares lurking in their shadowy depths. 'It was the way Sister Bright here swept her hair back,' whispered Sheri. 'It triggered off something in my memory.'

'What was that?' asked Robin. 'It must have been important . . .'

'I didn't know what to do; who to tell. I can't stop my treatment. I don't want to say it over the phone. I have this feeling of being watched all the time. I didn't know who else to tell.'

'You did the right thing calling me,' said Robin, at her most reassuring and motherly. 'What is it you remembered?'

'The diver. The diver who held my regulator and waited for me to die . . .'

'Yes, dear?' asked Robin, though she knew in her bones what Sheri was going to say next.

'It was a woman. A woman with long blonde hair.'

And no sooner had Sheri choked the words out than the lights went out. All the power went off, in fact.

Hilly Johnson was sitting beside Steve's bed. Her hand was wrapped in his fist. The flat screen on the wall at his bed-foot was full of pictures of the grounded *Ocean's Bounty* still surrounded by the silently threatening warships. Sitting on the open area cleared when the containers went by the board when she ran aground, was a helicopter. Men were bustling about it, and no doubt the commentators were speculating as to precisely what was going on. But the volume was turned right down.

The room was silent but for the gentle wheezing of Steve's iron lung, and Sittart's breathing, which had gown extremely heavy for some reason Hilly could not understand.

When the lights went off, it was an instant before the shock really registered with her, for there were windows and it was not yet dark outside. And the fact that the lights had flickered and the flat screen dulled did not seem at first so critical. Until Steve's fist closed on her hand with a grip like Death and she realized that the only sound in the room was the sound of Sittart's breathing. And the thunder of her heart.

'Now,' whispered that voice that reminded her so terribly of Gollum, close enough that she could feel the rain of spittle on her cheek. 'You sit there and watch your precious brother for a while. I have someone else to see to . . .'

Dr Jurong stood on the bridge wing outside *Ocean's Bounty*'s command deck with the captain and the captain's wife at his shoulder. He was looking down the full length of the foredeck at the Sultan's helicopter. The Sultan himself, the doctor knew, was in the container they had both bought at such huge expense.

If Jurong closed his eyes he could almost see what the Sultan must be seeing, a small room walled with aquariums. Each aquarium full of priceless, irreplaceable, unique, utterly collectable specimens. Later they would get together and go through the list. What a tragedy the other two containers full of smuggled fish had been lost overboard. What a blessing that the survivor had been theirs.

Dr Jurong blinked, clearing his vision. He focussed instead on the middle distance where the pirates, laden with the massive bundles of US dollar bills he and the Sultan had brought with them, were moving like ants amongst the ill-secured containers, climbing down into their boats. They were moving swiftly and silently, all too well aware that they were still beneath the silent guns of the Corvette, the Frigate and the smaller ships.

Jurong turned to face the captain and his surprisingly attractive Nordic wife, all long blonde tresses and ice-blue eyes. 'The briefcase?' he asked. The captain nodded and handed it over. As agreed, the pirate leader had given it to him the instant Jurong and the Sultan had handed the ransom money to the sulky, red-eyed, swollen-faced boy. He took the slim, smart leather case from the captain now, and was just about to call the captain of the Corvette to arrange the final double-cross of the naive and all too short-lived pirates, when it occurred to him to check the contents. Accordingly he keyed in the code which only he and Sittart were supposed to know, and opened the top.

The case was empty.

He dropped the useless thing on the deck and swung round, mouth open to shout – he just didn't know what to shout. Or to whom.

And then it didn't matter any more.

For the drill of the oil rig struck then. But it did not strike oil. It struck a massive magma chamber lying on the outer edges of the enormous volcanic network that made up the mighty Guanung Surat. The chamber exploded like an underground balloon punctured by a pin. But balloons are full of air which dissipates harmlessly into the atmosphere. The magma chamber was full of molten rock at almost unimaginable pressure, which boiled out of the little hole incredibly quickly. The heat and pressure behind it were enough to keep the first great pulse of magma molten and moving. Unlike the chamber punctured some years ago off Hawaii, the rock did not set and seal itself before it reached the surface. Instead it roared up the borehole like a bullet train coming up a tunnel and fountained up into the rig itself.

The entire platform exploded. The whole of it vaporized in a nanosecond as though there had been a nuclear bomb at its heart. The ocean all around it rose as though the water itself were going to make a volcanic mountain there and then. A ring of force shot out across the Java Sea that very nearly echoed that which had come when the top of Guanung Surat had blown right off. It was therefore the second loudest noise heard in the area since Krakatoa exploded a century ago. And, behind the ring of force, there came a wall of water nearly thirty metres high.

THIRTY-TWO
Wave

It is sometimes said that there is a fourth dimension beyond height, width and depth. That fourth dimension is time. The wave generated by those cataclysmic moments before the leak in the magma chamber sealed itself, was best measured in the fourth dimension. It began at the moment of the explosion as a tsunami thirty metres high, moving in a perfect circle expanding exponentially across the Java Sea. It lasted four minutes to the second.

Although the crest was thirty metres high, the disturbance it caused beneath the surface caused currents like hurricanes beyond fifty metres deep. Yet, because it was perfectly circular in form – to begin with, at least – it was not so easily measured by width. And as for breadth, it was here that time became involved. Because it took four minutes for the explosive leak to seal itself, that was how wide the wave was: four full minutes wide. And because there was enough clear water between the dying oil platform and the outer precipice of the reef for the leading edge to run forward undisturbed for nearly five minutes, the wave had a perfectly parabolic form – to begin with at least. Its profile was shaped like a tall hill with an up-slope at the front that moved forward at nearly a hundred miles an hour and a down-slope following behind it at the same speed, 280 seconds later.

The first thing that the wave encountered was the Sigma Class corvette. Although the wave was four minutes deep, it was nevertheless steep on its leading face. And indeed it was becoming steeper as it encountered the outer edge of the reef. It simply swept over the corvette, therefore, rolling it under and stamping it down like a giant treading on an ant. The two small gunboats stood no more chance. And although the old Tribal Class frigate lasted longer in the heaving maelstrom, it was a matter of moments. And no-one survived.

The leading edge of the wave slid under *Ocean's Bounty* next, lifting the vessel clear of the reef in an instant. By a fluke, the container ship was gathered up a slightly less steep face. She was much larger than the naval vessels, much more heavily laden and consequently steadier in the water. So that when she rolled, she rolled gracefully like a lady.

Dr Jurong had several moments to enjoy the stark terror of his impending death. Deafened and disorientated, he remained aware of the wave only as a great green shadow sweeping out of the sunset on to the tilting deck of the suddenly rolling ship. He saw the Sultan's incredibly expensive helicopter pitch into the water like the toys from the first containers lost overboard. He saw several more containers – the one he co-owned among them – take flight like rats abandoning the proverbial sinking ship. He became aware that the deck beneath him was suddenly impossible to stand upon. He looked back to see the captain and his snow-queen wife go sliding away like skittles on ice and he suddenly found he was following them.

When he hit the safety rail on the outer edge of the bridge wing, by chance he was able to hang there for a second, watching the captain and his wife a few scant metres below. And then, incredibly, several screaming children spilled out of the bridge beside him and rained down upon them like human hail. Then the far side of the bridge exploded inwards as the sheer weight of water shattered the clear-view windows. And the glass-fanged mass of it rained down upon him like a waterfall of razor blades. Screaming, he let go his grip and joined the doomed family below for the last few seconds of their existence.

The Sultan of Sabah was not so lucky. He was standing at the back of the container he co-owned with Dr Jurong looking lustfully up at a particularly striking Rajah Laut when the first great heave of water lifted the whole thing gently off the deck. In the Sultan's hand was a fabulously expensive notepad computer into which he had just keyed nearly 200 species, counted from the glass-sided tanks all around him. There were scorpion fish, stone fish, blue-ringed octopi; two tanks of box jellyfish and two more literally alive with various types of cone shell. And then there were the five containers full of varicoloured sea snakes. But it was the magnificent specimen of Rajah Laut that caught his attention just at the fatal moment when the great wave struck.

The inner lights went out at once. The Sultan turned, not yet terrified, to find that water was cascading in through the open end of the container. The whole thing remained steady for long enough to allow him several steps towards the open door. Then the weight of the water simply swept his feet from under him and washed him helplessly back. By this time the container was floating independently of the stricken ship – floating only in the sense that the water was not yet flooding in fast enough to sink it at once.

Even so, the Sultan, in his Savile Row finery, his double-weave silken shirt and hand-painted tie, his handmade Italian shoes and his personal jewellery by Tiffany's of New York, was being hosed by thick green brine as though he was a fire the brigade had come to put out. The floor of the container fell away and he found himself briefly afloat. Shouting for help at the top of his lungs, he struck out for the door with the rough but powerful technique that had almost earned him a swimming blue. After half a dozen wrenching strokes he realized he was outmatched here. And he vaguely began to wonder why his life was not yet flashing before his eyes.

Then the roof of the container bashed him almost decorously on the crown of his head, like a flunky reduced to unusual measures to attract his august attention. And as it did so, he suddenly felt something moving against him. Something more electrically vital than the water. And he screamed aloud, beginning to try and calculate in his rapidly surrendering mind exactly what rare fish had been imprisoned in the aquariums by which he was surrounded. How many of them were meat eaters? How many of them were poisonous? The container gave a lurch. A wall of fine glass boxes fell on him with stunning force, ballasted as they were with water weighing one kilo per litre. The combination smashed him beneath the surface – and gave him an agonizing glimpse of hope. The current was equalizing as the container filled. There was even a backwash powerful enough to push him almost gently out into the heaving sea.

Surrounded by his trophies and swimming for freedom as wildly as they were, the Sultan fought free of the falling container. He was deep beneath the surface by now – though the surface had been raised by more than thirty metres because of the wave. The blue-ringed octopi headed for the seabed and left him well alone. So did the cone shells. Had the sea snakes wanted a bit of him, the thickness of his clothes and the narrowness of their mouths would have made it impossible.

So it was left to the hammerhead shark to take him. It hit him like an express train. Its great jaws closed around his athletic waist. Row after row of teeth simply desecrated the iguana leather belt with its solid gold buckle, the alpaca of the suit's weave, the Chinese silk of his shirt and the Thai silk of his tie. Not to mention the pampered skin, flesh, bones and organs so elegantly contained within them. The last sound he heard, apart from a distant distorted screaming, was a shockingly intimate crunching sound, which he never quite realized was his ribs. And the hammerhead bit him neatly in half.

When the wave hit the reef it gained in height. Had it been a mere thirty seconds wide, like an ocean roller, say, it would have crested, broken and collapsed into foaming surf. But it was a far more majestic and powerful being than that. And nearly ten times as deep. Instead, its leading edge slowed and its after edge came on so that it narrowed to three minutes wide – then perhaps two – as it rose to a towering forty metres high. Cobb on the beach saw it coming and knew that he was dead. Ridiculously, his last wish

was not for miraculous survival but for a surfboard. There was a
phone on the bar of his kiosk and he snatched it up – not to call
anyone but to get a picture of the monster. But it was far too fast
and he was way too slow. Then it was upon him and he shouted
out with something lost in the wilderness between frustration, joy
and terror.

Distorted by the reef, the wave swung inwards, twisting out of
the perfect circle of its birth. The section above the reef attained
nearly forty-four metres before it exploded against the wooded slopes
behind the beach, throwing spray so high it started a rainstorm like
an eruption from the Guanung Surat. It would have destroyed the
late Dr Jurong's jungle hideaway, but the airborne wave of force
generated by the explosion had arrived at the speed of sound in a
blast wall that had simply shattered it already. Still, the deluge of
water from the in-wash of the wave and the downpour of the rainstorm was enough to dislodge the stout top of the desk Sittart had
sat at to admire his secret naked pictures of Sheri Aru. Leaving the
shattered remnants of its legs in the hollow wreckage of the house,
the desktop was whirled like a leaf above the treetops to fall on to
what little was left of Cobb's beach.

And it was this, they determined later, that the dying Cobb was
able to cling to in the roiling backwash of the aftermath. So that he
nearly got his wished-for surfboard after all. And so he did not die.

The outer edge of the wave, however, ran on south of the reef
and west into the mouth of the Sangsang River. The tide beneath
it was still sluggishly on the make. The outwash of the river itself
did not really get to grips with the massive inrush for a couple of
miles upstream past the heart of Bandar Seri. And so as it ran
through the midst of the town itself, the wave remained thirty metres
high. And four full minutes deep.

Richard was in his cabin when the oil platform went up. His
windows looked out over the harbour and the reef so he actually
saw the moment of the cataclysm. He – perhaps he alone – saw
the column of white-hot rock that suddenly soared skyward like a
searchlight beam for an instant. He realized that it was rising through
the middle of the distant platform like a rocket lifting off. A feeling
deep within him warned that whatever was going on here would
end in something overwhelming – though at this stage he wasn't
sure what. He hurled himself into action before his reeling mind
really registered what he had seen. He was out through the cabin
door – with the solid portal mercifully slammed tight shut behind

him – when the wave of force blasted the windows across his cabin like shrapnel from a bomb. Even so, the blast wall blew him twenty feet forward along the deck as the tall masts above him reeled like saplings in a gale.

Then he was on the bridge. 'Full power!' he was screaming. 'We need full power now!'

Captain Tom Olmeijer knew better than to argue. He hit the engine room telegraph and shouted the order into the mic that communicated with the engine room as he did so. The chief was shocked by the order to come to full revs without the usual warnings and procedures – especially as *Tai Fun* was still tied up in dock. But he recognized the captain's voice and the urgency it contained, so he hit all his starter buttons without a second thought, yelling, 'Full ahead all,' into his own mic as he did so.

The water under *Tai Fun*'s counter boiled. She strained at her mooring ropes, trying to turn her head and swing out of the dock. A couple of dock-workers who had unaccountably both fallen over at once picked themselves up. Although it sounded as though there was thunder somewhere nearby in the clear blue of the evening sky, they heard the bellow of Richard's barbarous Bahasa Indonesia calling, 'Let go all,' and mercifully, they obliged. The tall, elegant ship began to back out of her berth at once.

The wave had been twisted out of shape by the interaction with the reef. The effect of this on the section that ran round the south of the reef and into the dock area on its way towards the river-mouth was to make its leading face lean back. The wave became shallower, if longer. Its angle of attack went from head-on, coming in at ninety degrees to the shore to an angle of sixty degrees. The north end of the dock surrendered first as the great wave swept unstoppably in. It ripped up rank after rank of quays and piers, beginning to waste some of its energy upon them as though they had been breakwaters put there for the purpose. It tore ships and boats of all sorts up out of their moorings, rolled them over, threw them bodily into the dockside warehouses and into the city streets beyond as it heaved relentlessly ashore, half as high again as the tallest of the houses.

Tai Fun's dock was the southernmost – little more than a low pier leading out into the bay as though it was trying to extend and contain the mouth of the Sangsang. The section of the great wave that arrived in the docks here swept in under that foaming counter and lifted the racing vessel bodily over the pier and out into the width of the estuary itself.

Here the physics of the seawater's motion changed utterly. Right to the very point of land where the harbourmaster's new office stood – stood briefly until the wall of wreck-fanged liquid almost literally tore it from its foundations – there had been the slopes of the island's shore. The wave had gathered up against these, the down-slope of its after edge pushing the up-slope of its face relentlessly and destructively inwards like the rear of an army keen to attack an enemy the front ranks feared to engage. But abruptly, where the Sangsang opened, the resistance suddenly vanished. The great wave seemed to settle back; its up-slope became shallower still as a new section opened in the twisting circle, bowing out into the estuary itself. Its crest sank to twenty-five metres and, with *Tai Fun* racing across its inner slope, it hurled itself upriver.

Richard had wedged himself in the command bridge door because he needed the widest possible view if he was going to help get the ship out of whatever was happening here. He therefore saw the wave coming. He watched, frozen, as his mind strove to cope with what he was experiencing. He saw the crest of it rising unstoppably against the sky as it hurled forward with a sound that would have drowned out a thunderstorm. He saw the uprush of foam that reached the clouds above Cobb's beach. Saw the solidity of the massive heave come hurling out of the skirts of the downpour, turning everything before it into kindling and splinters like a rolling barrage from some distant cannons. He saw the far side of the docks consumed, and the buildings behind them swept away inland on the mountainous bosom of the thing.

And even as Richard registered this, the cataclysm came pouncing forward at a mind-numbing speed. Rank upon rank of solid wooden pier exploded upwards. The vessels secured to it tore themselves shorewards, smashing into the roofs of houses well inland. Chunks of concrete the size of trucks flew like hail, some sailing inland from the docks, some washing back out of the houses.

Richard felt the leading edge reach under *Tai Fun*'s racing hull. Felt the beautiful vessel lift and start sliding wildly out into the estuary. Felt her hesitate, bobbing gamely as the physics of the disaster seemed to change. He saw the harbourmaster's office take off like Dorothy's house in *The Wizard of Oz* and vanish into the roaring jaws of the monster, utterly destroyed in an instant. Then *Tai Fun* too was off as the full weight of the wave seemed to claim her. Richard's stomach heaved as though he was caught in the fastest

elevator ascent in history. The wind howled into his face as the wall
of foam-laced water seemed to hesitate beside – above – him and
then decide it didn't want to come aboard after all.

So, with Richard wedged in the doorway, *Tai Fun* went racing
forward at full speed across the slope of the twenty-five-metre
wave that was washing upriver at more than sixty miles an hour,
pushing *Tai Fun* sideways as it did so. Sideways past the police
station; sideways past the Irian Garden Hotel; sideways past the
polio clinic, dragging its four-minute width behind it. And it was
only when he saw the hotel away on the southern shore far ahead
explode into the fangs of the foam that Richard thought about the
clinic on the northern shore behind him. And began to wonder
about Robin.

THIRTY-THREE
Breath

Hilly was sitting, seemingly as powerless as her surround-
ings, listening to her brother losing his terrible fight for
breath, when the oil platform exploded. Van Leir's left hand
was like iron on her shoulder. The ice-cold muzzle of his gun had
been pressed to the back of her head since she had first, briefly,
fought to get free of him. To add to the brutal agony of her situation, the departing Sittart had rolled an oxygen tank into a beam
of bright red evening sunlight on the far side of the bed and left
its mask dangling just beyond Steve's reach.

The wall of force that came smashing through the air at
the moment of the explosion moved at the speed of light. It therefore arrived some time before the sound. And nearly five minutes
before the wave itself. It hit the back of the clinic in utter and unexpected silence. Only when the incredible power of it smashed all
the north-facing windows at the front of the building and ripped
several sections of the roof free did any sound really begin. The
building shook as though suddenly in the middle of an earthquake.
The crash of shattering windows was echoed by the noise of glass-
ware, silverware, steel and crockery all tumbling off shaking shelves.
The shuddering and shattering was followed by a cacophony of

screams as staff and patients alike found themselves swept by crystal shrapnel almost as deadly as Kei's firestorm sweeping the pirates off *Tai Fun*.

Van Leir staggered as the floor heaved and he turned, his grim concentration on the weeping woman and her choking brother broken by the mayhem immediately outside. Hilly went for his gun hand like a crazed wildcat, all her combat training forgotten in an instant. Both hands clawed at the security man's wrist. Her teeth fastened on the bony flesh between her grasping thumbs. The gun went off at once, the flat report adding to the loud confusion all around. The bullet punched a splintered hole into the floor at the foot of Steve's bed. Gun smoke billowed and suddenly all three of them were choking.

Through clenched teeth, in spite of the blood in her mouth, Hilly was screaming almost uncontrollably. Partly because the gunshot had come near to bursting her left eardrum. Partly also because Van Leir was punching her as hard as he could with his left fist.

Van Leir at last succeeded in tearing his gun hand free of the stunned and screaming Hilly. He stepped clear and brought the bleeding fist up. Blood was pumping from his bitten wrist but the weapon hardly shook at all. 'Little change of plan,' he said flatly. 'You die first after all.'

When the lights flickered and the power died, Robin crossed to the window and looked out, frowning, as though the answer to what was going on might be found in the broad reach of the calm estuary. She noticed that the ferry was midstream, that there were some little skiffs and cockleshells out, fishing probably. There was no hint in the peaceful scene of anything untoward at all. And yet her blood was running cold and there was the most disturbing sinking feeling in the pit of her belly.

The first she knew of the platform's explosion was when a section of the roof flew out across the river like a big square bird, dissolving into beams and slates as it went. At once, the room began to shake and there was the most almighty sound of breaking glass. Robin had the strangest feeling that the double glazing of the big French windows, which opened out on to the balcony, was flexing like a soap bubble being blown by a child.

She stepped back, turned. Someone somewhere started screaming. Someone else joined in. *Everyone* else, it seemed, joined in. Robin took another step towards Sheri's bed, which seemed to have become possessed – it was skittering across the floor as the nurse stood, her hands raised, watching her patient being spirited away. And somewhere, just beneath their feet, a gun went off.

At the sound of the gunshot, Robin was in motion. Time and again, she and Richard had faced dangerous situations and he had always been so specific. *'You know life isn't like the movies, darling,'* he would say. *'People who look for trouble usually find it. And trouble with guns means people shot and killed. Stay away from it. Run. Hide. Close your eyes and pray. But don't ever go looking for it.'*

On this occasion, the fact that she took no notice of his wise advice at all in fact saved her life. For as she went out of one door, Sittart came in through the other. He was armed and insane. He had a silencer on the barrel of the gun he used to kill the nurse as he entered, so, although Sheri heard it, Robin did not. And she did not find out until later that she would have been shot through the head at once as well.

Robin ran down a flight of stairs that took her directly to the room beneath, where she thought the gunshot must have come from. The room that housed Hilly's brother Steve. And someone in there was screaming in a high, weird, deeply disturbing tone. Wordlessly, as though through clenched teeth. It was only when she actually had her hand on the doorknob that her common sense caught up with her. She went down on one knee and leaned back as she swung the door wide.

There was an immediate shot and Robin hurled herself flat on the floor, suddenly finding it almost impossible to breathe. There was the most enormous roaring in her ears – so loud and relentless that she thought her racing heart must be about to burst. She did not raise her reeling head until she heard the thud of a body hitting the floor and a very masculine shout of pain. The she risked a quick look into the room.

Hilly was standing, choking, stricken at her brother's bedside. Jahan Jussif Kalla was standing behind her with a gun still smoking in his fist. And, level with Robin herself, Van Leir was writhing on the floor, clutching what looked to be his badly broken calf. It was the sight of Van Leir's gun lying safely against the wheels of an oxygen trolley nearby that galvanized Robin into action. But by the time she had picked herself up and staggered into the room she had realized that it was not the firearm that was vital.

She kicked the gun aside and rolled the trolley to Steve's bedside. She grabbed the facemask and pushed it into place, turning the pressure on full as she did so. It was only when the gas started to inflate his chest that she reached over to slip the strong elastic strap round the back of his skull, holding the mask tightly in place. She lifted the bottle off the trolley and put it on the bed itself, so there would be a minimum of strain on the tubes connecting Steve's face-mask to it. She looked up into Hilly's overflowing eyes. 'CPR,' she said. 'Keep it up until the power comes back.'

'If it comes back at all,' said Kalla. 'Have you seen it out there? It's mayhem. Blast damage like you wouldn't believe! The oil plat-form out in the bay just blew up like a frigging atom bomb.'

'*What?*' Robin froze for just an instant. She was a seafarer and Kalla was not. She knew water and the simple physics of hydraulic forces by experience as well as by education and training. She saw at once the implication of his words where he simply had no idea. 'Jesus! Hilly! Kalla! We need to get up to high ground! As high as we can!'

It had never occurred to Sheri in the wildest of her nightmares that a single shot would make a gun barrel so hot. But the heat of it as Sittart traced it up the back of her naked thigh was almost like a branding iron. He was standing where Sister Bright, the nurse masseuse, had stood before he blew a good deal of her brain out through her forehead. Her corpse was now lying like a bundle of dirty washing at his feet. One hand was holding Sheri ruthlessly in place, forcing her face into the pillow, while the other trailed the gun barrel up her leg and on to the right cheek of her bottom. Pushing the modest towel away. Wandering up almost to her hip, then down over the dimple above her buttock. He was talking quietly, wandering from one language to another, to a third and back again, raining her burning nakedness with drool and spittle almost as hot as the spray of blood and tissue had been, making very little sense indeed.

But when the second gunshot rang out from the room below, Sittart's multilingual muttering stopped. 'Miss Johnson *and* her brother,' he said distinctly in his oddly accented English. Sheri bucked spasmodically, but he held her fiercely still, smothering her ruthlessly until she quietened. 'Let's hope they rest in peace,' he continued as though she hadn't moved or fought him at all. As though she had sat there completely within his power and listened like a good little girl.

'But no,' he corrected himself at once. 'Let's hope they don't rest in peace at all. Let's hope there is an afterlife for her at least. Full of red-hot pokers and such.'

The hot circle of the gun barrel settled on the point of her coccyx, where the base of her spine curled into what would have been a tail, lost long ago through Natural Selection. There was a crisp click as he cocked the weapon. 'The first one should go here, I think,' he whispered. 'But not quite yet. Let's savour the power of the moment a little, shall we?'

Hilly and Kalla grabbed Steve and the air bottle. For reasons she would never really understand, Robin kicked aside the Glock on the floor and grabbed Van Leir – though she suspected that she would be far better taking his gun and leaving him. She hauled him to his feet, though only one of them was working at the moment. Then, using all her wiry strength, she dragged him out into the stairwell behind Kalla, Hilly and Steve. 'Go up, *go up!*' she bellowed over the gathering thunder outside. 'And keep going no matter what!'

Something clattered down the steps beside her and she realized that it was surprisingly bright in here, especially as the power still seemed to be out. With Van Leir's arm draped over her shoulder and round her neck like a scarf, she looked up. The stairwell immediately above opened on to a landing outside Sheri's door – then went on up again. Like the landing below them, Sheri's had a solid, square double-glazed window that looked out across the Sangsang River. Robin did not waste her time looking at the view now. She looked on up above her head instead.

The stairwell should have ended in some kind of door opening out on to the roof, Robin realized. But of course! She had seen the roof flying away over the river. How long ago had that been? Four minutes? Five? The stairwell opened on to the evening sky now.

Except that for a flickering millisecond the whole of her upward view was darkened by a strange green shadow. As though a huge, thick sheet of bottle glass was passing in front of the setting sun.

'NOW!' she screamed at the top of her lungs.

The whole clinic jumped forward towards the river. Robin twisted as she fell helplessly and landed on Van Leir.

The clinic jerked back again and then jerked left towards the inland mountain peaks. There was a vibration running through the fabric of the place strongly enough to make their teeth start chattering. And probably a groaning sound to go with it – but it was lost in the overwhelming torrent of all the other sounds around them. Then it leaned, like the deck of a heeling ship that was just beginning to roll.

But by the time Robin registered the second lurch and the strange new angle of what should have been a perpendicular stairwell, she was up to her waist in water. Now she did risk a glance out of the window on Sheri's landing. It was full of foaming water, like a porthole in a diving submarine. And she realized that the whole of the clinic around her was behaving exactly like the *Titanic* – and seemed to be sinking fast.

In his increasingly lurid fantasies during the last days and hours, Sittart had calculated that the moment before the beginning of her death would be the worst moment of Sheri's life. Naked and helpless, dominated by someone unimaginably more powerful than she, her legs useless and her crutches beyond reach, he would allow her to understand the full depth of her helplessness – and then he would begin to kill her.

The shot through the base of her spine would be the prelude. The perfect beginning in a number of ways – each one more deliciously perverted than the last. Then there would be a lingering sequence of assaults that would make her more agonizingly helpless still – and Sittart himself more rampantly powerful. Until she was finally dead, he was utterly satisfied, and the poor pathetic creatures who ran this place with his permission and at his command, cleaned up the mess and swore themselves to eternal, terrified secrecy.

Sittart leaned forward, putting his full weight on the gun as he ground it into her tender flesh, feeling the glorious, delirious insanity of Caligula, able to do *anything* to *anyone*.

And then his whole world lurched forward. A massive vibration shuddered through the room. The bed and the woman on it started skittering wilfully away from him. 'STOP!' he ordered, but even as he did so he realized the sound of his voice would be lost in the unimaginable roaring all around him. He looked out of the big French windows with their almost unbreakable double-glazing and saw that the balcony outside, which had once stood ten clear metres above the river, was awash with foaming water that seemed to be rising exponentially.

Surprisingly close at hand, appearing to swoop magically into the air as he watched, bemused, a beautiful four-masted ship seemed to be sailing away across the river, its stern towards him. But the open end of the shattered poop was level with his open mouth. The pair of them gaping at each other. Then the ship was gone, slipping sideways upstream at an incredible rate. Seemingly propelled by a mountain of thick green shadow. There and gone in a heartbeat. The picture of it was burned into his memory for the rest of his life.

Still battling to keep firm hold of the woman he was fighting to control, he looked back in and focussed his disbelieving gaze down the length of the heaving room. As the door into the stairwell burst open, letting a wall of water wash in; a strange indoor offshoot of the liquid enormity racing past outside. 'No!' shouted Sittart. 'Stay back!'

Suddenly he felt more like Canute than Caligula.

He raised his gun from Sheri's naked back and actually shot at the oncoming wave as it boiled relentlessly in through the door. Then the water swept his feet out from under him and, although the French windows, and the wall they were set in, held miraculously firm against the massive forces sweeping past, the balcony outside was ripped from its footings. And then the entire floor gave way.

THIRTY-FOUR

Air

The DelMonte Medical King Jayavar Memorial Polio Clinic might have been located in an old building, but it had been recently refurbished. As a public building designed to house vulnerable people with mobility problems on a volcanic island in the middle of an earthquake zone, some of the floors might have been a little suspect, but the stairwells, super-strengthened when the new lift shafts went in beside them, would withstand the end of the world.

Robin looked up as the roaring water rose over her head, shooting up towards the sky like a geyser. But the sky was gone in an instant and Robin found herself holding her nose and blowing, trying to equalize the pressure in her ears. And the vision of the wreckage being whirled across the square of dull green light that was all that remained of the opening on to the roof convinced her that they had better stay here and follow some of Richard's sage advice. Even if it was a case of too little too late. She started to pray, but she was never really going to consider closing her eyes.

Van Leir ran out of air first, for he was in shock from Kalla's gunshot in his leg, and had been breathing swiftly and shallowly, not really registering more than the overpowering pain he was in. As she saw the desperation entering his lean, drawn face, Robin pressed her mouth to his and gave him the kiss of life.

This isn't going to work too well if we're submerged for any length of time, she thought as he filled his lungs with her breath and settled for the moment. *What we really need is a scuba tank.*

But then Kalla tapped her on the shoulder and she turned to see Hilly's mouth fastened over Steve's and the big security man offering her the bubbling facemask from the oxygen bottle.

At the first splash of icy foam, Sheri took the deepest breath of her entire life. A second later she was under water. The mattress was wallowing somewhere between her and the madman with the gun while the iron frame of the hospital bed went down like a lead-weighted stone. Her crutches followed much more slowly, strangely buoyant. Sheri paid them no more attention. She was in her element, and as much at home as any fish. She swirled away from the clinging bedclothes, narrowed her eyes in the gloom and tried to see what was happening.

Even her nakedness was an advantage now, for she saw at once how Sittart was simply strait-jacketed by the expensive clothing he had on. His shirt and jacket bulged and bubbled, slowing his every movement. His shoes and trousers not only slowed him but also weighed him down, pulling him relentlessly through the shadowy space where the floor had been.

On the other hand, Sheri moved with the ease of a hunting seal. She only had to be careful of her all too vulnerable skin in the face of the shattered planks, splintered shelves and shards of other wood-work which were still whirling about as the incalculable pressures equalized within the hollow shell of the sunken building.

She was wearing her watch – waterproof to 100 feet and guaranteed to keep going long after its owner drowned, as she was fond of saying. She guessed it had been about half a minute since the floor gave way. She'd better start looking for a way to get out, find the surface, or lay her hands on a scuba set soon, she thought.

But she knew her limitations and began a mental count. She could hold her breath for four minutes at a pinch. She needn't start panicking for another two minutes or so, all things being equal.

But things were not equal. Sittart grabbed her ankle then and she nearly lost a good deal of precious air in a scream of surprise. But she controlled herself and looked down at him. She could see only his vague, unfocussed shape as she had no facemask or goggles. She could see enough, however, to understand that he was fighting to bring the gun round, still driven by his mad desire to shoot her at point-blank range. She kicked him in the face as hard as she could. Even the pain of wrenched muscles in her thigh, groin and belly had a certain satisfaction to it as her instep connected with his nose as though she were a footballer taking a penalty. His grip broke and she whirled away, looking for an escape route.

She saw a door gaping invitingly in front of her and went into it like an eel into a cave mouth. It was the door into the opposite stairwell to the one that Robin was in. Apart from the fact that it was empty, it was identical. Sheri began to swim upwards towards the square of brightness leading out on to the roof. But like Robin, she hesitated. Even with the limited vision she had underwater, she could see the tornado of deadly debris whirling above the stout shell of the building. And much more acutely than the huddled group of well-clothed people in the stairwell opposite, she could feel the dangerous tugging of the currents intensifying as she rose. She didn't need to see the madness outside the stout little landing windows or through the hole in the roof above to know the force of the water. And understand the way it was threatening to suck her out of the protection offered by the thick walls and into the deadly maelstrom the better part of twenty metres above.

She checked her watch. Two minutes. Two more to go. One more before she really started running into trouble. Now where in the name of Allah could she find something that would allow her to breathe? The only place she could think of was the kitchen. Surely the kitchen would be full of pots and pans – some of them very big indeed – many of them with lids that might stay secure, even in the face of this. She up-ended with a practised flip and started pulling herself down the stairwell, hand over hand along the banister. As she passed the door again she looked in. This was a foolish thing to do, but she had never received the benefit of Richard Mariner's wisdom on the subject.

Sittart was immediately inside the room, swimming forward with the gun already levelled. He fired at once and would have killed her on the spot but for the fact that the density of the water all but stopped the bullet, and the wetness flooding into the chamber after the shot made the whole thing seize. Sittart threw the useless weapon at her and at once began to panic, his mad fixation over and his air all gone.

Sheri turned in a swirl of long dark hair and pulled herself on down. She didn't need to consult her watch to know that she was passing from the third minute into the fourth. At the bottom of the stairwell she slid out through the doorway into a wilderness of wreckage. She grabbed the nearest solid-looking thing – one of a series of bed frames lying scattered amid the debris on the floor – and started to pull herself in what she hoped was the direction of the kitchen.

But she saw at once that she would never make it. The destruction was just too total. Her progress was simply going to be too slow. And if she let go of the bed frame and started to swim, her body would drift upwards relentlessly, buoyed by the air in her lungs. Until there was no more air in her lungs. Then she would sink to the bottom, like all of the other dead people here.

That was when the panic hit.

But even as it did so, she saw something that struck her as being at once strange and strangely familiar. It was the long tubular shafts of her crutches. They were standing upright but inverted, with the round rubber stoppers of the ferrules pointing at the distant ceiling and the arm clips just brushing the debris on the floor. And she understood at once why they had been so reluctant to sink. Why they were standing upright now.

There was air trapped inside them.

Suddenly flushed with hope, she pulled herself across towards them, her pain and panic forgotten, really expecting that she would pull the ferrule off each one and fill her gaping mouth with the life-giving air trapped inside them.

But she never had to try. For as the fourth minute of her underwater ordeal went past she discovered the truth of the great wave's breadth. Even as she reached the crutches, the water began to wash away. But as it did so, of course, the fabric of the clinic, which had remained miraculously steady when filled with water, began to surrender to gravity with no support but thin air to hold it up.

Although the base was four minutes broad the wave was shaped in a ballistic curve; the top was thinner, and the time it remained was shorter. Robin's head broke through the surface before Sheri's,

therefore, simply because she was higher in the wave. She felt the
weight of the water sucking down the chimney of the stairwell as
the down-slope of the wave's back swept past. As she emerged it
felt to her as though she was caught in the middle of a whirlpool,
for the trapped water could not just sweep upriver like its liber-
ated brother outside. It had to move vertically, cascading down
stairs, flooding out through gaping doors because the solid walls
would not let it past. The sudden change in the physics caught the
window on the lower landing at last. Robin heard one distant, half-
understood shattering sound as the heavy water smashed its way
out through the double-glazing at last.

But at least Robin's face was filled with cool evening air as the
water drained away. Her body attained weight even as her clothes
became icy. The oxygen tank that had rested so lightly on her instep
as Steve was force-fed air suddenly came near to breaking her foot.
Her eyes cleared and she realized her ears were water-clogged. And
her nose wrinkled automatically at the strange, seriously misplaced
sea stench all around her.

Without the support of the water, the chimney of the stairwell
wavered slightly, and Robin cleared her throat. 'Better go down,'
she suggested, and led the way immediately. Van Leir had
suddenly put on more weight than seemed fair or natural too, but
she toiled downwards, following the departing swirl of water until
at last there was nowhere else to go. She sat Van Leir on the
bottom step and looked up. Hilly, Steve and Kalla collapsed on
the next few steps above, their heads and shoulders framed in the
gap where the landing window had simply been torn out of the wall
and washed away upriver. And they would probably have stayed
like that, but for the crashing and the screaming immediately
outside.

As it was, the moment the strange sounds started, Robin pulled
herself to the door and looked out into what had once been the
reception hall of the clinic. It was a mess of wreckage seemingly
full of corpses now. But there in the middle of it stood Sheri, stark
naked, fighting to get her crutches in place and find somewhere to
hide as the walls around her began to cave in.

Robin swung round, her mind racing.

The north wall of the clinic fell outwards. This was merciful if
unexpected – it had been the wall that had received the incoming
blast of the explosion and the inward rush of the wave running
across the docks. But as the last of the water drained away upriver,

the north wall fell outwards across the parking area and into what little was left of the square beyond. The noise it made galvanized Sheri. She started fighting to get her heavy, sluggish body up and moving – she just didn't know where she was going to move to or how she was going to move through the dripping mess of corpse-strewn wreckage she was trapped in. *First things first, girl,* she thought to herself as she started to get herself mobile. She was utterly unaware that she was shouting at herself with every shuddering breath she took.

But then, out of the only doorway left standing anywhere nearby, came a simply beautiful man. He was more than two metres of perfectly moulded mahogany flesh in a light cotton shirt that might as well have been painted on to his torso. He stepped through the wreckage as though striding across his own back yard and he made his way to her side. He looked her straight in the eye and he said, 'I don't know if we've been introduced, but my name is Jahan Jussif Kalla, and I'm here to help you, ma'am.'

Then, before she could say or do anything, he took her under the arms and swung her over his shoulders like a child. With the crutches dangling from their clips up by her elbows, she simply locked herself around him. He strode back to the doorway with her riding on his back, exulting in the way his flesh seemed to burn against her, filling her entire being with warmth and energy. She did not feel naked or ashamed; she did not feel powerless or patronized. She felt like one generation described by the Greek philosophers, riding on the shoulders of another.

Inside the door she recognized Hilly immediately. The desperate woman was focussed on force-feeding oxygen into her brother's flaccid chest, though he looked to Sheri to be dead already. The iron lung lay on the steps beside him, useless in the face of the lack of power. The other man there was also fainting, his face pale and drawn, his eyes closed.

Robin was more careful of Sheri's modesty than the dazzled disorientated young biologist was. She eased Van Leir's jacket off his shoulders and down his arms. The wounded, half-drowned man stirred and seemed to be fighting her for a moment. But he had lost a lot of blood and the pain had weakened him. In a moment she had freed the garment. Then she offered it to Sheri who slipped it on and buttoned it up. 'Oh!' she said, shocked. 'It's freezing!'

But her words were lost in a rumbling crash as the riverside wall of the clinic fell in. There were three full storeys of it. Each one weighted with double-glazed French windows in heavy aluminium frames. The noise was colossal. The impact shattering. Even the all but indestructible stairwells wavered.

'We can't just sit here,' Robin decided. 'We have to find a way out.' She looked up at the gaping hole in the wall where the window had been and dismissed it for the time being. Outside there, she calculated, would be a vertical wall reaching in a little cliff of brick straight down into the river. She had seen the wooden walkway that had once been secured to it wash away. She would need to be very desperate indeed to lead a man in an iron lung, a man with only one functioning leg, a girl on crutches, plus the exhausted Hilly and Kalla over that twenty-foot drop into the river.

Instead, she went down to the inner door and looked across the inner area of the clinic. All she saw at first was the sort of thing her children had studied in history books dealing with World War Two. It was a perfect bombsite. Mounds of brick and shattered glass lay strewn as far as she could see from the open riverside to the empty car-strewn square inland. On the far side of the wreckage, a kind of mirror image of where she was herself, the opposite stairwell stood like a tall square chimney pocked at regular intervals with gaping doorways, leaning against the eastern wall. And even as she looked, two things happened. In the upper-most doorway, thirty feet and more above her, there appeared the figure of a man. He stood there, framed – almost crucified – his bald head glistening, his pale suit looking like soiled tissue paper wrapped around him. It took a moment for her to recognize Professor Satang Suang Sittart.

And, in the moment that it took her to understand who it was away up there, the whole crazy chimney of the stairwell toppled sideways, taking the third wall of the clinic with it. It fell out towards the river, like a tree felled by a logger's axe, bending as it went into an almost perfect bow. Over the twenty-foot brick cliff of the riverside and down into the heaving Sangsang with a rolling thunder of noise and spray. The destruction of the eastern side of the building opened up Robin's view exponentially, for none of the buildings along the riverside had been renovated like the clinic. None of them was standing now. When the wall went down, Robin could suddenly see as far as the jungle-clothed hill slopes and the distant watershed peaks beyond where the River Sangsang was born.

And there, nosing in through the wall of water thrown up by the falling wall and stairwell, pitching over the waves that raced upriver in the wake of the huge wave she had already conquered, came *Tai Fun*.

THIRTY-FIVE
Plank

R ichard had been standing in the forepeak with his hand against the furled foresail foot, straining his eyes and praying ever since he had managed to turn *Tai Fun* and bring her safely down the back of the heaving in-bound wave. A pair of binoculars dangled round his neck, but just at the moment he was trusting his naked eyes.

Richard was by no means alone up here – Captain Tom Olmeijer had ordered a keen lookout, all too well aware that the waters they were sailing would now be full of dangerous rubbish and wreckage. And Richard, who had been involved in the terrible flooding of the Yangtze after the Three Gorges dam burst a couple of years ago, knew exactly what the dangers to the delicate hull might be. Sailing Master Larsen was at one shoulder – surplus to requirements because they were proceeding under power. So was navigating Officer Gruber – also temporarily useless on the bridge because the wave would have negated all of her river charts. The three of them all had Bluetooth headsets in constant communication with the command bridge behind and above them. Everybody else aboard who wasn't vital to the conning of the vessel – and that included Nic, Gabriella and even Sailendra himself – was preparing the medical facilities as best they could to welcome aboard any homeless, lost or injured people that they found. And Richard, for one, was expecting hundreds – if not thousands.

The toppling chimney of the clinic's stairwell was the first sign of life Richard saw. Because of this, he pressed the binoculars to his eyes and, as the spray cleared, he surveyed the utter destruction of what had been the polio clinic. Given his relationship – such as it was – with Sheri, Steve and Hilly, he would have been careful to look there in any event, just in case. And what he saw made his heart leap. There, framed in the lower doorway of the last standing remnant of the place was the unmistakable glitter of Robin's golden curls. Suddenly feeling he was drowning in the thick and stinking air, he called, 'SURVIVORS! I see survivors! Can we come starboard hard against the shore?'

'Is that second tower safe?' demanded Tom's voice in his ear. 'I don't want *Tai Fun* anywhere near that one if it goes as well.'

'Robin's there, Tom,' said Richard, his voice trembling. 'I don't know who else . . .'

At once *Tai Fun* swung right and began to approach the vertical cliff of the brick-clad shore. Richard was scanning the shoreline, looking for a likely landing place. But all he could see was the square gape that must at one time have contained a window. And then Robin was there, framed against the darkness, waving for all she was worth. Reluctantly, Richard dragged his gaze away from her, checking the square column of brickwork towering above her. It seemed steady enough for the moment, he thought. But his mouth was dry and his heart was racing.

Tom Olmeijer echoed that vital word almost eerily in Richard's head, though he was talking to the helmsman. 'Steady,' he said. 'Steady as she goes . . .'

As *Tai Fun* edged towards the shore, Richard tore himself into action. The tension of standing there helplessly watching the approach was too much for him to bear. *Tai Fun* had lost one gangplank when the wave had torn her out of her berth, but she had another. With a shout of command to Sailing Master Larsen, Richard was off. By the time he reached the ridged and railed bridge of wood, the bearded Viking officer was at his shoulder. They swung the gangplank round and got ready to run it out.

It would be tricky to put it mildly, Richard knew. There would be no opportunity to run lines ashore and hold the vessel still. It would require all of Tom Olmeijer's seamanship to hold his command in one place against the current and the tide, for however long it might take to get the gangplank out and Robin and whoever was with her safely aboard. All the time praying that the added weight of the wooden bridge, the force it might exert on the trembling wall, the damage that the side of the vessel itself might do to the whole of the structure, were not enough to bring the whole lot down on their heads.

But they simply had to run the risk.

With Richard at one side and Larsen at the other, the gangplank

eased out beyond *Tai Fun*'s rail as Tom brought her under the
shadow of the towering stairwell. Robin was joined in the rough
gape of the window by Kalla, and the pair of them reached out for
the end of the plank. But it was frustratingly difficult to hold *Tai
Fun* still enough to allow those vital moments of contact. At last
Richard spoke into his Bluetooth: 'It's no good, Tom, we'll need
to throw them a line.' He raised his voice and shouted across the
frustratingly narrow stretch of water, 'Robin! Is there anything there
you can make a line fast to?'

'Banisters,' she called back. 'Newell posts. They're metal and
look pretty strong.'

'Right. There's a line coming over. Get ready.'

They caught the messenger line on the third attempt and pulled
the lightest of *Tai Fun*'s cables over, hand over hand. Then Robin
dragged it into the shadows and a moment or two later she was
back, calling, 'That's it!'

There was a gang of half a dozen hands behind Richard now
and they took the strain at once. The cable stretched taut, bending
round the downstream brickwork as *Tai Fun* was pulled back against
the falling tide and rising current. The rope creaked. The wall trembled. The first few bricks tumbled into the water, torn loose by the
movement of the rope itself. 'EASY!' bellowed Richard, and the
whole crazy edifice seemed to tremble with the power of his voice.

But the end of the gangplank slid neatly into the hole. Richard
and Larsen allowed some of the weight to go off their shoulders
at last, but it was obvious that they would have to hold the plank
in place, for there was no way it could be safely secured at Robin's
end. And the way the single line was flexing and the wall was
beginning to crumble meant that the whole jerry-rigged contrap-
tion needed constant adjustment if it was going to be anything
like safe.

'Go! Go! Go!' shouted Robin as Richard and Larsen eased the
plank home.

Hilly appeared in the hole, and pulled the fainting Steve up behind
her. Kalla lifted the oxygen bottle as though it was a feather and
gave Hilly a hand. The weight of the three of them made the uneasy
bridge of the gangplank settle threateningly. The brickwork beneath
it began to crumble. Richard and Larsen took the strain once more.
But the three staggered down the slope on to the deck where two
of the deckhands grabbed Steve and rushed him below. Hilly hesitated. 'Go with him,' ordered Kalla, and nimbly ran back up the

gangplank. *Tai Fun* heaved. The wood of the bridge slid in and out dangerously. Had Richard and Larsen not acted so swiftly, the whole thing would have fallen into the roiling water.

Van Leir came next, again in Kalla's arms. The tall security man was beginning to wake up now and was clearly agitated about something. As soon as Kalla handed him down on to *Tai Fun*'s deck, the two who had taken Steve below reappeared ready to take him, too.

'No!' he barked, hopping unsteadily and holding on to the gang rail just by Larsen's hand. 'I'll wait.'

Sheri came next. The way the jacket of Van Leir's suit swamped her made it impossible for her to use her crutches. Kalla offered to lend a hand but was shrugged off. The jacket was unbuttoned and swung across her shoulders instead. Her modesty was protected as the buttons were re-secured, making the whole thing like a cloak. Then she was ready. But as she stepped up on to the plank, the over-taxed buttons gave way and the jacket fell back. The gangplank shuddered as a swirl of gathering river-flow tried to push *Tai Fun* back out to sea. Sheri staggered. And Kalla was there beside her, half-carrying her forward as Robin too leaped up.

'No!' shouted Van Leir.

Richard felt his shoulders popping with the effort of holding the gangplank in place and Larsen actually bellowed with the strain like a bull going to slaughter. Bricks popped out of the wall as the cable ate through it like a wire cutter chopping through cheese. Bricks cascaded out of the square frame below the plank as it twisted like a living thing.

Kalla swept Sheri off her feet and leaped the last metre down on to the deck. Her crutches went flying. One of them hit Larsen in the face and he staggered back. The plank began to tear itself out of Richard's grasp but he would not let go until Robin had stepped down on to the safety of the deck.

But just as she did so, Van Leir launched himself past her. He had grabbed the crutch that had stunned Larsen and forced it on to his arm. Using it to support his shattered leg, he scuttled, crabwise, along the plank to leap back ashore. He just made it as the whole thing tore loose and tumbled into the water. Then he was standing unsteadily, framed in the crumbling gape of the window. He had his jacket in one hand. And in the other, pulled out of its pocket, what looked like two silver computer discs.

Sittart might have recognized them as the discs containing Yoshimoto's groundbreaking work on algae and biofuel stolen from the empty briefcase Van Leir had let the pirates escape with, had he been there.

But he was not.

And then it became academic in any case, because the stack of the stairwell collapsed. Unlike its companion on the far side of the clinic, it collapsed in on itself, raining bricks and masonry, concrete stair blocks and the structures that had held them in place, all precisely on to the spot Van Leir was occupying. And then the west wall fell in on top of that.

Richard stood rooted to the spot with Robin crushed in his shaking grip. The line whipped past them, one end trapped beneath the hill of rubble that entombed Van Leir, the other simply torn out of the crewmen's hands. *Tai Fun* surrendered to the lure of the falling tide and swept out into the mouth of the estuary, like the first arrival in the heart of Hiroshima after the bomb. The others started coming up on to the deck, stunned by the damage all around.

Richard surveyed the enormity of the destruction and turned to Sailendra, who was standing silently beside him. 'There's a hell of a lot of work to be done here, Your Majesty,' he said. 'I think we'd better get our sleeves rolled up.'

'A hell of a lot of people needing help and attention as fast as we can get it to them,' emphasized Robin, her voice trembling, her tone gritty with determination.

'And a hell of a fortune to be spent just getting the infrastructure back,' added Nic Greenbaum ruefully.

The young prince looked west into the sunset, his eyes beginning to fill with tears, his face uncharacteristically devoid of hope. 'Where on earth can I hope to get a fortune such as we will need?' he asked, his voice beginning to break.

But even as he asked the question, the long hull of the lovely vessel swept past the first corpse floating in the water. It was the body of the pirate leader, swept ashore with all his friends and confederates by the power of the wave that killed them as they sailed away from *Ocean's Bounty* with their ransom.

And secured safely and immovably in oiled, waterproof packets around his still and lifeless chest, was his part of the loot they had all shared just before they died: his cut alone was the better part of five million US dollars.

GL
21/10/09
Sk
2/7/10